THE
OATH

THE RANGER'S MAGI, BOOK 3

THE OATH

ESKAY KABBA

4 Horsemen
Publications, Inc.

DEDICATION

To the ones who see Magic all around us.

Content warnings: sexually explicit content, discussions of sexual grooming, incidents of violence and death

CONTENTS

CHAPTER 1

Reflections

Ciaran woke up and opened his eyes. His entire body was sprawled across Christopher with his head on Chris's chest. He didn't want to move just yet. It was the safest and calmest he had felt in five full days. Because just hours ago, Ciaran Beals, the Dragon Tamer, had been facing prison time.

Just the night before, he had been sitting on his cot in the tiny, cold, stone cell with antimagical wristband tattoos on, thinking about all the decisions he made that led him there. And he concluded he would do all of it again.

Because Ciaran Beals, the Magus, was deeply in love with a Commoner, a non-magical human.

He listened to Chris's heartbeat and thought about the day they met, stumbling into each other because Robetta, the baby dragon, escaped from the dragon reservation. How Betta blew fire at the ranger and Ciaran slammed into him and rolled him out of the way to save his life.

He remembered Ranger Jenning's face when he told him that it was a dragon. How in awe he was. How right before he was to *abscondo* him—conceal his memory of the entire incident—Ranger Christopher Jennings turned around with his wide brown eyes, grabbed his wrist, and pleaded, "Don't."

Ciaran gently caressed the soft hair of Chris's brown arms and remembered how he felt in that moment, staring into Chris's eyes. He had lowered his *rodulé* and agreed not to at that moment. Or any moments after. And it was the best decision he ever made.

He smiled, thinking of their friendship, how they talked and walked, played games, and shared food and experiences. While lying in the dark, Ciaran smiled even harder, remembering Chris kissing him for the first time under the lamppost. And the other things they did that night, solidifying their physical and emotional connection.

He remembered how confused he had been about his feelings for a man. It was the first time he had felt like that in his life. But the closer they became, the more it didn't matter.

He thought about how hard it was when they were physically apart, learning that they had this rare magical connection called *Ardenti*. He thought about the possibility that they could have been apart for months, even years, if Ciaran went to prison, which, because of *Ardenti*, would have destroyed them both from the inside out. It was a strong possibility.

But even that didn't matter at the time. The bond between them was unbreakable, fixed, and soul-binding. He felt it in his heart. In his soul. His soul was clinging to Chris's and would be for all eternity, slowly melting together like two pieces of wax until they became one.

Ciaran might have been trapped in Claustra, the Magi prison, for breaking the most sacred Magi law, the Law of Secrecy of the magical world from non-magical humans, Commoners. He could have been separated from his love for a long time. It was nothing short of a miracle—and a couple of extremely loyal friends—that he was only given sixteen months' probation instead of ten years in prison.

But it was worth it.

After a couple minutes of listening to the sound of Chris's breathing, he rose and kissed his lover's forehead. Then he tucked him deep in the covers to keep him warm on that late December evening.

Yeah, he thought happily, watching Christopher Jennings sleep. *I wouldn't change a goddamn thing.*

CHAPTER 2

Puppies and Kittens

Ciaran shaved the hair he had grown on his face for the last five days and took a long, hot shower. He quietly got dressed before he checked on Chris, who was still sound asleep. He gave him one last lingering look before he went down the stairs to find his brothers Ted and Sean, sister Diana with her husband Quentin, his cousin Rob, and Chloé, his girlfriend, in the kitchen with open boxes of pizza and beer.

"There he is, the ex-con!" Sean, his younger brother, said first with a grin.

Ciaran sat down and grabbed a lukewarm pizza slice. "How long have I been out?" He took a big bite, realizing how hungry he was.

"It's a little after 9 p.m., so I guess a few hours," Ted said. "Here." He handed Ciaran his *dulé*. "Alastair dropped by to give this to you. He hung around, and I think he wanted to talk to you for a bit."

Ciaran nodded, thankful for his cousin Alastair's thoughtfulness. "I will go see him one day this week at the office."

Ted nodded as well. "He'd like that. Since Shane... well ... Shane always knew how to get him to soften. Alastair has been having a hard time these last few years, and Savannah's words affected him more than he let on."

Sean interjected in their conversation, not wanting to talk about his dead twin brother. "So now that the nightmare after Christmas is finally over, New Year's Eve plans, yes?"

Ciaran smiled. He was looking forward to spending New Year's with Christopher and his family in Kingsbridge at his parents' home. But it seemed like his little brother had other debauchery planned. "Out with it," he said simply.

"Max's Top-Notch New Year's Eve party," said Sean with a smile.

Chloé and Rob groaned. But Quentin said, "Actually, I've never been. Too busy hiding from my maternal family, fighting in battles, then training to be a Magi Commander." He turned to his wife of six months. "We should go."

"Only if you leave the *Nigri Veneficus* shit at home, Quentin," said Sean. "No seeking out dangers everywhere, because trust me, there will be a lot of Magi law breaking. That means you too, my Magi spy little sister. If you can't just be a young adult doing young adult things, stay home."

Diana and Quentin looked at each other and smiled. Diana turned back to her brother. "We'll be fine."

"Good." Sean turned to his older brother. "And you?"

"I'll check in with Chris when he wakes up to see what he wants to do," said Ciaran. "I'm letting him get some rest."

"That's good," said Ted. "Because I don't think he got any sleep these last few days."

"So, the baby needed you to put him to bed, innit?" Sean winked. "Diana told us about the clothes thrown about the house, from the front door to your bedroom."

Ciaran laughed. "Do you have to be so crass about everything all the time?"

"Precisely," said Sean.

"I'm just glad we weren't around to hear it this time," Rob said and made a face.

"Oh, I don't know," Diana said. "I rather enjoyed it."

"You enjoyed hearing your brother have sex?" Ted asked their youngest sister.

"She did," Quentin chimed in. "But of course, we didn't get the full brunt of it."

"Oh, my stars, be thankful of that!" Chloé said. "It was…" She was trying to find the words.

"Passionate," Diana said.

"Animalistic," Chloé said.

"Endearing."

"Pornographic!" Chloé argued back with her friend.

"Sexy!"

"Obscene!"

"Romantic!"

"Indecent!"

The girls burst into a fit of laughter. Then Ciaran said, "Chloé, I do want to apologize for it. It was inappropriate and callous."

"Petty!" Sean exclaimed, wanting to join in.

"Well," Chloé said, "It wasn't that awful. Maybe a bit passionate."

Ted groaned out loud. "Uhhh, this conversation, while stimulating, is something I don't really care to talk about anymore. So, whisky in the parlor?"

They agreed and moved down the hall to the sitting room. Ted sat in the armchair, Quentin on the floor with Diana between his legs as Sean and Ciaran claimed the couch, and Rob and Chloé claimed the other armchair, with her curled up in her boyfriend's lap. Ted used his *dulé* to conjure the glasses and filled them with whisky to pass around.

He raised his glass. "To Chloé, the brightest and fiercest Mage of this generation. Thank you for representing Ciaran at trial and for saving our brother."

Everyone raised their glasses to "here, here!"

"Well, I had to," she said. "I know you all think I'm very black and white when it comes to the law because I know that justice and good will prevail when we do the right thing."

"And what if it didn't?" Sean challenged her. "What if that bitch Mage Brickenhouse got her way and Ciaran ended up in prison?"

"Well..." She took a sip before she answered, "Magna, Lucy, and I had a plan to intervene in the transport and get Ciaran out of the country with Christopher to the Dragon Reserve in South America."

They all looked at her in shock. "What?" she said innocently. "Just because I believe in the law doesn't mean I can't see when people distort it for their own personal gain, like Savannah Brickenhouse. In those cases, we must take justice into our own hands."

"Well, look who is learning how to live in the gray with the rest of the undignified?" Quentin teased his friend. Chloé stuck her middle finger at him.

"I guess there was a Plan B and a Plan C to keep Chris and me together, innit," said Ciaran. He looked around the room and said sincerely, "Thank you. Truly."

"Well deserved, mate," said Sean seriously. "*Ardenti* notwithstanding, you and Christopher belong together. Just like Ted and Elodie. Diana and Quentin. Even Chloé and that dummy over there."

They chuckled as Rob also stuck his middle finger, this time at Sean.

"When are you going to make an honest woman out of this amazing woman, Robert?" Ted said.

"Aunt Elspeth saying they are living in sin is hilarious." Diana giggled.

"It's not me," Rob said. "Chloé doesn't want to get married."

Chloé turned to him in surprise. "I didn't say that. I just wanted us to be more settled and ready. We're still living in Quentin's house like we're all dormmates at Campus."

"To which, by the way, is perfectly fine. Stay as long as you want. Stay forever if you want to," said Quentin. "I never wanted to be in this big, lonely house by myself anyway."

"And while we appreciate the sentiment, you and Diana will probably start a family soon, and you're going to need the extra rooms," Chloé said.

"Not quite yet, actually," said Quentin.

"And we might not have children at all," Diana admitted. "We're still so young. Let the notoriety of Quentin James, the youngest commander in the Magi Mercenary Unit, die down a bit before we decide to bring children into it."

"I don't think that's ever going to happen," said Rob. "The James boy who defied his aunt Talindra and his maternal family to stand on the side of good. It will make a fine movie one day."

"Yes, and I don't want my children on display because of it," said Quentin. "The more I think of it, the more I'm grateful that my father left this place in my name. He must have known that at some point my mother and her entire family would go off the deep end. Thank God he died before he witnessed any of it," Quentin said bitterly.

"Have you heard from any of them?" Sean asked.

"Just one cousin," Quentin said. "He's here at the University of London, Rugby scholarship. We've had one awkward lunch once and made promises to keep in touch. He was never one of the dark ones."

"Good," Ted said. "Family can be great or terrible, but it's still family. Reconciliation, if possible, is important. We're all we got, puppies and kittens. All of us in this room, this house, we're family. Doesn't matter if your last name is Beals, or Livingston, or Abbottsford, or James, or even Jennings. And we defend and protect our own, no matter what."

"Puppies and kittens? Are you drunk, Ted?" Ciaran asked their eldest brother.

"No," Ted said. He finished his second glass. "Maybe a little." His siblings laughed at him.

The parlor door opened, and Chris came in. He had showered as well and went to find Ciaran. He smiled upon seeing the whole family piled up in the parlor. "Good evening."

"Good evening," they all chorused back.

Except for Sean, who teased, "Did baby have a nice nap?"

Chris ignored him and sat on the arm of the couch closest to Ciaran. "Hello, love."

"Hey, you," Ciaran replied. He pulled on Chris's sleeve, motioning him to lean down for a kiss, which he gave.

Sean teased him again. "C'mon. You know you want to." Chris looked over at Sean, who was grinning. "You know you want to slide in and sit on his lap. Just do it. No one will judge you, big guy," he said sweetly. "Or should I say, little lady?"

Ted smiled, and Rob snickered. Chris grinned and indeed slid into Ciaran's lap sideways, then kicked Sean hard on his thigh. Sean howled, "Oooowww!" and rolled onto the floor.

"Arsehole," Chris muttered to him, and everyone laughed.

Chris moved to the floor between Ciaran's legs. Ciaran, who was confused by the exchange, said, "I don't get it."

Chris told him, "Your amazing brothers are insinuating that I am the female in this relationship."

Ciaran laughed loudly, then caught himself. "What the fuck are you laughing at?" Chris said in feigned annoyance. The rest either snickered or tried to hold back their laughter.

"I'm sorry, it's not funny," Ciaran said with a smile.

Chris looked around. "Fuck all of you, thank you very much." That made the room explode with laughter. He feigned anger and pretended to get up to leave, but Ciaran held him down.

"Sean is a git; you know I don't see you that way," Ciaran said, rubbing his shoulders. "We're two masculine men having a proper relationship." Chirs looked up, and Ciaran kissed his lips again.

"Speaking of Sean being a git, are you going to tell us what Plan B was?" Ted asked. "If Ciaran was found guilty and sent to Claustra, what were you two going to do?"

Chris looked at Sean, who shrugged his shoulders as he got back on the couch. "If Ciaran went to Claustra, Chris and I were also going to take a trip outside of the continent until his time was done, however long it would be."

"So you were just going to leave and not tell anyone?" Ted said, with his eyebrow raised.

"We were going to tell you, Ted," Chris said. "After we got there."

"Got where?" Ciaran asked.

"Senegal first," Chris said. "I have an uncle there. Sus out if I did actually have any magic roots in my family tree. Then make our way to South Africa, where Sean is comfortable. After that, no one knows."

Ciaran looked at Sean intently. He knew Sean left someone very special behind in South Africa, the sorceress that taught him his newfound spirituality and helped to make him whole again after the loss of his twin brother.

Ted asked, "So you were just going to hide for what, ten years or so? And do what, exactly, for money, food, and shelter?"

"Work. Hustle. Barter. Magic tricks. Do whatever we had to do to survive," Chris said.

"Speak for yourself; I was going for the relaxation and occasional shagging," said Sean. They laughed.

"Chris would not be shagging anyone, he would have been celibate, wouldn't you, Chris?" Diana said.

Before Chris could answer, Ciaran did. "Chris could never be celibate for ten years, and I wouldn't have expected him to."

Chris looked at him surprised. "I would have." Ciaran looked at him skeptically. "I would have tried." Ciaran smiled and kissed the top of his head.

"You would have probably stopped sleeping with men, but you certainly would have been sleeping with women," Ted said. "Fucking men would have felt disloyal." He winked at Chris.

Chris winked back. "Your assumption is correct, sir."

Rob was confused. "So you're not completely gay?"

"I'm pansexual," Chris told him.

"But you're with a man right now," Rob said, still confused.

"Yes. And I still find other people attractive, regardless of gender," Chris said.

"How? I mean. You don't have to answer that. But... how?"

"I just do," Chris said. "For example, you are one very lucky man. Chloé has beautiful eyes, perfect skin, and she is the prettiest when she does that sheepish smile she is about to do. But her inner beauty is what makes her shine the most. Her honesty, her ethics, her intelligence, her fidelity to you, Diana, and Quentin."

Chloé blushed and tried to hide her smile. "See? Beautiful is she. I notice beauty in people, and sex or gender has nothing to do with it. Ciaran is an amazing person. He's brave and kindhearted, selfless, sexy, funny, honest, sincere, empathetic, and he's everything I have ever wanted in a soulmate. I love his heart before I love any other part of him, including his *Vis*."

Ciaran smiled and kissed his head again. "See why I love him so?" he said to no one and everyone.

Diana put her hand over her heart. "The passion you have for one another is palpable. You two are perfect for each other."

"Agreed. So when is the wedding?" Chloé asked.

"No clue," Ciaran said. "We haven't talked about it yet."

"Soon though," Chris said. He turned to look at Ciaran. "Before the new year is out. I don't want to wait too long."

Ciaran nodded. "Okay."

They sat around and talked for the next couple of hours on the trial, what the others missed by being outside of the courtroom, and ended on what a top-notch New Year's Eve would look like.

CHAPTER 3

A Top-Notch New Year

On New Year's Eve, Chris and Ciaran were coerced into going to Max Morgan's Top-Notch New Year's Affair. Maxwell Morgan was a very wealthy Magus schoolmate from Sean's sixth form and very well known. Chloé and Rob wanted to spend their New Year's Eve alone, so Ciaran and Chris attended the party with Diana and Quentin. They fully expected it to have a lot of younger Magi, but they quickly realized it was anything but a regular party, even a Magi one.

The three-story brownstone was filled with hundreds of Mages and Magus under the age of thirty. The drunk adults were dancing to the loud music in what could only be described as Halloween costumes, some regular and some sexy. Chris and Ciaran looked out of place wearing regular jeans and long-sleeved sweaters.

Chris could feel and see the magic in the air, watching as people waved their *dulés* to make chairs move, appear, or disappear, Wisp'ing from one place to another, balloons suddenly appearing over their heads and popping so that confetti rained down. It delighted him tremendously.

As they walked through the dense crowd on the first floor, someone grabbed Chris from behind. He turned around, and a woman was looking at him seductively. She had long, thick, wavy black hair down to the middle of her back and big brown eyes, and was wearing a sexy maid outfit with a pointed witch's hat.

"You're adorable," she said loudly over the music.

Chris could not take his eyes off her large and perky breasts that were barely held in by her white sheer corset. "And you are … whew! Unbelievable. And very young."

"I'm nineteen." She smiled. "What's your name?"

"Chris. What's yours?"

"Whitley. You didn't go to Campus in England," she said. "I would have definitely remembered you."

"Well, you make me wish I did," Chris flirted back. She laughed with a girlish laugh much higher than her obvious voice.

Ciaran, who realized Chris was not behind him anymore, turned back and approached them. He heard Whitley say, "Are you here with anyone?"

Chris turned around just in time to see Ciaran walk back over. He pointed at Ciaran. "Yes. Him."

She rolled her eyes. "Ugh, great, another Beals."

Ciaran said, "Yup, throw a stone on any country, and you'll hit a Beals." He smiled, and Chris laughed.

Whitley rolled her eyes again and turned back to Chris. She put her hand on his shoulder. "You want to dance?" she asked.

Ciaran looked at him, amused. Chris moved a piece of hair out of her face and said, "Whitley, love, you are stunning. But in another life, sweetheart."

She moved closer and put her body up against his. "Want to do something else, then?" she said seriously.

Chris's eyes went wide. "Whoaaa ... what kind of party is this?"

Sean came from behind her and wrapped his arm around her stomach. He looked over at Chris and said, "The best kind." He winked at him.

Whitley looked behind her and rolled her eyes. "What do you want, Sean?"

"I want you to get your hands off my brother's boyfriend. Nope, fiancé."

Whitley slowly turned back to Chris, who smiled at her and nodded, with wide eyes. She looked past him at Ciaran, who did the same. She scoffed and started to walk away.

"Hey, I'm still available," he called after her. She gave him the middle finger and a smile, but kept walking. Sean said to his brother, "Yup, I will be in the bottom half of that outfit before the night is over." Then he turned to them. "Gentlemen! You made it! Follow me; I saved you a sofa."

They followed Sean up four flights of stairs to the rooftop deck and onto the platform section that had couches on it. Most were already occupied. Every floor they passed had a different atmosphere with the rooftop deck by far the craziest section. It was unseasonably warm for them to be outside, at least 22 degrees Celsius, but Chris rightly assumed it was magically temperature-controlled. Chris and Ciaran sat on a green oversized sofa as Sean left them to mingle. They sat, drank, and people-watched.

Chris enjoyed his first Magi party, as the pitcher of beer in front of them kept refilling itself and shooting stars and fireworks from *rodulés* burst everywhere around them. It was most amusing watching partygoers accidentally, or on purpose, falling off the roof or being tossed off as a joke, only to be propelled back up onto the roof with cheers from everyone. Ciaran explained what Chris had already figured out: it was a protection spell to keep anyone from actually falling off.

Quentin and Diana found them after making their rounds and sat with them on the couch. Others came by to sit and talk with them, especially Quentin, who was extremely popular, and Ciaran, who many hadn't seen in a while. Lucy Chesterfield, Ciaran's friend, Scholarly's Director of Magi Anime and Wildlife in Europe, and quite literally Ciaran's boss, came by to say hi with her boyfriend who taught Magi Economics at Campus. They talked for a few moments until she said, "Give Selma a kiss for me," and they disappeared into the crowd. She knew their next stop on New Year's Day was going to see their other close friend.

At midnight Ciaran and Chris kissed, then decided to explore the other floors, leaving Quentin and Diana to continue to kiss and paw at each other on the couch.

They found the stoner room that was full of smoke, courtesy of Sean's Amazonian strain, and the room on the second floor that had a fifty-inch screen playing porn that no one was watching, rather they were into each other. The air was infused with a magical aphrodisiac, and the sex was palpable, so much so that Ciaran and Chris left almost immediately before they too got caught up and started taking off their clothes.

They found the game room and the alcohol room and stayed in the dueling room for a while watching warlocks match up, men and women. Finally, they made it back to the first floor to the huge kitchen where the food was plentiful.

"How does food keep reappearing?" Chris asked as he grabbed another banana cake and one immediately appeared in its place. "Christmas dinner had me stunned."

"It's made in a different place or location," Ciaran explained. "The plate or tray is what is charmed. If the plate is empty, another is sent in its place. Eventually, it will stop, but probably not for a very long time. The Morgans are extremely wealthy and known for their lavish parties."

"Fascinating," said Chris with a mouthful of cake. "It's after 2 a.m., and we're not allowed back at the house until 3 a.m. Rob and Chloé's orders. So what do we do now?"

Ciaran took his hand. "Let's just walk."

Chris followed Ciaran out of the house and into the cold night air. They wrapped their scarves around their necks a little tighter, pulled their hats down closer, and held gloved hands while walking through the streets of London. They talked of future plans and the wedding, deciding to keep it small and intimate like Vlad and Alexi's wedding, and August 1st as the date: the day they met almost two years ago.

"I figure in five years I can buy land and start to build my house," said Ciaran. "Just trying to decide if it should be in the woods like I planned or by the sea for you."

Chris smiled at him. "Maybe we'll find a place for both of us. Would you want to leave Albania?"

"I don't think so, especially now that Dale wants to hand me the Reserve at some point and Lucy is all for that plan. I never saw myself leaving my job, although there are other smaller dragon reservations, like the Macfursty land in Scotland that guards the Cami's there. They have woods and the sea there. I would fit right in with my red hair. And I have family there on my dad's side."

"That would be helpful when we start having children," said Chris. Ciaran didn't respond. "But you don't want children."

"I never said that. I just said I would leave it to my partner to decide," Ciaran reminded him. "But I know you want them, so I want them with you. Little brown boys with red hair and C names. That's what we promised each other, yeah?"

"Or girls with 'C' names."

"Shit, what would I do with girls?" Ciaran scoffed.

"Play dress up," said Chris. "Tea parties, I did it all with Sis."

"Well, the girls can be your responsibility, and the boys will be mine."

Chris chuckled. "How many children?"

"Seven," Ciaran said confidently.

Chris laughed. "Bloody hell, Ciaran, how did you go from 'maybe I'll want to have children' to seven offspring? Who the fuck is having seven children?"

Ciaran laughed as well. "You act like you're giving birth to them."

"I thought you were going to say two or three."

Ciaran shrugged. "I'm pretty sure Ted is going for seven. Most Beals's families have five to seven kids."

"Good for Ted," said Chris. "Then we don't have to be the ones to populate the earth with magical redhead Beals."

Ciaran laughed. They walked and talked until they reached the docks and found a bench. Ciaran looked around at the quiet street before he raised his *rodulé* above them in a big circle and said, *"Temperatus mutare sursum."*

The air around them began to warm up, and they were able to loosen their scarves. The two men continued to talk about the places they wanted to travel, Ciaran to India and Chris to Senegal, both to the Americas. Chris was determined to track down his mother's ancestry to see if there was magic in his bloodline somewhere. Eventually, Chris checked the time, and it was after 4 a.m.

"Do you want to go straight to King's Cross?" asked Ciaran. "We have to get on a train in less than two hours, and we aren't sleeping now."

"But we do need to get our bags from the house," said Chris.

"Oh, that's easy," Ciaran said. He made a complicated wave of his *dulé*, murmured an incantation, and pointed at a space next to the bench. Their luggage materialized in front of them. Ciaran conjured a piece of paper and pen and wrote a quick note:

D&Q,

Sorry we never made it back to the house to say goodbye. Thank you for everything. See you at the Beals Residence in Kingsbridge in a few days.

All the best,
C&C

He crumpled it up and put it in his fist, then did another series of complicated hand gestures, tapped his *dulé* to his closed fist, and said some words, and his hand glowed. He opened it, and the paper disappeared.

Chris was in awe. "That's some advanced magic you've been doing in front of me there, Harry Potter," he teased.

Ciaran laughed. "Well, the cat's out the bag now. No reason not to." But Ciaran turned to him. "I can't wait until you take the Oath and I show you my world from Magi villages of three hundred people to Magi towns of ten thousand. Show you how we live, how we transport—"

"Except Wisp'ing," Chris broke in. "That literally almost did you in with the jurors, Wisp'ing with a Commoner."

Ciaran smiled. "We have other means of transport."

"I can't wait either," said Chris. "Not for the magic and to go into Magi spaces. But to do it all with you for the rest of my life."

They were quiet for a moment, staring at each other lovingly. "Will you miss being with a woman though? Soft, feminine, wet? Like Whitney?" Ciaran asked.

Chris smiled a little. "Maybe at times. But so what? I know you're all I will ever need, in or out of the bedroom. What about you?"

"I don't know," Ciaran said honestly. "The truth is, I couldn't take my eyes off Whitney's breasts." Chris laughed out loud, knowing he couldn't do the same. But Ciaran said, "Don't tease me. I'm still confused sometimes on who I am. What I am."

"You're Ciaran," Chris said simply. "Does it have to be more than that?"

"No, but you confidently say you're pansexual, like you did with my family. You know how to define it for yourself. I don't know if I can confidently say anything myself. I still don't look at other men like that. And despite me still admiring the female body, I'm definitely not interested in other women. Just you, Christopher. You're the only one who sets my body on fire. Quite literally."

"You did at the strip club. American Rodeo," Chris reminded him with a tease.

Ciaran chuckled and turned away. "Okay, I did get aroused, yes. But I was really drunk. And at the end of the night I still just wanted you. So does that make me gay? Or will I always only want you? Will I still desire women ten or twenty or thirty years from now? I still have no idea, and I don't know if that's fair to you, to not know who I am but still plan forever with you."

"Look at me," Chris said. Ciaran did. "Did you mean it when you said you would love me forever?"

"And three days after that," Ciaran said automatically.

"And did you mean it when you said I was your future? That you couldn't imagine a life without me in?"

"Absolutely."

Chris asked him, "Despite the *Ardenti*, do you think that will ever change for you? That if we weren't connected in this cosmic way, a day would come when you wouldn't want to be with me, love me just as much as you do right now?"

Ciaran stared into his brown eyes, thinking of how he felt just yesterday morning waking up lying on Chris's chest. "Never."

"Then fuck the labels," said Chris. "What does it matter if you are gay or bi or even kind of straight? Whether you still like women or whether you don't like men at all? I just want you to keep loving me. Because I'm going to keep loving you. There is nothing you can say or do that will change that for me."

Ciaran smiled at him. "You make it so damn easy to love you."

"It's not me, remember? It's this soul-clinging-to-you thing I got going on," Chris joked.

"Oh, love," Ciaran said. "My soul is clinging right back."

They kissed softly. Held hands. Talked a bit more. Kissed a little more. Sat in silence and watched the sun rise over the water on the first day of the new year.

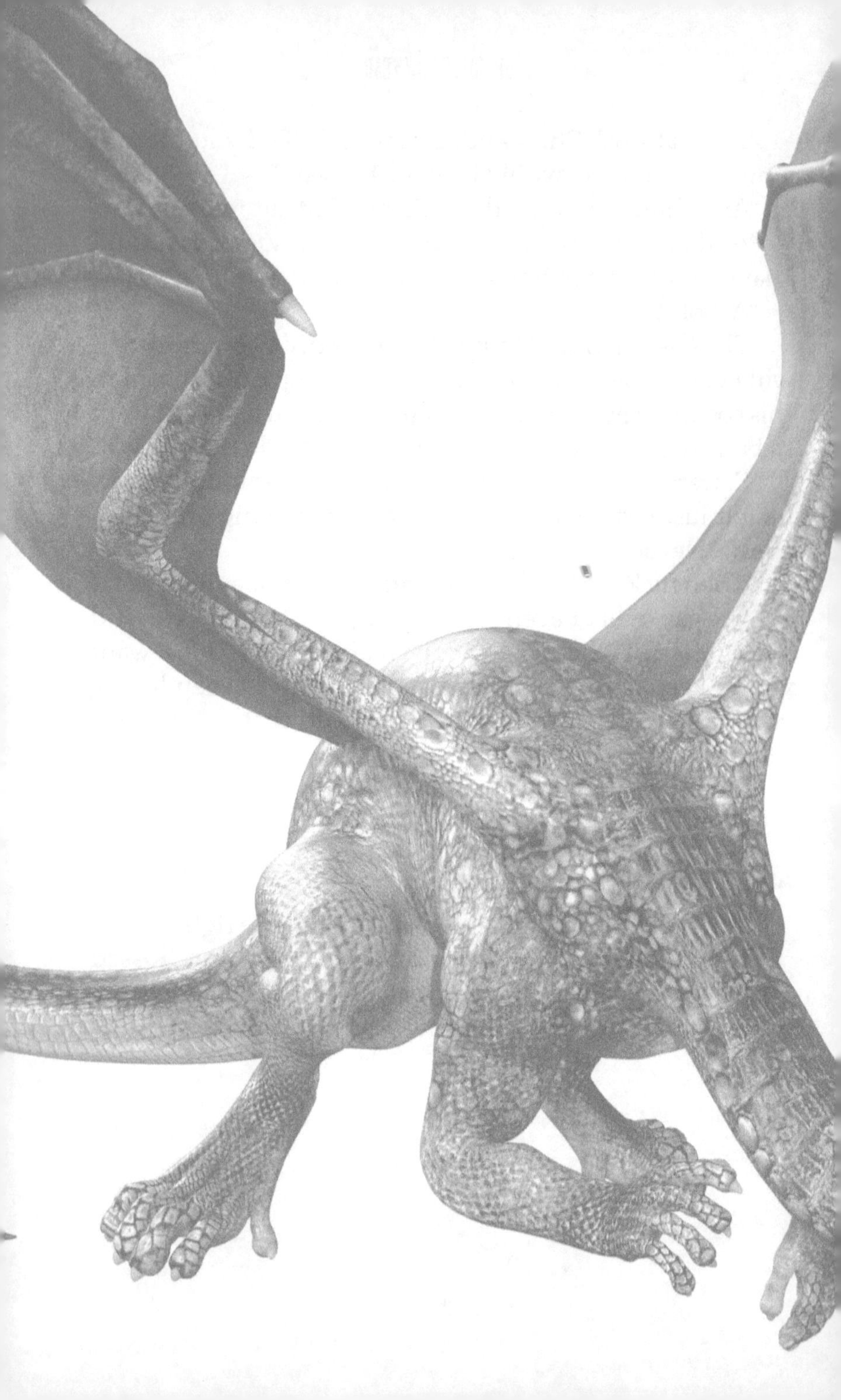

CHAPTER 4

Living like Commoners

They left the bench, dragged their luggage to the nearest road, took a taxi to Kings Cross Station, and were there by 6:30 a.m. As they were waiting for their train, Chris remembered. "Shit, Ciaran! We left the tickets on the dresser!"

"No worries," Ciaran said. He held up his *dulé* slightly in a crowded station and murmured, "*Cedo.*"

Chris slapped his hand down. "There are people around, and you have a tracking on you, dumb arse! Are you trying to get tossed into Claustra five whole minutes after just getting off the hook?!"

Ciaran laughed. "Ooops!" He gave Chris a goofy smile and shrugged. But then he held out an open palm and waited.

"That's not really going to work is it?" Chris asked skeptically.

"Only one way to find out," Ciaran said with a wink.

Thirty seconds later a huge gust of wind came through the station blowing everything, including people, around. When the wind died down, two white tickets floated into Ciaran's hand. Chris stared in shock. Ciaran laughed.

"Fucking magicians," Chris muttered, shaking his head in awe. "I think I'm a bad influence on you. I've matured, and you've gotten reckless."

They boarded the train and headed to Brighton. Ten minutes into the ride Chris fell asleep, but Ciaran did not, thinking of all they had discussed in the last few hours. What Chris didn't realize was that Ciaran had been holding back magically those last sixteen months. The little bit of magic that Ciaran had been doing around Chris didn't even scratch the surface of what he could do. There was so much for Christopher to learn, and he was happy to be his guide in that uncharted territory. He just had to get through probation.

Ciaran woke Chris up a couple of stops before their stop so they could gather their luggage. As they exited the train, Ciaran took his phone out to make a phone call when he heard a familiar voice call out, "Ciaran Beals! Taking the coaches like a Commoner. Be still my beating heart!"

He turned to see one of his best friends, Selma, walking toward them. Selma was average height, dark-brown skinned, and beautiful.

"Selma, my darling!" Ciaran ran up and gave her a hug, picking her up and spinning her around like he did with Lucy.

She walked back over with Ciaran holding her hand and looked at Chris. "And let me get a good look at *you*. See what all the fuss is about." Selma got close to him, looked him up and down over her gold-rimmed glasses, then walked around him slowly. "Hmmmm... Magna was right about you. Gandalf be damned, you are stunning."

Chris blushed and smiled at her. "Hello, Selma," he said as she made it back to the front of him. "I've heard wonderful things about you." He opened up his arms, and she walked into them, also hugging him.

"Cheers," she said and patted his back. "Come on, Commoners, let's get a ride."

They followed her outside to where her car service was waiting and got in. As they piled into the SUV, Ciaran asked her, "How did you know we were taking the train?"

"Well, Magna told me there was no way you would be *stupid* enough to Wisp, so I called Ted and he told me when and where."

Chris chuckled. "Seeeee? No Wisp'ing," he said, pretending to scold his boyfriend. Ciaran chuckled too.

Selma told them that they rented a penthouse in Brighton. Andres was dropping the children at his parents and picking them up tomorrow because they had to head back to Spain sooner than expected. "Andres officially got tapped for Liverpool," she said. "It's really just a formality; they've been poaching him from Barca for a while now, almost the entire seven years that he's been playing football there. It would be nice to officially come home." Ciaran and Selma talked football while Chris took in the sights.

When they got to the penthouse floor, Andres was waiting for them in the hallway. He rammed into Ciaran before Ciaran made it off the lift. "Keeeeyyyyyaaaaaraaaaaan!" he roared.

They embraced like old friends, talking so fast over each other, arms around their necks as they walked ahead of Chris and Selma. She rolled her eyes, but Chris could tell it was all in jest.

Once in the apartment, Ciaran turned to Chris. "Andres, this is Christopher. My best friend, my partner, my absolute everything that matters."

"Nice introduction, mate," Andres teased. He reached his hand out and gave him a handshake. "Good to meet you, finally."

"Likewise," said Chris. "The only pictures Ciaran has of you are of you two as teenagers. It's nice to see you all grown up."

"He's not all grown up," Selma deadpanned. "Especially now that Ciaran is here. You just watch."

Andres responded by rushing into his wife, who yelped, and carrying her around the room on his shoulder. She feigned annoyance at him, slapping his back, before he dropped her on the couch.

"Wanker!" she scolded him with a slap on his leg.

Andres stood straight up with his knuckles on his hips and looked at Ciaran and Chris. "Breakfast anyone?"

They sat down to an English breakfast and talked football, Andres' career playing for the Spanish team, and how they were ready to come back to his home. As their bellies filled and conversation died down a little, Selma started on her oldest friend.

"So, my darling Ciaran. Start talking. Because imagine my shock to hear that one, you're dating and in love with a man; two, you're dating a Commoner; and three, you broke all kinds of Magi laws to be with him. We've been exchanging posts for months. How could you not tell me?" she scolded him.

Andres leaned back as if to stay out of the conversation and looked at Chris to do the same.

"I don't know, Selma," Ciaran said. "I didn't even know how to tell myself these things. If we were around each other, maybe—"

She cut him off. "That's no excuse," she said sternly. "You should have told me. Did you think I would judge you for it? Any of it? We've been friends for twenty years, Ciaran."

"No. I... I don't know. Lucy asked me the same thing. I knew I couldn't pull anyone else into this web I created. Especially since I didn't know how to get out of it."

Selma reached over and touched his hand. "And that's why you should have called me. Because Magna is a Council official and also my best friend. And, as you now know, she actually heads her sector in the Magi Law Enforcement. She simply would have flown to Albania, given Chris the Oath, and nobody would have been the wiser, all because I would have asked her to. And nobody would have gone to Claustra over it." She patted his hand like he was a small child she was explaining things to.

Ciaran opened his mouth, but nothing came out. He looked at Chris, who was equally surprised. He turned back to Selma, who had an eyebrow raised. "I didn't think about that," he said.

"Because you're stupid, Ciaran," Selma said sweetly. "And that's why you have me, so you won't be so stupid." She patted his hand again. He smiled at her, and Chris snickered.

She glanced at Chris, then looked back at her friend. "So are you over it yet? Being embarrassed over your feelings for a man and Commoner?"

"Who says I was embarrassed?" Ciaran asked.

She ignored him and turned to Chris. "Is he over it yet?"

Chris hesitated, but then said, "He's... he still struggles a bit, but he's getting there."

"Hmm... It will be easier the deeper he falls in love with you. He'll forget it all."

Ciaran was affronted. "You don't think I'm in love now?"

"Oh, I do," Selma said. "The *Ardenti* that I keep hearing about makes it so. But it will grow deeper, less whirlwind romance and soul-burning passion, more tangible. Love becomes less about the outward affections and more about the internal connection. Especially after you complete the tie-bind and you can hear each other's thoughts as others who have experienced *Ardenti* can do. Congratulations by the way. Another thing I didn't hear directly from you." She raised her eyebrow again.

Ciaran laughed. "It literally happened three days ago. Of course, I came here to tell you."

"Just make sure you send me an invite," she said.

"Yours will be the first in the mail." They smiled at each other.

Andres leaned back in and threw a fist into his palm. "Alright, are we done with the scolding and berating? Because I'm ready to fly."

Ciaran's eyes lit up as Andres got up and walked over to the broom closet, taking out two brooms and two cloaks. He stood up as Andres walked back over and handed one of each to him.

"When was the last time you rode?" Andres asked him.

"God, it's been years now," Ciaran said, putting on the cloak. "Brooms are so cliché."

"Seriously?" Chris said in surprise. "Like every single fairy tale about witches on flying brooms is real?"

"Of course," Andres said seriously. "How do you think we Magi got around before planes were invented?" He didn't wait for Chris to respond. "Let's go, mate," Andres said and started walking to the patio deck. Ciaran followed him, and they stood side by side. They both kicked out their left leg at the same time, and, in a flash, they took off together.

Chris was again in awe. He started walking to the patio, and Selma followed him. "I've never seen him on a broom," said Chris. He looked up to the sky but could not see them at all. "And apparently I still can't," he joked.

"Ciaran was one of the best broom racers the entire six years we were at Campus, second only to Andres. But even Andres would say Ciaran was a better racer than him," said Selma. "Then in our fifth year, I foolishly took Ciaran and Ted with me into a nearby woods over holiday, and we came face-to-face with a dragon, the very thing he'd been fantasizing about for ages. He was already obsessed, but it became a mission for him after that, to ensure every dragon got to live a safe and happy life like any other animal. After their military experience, Andres went on to play professional football, and Ciaran went to the Reserve and never looked back."

Selma turned back around. "Come with me," she said to Chris. She grabbed two cloaks and a broom from the broom closet and brought them back to the patio deck. "Put the cloak on first," she said as she put hers on. "The broom is enchanted, but it's the cloak that will keep you in the air."

"Oh. Okay," said Chris, putting on the dark brown cloak and fastening the buttons.

"Now, I'm good on a broom, but you must hold tight to my waist. Like if you were on a motorcycle." She mounted and waited for Chris to slide in behind her. Once he wrapped his arms tightly around her waist, she rose slowly.

"Don't look down," she told him.

They went higher and with a little more speed, and Chris kept his eyes up. He wasn't afraid of heights, but he wasn't going to test his fate either. It felt like he was on an extremely high Ferris wheel with his feet hanging out. He held tighter to Selma who was completely at ease transporting him. He got used to the feel of the air blowing past him as she sped up and flew around thousands of kilometers from land and through the clouds.

"It's like being on a motorcycle with no ground," he found himself yelling.

"Yes," Selma acknowledged. "Just like that."

Chris started seeing Andres and Ciaran another couple of kilometers up, moving so fast they were almost blurry. Chris got to see how skilled Ciaran was even though he had not been on a broom in years. He was a natural and liked to do tricks, hang upside down, and loop around in the air, his laughter flying in the wind behind him. Selma and Chris circled them a bit, staying slightly below them.

After about an hour, she flew up to the middle of them, startling Chris, but he hung on. She yelled to them, "Okay, boys, we have to get there in forty-five minutes. And, thanks to Chris, seeing as how we have to act like Commoners and travel there, we should get going."

Selma turned around and headed back to the balcony. Chris's legs felt wobbly as they landed. As happy as it made him, he was even happier to have his feet on solid ground.

Chris watched Ciaran and Andres land on the balcony together. Ciaran's face was red and flushed, and he was grinning with all his teeth. He kissed Chris hard on the lips before he followed his friend inside. It was the happiest Chris had ever seen him, fully immersed with his Magi friends doing magical things.

They took the car service and drove to West Pier where a sailboat was waiting. Chris's eyes lit up as they walked toward it. Selma turned to him and said, "Ciaran told me you like boats. We thought we'd take you both on a long ride."

Chris turned to Ciaran who was smiling at him. He turned back to Selma. "I do. I love the open water."

They boarded, and when inside, Chris was shocked, although he knew he shouldn't be, that the space wasn't small at all. It was a room large enough to fit ten humans, and it was springlike weather too. There were different kinds of chairs from lounge chairs to benches to a long couch along the right side. Chris went right to the front window so he could see everything. He pressed his hands and face to the glass as the boat began to move.

Ciaran grinned and turned to his friends. "How long are we out here for?"

But Andres said, "No questions, mate. Just enjoy the ride."

Selma smiled at him and kissed him on the cheek, then followed her husband to the bar in the back of the boat. Ciaran sat back and relaxed on the long couch. As the boat left the harbor, eventually Chris plopped himself next to Ciaran and leaned on his shoulder. Ciaran lifted his arm around Chris's neck so that Chris was cradled against him. They silently watched the boat sail through the English Channel. Within minutes, Chris began to feel the rumbling of Ciaran's snores against his back. He didn't bother looking at him. He stared at the bright sky and the waves until he too fell asleep.

CHAPTER 5

Home Again

Andres tapped them both awake hours later. "We're here, mates."

Chris leaned up, and Ciaran rose and stretched. He looked out the windows, confused at first, but then realized where they were. He turned to Selma and Andres. "I can't believe you brought us all the way here." He hugged his friends individually.

"Where?" Chris asked.

He looked at Chris. "Home." Chris grinned in understanding.

Ciaran led Chris off the boat and onto the pier. "Christ, my balls just shriveled up," Chris said as the ice-cold wind blew around him.

"Welcome to Kingsbridge," Ciaran announced with a chuckle.

"It's exactly the kind of place that I imagined you grew up," said Chris, his eyes darting everywhere.

Ciaran took his hand, and they walked through the town together, with Andres and Selma alongside them. It had a small-town feel to Chris, as he watched fishermen and other buyers of goods milling around in the middle of the day. The road became less paved, and eventually Ciaran turned up a grassy road whose blades were ice between the salt water in the air and the freezing temperature. Chris could tell the walkway was rarely used, if at all, and the path was kept open for pretenses. He followed Ciaran through the trees and up the hill until Ciaran stopped and pointed at a bungalow, no more than twelve hundred square feet sitting on two acres of land.

"There is no way five kids and two adults lived in that little house," Chris commented.

"Pfft," Andres commented. "You should have seen the flat I grew up in in Sussex. There were eighteen of us in a structure that appeared smaller than this."

"Appeared?" Chris asked, still dumbfounded on how that could happen. But no one answered as Ciaran turned the doorknob and walked in.

Chris was immediately startled. The front entrance was grand with high ceilings and a spiral staircase at the end of the hall leading to the bedrooms upstairs. The door to his left was the sitting room, and the one to his right was the enormous kitchen with a similar long wooden table like Diana had in her kitchen. One day, after he took the Oath, he would investigate this enlargement magic fully, he decided.

Grace looked up from stirring her pot on the stove. "Oh, good, right on time. Go get cleaned up. Thanks for doing this, Selma. You and Andres will stay for dinner, yes?"

"Absolutely, Mistress Grace," Selma said.

"Yes, Mistress, we just had to bring a couple of Commoners along," Andres teased, giving her a kiss on the cheek.

"Oh, you," she said back.

Chris and Ciaran hugged Grace; then Ciaran said, "We'll be right back."

They went upstairs to the room he shared with Ted, leaving Selma and Grace to catch up. One thing Chris noticed as they walked through the house was that outside of the enlargement of the interior of the home, it was normal. No signs of magic anywhere.

Ciaran stopped at one of the first doors on the second floor and opened it. The room was huge, with two full-size beds on opposite sides. The posters were mostly red, but one side was covered in red and gold, and the other side was red and blue. Chris laughed at all the posters. "You two were serious about your teams, yeah?"

"Yeah, we were," Ciaran said, looking around. "It's his fault that I hate Arsenal. He jinxed his posters so that every time I tried to take them off, they would duplicate. I still don't know the spell he used. That's why he has more posters than I do."

Chris chuckled. "Clever boy."

"Want to shower?" Ciaran asked.

Chris turned to him and saw his sly smile. "In your parents' home? In your childhood bedroom?"

"I just said shower," Ciaran said innocently. "I was not thinking of sex."

"Sure," Chris said sarcastically. "I'll follow you into the bathroom. Just make sure you soundproof the room first."

"Can't," said Ciaran, taking off his clothes and walking to the adjacent bathroom. "The house is enchanted. My mum is alerted whenever any of her children use our *Vis* under her roof."

Chris laughed while taking off his clothes. "And a clever mum too."

They showered and changed, and by the time they made it downstairs, Hamish had arrived from work. The six of them feasted on stewed chicken and vegetables with rice and black beans, and the Beals told Andres and Selma about Ciaran's arrest and trial and then Chris's proposal to Ciaran in the crowded lift. They gave commentary, expressed shock and anger at Brickenhouse, but were grateful for the leniency of the jury and excited for the upcoming nuptials.

Afterward, they hugged Ciaran's friends goodbye. "We'll come to Albania in the summer, so let's make plans," Selma told them.

"You better," Ciaran said. "We're getting married August 1st, and you are officially the first person who knows."

Selma grinned and hugged him again. She and Andres held hands, stepped onto the back porch together, and Wisp'd right in front of them back to their penthouse flat in London. Chris took that time to walk around the house alone, looking at every picture on the walls, peeking in Diana's and the twin's childhood bedrooms, and going over the books on the bookshelves before he sat down in the sitting room with the other three drinking tea, feeling content with Ciaran in his family home.

Eventually, Ciaran bid his parents goodnight, and Chris followed Ciaran upstairs. They lay on Ciaran's full-size bed together fully clothed, staring at the ceiling, side by side.

"Tired?" Ciaran asked.

"No, not yet."

"Me neither."

"Tell me a bedtime story, love," said Chris.

"When I was a little boy," Ciaran began, "I used to be afraid of the dark. Ted never allowed me to have a nightlight because he can only sleep in full darkness. One night when I was six, and he was nine, I looked up at this very ceiling and said, 'I wish I had starlight,' and…"

The ceiling began to form little twinkles right above his bed. Chris smiled, staring at them. "Amazing," he said softly.

"It was the first time I used my *Vis*. It would disappear in the morning, but every night I would wait until Ted went to sleep and whisper, '*Stellarum*.' Alastair told me the proper name about two years later, after he and Ted went off to Campus. Then one day, I didn't need it anymore." He looked at Chris who was still staring at the miniature constellation above him. "I've never told anyone that before."

Chris turned to him. "Really? Not even your best mate, Selma?" Ciaran chuckled and looked up at the ceiling again. "I think Ted was right. I think there was some unspoken love between you and Selma," Chris said.

Ciaran was quiet for a moment, then said, "And I think you were once in love with your best friend Emiranda."

Chris was quiet for a moment as well. Then he said softly, "Cristobal is like a brother to me. And I would never betray my brother. So it never happened between us."

Ciaran rolled over, got on top of Chris, and said, "Well, this is going to happen because I've never had someone in my childhood bed before, and I'm not going to miss this chance now. *Arcanos susurrus*." He began to kiss Chris's neck as the walls, ceiling, and floors began to coat in a sparkly yellow film.

"Your mum's gonna know," Chris sang, but allowed Ciaran to relieve him of his shirt.

Ciaran didn't have a response. With the room sound-proofed, the door locked, and the lube floating over to the bed, they kissed and touched until Ciaran entered him. They made love, switched positions, and made love again, then fell asleep spooning on the small bed, all under the twinkling yellow stars.

In the morning, Chris came downstairs first, and Grace was in the kitchen. "Good morning, Mrs. Beals."

She smiled at him. "Good morning, Christopher. And call me Grace."

Chris smiled. "Do you need some help, ma'am?" he asked.

"No, thank you," she said politely. "It's just hog's pudding and kippers," she said.

Chris sat at the table. "I noticed that you don't use your *Vis* to cook all the time. Or for much of anything."

She smiled as she turned the sausage in the pan. "We Livingstons grew up in Mevagissey, Cornwall. My father was a proud seaman, and my mother was a baker. We were the only Magi in town. So my parents behaved as such and rarely used their abilities, unless they needed to, such as if there was a storm while my father was at sea to save others, or my mother had a last-minute wedding and needed the perfect cake. My parents taught us that magic doesn't solve all of life's problems, and we should learn to live and feel human first. It wasn't until my brother Malcolm and I went to Campus that we saw how much other Magi used their *Vis*. It was fascinating and opened up a whole new world."

She sighed. "But over the years and learning from my mistakes, John Dalberg-Acton's famous quote—who was a Magus, by the way—rang true for me. Absolute power does corrupt absolutely. I've watched it, been a part of it, and learned the balance of it."

"That's very profound," said Chris. "You have raised amazing children that all feel the same way about their *Vis*.

They lean into their humanity more than their supernatural gifts. And that's why they all stood on the right side of war."

"Yes," said Grace with a sigh. "For that, I am grateful. I watched how Elspeth struggled with her eldest son, Alastair, who bought into Talindra's propaganda that Magi should rule over Commoners. They were in his ear, telling him that he was going to be the next Grandminister once Graham was ousted. His ambition and his pride got in the way so much. It was Shane who got through to him, just months before he died."

Grace sighed again. "All that is in the past now. We're together again as a family. I've lost friends. I've lost family. I've lost a son. But we made it through."

Chris nodded. Grace continued to cook breakfast. After a long moment, he said, "I want you to know that I don't take for granted what Ciaran went through for me, for us."

"Well, Ciaran loves you, so…" She let a moment pass and then said, "He believes very strongly in what you and he have. Because of that, he would do anything for you."

"And I really do feel the same for him," said Chris.

"Yes," she said. "I heard you during the hearing."

Chris did not like the doubt in her tone. "I sense that you are still not convinced of Ciaran and me."

"I wouldn't say that," she said, turning around.

"Then what would you say?" Chris asked. "What do I need to do to convince you that I truly love your son? And I promise to be there for him and protect him, always and forever."

"Oh, Christopher," she said with a heavy sigh this time. Grace sat at the table and clasped her hands. "I think you've already proven that to everyone. I just…" She tried to find the right words. "I think I'll feel better after you've taken the Oath and become a part of our world fully. It will become real to you, what we've spent centuries trying to protect. Why my Shane died. Why Ciaran's small breach because of his love for you was so big for the Magi Community. It wouldn't just be about protecting Ciaran anymore. It will be about protecting all of us. And then you will understand."

Before Chris could respond, Ciaran came into the kitchen. "Good morning."

"Good morning," they chorused.

Grace put plates on the table. Hamish came downstairs, and the four of them ate together. "Ciaran, dear," Grace said, "After breakfast, I need some help decluttering; the fairies wreaked havoc in the attic on New Year's Eve."

"Okay, Mum," Ciaran told her. "We're going to pay him a visit first, then come back to help." His mother nodded in response. Chris was confused about who they were visiting, but didn't ask.

Hamish Wisp'd to work, and Ciaran tugged on Chris's sleeve. He got up from the table, and Chris followed him to grab their coats. But then Ciaran led Chris out the back door toward the right. They walked toward the trees and stopped at a huge oak tree with a boulder in front of it. Ciaran sat down and faced the tree, and Chris sat with him, puzzled. They were silent for a moment. Before Chris could ask a question, Ciaran began to speak.

"Hey, Shane. So this is Chris, who I told you about in June. I wanted you to meet him properly, the love of my life. Keep the sex jokes to a minimum, yeah? I got enough of them from Ted." Ciaran smiled, and Chris smiled with him. "I'm sure you saw what happened, and you know that everything is okay now. And now we have a future, which I am excited about."

Chris thought he was just talking out loud for a moment but looked down and noticed the flat gravestone right under the tree with the words engraved: "Shane Garvin Beals, Forever 21."

"I didn't realize he was buried here on the land," said Chris.

"Cremated," said Ciaran. "We mixed his ashes in with the soil and seeds, and then we accelerated the growth of the tree. So he's in the bark, in the wood, the leaves, and the yellow catkins that will always bloom, no matter what the season."

"It's beautiful," Chris said, looking up, watching the yellow flowers blow in the cool breeze. He reached over and took Ciaran's hand.

"He was the first person I told about you, admitted my feelings for you," said Ciaran, holding on. "You think I'm mad?"

"No madder than me talking to my mum under our tree," Chris reminded him. Chris turned back to the oak. "Nice to meet you, Shane. Although I get a good sense of who you were through your brothers, especially that twin of yours. How you shared a womb with that arsehole I will never know." Ciaran chuckled.

"I want you to know I'm going to take good care of this one." He kissed the back of Ciaran's hand that he held. "And be the best brother I can be to the others. I could never take your place as the fifth Beals kid. But I can be me and hope the void hurts a little less. I wish we met in person, but you can definitely count me as one of the many who is terribly sad you're not here anymore. Oh, if you see Ma Ami up there, give her a hug from her favorite son. Tell her I am doing alright here."

They sat in silence for a while; then Ciaran rose, taking Chris with him, and they walked back to the Beals's family home.

CHAPTER 6

Confessions

Clarissa picked up the phone on the second ring. "Chrissy, you're back? How was the trip?" She hadn't heard from her brother since New Year's Eve, and it was brief.

"Eventful," Chris said. "We just landed. Listen, Ciaran's parents came back with us. We're coming for family dinner tonight."

"Okay. We don't typically have a Sunday-like dinner on a Saturday, but I'm assuming that's what you mean by family dinner, correct?"

"That's exactly what I mean, yes," Chris said. "And they're coming with a family friend, so let's put on our Sunday best. It will be the seven of us, plus the children, for dinner. Do you need me to come over and help?"

"No, it's okay. Stay with Ciaran and his parents. I can get Charity to help. Bring everyone over at 6 p.m. That will give me time."

"Thank you," said Chris. "This means a lot to me." He hung up and turned to Ciaran at the airport in Tirana. "We're on. Fingers crossed."

They followed Graham, who was dressed in a suit with his two Magi bodyguards outside the airport. There was a Suburban waiting for the group to drive them back to Korçë. For a moment, Chris thought it was going to be stretched out or enlarged on the inside, but it was a normal large vehicle that seated all seven of them. Graham kept the conversation light, asking about Albanian tourist places, things to do, and any Magi-specific events.

The car dropped Chris, Ciaran, and the Beals off at The Atrium with the promise to come back around 5:30 p.m. for dinner. They went upstairs to freshen up and relax, but Grace had other plans, like berating her son Ciaran about his housekeeping skills and invoking Chris's help to clean up. But Chris didn't mind; he was nervous, so the cleaning gave him something to do. He had no idea what was going to be said or how it was going to be revealed, but he trusted Hamish and Graham, the experts who had done it several times over, to introduce the Commoners to the hidden world of Magi.

At 5:30 p.m., they made their way downstairs, and the same Suburban pulled up. Graham, now dressed in teal green African clothing and a kaftan cap, looked at ease. They rode in silence, everyone in their own thoughts.

Once arrived, Chris led the way to his apartment. Rudy, his five-year-old nephew who was looking out of the window, opened the door before he pulled out his key. "Uncle Chrissy!" he yelled and jumped in his arms.

"Hey, Rudy! I missed you, little guy!" Chris carried him into the main area.

Clarissa looked stunning as she was putting the finishing touches on the table, in black slacks and a soft white cashmere sweater. Charity was already seated, equally stunning in a soft pink sweater and long, black skirt. After Chris hugged them both, Ciaran introduced his parents and introduced Graham as "a leader in our community." The girls exchanged looks, but otherwise gave polite hellos.

They sat down to a large bowl in the center of the table of fish, veggies, and rice in tomato sauce. "It's thieboudienne, a traditional Senegalese dish," Clarissa told them. "I hope you like it. I tried not to make it too spicy."

"Oh. I did not realize your family hailed from Senegal," Graham said. "Chris did not mention it. My family originates from Ghana, but I was a little boy when we came to Britain many years ago."

They sat and ate, with Graham keeping the conversation light as he asked about their Senegalese background, their professions, interests, and hobbies. Clarissa and Charity asked Grace and Hamish questions about what Ciaran was like as a boy and growing up in England. Everyone seemed to get along well as they relaxed and drank wine. They took turns holding six-month-old Sierra, but she eventually settled into Ciaran's arms and did not want to be held by anyone else.

By 8 p.m. she had fallen asleep, so Clarissa took her and Rudy upstairs to put them to bed, and thirty minutes later brought the baby monitor down as they drank tea. As she sat down at the table again, Graham began.

"So I know you are wondering why I am here." He sat back, crossed his fingers, and smiled. No one spoke, but everyone gave him their full attention. "Clarissa and Charity, what has Ciaran told you about himself and our community?" he asked.

The sisters looked at each other. "Well... not much," Clarissa said. "We... we thought he belonged to a prejudiced community that would not accept Chris because he's African."

"But clearly that's not the case, seeing how you are one of the leaders and you are African," Charity said.

Graham told them, "I am not one of the leaders; I am *the* leader of our community in Europe." He let his words sink in for a moment. "And no, skin color has never been an issue in our community. What bonds or divides us goes beyond the outward appearance. So we don't worry about trivial things such as ethnicity, nationality, or sexuality, for that matter." He glanced at Chris and Ciaran at that last part.

"So what is it?" Clarissa asked. "Religion?"

"What do you know about magic, Clarissa?" Graham asked her plainly.

Chris's sisters were dumbfounded and exchanged looks again. "I don't understand; what do you mean by magic?" Clarissa asked.

"I mean, magic," Graham answered her. "Have you ever seen or heard someone say they can do magic or call themselves magicians, sorcerers, Magi, warlocks, or witches?"

Charity smiled. "Like Dungeons & Dragons? LARPing?" She turned to Chris. "Is this a joke?" Chris did not answer her, almost afraid to talk.

"Or are you Satanists?!" Clarissa stood up. "Is that it? You guys are some kind of Wiccan freaks?! Devil worshipers?! Well, I, for one, will not have it! We are good Catholics, and my brother will not be converted into the occult."

"Sit down, Clary, no one is worshiping any devils," Chris said with a roll of his eyes.

"Although. Wiccan is a religion that some in our world do practice," Graham said, raising a finger. "Others partake in religions such as Christianity, Judaism, Islam, Hindu, and Buddhism, depending on what part of the world you were born. I myself was raised Christian and still celebrate the holidays. But the vast majority of us are more agnostic than anything else, specifically in Europe, the part of our world that I lead."

Clarissa sat back down. "I'm confused. What is this about?"

"Let me go back to my original question, Clarissa and Charity. Do you believe that magic exists?" Graham asked.

Again Clarissa and Charity looked at each other wide-eyed, then back at Graham.

"No," they both said in unison.

"And what if I were to tell you that magic does exists, and I, Ciaran, and his parents can perform magical acts, mostly with the use of our wand." Graham took out his *dulé* from his side pocket and placed it on the table. "The proper name is called a *Rodulé*."

Clarissa's face was blank, but Charity smiled. "Okay, this is getting too weird. Chris, what is really going on?" Chris did not smile back.

But Clarissa, face still unreadable, said, "Show me."

Graham abruptly picked up his *dulé* and pointed to a glass on the kitchen counter. "*Cedo*," he said calmly. The glass flew across the room and landed in front of him on the table.

The women shrieked, jumped out of their seats, and held each other. "How the fuck did you do that?" Charity asked in fear.

Chris finally smiled. "Magic," he said. His sisters both glared at him.

"That's not funny!" Clarissa yelled at him. "Now whatever the fuck is going on here, I want it to stop now. And I want the truth! Real answers."

Hamish finally spoke, being used to having these conversations as it was his position with the Council. "The truth is, Ciaran is Magus, a person born with a magical genetic code in his bloodline. The Magi Community is a group of magicians across the world who are born with the ability to perform supernatural acts. Most of us come from generational families of magicians, such as us, the Beals, where either one or both of the parents are also Magi and direct descendants of Magi. I and my wife are Magi, and all five, now four, since one passed away, of our children are Generational Magi. Some others come from non-magical families, where one day a child will begin to show magical abilities with no seeming or direct ties to any Magi. Somewhere in their DNA was a dormant magical bloodline that reappeared. They are Commoner Magi. That is, we used to call them that. A few years ago we went through an intense civil war that was divided over fractions of Generational Magi versus Commoner Magi. Magicians versus Commoners—non-magical humans like yourselves."

Graham interjected. "And I have officially put a stop to that. We have taken those terms out of all future publications. We are all just Magi. It was time that the Magi Council took a stand to bring us all together. Allow me to reintroduce myself. I am Graham Agyapong-Yiadom, the Grandminister of the Magi Council of Europe."

Clarissa and Charity stood there, still holding each other with their mouths open, not sure what to believe. Everyone was staring at them, waiting for them to take it all in. Clarissa slowly unwound herself from her sister, walked back to the table, and sat down cautiously. Her younger sister followed.

"You mean to tell me," Clarissa began with her fingertips on the table, "that Ciaran is magician or Magi as you call it. And our brother, who is not a magician, is in a relationship with a man I have personally spent time with, who can do actual magic that no one here has ever, *ever* seen him do?"

Ciaran said softly, "I can show you now if that's what you want." He pulled his *dulé* out.

"No, I don't want you to show us more magic tricks!" Clarissa shrilled. She turned to her brother. "Christopher, what does this all mean for you?"

"It means," Graham answered for him, "that when Chris and Ciaran entered into a relationship together—which is not uncommon or forbidden as many Magi find Commoner mates—but when they did without notifying the Magi Council, Ciaran broke one of our most sacred laws by telling Chris who he was and about our world. The Magi Law of Secrecy and Concealment has been in place since the thirteenth century, protecting Magi from humankind and Commoners from us. We take it very seriously. So seriously, in fact, that Ciaran was arrested ten days ago and had to stand trial for his crimes and could have been sentenced to prison."

The women gasped. Ciaran held his head down, but Chris grabbed his hand and squeezed it.

"Oh, my God," Clarissa said with her hand on her forehead in an epiphany. "Now everything that Ted was saying makes sense. How people wouldn't want you to be together and how you'd have to decide to stay and fight or leave the community entirely."

"You were going to give up your magic, Ciaran? Your entire community, your birthright, for my brother?" Charity asked Ciaran incredulously.

Grace was stunned. "What? What is this talk? No, he could never do that. We wouldn't have let him."

"I would never let him, Grace. Please believe me," Chris told her seriously.

"So now you're what? Part of it all now?" Clarissa asked her brother. "Will you start to do magic too?"

"Ha!" Chris laughed. "I wish!"

Hamish told her, "No, it doesn't work like that. No one wakes up one day or hangs around magicians enough to have magic in their veins. Either you are born with it, or you are not. But regarding Ciaran and Chris, they have fought the charges and reserved the right to be together. So there is no more fear of retribution from the community. No one is giving up their magic here."

He looked at his son intently, also disappointed that it was even considered. Ciaran turned his eyes away. Hamish turned back to Clarissa.

"But there are some caveats. Ciaran was given probation for sixteen months. And Chris has been ordered to take the Oath, today in fact, to be sworn into the Magi Community as a Known Commoner, and he will be registered with the Magi Council of Europe. A known or registered Commoner is a Commoner that has ties to the Magi Community, usually through family ties and bloodline. This would make Chris and Ciaran family."

"And that's why you're here, right?" Charity asked as a lightbulb went off in her head, too. "Ted said something like we would need to be a part of it, too."

"Yes," Hamish said. "That is why we are here. Chris made it clear that he did not want to keep this a secret from his family any longer. Seeing as how the Beals will soon be your family too, this was important to him that you all embark on this journey into our world together. So you must decide whether to take the Oath with him."

But his sisters stopped listening halfway through, and both turned to look at Chris and Ciaran. "I'm sorry," Clarissa said. "What do you mean by 'the Beals will soon be our family'?"

"Ciaran, you proposed, didn't you?!" Charity squealed.

"No. I did," Chris said factually.

"What?!" the women exclaimed together.

Ciaran smiled. "He did. And it was perfect." They smiled at each other.

"Wait," Clarissa said sternly. "Are you getting married because you want to get married or because you have to get married because of the trial? Were you ordered to get married?"

Graham said, "We would never force two people to get married. Magi who mate typically stay together for life with a magical bond that seals them through the vows they share, barring any dangerous circumstances. We call a Magi marriage a Tie-Bind. Chris must take the Oath for the Tie-Bind to take effect. But," he looked at Chris and Ciaran, "it appears they have created their own magical bond, a soul-binding one." They grinned at him. Graham turned back to the two women. "So whether they marry or not, they are still family, and they are still bonded for life."

"So then, why are you getting married now?" Clarissa asked her brother.

Chris said, "Because there is no other person on this earth that I would want to be with. Ever."

And Ciaran repeated, "Because there is no other person on this earth that I would want to be with. Ever." They looked at each other and smiled, squeezing their hands.

No one spoke for a moment. Then Charity said, "So what do we have to do?"

But Clarissa cried, "Wait! We can't just..." She turned to Chris. "Are you sure about this?"

Chris became frustrated. "Did you not just hear me? That I was the one that proposed to him? I'm going to marry Ciaran Beals and be a part of his world. Now, you can either get on board or not, but this train is leaving the station."

Chris softened. "But I want you there with me. Otherwise…" He looked at Graham.

"Otherwise what?" she asked him. She turned to Graham. "What happens if we say no?"

"Then we conceal this conversation from your minds like it never happened, Chris takes the Oath without you, and he has to live out the rest of his life keeping this secret from his loved ones. Usually when that happens, the person ends up distancing themselves from their Commoner family."

"Oh no, we won't let him live like that," Charity said. "We'll do it. We'll take the Oath." She glared at her older sister.

Clarissa said slowly, "Yes… Yes, we'll take the Oath."

"Splendid," said Graham happily.

"But—"

"Clarissa!" her siblings yelled at her in frustration.

"Give me a goddamn minute!" she yelled back. Everyone quieted as she collected her thoughts. "What exactly is the Oath? What am I pledging to? Give me specifics."

Hamish said, "You are pledging to keep the Magi world a secret from the Commoner world and to uphold our laws and values."

"It's something we said every morning of every day while at Campus," Ciaran chimed in. "Even among us Magi, we pledge our fidelity to our community."

"And that's it?" Clarissa asked skeptically. "We just say the words, and that's it?"

"Well, it's a magical Oath, dear," Grace said. "You take the Oath, not just with your words, but with your entire being. You will feel it the moment it happens when you become a part of us."

"Let's not waste another minute," said Graham. He stood up and waved his *dulé* as three pieces of paper appeared in thin air and fluttered in front of Chris, Clarissa, and Charity.

"You can read over and memorize the words if you'd like. But first, say them to yourselves three times. Then you will repeat after me, one by one."

It was quiet as the Jennings siblings read the words to themselves. "Okay," said Graham. "Who wants to go first?"

"Wait!" Clarissa yelled again. "What about my children? They are too young to understand."

Graham told her, "Yes, and when children talk about magic, it's all make-believe. No adult will take a five-year-old who insists he saw magic being done in front of him seriously. But as they get older, you will have to explain to them that some family secrets will need to stay in the family. And as early as ten years old, they can also take the Oath. But as their mother, you can cover them until then."

"Oh. O-okay," Clarissa said, still seeming apprehensive.

Charity scoffed. "Clary, for once in your life, can't you just let go and take a leap of faith that everything will be okay?"

"Excuse me," said Clarissa, offended. "I've taken that leap more than once, thank you, and I got two little humans up there to prove it. I'm just weighing out all the risks for me."

"Well, it's not about you, innit?" Chris said, getting frustrated once more. "It's about me. What I want. What I need. I never asked you for anything, Clarissa. Never judged your choices like you judge mine. Never complained if you needed me to drop everything and be there for you because we're family. The plan, just so you know, was to handle this last June when I was to go with Ciaran to his sister's wedding, but I didn't go because you needed me here. Because that's what we do for one another. So here I am, asking you to do this for me. I love you, and I don't want to leave you behind. So, can you please do this for me?"

Clarissa realized her brother was right. She stood up and came over to Chris, who also stood up. She hugged and held him. "Thank you for always being there for me, Christopher." She let him go and faced Graham.

"I will go first." Clarissa moved to the center of the room.

CHAPTER 7

Magic Is Real

Graham stood in front of her, holding out his *dulé*. "Grasp the tip of my *dulé* with your right hand and place your left hand over your heart. Don't let go of the wand." She did as he instructed.

Graham said, *"Vis Sacramentum."* The tip glowed a bluish-teal color in her hand.

"Oh," she exclaimed, watching it. "It's warm."

"Indeed," he said. "Repeat after me."

Graham spoke the words of the Oath, and Clarissa repeated it, surprising herself that she knew it by heart.

As soon as she finished, she said, "Oh!" again. They all watched as the light from the *dulé* traveled just beneath her skin, through her hand, up her arm, past her shoulder, and across her chest to where her hand and her heart met. It glowed three times, then disappeared. When Clarissa lifted her hand back, she had a small tattoo of a *rodulé* with three stars below her wrist. She looked a bit alarmed at having a tattoo.

"No one can see it but Magi and other Commoners with a similar mark," Hamish said, answering her question. "That is how we recognize Commoners in the community."

Charity was in awe. "That was so cool! Me next!" she exclaimed.

But Chris was watching Clarissa stare at her tattoo. "How do you feel?" Chris asked.

She looked up wide-eyed, mouth opened. Then she grinned. "Oh, my God. Magic is real." That made Chris chuckle. He pulled her into a hug.

"No, really, my turn!" Charity whined, practically stomping her foot.

Clarissa stepped back, and Charity stepped forward. Charity mimicked Clarissa's hands with Graham and repeated the words. The same glow and then the tattoo appeared, but hers was on her left forearm.

She smiled brightly. "It's so pretty," she said, touching it with her thumb.

Chris hugged Charity too; then he stepped forward. But Graham said, "I think Ciaran should do yours."

Ciaran was confused. "How? I'm not a Council official."

"Well," Graham said. "Technically, when Dale made you a manager and part of the executive team at the Dragon Reservation of Albania, it made you a Scholarly official. A Minister of Scholarly, if you will. Therefore, I can grant you higher access and privileges, for let's say, the next twenty minutes. If you want to."

"Yes!" Ciaran said enthusiastically. "But never tell Dale."

Graham walked to Ciaran and tapped the center of his head and said, "*Tempus officialis viginti.*"

Ciaran chortled at the feel of warmth spreading through him. He moved to stand in front of Chris as they all watched and held out his *dulé*. Chris proudly grasped the tip with his right hand and put his left hand over his heart. "I'm nervous," Ciaran said. "Excited. But nervous."

"Right? Me too. This better work, Graham!" Chris scolded jokingly, then said, "I mean Grandminister Graham, sir!"

Ciaran laughed and then said, "Okay, here goes. *Vis Sacramentum.*" The tip of his *dulé* glowed in Chris's hand. "Whoa," Ciaran said in awe.

"Yeah... whoa," Chris said right behind him, also in awe, feeling the warmth of the glow. He also realized he could not remove either hand, as they were suddenly stuck to the *dulé* and his chest.

It was quiet as everyone waited. "You're ready?" Ciaran said gently, wanting to give him all the time he needed.

Chris finally looked up into Ciaran's eyes. "Absolutely."

Ciaran said, "Repeat after me."

"No need, I know it," Chris said. "I don't know how I know it, but I do. Maybe I memorized it."

Ciaran looked at him and smiled. "Did you? Like a real Magus, huh, with the *Vis* in your system, it immediately etched into your heart."

"I already feel..." Chris couldn't explain it, like his blood was bubbling on the inside. "I'm ready," he said to Ciaran.

"Let's say it together then, love," Ciaran said.

Together, they recited, "I, Christopher Macdougal Jennings, do hereby solemnly swear that I will uphold the laws of the Magi Plain, to protect and defend our people against those who wish to do harm, Commoners and Magi alike, and to keep the visibility of all magical people, objects, creatures, items, and beings from Commoner eyes for as long as I live, by the Order of Myrddin, the first of our *Vis.*"

A moment passed, and Chris was about to ask if it worked when he felt the warmth move from the palm of his hand. He, too, watched the glow travel through his body to his heart. A small pulse started and grew stronger until it came out of his chest like a small pebble and entered into his other hand. The light disappeared, but he could feel it travel back through his body to his hand to release the hold. When he could let go with his right hand, he looked down and watched the small *rodulé* and then the three stars appear on the back of his left hand.

Chris felt different somehow. Like he just *knew* all magic was real. Magic was wonderful, beautiful, and precious, and it was *real*. And he knew it would be his lifelong duty to protect the Magi Community, to keep it hidden. His vow, the solemn Oath that he just took, was etched as deep into his skin as the tattoo was on his body. He knew that was what his sisters felt, too.

But Chris also felt something else. Like there was magic inside of him, coded in his DNA, hidden, untapped, and unable to unlock for himself. His children would be carriers of the *Vis*, not because of Ciaran, but because of *him*. He was as sure of that as he was that magic was real. As sure as his love for Ciaran. But Chris kept that part of his epiphany to himself.

Ciaran was watching Chris's face intently, trying to gauge his reaction. "All good there, mate?" he asked cautiously.

Chris looked up. He grabbed Ciaran's face with both hands and kissed him on the lips. "All good." Ciaran laughed and kissed him back.

Chris found Grace's face and saw she was grinning from ear to ear. "I understand now," he said to her.

Grace smiled and nodded. "Of course you do, my boy." Chris reached one hand out and grabbed hers. She squeezed it. "Let's celebrate!"

"You forgot the important part, dear," said Hamish. He turned to the three. "You must eat the parchment with the words of the Oath."

"What?!" the Jennings siblings exclaimed.

"Once you do," Hamish explained, "your genetic code will automatically be placed on the Known Commoner Registry in Scholarly, the one located in London. So that no matter where you go, what Magi space you are in, if someone cuts off your left hand or attempts to burn your Magi mark off, you will be found in the registry as one of us."

"That was super dark there, Hamish," Chris said.

"But incredibly necessary," he said seriously. "Now eat the paper."

Chris chuckled as they moved back to the table. Chris picked his up, and his sisters followed. "This is madness," said Clarissa. But she crumpled the small paper into a ball and held it out. "*Santé!*"

"*Santé!*" they said behind her, and did the same. The three put it in their mouths and began to chew.

Chris thought it was going to be like eating paper, but it quickly dissolved like cotton candy, with no distinct flavor. The Jennings turned to each other and formed a group hug.

Grace pulled out her *dulé* and conjured uncorked champagne bottles and wineglasses which poured on their own, hanging in midair. "Now we celebrate."

Charity and Clarissa smiled, no longer afraid of magic. They all reached for their glasses.

Graham said, "Ciaran, you do the honors."

Ciaran looked at all the smiles around him. "To Magi and Commoners. And the love that brings us all together." Chris grinned and kissed his cheek.

"Cheers!" Graham said. They drank and hugged each other.

Clarissa brought freshly baked brownies and ice cream as dessert. As they sat down to dig in, Charity looked at the brownies and squealed alarmingly, "Ciaran!!"

She covered her mouth with both hands and looked at him with wide eyes. He knew that she remembered exactly what happened between them now, when she was high and came onto him, because of her knowledge of magic. Ciaran had cast a number of spells, from the barrier spell so she would stop trying to touch him, to the *stellarum* incantation that she followed all the way to her bedroom in awe. But he kept his face as puzzled as everyone else.

"What? What is it, Charity?" Ciaran asked.

Everybody waited. She took a deep breath and looked down. "Nothing. I just... I just remembered ... that... that I used to see your wand around the house. And I never thought to ask you. And... and now... now it all makes sense." She gave him a knowing look.

Ciaran kept his face neutral. "Yes. I suppose I did get lazy when I was here with my *dulé*. But thanks to Chris's present, I won't ever lose it again."

"Oh, you have a *dulé* retractor now?" Graham asked. "It's all the rage with the youth."

"Yes, two, in fact," Ciaran said, turning away from Charity to give her a moment to collect herself. "One for my place and one for his. Although I suspect we'll just be needing one now, since he will most likely move in with me and give Charity the flat here."

"About that," Chris chimed in. "I'm not going to move in with you. At least not yet."

Ciaran turned to Chris in surprise. "Why? I thought it's what you wanted."

"I do. But I'm an old-fashioned guy. I think I want to wait until after we are officially married."

Ciaran was confused and slightly annoyed, but tried not to show it. Grace said, "And when is that, dears? The wedding. Have you got a date?"

"Um, yes," Ciaran said, still annoyed. He turned to his parents. "We agreed on August 1st. Unless Chris wants to change that, too."

Chris gave Ciaran a side-eyed look of annoyance, but no one noticed, as they were too busy being shocked.

Clarissa said, "What? As in this year?"

Grace said, "That's less than a year!"

Charity said, "August is way too hot."

"OY!" Chris yelled. "There is a reason we chose the date, and we aren't changing it."

Ciaran told them, "It's kind of our anniversary, the day we met. The wedding will be at twilight."

"But you'll have to find a place, a venue, flowers, decorations, music, all of those things," Charity reminded them.

"Whoa," said Chris, holding his hand up. "We're keeping it simple. Just like Vlad and Alexi had, a pretty corner of the woods and reception at The Atrium."

"Absolutely not!" Clarissa exclaimed.

"Well, I don't know who Vlad and Alexi are, but at least he didn't say Nemo's." Charity rolled her eyes.

"Trust me, I considered it," Chris threw at her. Ciaran chuckled.

Grace said gently, "Ciaran, dear, I really think you should reconsider this idea."

Clarissa said, "You're my only brother, Christopher, and you need a proper wedding."

They all began cross-talking until Ciaran whistled to get everyone's attention. "I appreciate everyone's enthusiasm, but this is Chris's and my wedding. We want to keep it simple."

"Okay, we hear you," Charity said. "Simple, quick, cost-effective. Sure. But give us a chance, Grace, Clarrisa, and I, to honor your wishes for a small, no-frills wedding, but still make it nice and elegant? For example, a small corner of the woods, I heard you. So let us find a nice small corner that looks great at twilight."

Grace chimed in, "And if it's the Atrium you want, maybe we can do a tent reception where Phoebe can cater."

"What a great idea, Mrs. Beals," Charity said.

"And I'm assuming you're wearing white?" Clarissa asked.

Ciaran and Chris spoke at the same time with Chris saying, "Yes," and Ciaran saying, "No." They turned to glare at each other, having a conversation with their eyes while everyone waited in silence.

<No>, Ciaran told him in his head. <*I will not wear white.* >

Chris conceded out loud. "Fine. You don't have to. But I will wear white."

"White it is!" Charity said. "So, what are the theme colors? And do not say red."

"No," they both said simultaneously.

"Blue," said Ciaran.

Chris scoffed. "This is not the Reserve. We aren't doing blue and white."

"Reserve colors are blue and tan," Ciaran said with an attitude.

"And we aren't doing that either," Chris said.

"And what do you envision?" Ciaran asked.

"I don't know. Maybe a periwinkle or lilac?"

Ciaran scoffed. "Is that a fucking joke?"

"Ciaran!" his mother scolded at his language.

"Sorry, Mum," Ciaran said. "But there is no way I'm allowing bright colors—"

"Allowing!" Chris bellowed. "I don't need your permission to have a wedding that has more than black, blue, and brown in it."

"You do if you want me there," Ciaran said definitively.

"Fuck off with that, Ciaran, you will be there if I have to drag your ginger ass there, wearing fucking white!"

"Sod off—"

"BOYS! LANGUAGE!" Grace yelled at them.

"Sorry, Grace."

"Sorry, Mum."

"Now," Grace started again. "There are plenty of colors between blue and lilac. Observe." She waved her *dulé* and sixteen different flowers appeared in a row, from royal blue irises to actual lilacs. Charity and Clarissa were beside themselves with happiness at all the magic casually happening around them. "Pick your three favorite colors."

Ciaran chose brilliant blue, eggplant, and mauve. Chris chose iris, eggplant, and periwinkle. Grace said, "Looks like eggplant it is. And instead of pure white, why not go with silver? Silver and eggplant will complement each other nicely." They both nodded.

Then Ciaran said, "Honestly, I don't think I have the patience for this wedding planning stuff. So I will give my input if it's absolutely needed, but honestly, just tell me where to show up."

Charity said, "Grace, if you have some time tomorrow, let's look at some places and put together as many ideas as possible."

"I would love that. We're going to visit the Reserve in the morning, but the afternoon is great. Chris, will you be joining us?" Grace asked.

Chris gasped. "Can I?!" he asked Ciaran.

"Yes," Ciaran confirmed. "Now that you have taken the Oath, I can pass you in with my parents."

Chris could not contain his excitement and started bouncing around. "What's this Reserve you keep mentioning?" Clarissa asked.

"It's where Ciaran is employed," Hamish told her. "The DRA, Dragon Reservation of Albania."

Charity blinked twice. "Sorry, did you say, 'dragon reservation?'"

"Yes!" Chris said enthusiastically. "And now I can finally tell you the real story of how Ciaran and I met."

And he did.

At the end of the night, Chris walked them to the door, thanking Graham for everything. Ciaran lingered in the doorway after everyone left the home. Chris smiled at him. "This was like the best night ever, Ciaran. I feel ... so different. Like..."

"Like magic is real?" Ciaran asked, amusingly.

"Yes... but..." He was thoughtful in his words. "I feel closer to you. Like ... I get you now. I touch you and..." Chris touched the skin on Ciaran's arm, and heat flooded through him. "I *feel* you. I can feel the *Vis* running through your veins. I can feel it running through mine too..." He trailed off.

"Because of the *Ardenti*," Ciaran deduced. "Our souls are aligning, so you would feel it in me." He adjusted his hand so that he and Chris were caressing each other's fingers. "I feel it, too. The heat between us."

"I think it might be more than that..."

"What do you mean?" Ciaran asked.

He chose his words carefully. "Could I have an untapped *Vis* bloodline? Is that possible?"

"Yes. It's possible. I told you that. That's how Commoners become Magi," said Ciaran. "A child will suddenly have magical abilities. And when Scholarly does their research, they find the magical bloodline."

"Okay. I would like to research that at some point."

Ciaran nodded. "Sure. We can do that." Chris nodded too, falling silent. "I realize we haven't slept apart since Claustra," said Ciaran. "And I don't really want to."

Chris chuckled. "Well, unless you're telling your parents that you're sleeping at your boyfriend's house, I don't see another way."

"Fiancé," Ciaran corrected him.

Chris smiled. "Fiancé."

Suddenly Ciaran's face fell. "Why don't you want to move in with me?" he blurted out. "I just assumed when we got back..."

Chris wrapped both arms around Ciaran. "I do. And I will. I just want to leave a little mystery to it."

"There is no mystery. We practically live together now, just in different spaces at the same time."

Chris touched his ponytail. "Does it really make a difference, then? Won't we still see each other every day?"

Ciaran sighed. "I guess," he moped. Chris grinned. Ciaran kissed him. "I'll see you tomorrow. 7 a.m."

"Okay. But call me tonight so we can have phone sex," Chris said. Ciaran laughed and kissed him once more.

CHAPTER 8

One of Us

Graham had not arrived yet when Chris walked through the door to meet the Beals for breakfast at The Atrium. Elsie whispered to him, "Ciaran's parents are here! Is everything okay between you and them? I mean, do they *know?*"

Chris smiled and held up the back of his left hand. "See anything?"

"Oh my stars, oh my stars!!" Elsie screamed, grabbing his hand, "Mama!! Mama!! Chris is one of us now!"

She dragged him past the Beals's table, where he smiled at them apologetically to the counter where Phoebe came around it. She grabbed his hand and also shrieked. "Welcome to the Magi Community!" She gave him a big hug.

Lewis came out of the back room too and gave him a handshake to congratulate him. A couple of Atrium regulars came over to shake his hand, some who'd had no idea Chris wasn't already part of the Magi Community. Ciaran came over and received handshakes as well, congratulating them on their official coming out.

Then Ciaran said, "Oh, and we're getting married!" More shrieks, hugs, and handshakes followed.

Chris turned to Phoebe. "Phoebe, we would love it if you would cater our wedding. Please talk with Grace about it since she and my sisters are planning it."

Phoebe smiled and touched both their hands. "I would be honored."

After a few more hugs, they finally made their way back to the table to finish breakfast.

Graham came in when they were nearly done. "Apologies. I was on the phone with the Grandminister in the States this morning. Apparently, some crisis broke out in Puerto Rico. They believe the Santarias are a part of it. They are asking for Magi backup from Europe, so I will need to leave soon."

"Oh, I didn't know that Magi Councils in other countries support each other in that way," said Chris.

Hamish told him, "The United Magi of America, The Canadian Magi Council, Magus of Eurasia, and the Magi Council of Europe have a treaty in place to share resources, including academic and military."

"But not the continents of Africa or South America?" Chris asked casually. Ciaran resisted the urge to look at him.

"No. Both continents have their own Magi laws and resources. But the law of secrecy and concealment is universal across continents and councils," said Graham. He turned to Hamish. "I must go earlier than planned. But I will arrange flights for you and Grace on Monday. We'll spend some time at the Dragon Reservation to show my support; then I am off."

"Speaking of which," Ciaran said, "Chris, you left two work uniforms here. You should grab them now."

"Oh, that's right," Chris said. "I'll need them for next week. And I'll borrow a pair of trainers, too."

Chris rose, and Ciaran rose as well, chuckling. "Of course you will. I'll come with you."

They went back into the Atrium Residence and went into the apartment together. Chris went into the bedroom, and Ciaran followed. He chose a pair of red and black Converse sneakers to match his black jeans and red and white t-shirt and started changing his footwear automatically. As he bent over, Ciaran came to him and grabbed his waist.

"Now what was that you were saying last night on the mobile? About me bending you over?" he asked seductively.

Chris stood up slowly and turned around. "Your parents are right downstairs. You plan on keeping everyone waiting?"

"I can be quick."

"You don't do anything quick. Especially that."

"I guess I should start practicing then."

He kissed Chris passionately. Then he stepped back and started taking off his clothes while Chris watched. When he was completely naked, he moved backward and lay on the bed, stroking himself. That's when Chris began to strip.

"Aren't your parents sleeping on that bed?" he asked.

Ciaran answered, "Strip. Now. And cum inside of me."

Chris grinned the whole time as he took off his clothing. Chris lay beside him, and they kissed and touched. Chris moved behind Ciaran and bent him into a doggie-style position to penetrate him. Ciaran moaned loudly, and Chris wasted no time pounding him hard, slapping his thighs against his bottom. Ciaran moaned, and Chris grunted until he came inside of him.

"Now my turn," Ciaran said.

"By all means," Chris said as he lay on his back.

Ciaran entered Chris slowly, kissing and penetrating him. The pleasure was so intense for both of them that they forgot that they were supposed to be moving quickly. When Chris tightened his rectum around Ciaran's cock, Ciaran knew he had to cum. He pumped a few more times, then pulled out, and left ropes of cum on Chris's stomach.

"Why'd you pull out?" Chris asked with a groan. "I wanted to feel it inside, too."

Ciaran smeared his cum on Chris's chest and up to his collarbone. "I'm marking my territory," Ciaran replied.

Chris laughed. But Ciaran kissed Chris deeply and said, "I love you." He did not wait for a reply before he rolled off him and stood up, starting to put on his clothes. Chris grabbed the sheet to wipe the cum off, but Ciaran took his hand to stop him. "Don't wipe it off. Let it dry."

Chris laughed again. "You want me to hang around your parents smelling like your *sex?*"

Ciaran winked. He tossed Chris his own tank top, saying, "Wear this on top of it." Then tossed Chris back his red t-shirt and sweater. Chris grabbed the items, got dressed, and they went back downstairs, where Graham was finishing up his breakfast and talking with Phoebe. Ciaran checked his watch. They had been gone for a total of twenty-two minutes.

They took the car service to the parking lot under the Tank. One of the Magi bodyguards stayed with the car while the others trekked through the woods to the Dragon Reservation of Albania. When they got to the tree, Ciaran paused everyone and said, "I'm going in first with Chris. The alarm is going to go off because of Chris, so just keep your hands visible. Grandminister, please come in behind me so they see your face. Mum and Dad, take the rear. Everyone ready?"

"Splendid!" Graham said happily. "Happy to follow your lead. I have only been here once when I first took the post a decade ago, so this is exciting for me, too." Chris smiled at his giddiness.

Ciaran reached out for Chris's hand, and Chris took it. Then he turned around and walked into the tree, pulling Chris with him.

Chris half expected to bump into the solid wood he had touched many times. But as they passed through, Chris felt a rushing wind all around him, then the same cool air again. They stepped into an open area at the bottom of a short, grassy hill. Before he had time to comment, a loud roar sounded, like a dragon was right above them. Chris immediately looked up. But a bunch of Magi came running down the hill and made a circle around them with their *dulés* raised.

Mateo noticed who it was first. "Ciaran? *Culo, jefe*, why did you raise the alarm?"

"Is that Chris?" Lucas said in astonishment. "He can't be here!"

But Graham appeared right behind them. At the sight of him, they all dropped their *dulés* to their side and exclaimed, "Grandminister Graham!" "It's the head minister!" "The Magi Council Grandminister is here?!"

Ciaran's parents came through as Dale was walking down the hill with a scowl on his face. But upon seeing the head of the Magi Council of Europe, he grinned. "Grandminister Graham. What a great surprise! Please, please, gentlemen, give him room."

Dale walked up to Graham and shook his hand. Then he turned to Ciaran. "Ciaran, my boy, how was the holiday? Oh, and you brought a friend, splendid! Dale Babbit's the name."

He shook Chris's hand and then turned to Grace, turning up the charm even more. "Mrs. Beals, lovely as ever. And Minister Beals, good to see you." He kissed Grace's cheek and shook Hamish's hand. "Come. Let's head to the main area." Dale led them up the hill.

"That's Dale?" Chris whispered to Ciaran as they trailed behind everyone else. "I expected him to be a bit surly."

"Hmmmm…" Ciaran said, watching him warily. "That's 'company's over' Dale, I reckon."

When the group reached the top of the hill, it was Sarah and Felix who greeted them. "Grandminister Graham, it is a pleasure to have you visit us today, although unexpected," she said sweetly.

Graham grasped both her hands. "The pleasure is all mine."

Vlad came jogging over. "Ciaran, what are you… CHRIS!" he bellowed upon seeing his Commoner friend.

They slapped palms; then Vlad pulled back and looked at him curiously. "Does this mean…" He grabbed Chris's left arm before he could respond and turned his hand over. "HAAA!" he screamed again. "You're with us now!" Vlad threw his arms around Chris, who was much taller, making him laugh.

Dale had a tight smile. "Ah, boys will be boys. Vladimir, you have some work to do. Please return to your duties, lad. To everyone else, let me and Sarah show you around."

They walked around the main clearing, spotted with trees. There were men around doing different jobs: shoveling dung, practicing incantations, and skinning meat, but all stopped and stared at the visitors. They walked toward the barracks where the trainees lived when Dale turned around.

"Ciaran, a word, please? You don't mind, do you? You can bring your friend too, the more the merrier. Sarah, you don't mind showing them inside the main building, yes? Show them the trainee classrooms."

"Ah, sure," Sarah said, giving Ciaran a warning look, not wanting to leave him alone with Dale.

Dale patted Ciaran's back. "Come with me, son. I need to show you something. Bring your mate." He led him away, and Chris followed.

As they walked farther away from the building, Ciaran started talking. "Listen, Dale, I know—"

But Dale swiftly pulled out his *dulé*, pointed it at Ciaran and Chris, and growled, *"Flotus maxima et descendit!"*

Ciaran and Chris both went flying ten feet in the air and fell back down, landing on their backs.

Ciaran groaned. "Ooooooh, what the fuuuuuck?!"

Chris groaned too. "Ow."

Dale walked over to them and looked down. "You. You brought Magi officials to my Reserve, you candy-flavored cunts!" he growled nastily. "*My* Reserve! Crawling with them, asking questions about you and your cock-sucking cocksucker here. I should glue your balls together right now." He stepped on Ciaran's chest with his hard boot.

Ciaran could barely talk with the wind knocked out of him. "Dale ... I'm ... sorry..."

"Oh, you're sorry! Well, that solves everything, innit? *Erecto!*" Dale cried.

Both Chris and Ciaran were made to stand up like marionettes, their arms stuck to their sides. Dale continued to berate them, walking around their stiff bodies. "Motherfucking piece of shit-talking cunts, the both of you. You just had to open your mouths; you couldn't just be satisfied with your dicks in them. I told you, Ciaran, to keep your fucking mouth shut; I told you what would happen if—"

"Dale," Chris called his name, surprised that he was still able to move his lips and tongue. Dale turned slowly to face Chris, who was immobile. Chris muttered, "I know it wasn't the best way to handle it, but see, it all worked out in the end. Now I am one of you. So it's better now."

"Ooooh," Dale said with a feigned look of surprise. "You want to be one of us? Well, let me help you with that, you dumb fuck. *Alta volare!*"

"NOOOO!" Ciaran screamed through his parted lips.

But it was too late. Chris went flying upside down and high into the air at rapid speed, screaming. Reservers stopped working to watch the show.

"What the bloody fuck, Dale?!" Ciaran yelled at him. "He's still a Commoner!"

"No, he's one of us now," Dale said nonchalantly.

"Bring him the fuck down now!" Ciaran yelled.

"Okay," said Dale.

He made to point his *dulé* at Chris, who was upside down in the middle of the air, nearing the top of the pine trees, still screaming. But then Dale said, "On second thought, sod off, you maggot!" He pointed it at Ciaran instead, yelling, "*Avifors!* Now go join your boyfriend!"

Ciaran went flying in the opposite direction, high above the trees. "DAAAAAAAALE..." Ciaran screamed.

Dale watched them for a moment, then did a complicated hand move. "*Descendomora.*"

Chris and Ciaran flew downward face first, screaming the whole time, stopping inches from the ground side by side.

Ciaran yelled at him, "This is not funny, Dale! Stop this shit and stop it right now!"

"I think I just peed myself upside down," Chris cried. "Pee is falling down my stomach."

Dale walked over to them, but all they could see was the bottom of his shoes. "Next time you find yourselves breaking Magi law, you'll think twice. Because you won't need the Council for consequences, I'll kill you myself. In fact, let's knock some sense into you right now."

He did another complicated wave of his *dulé*, this time wordlessly, and walked back to the barracks, not watching the outcome. Chris and Ciaran rose in the air again, faced each other, then suddenly crashed headfirst into the other, and dropped to the ground. Everyone who was watching heard the midair crunch and cringed.

"Ooooooh!" Chris saw stars and blurry vision, and he knew there would be a knot on his forehead.

Ciaran groaned and turned onto his stomach. He looked at Chris and said, "Chris, meet Dale, the Dragon Reservation Ringmaster."

CHAPTER 9

Territorial

Vlad and Felix came over to help them up into a seated position. "Dale's exaggerating," Felix said, holding out ice packs for them that he'd conjured. "There were only two officials. They lined us up, asking if we knew anything. Of course, no one said a word. Then Bruno told them to sod off and almost got arrested. That was fun. Sarah offered them tea before they left that was surely going to give them boils in unpleasant areas. Dale grumbled for the next couple of days that if you didn't go to Claustra, he was going to kill you himself."

Vlad said, "Then we got the pigeon from Chloé asking us to write letters of support on your behalf, and the bird waited around for them. I wrote one and got others here to do it as well, which they were all happy to do so. Alexi wrote one too, and he got the staff at the Atrium to do a couple too."

"I really appreciate that, mate," Ciaran said, holding the ice to his forehead. "It really helped."

"Anything for a friend. I'm glad it all worked out," Vlad said.

"Speaking of friends…" Felix said. He looked over their heads.

Ciaran realized they were at the edge of the hill going into the valley and figured they had a visitor. He turned slowly to see Betta inching her way toward them on four legs.

"Chris, don't move," Ciaran said seriously.

Chris's eyes went wide, and he froze, his ice pack still over his right eye. "Okay."

"She missed you," said Felix. "She kept trying to come up to the hill to find you. Tommy had to keep her calm these last two weeks. He's doing a good job, but you can tell it was not enough."

When she was about three feet away, Ciaran stood in front of Chris, who was still sitting on the grass, his back turned to her. He could hear her breathe; Chris would never forget that sound. As eager as he was to see the dragon, he was also trembling with fear.

"Now do exactly what I say," Ciaran said to Chris. Chris nodded. "Come slowly to your knees." Chris did. "Move your head from side to side, then up and down. Slowly now." Chris moved his head side to side at first, then back and forth. "Good. Keep moving your head back and forth."

Chris mimicked the movements in front of Ciaran's groin; then he stopped. "How is this helping me or the dragon feel comfortable?" he asked.

Ciaran smiled down at him. "It's not. I just wanted to see you do it."

Chris scowled at him, and Vlad and Felix busted out laughing. Ciaran stepped around Chris and said joyfully, "Betta, my love!"

He walked over to the dragon, and she bent her upper half lower to the ground to be greeted. Ciaran touched her face gently, made some cooing noises, and rubbed the side of her chin.

Chris shook his head and looked up at Ciaran's friends. "My boyfriend is an arsehole." Vlad and Felix laughed harder.

Chris turned around and stood up. And then he gasped in awe. "Is… is that the same dragon?"

"The very same," Ciaran said, rubbing her behind her ears. "The one you named. Our Robetta."

Betta had grown at least five feet longer, or taller, since he saw her almost two years ago. Seeing the dragon in the light of day was also fascinating. Her skin was still blue-black and gleamed metallic in the sun.

"I'm going to head on down, check to see if Malik is here," Vlad said. "He's rarely without her now, and I don't want him coming up the hill, too." He began heading down.

"I'm going to head back to the office building," said Felix. "See you up there?" He didn't wait as he went in the opposite direction of the valley.

Ciaran was still petting the dragon on the left side of her face. She was enjoying all the attention from her first friend. "You can come closer," he said to Chris. "Just no sudden movements. Come to the right of her, and let her sniff you."

Chris breathed out all his air. Then he began walking. As he came closer, she let out a grunt that stopped him in his tracks. She lifted her head up, and he could see her nose twitching as she caught his scent in the wind. Suddenly she began walking toward him on all fours. Chris stood frozen, barely breathing, letting her come to him. Betta approached and stopped. She smelled him over and over again, her breath on his chest and legs.

Ciaran came closer and rubbed the bottom parts of her torso. "It's okay, girl. It's just Chris. You remember Chris, don't you? He's safe. He's with me."

Betta continued to breathe on Chris and sniff him until she was satisfied, then nudged his hand with her mouth. Slowly and trembling, Chris touched her very softly on the side of her mouth. Her skin was hard and scaly like a lizard's.

Ciaran stood next to Chris. "Stay to the side of her, never directly in front of her."

"Okay," he said, still petting her. Betta continued to sniff him, especially his torso. Suddenly Chris understood this morning. "Marking your territory, huh?"

Ciaran smiled and nodded. "You're okay with her because you smell like me, so it's familiar. She's not threatened by you. Plus, she most likely remembered your scent from a year and a half ago. Magnetites have great scent memories."

Chris continued to touch her. "Hey, beautiful," he said softly to her. She grunted.

"I'm going to ride, okay?" Ciaran said. "She needs me right now."

Not waiting for an answer, he went around to Betta's neck and hoisted himself up. He grabbed onto her scales tightly and spoke to her softly, then cried, "Hiyah!" and kicked her hard in the neck.

The dragon let out a small roar and rose with such force Chris had to back up. She flapped her massive batlike wings, and Chris felt the wind as if he were standing too close to a helicopter. He hid his face as she went higher and higher, above the trees.

Chris was paying so much attention to Ciaran and Betta in the sky that he didn't notice someone standing right next to him. "Oy," the man said, startling him.

Chris jumped. "Fuck, Tommy, you scared the shite out of me!"

Tommy looked at him. "Sorry there, mate." He looked up at Betta and Ciaran as they disappeared in the clouds. "So, nobody got *abscondo'd*. That's a good thing, innit?"

"Yeah, Tommy, it's a good thing," Chris said, still looking up for them. But just like Ciaran on the broom, he was out of sight and long gone.

"Yeah, that would have been awful because what if one day you meet up again, and Ciaran was with a woman, and you were with a man, and then the woman and the man met each other and fell in love, and then you both get cheated by your exes, and then you fall into each other's arms because you're so distraught, and then you get your memories back somehow and realize you had this whole great love, but it's like thirty years later, and you're both too old and gray to get it up; I mean how sad would that be?"

Chris slowly turned to look at him. "*What?*"

Tommy shrugged. "It could happen."

Chris did not even know how to respond at first. Then he chuckled. "Tommy, you are ... every bit of what Ciaran says about you."

Tommy scoffed. "I'm sure he just told you how much of a pain in the arse I am."

"Yeah, that too." They both chuckled.

"C'mon, mate," Tommy said. "Let me walk you back. Betta is Ciaran's for sure, but the other dragons belong to other Tamers, so I'm trying to keep the smell of Commoner from grabbing their interest."

"Fair point."

They walked over to the main grassy clearing to find Grace in the garden with Sarah and Felix and Hamish, Dale, and Graham talking Council stuff in front of the main building. He opted to hang out in the garden and learned a lot about healing herbs, roots, and potions. Ciaran returned about an hour later and joined the men.

They stayed for a few hours, then went back to the Atrium for lunch and drinks while Graham said his good-byes and left. Charity picked up Grace from there to go over wedding duties, and the men explored the town of Korçë. In the evening, Grace cooked dinner as a thank-you for Clarissa's hospitality.

At dinner, Grace and Charity talked about the clearing they'd found about two miles from the Tank with the back-drop of the mountains in the Reserve. Charity told them, "The terrain is owned by the city and rented periodically for events since the view overlooks the valley and the mountains."

"Yes, but the land hasn't been used in a while, and it's overrun with bushes and wildflowers," Grace said. "They're actually looking to sell it, but no one wants to buy it because it's not on the main road. We can clean that up in a jiff, rent a tent, and set it up nicely for the wedding."

"Thanks, Mum," Ciaran said. "You too, Charity. We really appreciate you going out of your way to make this a special day for us."

Chris was thoughtful. "Can I see the land? Before we decide?"

"Of course, but it's already been decided," Charity said. "I'll take you over there tomorrow, but this will be the one and only time you see it before we put it all together for you."

Chris looked at Ciaran, and he rolled his eyes. <It's their wedding, not ours,> Ciaran joked in his head. Chris rolled his eyes again.

At the end of the night, everyone hugged before heading to their prospective homes. Ciaran and Chris met at the door again. Ciaran pulled him close with one hand. "So tomorrow

I am going with them to Tirana and have some errands to run. I won't be back until it's time for me to get to work. We won't see each other until then."

"Okay," Chris said, playing with Ciaran's ponytail, lying against his shoulder again. "I'm going to see the land with Charity to make sure it's good for the wedding, and I can keep myself busy for the day."

Ciaran moved closer and put his head on Chris's shoulder. "I can't believe how crazy these last couple of weeks have been."

"I know. But we're free now. Free to live our lives and be together."

"Maybe you're free, but I'm—" He looked at Chris, alarmed. "Chris! Graham never put the tracking on you!"

"Ho. Lee. Shit. He didn't," Chris said, concerned. "So what now? Do you mention it or not?"

Ciaran sighed. "I'll tell my dad. Maybe he'll send someone to give you the trace, or Arslan will do it himself."

"Maybe he did it on purpose," Chris said, smiling slyly.

"Maybe," said Ciaran. "But after all we have been through, I think it's better to be safe than sorry."

"Right," said Chris.

They looked at each other and moved at the same time to kiss. <*I love you,*> Ciaran said in Chris's mind.

"You know, it's getting louder and louder," said Chris. "No longer a whisper, but like a low voice in my head. I heard you so clear at dinner, and even clearer now."

"Hmmm... The *Ardenti* is definitely getting stronger between us."

"But when am I going to start to talk to you telepathically?" Chris practically whined.

"I don't know," Ciaran said honestly. "It's not a typical Magi thing. There are very few Magi with that gift naturally, mostly witches. And you can teach yourself or spell yourself to be able to send your thoughts like Ted does with Elodie. But I don't know anyone else that can do it with their partner that actually has created *Ardenti*."

"Elodie's grandparents," Chris remembered. "She told me that her grandparents on her father's side could do it. They would sit for hours not talking out loud."

"Interesting. We should take a trip to France soon," said Ciaran.

"We should," Chris said back. "I would love to know how it all works. But also, the Eiffel Tower. I didn't forget."

Ciaran kissed him again as a response. Chris looked beyond Ciaran, and his parents were gone. "Go," said Chris. "They're waiting for you."

Ciaran kissed him a third time. "I love you," he said out loud.

"It sounds sweeter in my head," Chris said back.

<As long as you hear it in your heart,> said Ciaran.

Chris put his hand on Ciaran's chest. Ciaran Wisp'd, leaving black smoke in his disappearance. Chris closed his eyes, breathed in Ciaran's essence, and smiled.

When Ciaran made it home, his parents had already made tea and were sitting on his sofa. "Sorry for leaving like that. We wanted to give you some privacy," Hamish said.

"We made you a cuppa," said Grace, and handed him a cup of tea.

"Thanks," Ciaran said, as he sat next to them. "So. This has been the most eventful two weeks, innit?"

"Indeed, it has," Hamish said. "But I have to say, Ciaran, it was good getting a glimpse into your life here. We've always felt like you're the son we know the least about since you live the farthest away. So I'm glad we were able to meet Christopher and his family, see where you work, how you live. We're very proud of you. And we're happy for you and him."

"And Mum?" Ciaran said, turning to her. "Now what do you think of Chris since he's taken the Oath? And that you've gotten to know him and his family better? I hope you can see now that he's a bit of me."

"Well, he certainly is your match," Grace said. "It's good that he challenges you. That you challenge each other. Just remember that marriage is more than passion and banter. It's work to deal with another person's personality all the time, day in and day out. But, if you truly love each other, the work feels more like a journey than a chore. And, yes, I do see that you truly love each other."

"But do you—" Ciaran started.

"Yes," she answered before he finished. "I do like Christopher. And as you suspected, I like him more now that I've met his family. He comes from a good home, and I'm so happy they all took the Oath. They are family to us now." She paused, then said, "Although we didn't hear much about his father, who is still alive. Charity said he and Chris are estranged from each other, but she and her sister see him regularly."

"What's the story there?" Hamish asked.

"Yes," Ciaran said, not wanting to go into it. "That is a long story for another time."

CHAPTER 10

Fairies

After stopping at Chris's to say goodbye, Ciaran Wisp'd with his parents early Monday morning to the airport to see them off and then went shopping in the city. Chris and Charity drove through the woods halfway to the Tank, the ranger's station. They pulled over on a barely visible dirt road, and Charity directed him to drive as far down as he could go.

"This is a little creepy, sis," he commented as the trees became more dense, practically blocking out the sun.

"I told you this area has not been used in a while. Pull over here," she directed.

Chris did, mostly because the road became smaller, and he couldn't drive forward anymore. They got out of the car, and Chris followed Charity farther up the road. As they traveled deeper into the forest, Chris saw it, a colorful insect that flew past him. It was too big to be a butterfly. He turned and looked up. High in the trees was a nest of fairies.

He stopped Charity from walking with a grab on her wrist. "What?" she asked.

Chris pointed up with his other hand. "Do you see them?"

Charity looked up and saw colorful wings. "Butterflies?"

Chris shook his head. "No, look closer. They're fairies."

"Bullshit!" she exclaimed.

"Come on," he called to them. "We see you. We won't hurt you."

"Chris, what are you—"

"Shhh," he shushed her. "You don't want to scare them."

They waited. Eventually, one came down. Charity gasped. "It's ... Tinkerbell!"

The creature was no bigger than the palm of his hand, a human figure with yellowish skin and bright fluorescent wings that had colorful spots on them.

"I'm sure not all fairies are called Tinkerbell. Isn't that right, sweetheart?" said Chris. She began to squeak and squawk at him as she flew around his head.

"How did you know?" Charity asked, still in shock.

"Ciaran's apartment building has fairies in the Atrium," said Chris.

The fairy hovering in front of him squeaked again. Chris held out two open palms together. It landed on his palm. "I'm Chris," he said. "And this is my sister, Charity."

The fairy left Chris's palm and flew over to Charity. It hovered in front of her face, judging her. Charity stood there with her mouth agape. Suddenly it flew back up to its nest.

"Oh, my God," Charity said, turning to her brother. "I've been missing out on a whole world."

"So have I, apparently," said Chris. "I had no idea there were fairies in our woods. But I think you see them now too because you took the Oath. It makes me wonder what else—"

But Charity cut him off with a squeal. "Christopher, look!"

The rest of the fairies came down, about twenty of them, and flew around their heads, some landing on their hair and shoulders. Their wings beat rapidly like hummingbirds and made a buzzing, sweet musical sound when they were together. They were also all squeaking at the same time.

"Oh, my God," Charity said again as one lifted up a lock of her hair and sniffed it.

Then, just as suddenly, they left together, higher up in the trees. "That was bitching," Chris said with a smile.

Charity giggled as she continued to look up. "So fun." She grinned at her brother. "Come on, it's right there."

She took him through a few more trees until Chris saw the clearing. They walked into it together.

The clearing was at least an acre, with wildflowers of all colors, six inches tall. He walked around for a while, deep in thought. It was surrounded by tall pine trees and a cliff's edge that led to the river about a kilometer down. It was the same river that flowed from the Verdant mountains for the dragons' supply of water. It was also the same river near his tree, the Motus Willow. Chris looked up and squinted. From where they stood, the mountains of the Reserve were about twenty kilometers away. He waited. Eventually, he saw it: a batlike wing emerged up and into the clouds. If he'd blinked, he would have missed it. If he had not taken the Oath, he would not have seen it at all. That thought made him smile.

"What are you thinking, Chrissy? Is it a good place?" Charity asked.

"It's … perfect. In every way," he said to himself, mostly.

"Okay," she said excitedly. "I'll give Grace a call and begin to make the arrangements."

Chris turned to her and hugged her. "Thanks, sis."

Chris drove her home but then went back out to the municipalities office to make some inquiries. He went back to the land at twilight by himself and sat in the grass and cold until dusk, thinking of all the possibilities. Then he went home to change for work.

———————◆———————

Ciaran did not show up at the Tank until after Chris had completed his rounds. He came in as Chris was resting on the twin-size bed and silently took off his shoes and lay next to him. They were quiet for a moment.

Then Ciaran turned to him and gave him a mischievous smile. "Hey."

"Hmmm... Hey yourself. What did you do today?"

"Noooothing," Ciaran said unconvincingly. "What did you do?"

"Nooooothiiiiiing," Chris sang.

Ciaran laughed. "Okay, then. We both did nothing." They chuckled.

They lay side by side and talked about the last few days, Charity and Clarissa's faces when they discovered that magic was real, taking the Oath, Dale's admonishment of them, and seeing Betta together. "It's good that our families get along and that our friends are happy for us," said Ciaran.

"That reminds me: Clarissa asked us to go to lunch at the Atrium. Obviously, she has never been inside a Magi space before, but after Charity saw fairies today, now they both want to see the garden."

Ciaran yawned. "Okay," he said nonchalantly. But inside, his heart was pounding with excitement. He got up to go so Chris couldn't start to feel it. "Your place or mine tonight?"

"Yours. I'm tired of looking at my bedroom furniture," said Chris. Ciaran smiled and kissed his mouth.

———————◆———————

Chris spent the week at Ciaran's and barely saw his sisters. On Friday, they agreed to meet for brunch at the Atrium. Chris and Ciaran opted to eat light and sleep in a bit so they could be alert at 1 p.m. for their guests. They both put on casual jeans and long-sleeved shirts and went downstairs. To their surprise, his sisters were at The Atrium Restaurant, and Elsie had already seated them at a center table, different from the booth that Chris and Ciaran were used to.

They feasted on Albanian delicacies and talked about the Magi Community and the rare phenomenon of *Ardenti* that Ciaran and Chris were experiencing together. Charity excitedly told them about the fairy nest they'd found in the woods, and Clarissa expressed her frustration at not seeing anything yet. Phoebe had to come over and remind them that Commoners frequented The Atrium as they got loud and excited talking about spells and incantations, and the ladies laughed so hard tears were running down their faces at Dale's jinxes against them.

After the third time, Phoebe scolded, "Okay, time to go! Out, out, out!"

"Awwwww!" Clarissa and Charity exclaimed together.

Ciaran said to Chris, "Take the girls to the garden, but take them through the alley entrance so they can experience the whole thing since Clarissa hasn't seen anything yet. I'll pay the tab and meet up with you."

Chris said, "Okay" and took his sisters out of the building into the alleyway and through the dusty blacked-out glass doors with his key chain wand. The doors opened into the Atrium garden, and the ladies gasped at how beautiful it was. The Emmth came up to greet Chris, then sniffed the ladies. Once the animal was satisfied that they were not a threat, he allowed them to look around. Chris let them take their time, stop at every tree, touch every flower, and explore the denser parts of the Atrium. His sisters were in awe of the unusual and colorful trees and creatures roaming about.

They found a swing connected to a tree that Chris knew was another fairy tree. But unlike the ones in the forest, they were not happy with humans in their personal space. One fairy with gray skin fluttered angrily in front of them, squeaking and squawking.

"Yeah... let's ah ... move on, shall we?" Chris told his sisters. He steered them away from that tree. "They are usually friendlier than this, at least when it's just me. I wonder—"

But as they started walking toward the center of the Atrium, suddenly about seven fairies started flying around him, pulling at his hair and his ears, squeaking at him.

"Okay, ow! Ow, stop! Gerroff me!" He started swinging his arms widely as Clarissa and Charity laughed.

"I think they are trying to tell you something," Charity said.

"No. They just want us far away from their tree," Chris said, still swinging.

"No, it looks like they are moving you forward," Clarissa said.

"Let's follow them!" Charity said excitedly.

Chris gave them an exasperated look. Three fairies took the lead and motioned for him to follow while four fairies circled his head and kicked him every few moments for him to keep going. They kept edging him along until they got to the bridge and let him get a few paces on before they blocked his way. Then they danced around him some more.

Chris had had enough. "What the... Fuck off!" he growled at them. His sisters laughed again.

Suddenly piano chords began to play out of nowhere. The Atrium Residence doors on the other side of the bridge opened, and Ciaran came through. He had changed to a crisp white shirt with the two top buttons opened and tan pants with white loafers. The fairies parted as Chris got the full view of Ciaran walking toward them, smiling.

"Whaaaat...?" Chris said, surprised. In addition to the fact that he had never seen Ciaran wear anything white, he was confused about why he changed his clothes at all.

Behind Ciaran, others began filtering through: Phoebe, Esme, Earle, Elsie, Lewis, Rebecca, Alexi, Vlad, and a few other residents. Chris's mouth opened slightly as it dawned on him that it was a setup of some kind.

He turned to look at his sisters, who confirmed it with their big smiles as they held hands from the base of the bridge. Only Chris was standing in the middle of it. He also realized the fairies had moved away from him, flying high above him in circles. He slowly turned back to Ciaran, who had just made it onto the bridge.

Ciaran smiled out of nervousness and excitement, and Chris could definitely feel it. He inhaled and exhaled as he walked to Chris in the center of the bridge. Chris held both sides of the bridge to steady himself.

"What ... are ... you ... doing?" Chris said softly with wide eyes, although he knew exactly what he was doing.

Ciaran took a deep breath. "Christopher Jennings. There will never come a day that I would ever want or need to be without you," Ciaran said seriously. "I told you that you're my future. You made it real when you asked me first. Now let me make it official, yeah."

Ciaran got down on one knee and pulled out a red velvet heart-shaped box and opened it. Chris's mouth dropped open completely. Inside was a black meteorite ring with a diamond-encrusted center strip.

Ciaran looked up at him. "Christopher Jennings, will you marry me?"

Chris ran his fingers through his hair, which had been growing out all winter. He slowly sank to his knees and touched both of Ciaran's arms. Ciaran adjusted to where he was also on both knees, and they faced each other. Chris gently took Ciaran's face in both of his hands; kissed his forehead, his eyelids, each cheek, his nose, and his mouth; reached down to hold his hands; and kissed them each.

Then he looked up at Ciaran and said softly, "Yes." He kissed Ciaran's lips again and again; then they hugged.

"Wait!" Clarissa cried. "We didn't hear the answer!"

"Yeah, mate, did you say yes or what? We gotta get back to work!" Vlad yelled at them.

Ciaran laughed. Chris, still holding onto Ciaran, leaned his head back and yelled, "YEEEESSSSS!!!"

The response was instant. Vlad and Alexi ran from one side, and Clarissa and Charity ran up from the other end, all colliding with the couple on the tiny bridge, hugging and falling all over them.

After a few minutes of celebrating that way, they all stood up. Charity said, "I want to see the ring! I just found out about this last night!"

"I barely got a chance to see the ring. Wait your turn!" he told his sister.

Ciaran handed the box to Chris. Chris pulled the ring out and showed it around. "It's perfect. Simple, but a bit glammy like me. I love it. And I love you."

Ciaran explained the design, saying, "My ring is identical. And the meteorite was made from Robetta, our dragon. Symbolic of us, I reckon. And both are inscribed."

Chris held up the ring for a closer look to read the engraving on the inside: "*...and three days after that.*"

"Three days after what?" Clarissa, who was over his shoulder, was also reading it. "I don't get it."

"Because it's not for you to get," he said to her sternly.

<*I love you*,> Ciaran said in Chris's head. <*Forever.*>

Chris turned to him and grinned. "And three days after that," he said out loud. They kissed again and held each other again.

CHAPTER 11

A Bit of Traveling

Ciaran received the *Amina* from Ted mid-January while he was on the Reserve in the middle of the night. *"It's a girl,"* the Barnaby lion said. *"Elodie is doing great, and Charlene is perfect. Ten perfect fingers and toes and a head full of strawberry-blonde hair. I think I'm crying more than both of them are. My girls."*

Ciaran told Chris, and instead of going straight home after work, they went shopping for gifts for Elodie and Charlene to send to London. When they arrived at Ciaran's flat, he called for a mail pigeon while they arranged the gifts in the box.

It was quiet until Chris said, "I can't wait to have a newborn of our own." Ciaran didn't respond, so Chris looked up at him. "We are having children, yeah?"

Ciaran put the rattle with the bow on it in the corner of the box. "We agreed, yeah."

"I think I just need to hear you confirm the words to me. 'Yes, Christopher, I would love to start a family with you,'" Chris modeled for him.

Ciaran looked up. "Yes, Christopher, I would love to start a family with you." Chris grinned. "Later." Chris frowned.

Ciaran scoffed out a laugh. "What? Do you already have a surrogate picked out?"

"I don't have a surrogate picked out, thank you very much," said Chris with a huff. "But I would like to get started sooner rather than later."

Ciaran touched Chris's hand. "Can we do some traveling on our own before we begin moving through Magi communities in Africa with babies on our chest, please?"

"On our back," said Chris, correcting him. "With beautiful African prints holding them against our bare skin."

Ciaran began rubbing his hand. "Is it wrong to slow it down a little and just enjoy the ride?"

Chris slid his hand away. "No. Not wrong. But we are having children right away." He added the folded-up cloth nappies to the box.

Ciaran watched him touch the items gently, longingly, and decided to leave the conversation alone for now. Especially since the tapping at the window alerted them that the pigeon had arrived.

Chris folded the items in the box and closed it. Ciaran opened the window, pointed his *dulé* at the box, and murmured, *"Emarcesco."* The box instantly began to shrink until it was the size of a €2 Euro coin. The mail pigeon waited patiently for Ciaran to tie the tiny box to its leg, then put a treat in its mouth. The pigeon squawked a thank you and flew back out the window.

Chris watched it fly away. "So? When do we start going into Magi communities?"

Ciaran smiled. "As soon as an opportunity presents itself, we'll explore it together."

Tap tap tap… Tap tap tap…

Ciaran was on his stomach and his arm stretched across Chris's chest when a tapping noise woke Chris from his sleep one morning in March. He gently moved Ciaran's arm and went to the bathroom first to relieve himself. The tapping noise was louder in the main area. Chris's eyebrows scrunched in as he used his ears to follow the sound and ended up in the kitchen. Chris looked around until he saw a shadow of a bird at the window. He drew back the curtains and saw a large brown buzzard tapping on the glass.

"Oh," he said out loud. He opened up the window, and the bird came flying in. "Good morning."

The bird sat on the table and lifted up its leg. Chris gently untied the two tiny silver envelopes. He knew to hold steady as they grew to regular size in his hand. But what surprised him was that one of them was addressed to him at Ciaran's flat. He opened the one with his name on it, and the air was filled with silver, sweet-smelling glitter.

"Wow," he said in awe. "I love this Magi shite."

Chris pulled out the card and read it aloud.

> Dear Commoner Ranger
> Christopher M. Jennings,
>
> The Cordonnier Family invites you to the Eightieth Wedding Anniversary celebration of Fabien and Elinore Cordonnier at Le Musée Bruguière in Maison-de-Charme, Marne, France, on the second of April. Please dress in black-tie attire and come for a night of love and festivities.
>
> Sincerely, La Famille Cordonnier
> Notre âme brûle pour toujours dans les étoiles.

Chris was confused. He picked up Ciaran's envelope and walked it to the bedroom. "Ci?" he called out.

"Hmmm?" Ciaran moaned, mostly still asleep.

"Who are the Cordonniers?"

"Hmmm..." Ciaran groaned again. "Elodie's family. Why?"

"Because we've been invited by the Cordonniers to France next month."

"What?" Ciaran finally lifted up his head in confusion. Chris held out the unopened envelope. Ciaran moved one finger, and the envelope left Chris's hand and landed in Ciaran's.

"You're getting better at that," Chris said, sitting on the bed.

"Yeah, I know," Ciaran said as he opened up his envelope. "Bloody hell," he exclaimed as glitter burst out all over his face. Chris giggled as Ciaran swatted it away, then read his own card.

"Interesting," said Ciaran. "My guess is Elodie set this up so we can meet her grandparents."

Chris's eyes lit up. "That's right. The only other couple in our circle that has *Ardenti*." He smiled at the paper. "I'm going to learn all that I can from them. Maybe they can teach me how to talk telepathically to you."

Ciaran lay back down and closed his eyes. <*Good, because you talk too much outside my head anyway.*>

Chris turned to him. "I heard that, arsehole."

"You were meant to," Ciaran mumbled. Chris stood up and did a swan dive on top of Ciaran.

———

"Where are we going?" Chris asked as Ciaran steered him toward the old airfield in Korçë.

They had been to the airport in Tirana before, just last Christmas, and Chris assumed they would be driving to Tirana, the main airport for their flight to France. But all Ciaran said to him was that they were leaving from Korçë and put the address into the GPS.

They drove as far in as they could until they spotted the end of the road blocked by a metal fence. "This hasn't been open in years, love," Chris reminded him.

"I know. The Albanian Magi Division took it over as a Magi transit station," Ciaran said simply. "Keep driving, right through the fence."

"Ciaran—"

"Keep going. Don't stop."

Chris kept his eyes open as they continued down the road and went right through the fence as if it weren't there. "Ho. Lee. Shit." said Chris, looking behind him.

Ciaran chuckled. "Eyes on the road. Go toward the first building and park the car in the lot."

Chris did as he was told and pulled into one of the hundreds of open spaces. Ciaran stepped out of the car first, pulling their suitcase out of the back. "Let's go."

Chris was still confused. "Go where? That building is decrepit. And we're just to leave the car here to get stripped, is that it?"

"The car will disappear as we walk away. Now follow me," said Ciaran.

Chris looked at it, then back at Ciaran. "How?" he asked skeptically.

"Magic," Ciaran said with a smile and kept going. "Let's move so we don't miss our plane."

Ciaran was walking toward the dusty metal doors. But Chris walked backward, keeping his eye on his precious vehicle, waiting to see what would happen. When he was at the edge, he felt his shoe brush against something and accidentally looked down.

"Crap!" Chris said when he immediately looked up. But as he suspected, the car was already gone.

"You're done playing around, mate?" Ciaran asked, amused. Chris turned to him and grinned. "C'mon."

Ciaran touched the handle of the dusty metal door and murmured, *"Superno introitus."* The handle turned for him. He yanked the door open and held it for Chris to step in behind him.

It was an airport. A large open space with bright and airy high glass ceilings and a hundred chairs in the middle for seating. Like an airport, all kinds of stores and eateries were available, along with bookstores, clothes, jewelry, and even duty-free alcohol. But there were other stores, like Cloak and Daggers, which sold cloaks for flying; Sweepers, which sold brooms of every size, shape, and color; and a *rodulé* shop, in case someone forgot theirs at home.

Chris's grin increased. "Why didn't we do this before?"

"Well, we couldn't; you were an unregistered Commoner," Ciaran reminded him. "Plus, we drove to Vlore to fly out from there. Now we don't need to drive anywhere to get to an airport. This is our closest Magi transport station. It's how we teleport."

"What do you mean?" Chris asked. "Magi teleporting?"

Ciaran pointed to the terminal booths in between the shops. There were eight of them, all listing the names of the other airports in Albania. "That's ours," he said of one that said Tirana International Airport across the top.

"I don't understand," said Chris. "Are we Wisp'ing? Or is there a revolving door?"

"We're getting a Lift," Ciaran said as he walked over.

"I assume you don't mean an actual taxicab," said Chris, following him.

The Mage at the desk smiled at them as they approached. "Welcome to Tirana International Airport. May I see your passport and boarding pass?"

Ciaran and Chris handed them over. She checked them against her system as Chris noticed a man in a suit walk past them to the elevators behind her. Instead of buttons, there was an insert to put in his ticket, which he did. The ticket scanned, the lift doors opened, he stepped in, and the doors closed behind him. The light above went red for a moment, then went back to green.

"Mr. Beals, welcome back. And Mr. Jennings, it is lovely to have you join us today," she said, bringing his attention back to her. "Any checked luggage? Do you need Avian services?"

"No, thank you," Ciaran responded for them. "Carry-ons only."

"Very well." She stamped their boarding passes with an invisible ink and handed them back to them. "Your Lift leaves promptly at 10:22 a.m. Boarding will begin at 11:40."

"Thank you," Ciaran said.

"Thank you for using our service," she said with a bow.

Ciaran steered Chris back to the main area, but not before he saw a woman with two kids do the same with their tickets at the elevator behind the desk. The children pulled their smaller carry-ons into the elevator, and the doors closed. Chris grinned again and couldn't wait for their turn as he looked at his watch.

Ciaran saw the awe on his face. "Let's ward our bags and explore. We have some time."

Chris followed him to two empty seats and placed their bags on them. Then Ciaran took out his *dulé* and said, "*Nulla tactus inpulsa.*"

Chris saw the wave of the force field cover the area, then disappear. He reached his hand out. "I can still touch my luggage."

"Of course you can. It's your luggage," Ciaran replied. "You just can't touch anyone else's." He pointed to a purse on the chair. "Try it."

Chris looked at him. "No. What will happen? I get shocked?"

"Shocked, burned, pus, boils, whatever hex the Mage put on it. Most Magi know not to touch another Magi's stuff. It's usually warded."

"So what happens if they touch our stuff? What hex did you put on it?"

"You don't want to know," Ciaran said simply.

They explored, ate, and bought some things, and at 10:20 a.m. they walked back over to their Lift. There was a group of men in front of them. Once the men went into the elevator, they waited for it to turn green again, and then Ciaran stepped forward. He inserted his ticket, then Chris's, and when the door opened, they stepped inside.

It was a regular elevator, but inside there was only one button, no numbers or letters on it. Chris pressed it, and the door closed. He felt it move, but was unable to tell if they were going up, down, or even sideways, and then it stopped. The doors opened, and they were in the terminal section of the Tirana airport, right near the gates. Chris stepped out slowly as others pushed past him to get into the elevator to take them to the lounge they had just come from.

"We passed check-in and security?" Chris asked, looking around.

"That was all done in the transit station and through the Lift," Ciaran explained as they walked over to Gate 3. "You saw us check in, and if we had anything that would not pass through Commoner airport security, like a gun or knife, the Lift's body scan would have brought us back to the transit station for review. Remember, Magi need to stay inconspicuous. Just because we can get through security doesn't mean we're reckless with it. We still follow human, Commoner, rules and law."

"Got it," Chris said.

The flight was uneventful, except for when an older man was walking toward the bathroom and lifted his hands up to give room to another woman passing him in the aisle. Chris saw the *dulé* and three stars on his left wrist. He couldn't help but gasp. The man looked down at him curiously as the woman passed. Chris waved hello, but with his left hand, then turned his hand around. The older man smiled at him and gave him his left hand to shake.

"*My daughter and grandchildren,*" he said in Albanian.

Chris smiled and shook his hand with his left hand, too. "*My partner,*" he said with his head motioning toward Ciaran. Ciaran looked up in confusion. "*Just a few months ago.*"

"Ah," he said. "*It's only just begun for you. You're in for a wild ride.*"

"*Indeed,*" Chris said and chuckled. The man walked on to the bathroom.

"What was that about?" Ciaran asked, curiously.

"Just a Commoner conversing with another Commoner," Chris said.

CHAPTER 12

Soit en Paix

Upon arrival at Paris's Charles de Gaulle airport, instead of heading out toward the entrance, Ciaran took Chris through the Connecting Flights path to get a look at the other terminals. "I haven't been to this airport in years, so I have to look for it," he explained.

"Look for what?" asked Chris.

"The transport station," Ciaran said. "There." He pointed to an exclusive airport lounge named Salon de l'épée de Charlemagne.

"How do you know?" Chris asked as they walked over.

"Charlemagne is the most famous magician from France and was one of the most powerful Magi in all of Europe."

"He was Magi? Wow! Wasn't he a king?" Chris asked.

"An Emperor," Ciaran corrected him as he opened the door to the lounge. There were a few people there, some at the counter and some waiting to get into the large elevator on the side. Others were sitting in chairs watching the big screens.

"So much I didn't know," muttered Chris.

Ciaran walked up to the counter. "*Bonjour. Parles-tu anglais?*"

"*Oui,* very little," the man at the counter said in a strong French accent.

"Okay. We need to get to a transport station near Marne. I believe it's *Canton de Bourgogne.*"

"*Oui.* Transfer ticket, please?"

Ciaran handed the man his and Chris's tickets. He went into the computer and looked it up. "*Oui,* Canton de Bourgogne is the closest. We can get you into the queue in *dix* minutes. *Est-ce que ça marche pour toi?*"

"Pardon?" Ciaran asked.

But before he could ask again, Chris responded, "*Oui, c'est le bon timing, merci.*"

The man smiled at Chris. "*Tu es le bienvenu.*" He handed Chris their tickets.

Chris steered Ciaran away from the front desk. "Our Lift leaves in ten minutes," said Chris.

"I heard that part," Ciaran said.

"I know. It just makes me feel better that I'm a part of a world that you aren't. The francophone world," he said smugly.

Ciaran kissed him. "Shut up."

They took their turn on the Lift, and again, Chris could not figure out what direction it was moving in, just that it was moving. When it opened, they were on the ground floor of another Magi transport station. It was similar to the one in Albania, with different shops. But instead of exploring, they headed right out of the revolving doors. When they stepped out, Chris looked up, and it was a stone building. He decided to take the revolving door back inside and saw it was a bank. He smiled and revolved back out onto the street.

Ciaran looked at him with amusement. "Having fun?"

Chris grinned. Before he could respond, a silver Peugeot honked, and they both turned to it. *"Bonjour mes frères!"* Ted yelled as he stepped out of the passenger side.

Elodie stepped out behind him. "I'm so glad that you are here," she said happily, running up to Chris first.

Chris hugged and spun Elodie around. *"Magnifique!* You were glowing with Charlene, but that body is slapping post-natal."

"Merci!" Elodie said and kissed both of Chris's cheeks.

Ted slapped palms with Ciaran and gave him a brotherly half-hug before putting their suitcases in the trunk. "Hey!" Ted said to Chris in faux anger. "I told you to keep your grubby hands off my wife."

"She kissed me first," said Chris, as he grabbed Ted into a brotherly hug as well.

Elodie opened up the car door and hopped inside. "Let us go!"

Ted smiled at them. "She's really excited to show you her town."

"I'm really excited to be here," said Chris, getting into the backseat next to Ciaran. "I've always wanted to see Paris."

"And you shall," said Elodie, pulling the car into gear and screeching onto the road, barely missing another car.

Elodie talked and drove, a bit madly, through the small streets. "The Magi town is called Maison-de-Charme, hidden in Marne. It's a young village, less than a thousand years old, founded by two French Generational Magi. Gérard Bruguière and his best friend Jaques Lemaître built their homes and a primary charms school for young Magi children, ages four to ten. They called it The Charm House."

Ted cut in as she braked hard to avoid hitting the car in front of her and screeched around it. "El, my love, don't you think you should concentrate on the road? Chris can hear the story later."

"Hush, *mon roi*, this is important," said Elodie, dismissing him with one hand and swinging forcefully around a curve on the small street, forcing all three men to steady themselves.

"I will tell you the truth," said Elodie as she sped down the main road. "There was prejudice in their thinking. They wanted Generational Magi children to be more prepared than Commoner Magi children when they entered Campus for the first time. More Magi families with the same thinking moved to be closer to the school, and within a hundred years of its opening, suddenly it became a Magi village. Today it pretends to be a private gated community of around twenty thousand Magi, so Commoners are never allowed in there."

"Fascinating," said Chris, holding tightly to the handle over the window.

"Back then, the only way to enter the village was with pure Magi blood spread across one of the two landmark stones. It was very primal. Now it is a more modern city, and we have an incantation that only someone from the village with pure Magi blood can say."

As they passed the two boulders, Elodie raised her right hand and said, *"Bruguière et Lemaître, je suis chez moi."* The twenty-foot-tall gate in front of them opened and allowed the car to pass. The gate immediately closed behind them.

"Welcome to Maison-de-Charme," she said dreamily. "My home."

They went through a series of townhomes until it opened up, and suddenly there were buildings everywhere. As they drove through, it appeared to be a normal French city, with medium-sized buildings, main roads paved, and smaller cobble or stone roads. But it wasn't. There were barely any cars on the road, so Elodie's driving was no longer an issue. Instead, Chris saw clouds of smoke as people disappeared and appeared on the streets, people on brooms, or people gliding past them wearing cloaks. As Chris had noticed when in Myrddin, the older generation appreciated Magi robes and cloaks, but everyone under thirty wore regular, modern, and fashionable clothing like Elodie.

Elodie pointed at a mansion on a hill. "That was the original charms house. It was Bruguière's home on the third floor of the estate, with classes on the first and second floors. Now it is our historical museum."

"Does the charm school still exist?" Chris asked.

"*Oui*. It is now at the chateaux where Lemaître lived with his family. We will pass it on the way to my longères."

"Longères?" Chris asked. "Your father was a farmer?"

"*Fleuriste de l'agriculteur*," she corrected him. "My father grows and creates flowers. My mother sells them at her shop in town."

Elodie pointed out the current charms school, which was a mansion in the center of the main road, of at least twelve thousand square footage. It was a large stone structure with peaks like a church. Since it was midday, young children were playing in the gated playground. Chris noted that they were wearing white tops and red bottoms: pants for the boys, pleated red and blue skirts for the girls. Some of them had mini *rodulés*, even the smallest among them, running around and doing target practice, but most were enjoying the sun and playing tag with their peers. Chris smiled, thinking of his own son or daughter attending a charms school one day.

Elodie swung a hard left onto a narrow street, making everyone abruptly lean to the right. Ted tried again. "Elodie, can you get us to the chateau in one piece, please?"

She turned her neck and gave him a long, hard look. So long that even Ciaran had to yell, "Watch out!" Elodie looked at the road and swerved around a goat that was crossing the street, making them all lean to the left.

She turned to Ted again. Ted quietly faced forward and continued to hold on to the handle of the door.

The houses became less close to each other, with more farmland in between. Soon, she turned onto a stony road that had a simple sign: Chateau Cordonnier: *Soit en Paix.*

Elodie drove up to the front entrance of the large white-stone home with beautiful star jasmines growing down the wall and along the side, white flowers dotting the green. They followed her out of the car as she went to the double wooden and glass French doors and opened them dramatically.

"We are home," she said with a grin.

The house was quiet. Elodie explained that mostly everyone was at the museum getting ready for the event in two days. As they passed down the hallway to the stairs, Chris commented, "Everything is so ... French. From the millwork, limestone floors, the high ceilings, and the large glass chandelier. It's almost timeless and modern in here."

"*Oui,*" she said happily. "Ted will show you to your room, and then come have lunch with us in the garden. My *grand-pères* are excited to meet you." She kissed them goodbye and kept going out of the French doors on the other side of the hallway into the garden.

Ted took them up the grand staircase to the left and opened the door toward the end of the hall. "This is your room. Elodie and I are just a few doors down from you. The children are next door to us. They're with Elodie's mother right now, except Charlene, who is with Fab and Eli. I can't wait for you to meet my daughter," he said happily.

Chris and Ciaran both marveled at how beautiful the room was, with seating in front of the fireplace and its own bathroom. "Take your time; freshen up," Ted said, and he closed the door.

Chris smiled. "*Si magnifique*. It's so peaceful here."

"It is," said Ciaran curiously. "I wonder if it's a charm or spell of some sort because from the moment we walked in, I felt at ease."

"Yes, that's it," said Chris. "*Soit en paix*. Be at peace." He looked at Ciaran with a grin. "We're under their spell."

Ciaran smiled. "If we are, it's a good one." He changed the subject. "So tomorrow do you want to go into Paris, or do you want to explore Maison-de-Charme first?" he asked as a small rustling sound took his attention, and their suitcases appeared by the door.

"Definitely Paris. We can explore this town anytime." Chris walked toward the window and looked out at the garden.

There were symmetrical stone pathways in an intricate design, surrounded by patches of greenery with different flowers in each center. The garden was surrounded by small trees and shrubs all green except on one side. He noticed the row of red and white rosebushes along the back end acting as a fence to the land behind it that was covered in wildflowers, colors bursting from the vast landscape. In the center of the garden was an octagonal gazebo with couches built along the side. Elodie was standing there holding her two-month-old daughter. Chris could not tell who else was in the gazebo.

Chris and Ciaran both changed out of their comfortable traveling clothes to be more presentable and came downstairs and out the French doors Elodie had left open. They followed the path, but Chris stopped to touch every flower he recognized: white lilies, purple lavender, and pink peonies. As they made their way closer to the gazebo, they could see the table was set for six. An older couple was already there, looking at each other and not talking. Ted was walking around holding his newborn daughter and Elodie was straightening up the table.

"Ah, you're here now," she said loudly, getting her grandparents' attention. Chris and Ciaran walked up the small steps of the gazebo into the shade. The seniors got up and stood together.

Elodie introduced them. "This is Fabian and Elinore Cordonnier. *Grandmère*, *Grandpère*, this is Ciaran, Theodore's brother, and his fiancé, Christopher. The ones I told you about."

"Of course, please sit down and join us," Eli said happily as Fabian shook their hands.

Elinore was small framed and had a heart-shaped face, the same as her granddaughter. Her hair was snowy white and stringy, but down to the bottom of her back. She wore a pink wildflower in her hair that matched her white and pink flowery dress. Eli had lots of age lines and wrinkles, but her bright, beautiful smile was all they saw when they looked at her.

Fabian, they could tell, had been tall in the prime of his life. Now at almost a hundred, his back was hunched over. His eyes were dark blue and watery, his hands, face, and arms covered in age spots, and the only hair he had left was circled from his ear across the back of his crown to the other ear. But they quickly saw that both Eli, and especially Fab, were lively, spritely, and fun to be around.

Lunch was a spread of food from a charcuterie board of several different cheeses, meats, and grapes, to actual salad, pasta, mixed vegetables, and soup, along with a basket of bread. Again, Chris noticed that when a plate was empty, it magically became full again. But he was used to it now, understanding the magical mechanics. They took turns holding baby Charlene, passing her around as they ate and talked.

"So, how are the wedding preparations going?" Eli asked.

The men looked at each other and smiled. "We don't know a whole lot of it just yet," Ciaran answered. "We have allowed my mother and sister and his sisters to take over."

"We know where it will be," said Chris. "They found this beautiful piece of land that overlooks the valley and the mountains in the Verdant Forest. We're building a make-shift tent in the middle of it that can house around a hundred people."

"Of course you're invited," Ciaran chimed in. "And thank you for inviting us to your ceremony."

"Eighty years together is quite an accomplishment," said Chris. "We have promised each other forever—"

"—and three days after that," said Ciaran.

Chris turned to him with a smile, then back to the couple. "But you are actually living it."

They also turned to each other and smiled. Fab turned back to them first. "It's not much of a choice anymore at this point. What we have was solidified the day we met. As I'm sure you already understand."

"We were innocent bystanders in the plan of the Fates," said Eli. "Our souls chose each other. We complied."

"Well, I complied. She resisted at first," teased Fabian.

Eli turned to him with a stern look. After a moment, Fabian laughed. He turned back to the table. "She's scolding me, in case you didn't know. We haven't had one vocal argument in eighty-one years."

Chris and Ciaran both chuckled. "How did you meet?" Chris asked.

"Oh, it was at the tail end of World War II," Fabian began. "My platoon was making its way to a battle when were trapped by enemy fire. We had to split up, and I ended up in a village outside of Rouen. There was a woman who got caught up in the melee hiding behind a cart, but a soldier found her and was dragging her to the alley to do god knows what. I didn't have my *dulé* on me, but it didn't stop me from using my *Vis*, pushing him back so forcefully he hit the wall, and it knocked him unconscious. I was ready to *abscondo* her for what she saw me do, but she screamed, 'I'm a Mage,' and burst into tears.

"I picked her up with my two hands, and she grabbed onto me sobbing, so frightened. I had to calm her down enough for her to tell me where to take her because I had no idea where to go in the village. She pointed me in the direction of her cousin's home. As soon as I stepped in, I knew it was a Magi household. Her cousin, Nicholette, was also frightened; her husband was killed the day before, and she couldn't find Elinore anywhere as troops were coming in. She feared Eli was dead too, and she was so grateful to me. I revealed myself as a warlock and ended up staying with them for another three days until the troops had passed on their way to Normandy, where I was supposed to be. Eli kept saying she wanted to go home, but Nicholette would not let her go. So I agreed to accompany her."

Eli chimed in, "At the time I was sixteen and afraid to Wisp. As a young girl, I had a friend who accidentally Wisp'd herself into the sea. It is still not something I am entirely comfortable with. So I needed to go on foot. It took us two days to get here."

"We went through so much in those two days," Fab said. "Rough terrain. Dodging soldiers because, technically, I was AWOL. This one thinking she knew everything." Chris and Ciaran smiled as Eli turned to him with that look again. He grinned without looking at her. "But I brought her back home safely in one piece. She wanted me to stay. I told her I couldn't; I had to get back. I had to report to the French army."

"He likes to remind me that it took him a few hours, Wisp'ing a little at a time, what it took over two days for us to do together," she said with snark.

"But I could not get her out of my head," Fab said, looking at her. "I wrote to her every day. She wrote back every day. Short letters, long letters. I could not go back to see her for a year, although we were in the same country. I knew if I did, I would never want to leave her side. But when I did, it was like fireworks between us. The words we shared in our letters were... let's just say inappropriate in those days."

"In those days, people weren't so free with their bodies," Elinore said, turning to them. "But the night he appeared on this very doorstep after he marched to my father to ask for my hand in marriage, I gave myself to him right behind that rosebush," she said, smiling, making them all laugh.

"*Grandmère!*" Elodie feigned shock.

"That was also the night we discovered our internal voice," Fab said. "I held her and thought to myself, 'I love this woman.' And she said in my head, 'I love you too.'"

They looked at each other and smiled again.

"So you were always able to hear each other?" Chris asked.

"It was a whisper," Elinore said. "A whisper in the back of my mind, but his voice. At first, it was only after we would make love. Then we started hearing each other when our emotions were the most heightened. If one of us was hurt or in pain, or even experienced extreme joy or sadness, we would be able to feel it, first emotionally and then physically. He stubbed his toe once, and I cried out." They chuckled at that. "Within a few years, it became our norm. We could talk to each other, feel each other, anywhere, no matter how far apart we were."

"They would sit for hours," Elodie said, "and not talk to anyone but each other. My father said as a boy growing up, he just thought his parents were quiet people. But when he discovered their *Ardenti*, he learned telepathy and would be able to communicate with his parents just as they communicated with each other. All three of them talking in the same mind."

"That's so fascinating," said Chris. "I wonder if we would be able to do it with our children one day."

"Well, first we have to grow deeper in the *Ardenti* so that we can talk to each other," said Ciaran.

"So it hasn't happened yet?" Fab asked.

"No, unfortunately," Chris said, trying to keep the sadness out of his voice.

"Maybe it can be taught," said Ted. "It was Scholarly who sent me to China on a mission where I met a telepathic Magi there. That's how I learned it."

"But it is creepy," Elodie said. "The first time Ted did it to me, I thought I was going crazy in the head."

"'Tis not a normal thing," said Fab. "The *Ardenti* is extremely rare. Have you tried to mold your minds together yet?"

Chris and Ciaran looked at each other in confusion, then back at Fab. "How?" they chorused.

"If you can feel each other's feelings, you should be able to transfer those feelings into scenes," said Eli. "Think about it like this: I can close my eyes and think of something that makes me happy. Like the peonies behind me. Try it now, Ciaran, touch his hand, and bring Chris into your mind."

Ciaran closed his eyes and thought about the last time he rode Betta into the mountains. He could feel the rush of the wind all around him. He reached over and touched Chris's hand.

Everyone was quiet as Chris closed his eyes. At first, he saw nothing. He could feel Ciaran's excitement and joy, but it was darkness. Then something flickered. Sunlight. The horizon. He began to feel the roughness of Betta's skin underneath him, the curl of his fingers as he grabbed onto horns. A bigger flashed happened, and he saw himself coming toward the mountain in the sky. It was like he was Ciaran. Then it disappeared.

"I saw it, Ciaran," Chris said breathlessly. "We were flying on Betta, headed to the mountains. I lost it. It was quick, but I saw it."

Ciaran smiled. "That's incredible."

"Okay, now stay in sync," Fab instructed in a low voice, "and, Chris, you begin to think of something. Anything."

Chris saw himself standing under the Motos Willow. The leaves were pink, as if it were summer. Sunlight streamed through the hanging leaves as they swayed so softly. He thought he was alone, but then he turned around. Ciaran was standing there.

"I'm with you, aren't I?" Ciaran said. "Under our tree."

"Yeah," said Chris softly.

"It was just a flash, like you said, but I know where you were in your head. And somehow I was there with you."

Chris opened his eyes and noticed everyone was watching them. "Whoa," Ted said softly, in awe.

Ciaran opened his eyes, too. "Does that mean we can enter into each other's dreams?" he asked.

"Eventually, yes," said Eli. "Sometimes you will dream the same dream. Other times, you will begin a dream and bring the other into it. Or be in a dream state, and your love can enter it."

"This is extremely intense," said Ted. "I've never heard of magic like this."

Fab nodded. "Love magic is intense magic. But the *Ardenti* is sometimes thought of as dark magic, to invade one's thoughts, to bind one's soul to yours for all eternity. The intensity of your emotions toward the other is so great, you will easily want to give your life for the other, or kill anyone who stands in the way of the two of you being together. We kept it to ourselves for many years, even after we were married. We didn't want to give Jean-Paul another reason not to like me and deny me his only daughter."

"Did he really not like you, Fabian?" Ted asked. "You saved his daughter's life, for god's sake."

He shook his head. "Jean-Paul was not thrilled with the match. I was poor. My mother owned a small flower shop in the south of France, raising four troublesome boys by herself after my father died. I went into the army to support her and my brothers. But yes, saving his daughter's life was key for him, so he allowed it. We married here in the garden, and I moved into the chateau with her family, the St. Pierres. I knew gardening, especially Magi gardening, so I opened up a shop here, just to show that I was not going to live off them. They allowed me to grow outside of the garden, so I grew my flower farm there. My business grew, and I became a self-made man. When the house was passed down to Eli, we renamed the estate."

"How do you believe the *Ardenti* came to be for you?" Eli asked them.

Chris and Ciaran looked at each other. Chris said, "Well, after hearing your story, it could have been the first time we met. You literally saved my life from a dragon killing me."

"It also could have been our encounter with the CV," said Ciaran. "I saved your life then too."

"Eh, we saved each other," said Chris. Ciaran chuckled. "We just didn't realize how deep it was because I felt connected to you even then."

"It sneaks up on you," said Fab. "One day you are fine, and the next day your very core is consumed by the other. But it's not lust. It feels like it, a primal yearning to be together, but it's something more. Something deeper."

"Then it was formed the night we met," Ciaran said. "The duel with the warlock was the first time I realized that I was connected to him too, deeper than friendship." He turned to Christopher. "You were right during the hearing. I felt something right then and there, a yearning to protect you and keep you safe. Like a man would with his partner. So it was already brewing between us by then."

Ciaran turned to the older couple. "And he was just as stubborn as Elinore, I might add. Forging ahead without me and almost getting himself killed by a *Caerulus Veneficus*."

"I agree with you," Chris said with a chuckle. "Because I, too, felt the need to protect you, which was why I forged ahead. But after that, those next moments between us were definitely lust."

"What do you mean?" Ciaran asked him curiously.

"The massage," Chris reminded him.

"Ooooh…" Ciaran started to chuckle. "Yeah, mate, that was primal lust," he said. "The things I envisioned doing to you that night—"

"Ooookay, we got it," Ted said, cutting his brother off with a faux look of disgust, making the others laugh.

"But the lust is a part of it. Your bodies are yearning to connect, every day," said Fab.

"And still do," Eli said slyly, reaching her hand into her husband's lap, making his white face turn pink.

"*Grandmère!*" Elodie feigned shock again. Chris and Ciaran cackled.

Eli laughed. "Because it is the souls inside of you that are trying to fuse together. Burning with passion for one another. The farther apart you are, physically and emotionally, the more the souls cry out for one another."

"That's why it's hard being away from you for days at a time," Ciaran said to Chris. "I left your side for that first dragon mission, and I could still feel you. I could smell you. Taste you on my tongue. I needed to push it down when we arrived so I could do the task at hand, but every quiet moment I had, you consumed me. I can't even explain how it feels to be away from you."

"I can explain," Chris said. "It's like a feeling of something is missing inside of me. A hollow place that I can't fill. Like I'm not getting enough oxygen, not enough blood pumping into my heart, not enough feeling in my fingertips. And when we come together, it's like an explosion."

"Too right it is," Ciaran said, staring into Chris's eyes.

"That's how I was for an entire year," said Eli. "I wrote to Fabian every day just to release that pain I was feeling. And masturbated twice a day."

Chris and Ciaran laughed. Ted groaned loudly. Elodie once again scolded her grandmother for her crass behavior.

"That's why your *Amina* helps," said Chris when the laughter died down. "Because it's a part of you, your essence. When it's near, my soul is happy again. I am happy again."

"Ah, yes, I know that feeling all too well," said Fab. "A year apart was all I could muster. I needed to quit the French army and be close to my love."

"A year apart." Ciaran took Chris's hand and kissed his knuckles. "I couldn't even imagine—"

"Neither could I," Chris said right behind him. But then Chris turned to the older couple and asked, "Could it be broken? The *Ardenti*?"

The older couple looked at each other. "It can, technically," said Fab. "We spent decades researching and studying this type of love magic. As it takes time to grow, it takes time to break apart, piece by piece."

"The only ones that can break it is you," said Elinore. "No one can separate your souls unless you allow it to happen. It is still a choice. You could have chosen to reject those initial feelings and stayed away from each other. Ignore the empty, hollow feelings when you are away from one another. It will drive you to madness, and that's if you survive it. But you could walk away from each other and never look back. Even if it kills you."

"And it will kill you," Fabian said. "There are stories. People who have walked away from their pull of the souls because of societal things. Commoner blood. Different cultures. Different religions. An outside force that unintentionally severs their physical, spiritual, or emotional connection. Even family obligations, if one has an arranged marriage or one is already married. If you leave it early on, you have a chance of survival. Those who didn't separate when they first started feeling the effects, but tried to separate years later have died not too long after that. Heart attacks, cancer…

It's like your body has given up on you. Like your soul begins to die without its other half."

Elinore said, "The soul wants what it wants. But you can make the choice to rip them apart again. You would have to do it now, however. It's only been a year or so for you. If your souls are separated now, eventually the burning will fade out to emptiness."

"I could never," Ciaran said, squeezing Chris's hand.

"Yeah, of course not," Chris said quickly. "I just wanted to make sure nothing and no one would be able to come between us."

"Not unless you let it," said Fab. "Remember, the longer you stay together, the more your two souls become one. At this stage of our lives, we truly have one soul. We know that if one of us dies, the other will as well."

"And our soul will live on together, for all eternity, just as the Fates intended." They looked at each other silently, longingly.

"Whoa," said Ted softly again. He looked at Ciaran. But Ciaran was looking at Chris, who stared back at him.

They heard the doors of the home open, and a couple of people spilled out into the garden: Elodie's mother Annabelle and younger sister Janie with Ted and Elodie's children, Teddy and Victoré, who ran over to their parents screaming "Mama, Papa!" Jean-Paul, Elodie's father, and Florent, Elodie's brother-in-law, were right behind.

Ted conjured more chairs, and they gathered around the table to join in lunch with no more talk about *Ardenti*.

CHAPTER 13

Creatures

"Where are you going?" Ciaran asked from the bed. After a rousing lovemaking session and a long day of traveling, Ciaran had turned over to sleep. But he felt the bed move and turned back to see Chris putting on clothes.

"The garden is beautiful," he said. "I want to see it at night."

"Okay, then," said Ciaran with a yawn. "I'll be here."

Chris quietly walked through the home, down the steps, and then out the back door to the garden. He could tell it was pretty from the window, but seeing it up close was even more beautiful: every flower had a soft glow to it. He walked over to the corner of the garden where the low shrubs met the rosebush and looked out onto the open rolling hills filled with wildflowers that twinkled like stars on the ground. It reminded him of the clearing where they were to have their wedding.

"Ma Ami, I hope you can see this with me," he said softly. "France is even more beautiful than you could imagine."

There was a noise behind him, closer to the rosebushes. He looked over but didn't see anything, so he turned back to the sight before him. Then he heard a low growl.

Chris's instinct checked in. He turned back to the closest bush and stared at it. It was silent. He waited. Then he heard it again, a low growl of an animal. Chris slowly backed up to the gazebo. But then the growl turned into words.

"Whoooooo are yooooouuuu mmmmrrrr..."

Chris stopped in his tracks, his eyes wide with fear. "W-*what*?"

"Mmmmmrrrrrr... Who are you?!"

Chris gasped. "Who are *you*?" he asked back.

"I will rip your throat out if you don't tell me what you're doing on my land," the voice said clearly, then went into a low rumble.

"Your land?" Chris said, still staring into the bush. "I'm with my brother-in-law's family, the Cordonniers. And who the fuck am I talking to?!"

"You smell ... huuuuuman. Commoner. Commoners do not trespass in Maison-de-Charme. Commoners do not come onto this land."

"Well, there's a first for everything," Chris said sarcastically, getting more annoyed than afraid. "Show yourself. Now."

A sadistic laugh echoed around him. "You dare make demands on me, you Commoner filth?! I could kill you in an instant."

"You think you're the first warlock I've faced down?" Chris said bravely. "You Magi are all alike. Put down your stick and fight me like a real man."

"I am not a Magus. And I am not a man." Two yellow circles glowed through the bush. The growl came again, this time with a snarl.

Fear gripped Chris in the center of his chest. He started backing up again, keeping his eyes on what was watching him.

"Chris?" he heard a voice call out behind him.

Chris turned around to see Ted standing in the doorway of the kitchen. "You okay—"

But Ted was cut off by sudden movement. They both turned back to witness something—someone?—leap out of the bushes and fall against Chris, knocking him to the ground. Chris immediately grabbed it by its shoulders to push it off, but it was heavy. Thick. Hairy. He could see its face as it raised its hand and took a swipe at him.

It was a man, but it wasn't. Its face was covered in long brown hair. Mouth elongated. Teeth bearded with sharp canines. Like a dog.

Like a wolf.

It tried to strike Chris again, but he raised his arm instead and was scratched across his forearm.

Ted, who had sprinted over at full speed, pointed his *dulé*, and yelled, *"Retroago!"*

The thing was forcefully pushed off Chris as if a gust of wind came by. It yelped and slid across the grass into a pile of peonies. Ted came over to Chris and held his free hand out to lift him to his feet, but his eyes were still on the monster that had attacked him.

The thing shook itself off and stood on two legs. It lumbered over to them in jeans and nothing else. He had a hairy chest, his arms and bare feet covered in hair. His long brown hair was swinging behind him.

Ted stepped forward, his *dulé* still poised. "I know it's in your nature to be a fucking animal, but do not attack anyone here ever again, or you'll have a problem with me."

Chris looked at Ted in confusion that he was talking to the wolf-man with such venom. And he was even more surprised when it spoke back in a normal voice.

"Fuck you," the hairy man growled. "He's a Commoner. What is he doing here?"

"He was invited," Ted told him. "He's a registered Commoner and soon to be my brother-in-law."

The man scoffed. "Just because the Council tags and tracks them doesn't make them any better."

"Yes, we know how you feel," Ted said in a bored manner. "Why are *you* here? Who invited you?"

"My *grandmère*," he said proudly. "She wants me here for the ceremony. She didn't throw me away. To the *wolves*."

"You threw yourself away, Zach," Ted reminded him. "You walked away from your family."

The man practically leaped from his spot to directly in front of Ted. Ted did not flinch as they stood face to face. From behind Ted, Chris could see the yellow outline of his light blue eyes.

"They are not my family, and neither are you. Go back to London, where it's safe from people like me," he snarled.

Ted still had his *dulé* in his hand and pushed it against the man's stomach. "Go find a hole or cave or forest to stay in until the celebration, and don't come back here again. Or you'll have me to answer to."

Chris watched them stand eye to eye. Zach relented first. He stepped back and looked at Chris. Then he snapped his teeth at him. Chris flinched. Zach smiled and turned back to Ted.

"Tell my sister I said, '*Bonjour, mon soleil.*'" He turned around and began walking, then jogging, almost on all four limbs, jumping over the rosebush like it was nothing, and disappearing into the wildflowers.

Ted turned back to Chris, who was stunned. "Are you okay?" Ted asked.

"What the fuck was that?" Chris asked his own question, touching the blood from the scratch on his cheek.

"That was a werewolf," Ted said calmly. "Tea?" He walked around Chris and went to the door.

Chris was still stunned. "W... w..."

"Yes, yes, they're real," Ted said, holding open the door. "Coming?"

Chris found his feet and followed Ted into the kitchen. He sat at the table, and Ted went to the stove to heat up the kettle. Then he went underneath the island cabinet and pulled out a first-aid kit.

"Give me your arm," he said.

Chris did, and Ted gently cleaned the three shallow scratches. "Am I gonna turn?" Chris asked quietly, fearfully.

Ted smiled a little as he wrapped a gauze around his arm. "No. It doesn't happen like that. Plus, he wasn't trying to turn you. He was trying to scare you. Zach is an arsehole, not a murderer or a sire. He's too self-preserving for either."

They heard footsteps, and both turned to see Ciaran come into the kitchen. "Hey! I woke up, and my heart was racing. It took me a moment to realize it wasn't me, so I came down to find you. I don't know what you were doing out there. Are you okay?"

Before he could respond, Ted said, "No. He encountered Zach."

Ciaran's eyes went wide. He looked at Chris's face, still drained of color, then at Ted. "What the bloody fuck is he doing here?"

"Elinore invited him," Ted said sourly.

"God, that woman and her soft spot," Ciaran bemoaned. He went over to Chris and touched the drop of blood on his cheek. He looked at his wrapped arm. "What happened? Did you fall running from him?"

"No," Ted answered for him again. "Zach swiped at him. Twice."

"What?!" Ciaran yelled. He started walking toward the door. "I'm going to kill him."

Ted got up and stood in his path. "Calm down, little brother. He's gone now. He won't be back until the ceremony. Then hopefully he'll disappear again."

"God, I hate that arsehole," Ciaran said in anger.

Ted scoffed. "And he's feral now. He actually looks like a monster. He better shave it all off before the ceremony."

"Excuse me," Chris said. They turned to him. "*Werewolf?*" he asked in astonishment.

Ted looked at Ciaran. "He doesn't know what's real and what isn't?"

Ciaran shrugged. "We haven't had that conversation."

"Well, you should have it now," said Ted as the kettle began to whistle. "Because of the Oath, he's going to notice things, see things. He's fully in our world, and he should know what to expect."

Ciaran sat at the table next to Chris. Chris waited expectantly.

"Werewolves are real," Ciaran began. "Most are born. Some are created with a bite, a transfer of saliva in the blood stream. The ones born are less feral. They fit into society like everyone else. As they get older, they can choose whether or not to turn, and the lunar cycle doesn't control them as strongly, but they still must turn at some point. The ones bitten are more aggressive. Angry. And they turn for three days a month under the full moon. Zacharie, Elodie's younger brother, was bitten when he was a teen. They have tried everything, but it's just gotten worse over the years. He's angry at the lack of control he has over his life."

"Well, it looks like he found a way to live with it," Ted said, pouring three cups. "He's given into the beast inside of him. You had to see him, smell him, Ciaran. He's more wolf than man now." He brought the tea to the table and passed around the milk. "What else do you want to know?" Ted asked Chris.

Chris chuckled nervously. "Do I want to know?"

"Ted's right," Ciaran said. "You're going to encounter more creatures and see things now that you've fully stepped into the Magi world. Things you might not have noticed or your eyes weren't open to it before you took the Oath. You should know what to expect."

"I read all your textbooks, Ciaran. Nothing in there mentioned werewolves."

"Because the Magi Council of Europe forbade it," Ted said simply. "It's one of the many things that the Council and Scholarly disagree on, how much information should be out there. We didn't learn about werewolves at Campus, although we knew they existed. And they don't come to Campus. They are typically homeschooled or schooled by their pack."

"We don't have many of them in Britain," said Ciaran as he took a sip. "They aren't welcomed, unfortunately. There are plenty in the Americas, North and South. Some Eurasia countries, but not many. They like forests and bodies of water."

"Any in Albania?" Chris questioned. "In our woods?"

"I don't know about Albania in general," Ciaran answered. "Arslan would know. None in our woods. They don't fuck with dragons."

"Nobody fucks with dragons," Ted said with a smile.

"Okay. Werewolves, real," said Chris. "Dragons, real. Fairies, real. Vampires?" he asked with his eyebrow raised.

"Ask Ted; he hangs with them," Ciaran said with a grin.

Chris gasped. "What the fuck?!"

Ted raised his hand casually. "Actually, full immortal vampires are extinct as far as we know. The one time werewolves and Magi were aligned was in the fifteenth century to hunt and kill anyone even suspected of being a vampire, and it was successful. But when they were around and would breed with humans, they created daywalkers. They are human, but they do need blood to survive and for their immortality, so they blended in. Daywalkers usually mate with each other, creating more daywalkers. It's an entire race that the Council pretends doesn't exist."

Chris could not pick his mouth off the floor. "And where are they?"

"Everywhere," Ciaran answered for him. "They, like werewolves, can smell the *Vis* in our blood, and they stay away from Magi. Except Ted."

Ted smiled. "I've encountered a few on my travels. Learned their language, Gareshani. It's very old, around the time of Aramaic. They don't have the *Vis* per se, but other supernatural talents, like flash walking, long-distance hearing, levitation, telepathy, and telekinesis. I've spent time in their community and participated in their customs."

"And by participated, he means group orgies," Ciaran said with a straight face.

Ted chuckled. "Obviously before my beloved Elodie came into my life."

Chris turned to him. "You fucked vampires?"

"Daywalkers," Ted corrected him again. "Only the females. The males were busy fucking each other."

"But would have fucked a male?" Ciaran asked his brother. Chris also leaned in.

Ted blushed and sipped his tea. "It never got that far." Ciaran and Chris laughed loudly.

"Okay... um..." Chris was thinking of all the fairy tales he'd ever heard of. "Wendigos?"

"Totally fake," Ciaran said.

"Not totally," Ted said, happily in his element and skill set. "They were real, mostly in the Americas and the Caribbean, and have roots in native American history. But, again, are extinct, according to the United Magi of America."

"It's folklore, Ted. No one has ever seen one."

"No one has ever seen a dinosaur, either. It doesn't mean it didn't exist then. Dragons and dinosaurs come from the same genetics."

Before they argued again, Chris said, "Elves?"

"Elfsten," said Ted. "Descendants of elves. They look just like us, just smaller in height. Nowadays, they go through a cartilage circumcision when babies are born so their ears aren't pointy and they can fit in as little people."

"So then how do you know if you're encountering an Elfsten or just a little person?" Chris asked.

"You don't," said Ciaran. "But Elfstens have the *Vis*, just like Magi do. They can make things move and perform incantations."

"Interesting. Goblins?" Chris asked.

"Fake," said Ted.

"Real," countered Ciaran.

"Fake," Ted said again. "They're just Elfstens being assholes. Just like leprechauns. Anything that's short, has magic, and an arsehole streak has Elfsten origins."

"Golems?" Chris asked.

"Real," the brothers said together.

"And deadly," said Ciaran.

"Do not fuck with descendants of Hebrews," Ted said seriously. "You don't know who has a golem or not."

Chris nodded. "Mermaids."

Ciaran looked at Ted with his eyebrows scrunched in. "Extinct?"

"The jury is out," he said with a wave of a hand. "No one has actually seen a mermaid in centuries. There have been sightings, but those who are deep at sea, like the Mediterranean, or Artic, or the Caribbean Sea, and usually they have been at sea for a long time, so nothing confirmed. If they aren't extinct, they have absolutely no contact with land or humans. But I believe they are still down there, under the sea, if you will. There is a whole department in Scholarly dedicated to mythical marine biology."

Chris smiled. "So, are they studying the Loch Ness Monster?" he asked in jest.

"Actually, yes," said Ciaran.

Chris's mouth dropped. "No way that's real!"

"It's a kelpie," Ted confirmed. "A very large one. But it was moved by the Council in 1977 after that idiot Magi claimed he could bring it to the surface for the world to see. The Magi Council coaxed it closer to Iceland. It hangs out in the Norwegian sea."

"Did he go to Claustra for that?" Chris asked.

"Unfortunately, no," said Ciaran. "Because technically it didn't happen, so he didn't break the law."

"But he had to go before the Council and explain himself, especially afterward when he went ahead anyway with some fake thing and took pics of it to sell to a local newspaper."

"So interesting," said Christopher. "I always wanted to know about that one. What about Centaurs? Half man, half horse?"

"Fake," they said.

Ted continued, "It was a very bad Magi experiment that went wrong about a thousand years ago."

"Unicorns?"

"Real," they said.

"Endangered though, less than a hundred in the entire world," said Ted. "There are sanctuaries and reservations on every continent for them, just like dragons."

"Chimeras real, yes?" said Chris. "You encountered one."

"Yes, chimeras are real," Ciaran murmured, not wanting to relive that experience.

Ted said, "So are sphinxes, griffins, and manticores. They are found in caves and usually protect some kind of treasure. But these animals were created, not born, by very powerful magic and can live centuries."

"Hmmm... Okay," said Chris. "Giants?"

They both hesitated and looked at each other. "Yeesss..." Ted drew out. "They are also endangered though and very, very deadly. But unlike unicorns, they don't want help. They hibernate in the mountains and never come out."

"And, yes, there is one in Verdant," Ciaran confirmed.

Chris gasped and turned to him. "Ho. Lee. Shit! Seriously?"

"Most have never seen it," said Ciaran. "I have, but only if I'm in flight with a dragon. They like watching them fly."

"Bigfoot?"

"Another Magi experiment gone terribly, terribly wrong," said Ted.

"Ghosts?"

"Yes," Ted said while at the same time Ciaran said, "No."

They looked at each other. "Ghosts are not real," said Ciaran.

"Spirits are real," said Ted.

"Ancestors are real, yes. Being able to communicate with your ancestor or having your ancestor reach out to you is common. But people who die and then come back to haunt? That's not real," Ciaran said, shaking his head.

"Ciaran, you were just on this mission with me. The spirit of Hajj Maji in the chimera was blocking the path."

"It wasn't her spirit, Ted; it was her pet. Chimeras live thousands of years, as you just said."

"You haven't encountered all that I've encountered, Ciaran. I believe in ghosts."

Ciaran scoffed. "And I thought I was the naïve one."

"Okay, so the jury is out on that one, too," Chris said, cutting off their debate. He stood up. "This has been enlightening, yeah, really it has. But, honestly, as long as I don't come across that thing that just jumped me, I will be just fine."

Ciaran stood up, too. "Don't worry about that. If that Zach comes anywhere near you again, I'm going to rip his fucking head off," said Ciaran.

"That's still my brother-in-law, Ciaran," said Ted, with an eyebrow raised. "We already had one incident where Shane had a go at him at Teddy's christening. Can we not have another Beals/Cordonnier showdown?"

"Then that mutt shouldn't have taken a swipe at my fiancé," Ciaran said stonily. He turned to Chris. "Let's go to bed. We have Paris tomorrow."

He took Chris's hand and pulled him along. Ted gave him one last look and sighed.

CHAPTER 14

Heart of France

After breakfast, Ted drove Chris and Ciaran back to the transport station in Canton de Bourgogne. They did not go toward the airport section, however, but to the other side where a series of revolving doors were, naming different parts of the country for teleporting. Ciaran steered Chris to the entryway with a simple sign above that said "PARIS." It was by far the longest line, and there was an attendant making sure that the Magi spaced themselves out and moved discreetly through the doors to the other side.

When it was their turn to exit through the revolving doors, they ended up coming out of a municipal building in the city. Chris wanted to stop and look around like he did before, but Ciaran gently kept them moving as if they belonged there. It was cloudy with a small drizzle in the air but Chris smiled brightly. With no destination in mind at the moment, they walked through the streets of Paris, not doing a lot of talking except for Chris happily saying, *"bonjour,"* and greeting other passersby in French. While English was Chris's first language, and he was fluent in three others—Albanian and Irish Gaelic included—French was the one that was dear to his heart because it was his mother's tongue. Just being able to hear it all around him made him feel close to her.

It was busy and bustling on a Friday with people getting to school and work and tourists snapping pictures. And Ciaran made sure they blended in with the tourists, with big backpacks on their backs and selfie-sticks attached to their phones. They did some shopping at the Avenue des Champs-Élysées, picking up clothes and jewelry for their sisters and cologne for themselves. While there, Chris asked about the Magi areas of Paris.

"Is there a section like Myrddin?"

"Yes, it's called d'Arc. Unlike Myrddin, it's just for shopping. The French Magi Division is in an undisclosed location elsewhere, and their Scholarly office is also not located there. I don't know exactly where d'Arc is, but I can find it if you want to go."

But Chris looked around and said, "Another time. Right now I want to explore regular old Common Paris: the Louvre, the Arc de Triomphe, Notre-Dame de Paris, and, of course, the Eiffel Tower."

Ciaran smiled, but had plans for that last stop and told him that they would not go there until right before it closed. Chris happily agreed.

They made their way through the famous arch and went to the Notre Dame Cathedral, climbing all 350 steps so that Chris could take a picture with an ugly gargoyle, as he called it. After the picture, Chris looked at the statue and then at Ciaran. "Real?"

Ciaran smiled. "Yes. But that one is a statue."

Chris gasped. "How can you tell?"

Ciaran moved Chris out of the way so the people behind them could take pictures and spoke quietly. "I would be able to sense the magic within. Gargoyles are a type of ward created by Magi to keep anyone with evil intentions from entering a building. They are guardians, stone by day, protectors by night."

"So a real gargoyle would actually come alive and fight, even kill, if it had to?" Chris asked, also quietly.

"If it had to, to protect the person or things it was created to protect, yes. Early Christians used them to ward off evil spirits. And like a chimera, some Magi might infuse their own spirit into one upon death to protect their family for generations to come."

"Fascinating," said Chris. He was quiet for a while as they made their way back down. When they got to the bottom, Chris looked up at the statue. It didn't seem so ugly anymore. "When we build our house, I want you to put a real gargoyle on top of it."

"Seriously?" Ciaran said.

"Seriously," said Chris. "To protect our home and our children. Anyone who wishes to do us harm on our own land or to come into our home with evil intentions will have to face them. Can you do it?"

"I..." Ciaran was thoughtful. "Maybe. I've never tried, and I don't know anyone who has them on their dwelling. I'll be sure to ask Felix when we get back."

"Okay," said Chris. "I know it seems silly; it's not like we'll have some ancient artifact to protect. But nothing in this world is more precious to me than family."

Ciaran paused Chris to kiss him on the stairway. "I agree." They kissed once more before continuing on.

They made their way to the Louvre and spent most of their time there, with Ciaran telling Chris that Leonardo

DaVinci was indeed a Magi and that there is an actual DaVinci code having to do with the world of Magi. They stared and stared but could not see it.

Afterward, Ciaran took him to the Latin Quarter for a late lunch with Chris commenting that they were at a real French café eating real French food. And Ciaran could see how happy Chris was. He had many surprises planned for the day and introduced the first one.

As they sipped their café au lait, Ciaran said, "So, as I said earlier, I don't know where the French Division of the Magi Council is, but I do know that Scholarly is right around here. Want to visit Scholarly in Sorbonne?"

Chris looked at him in surprise. "Could I go, really?"

"Of course you can," said Ciaran. "For one, you are a registered Commoner now, so you can get into most Magi spaces. As a visitor, of course. But two, you're with me. And I know people who know people who can get us both into more inconspicuous departments. For example, the French Scholarly focuses a lot on humanities. Do you want to see if you really do have the *Vis* in your ancestry?"

"Ho. Lee. Shit," Chris said in anticipation. He looked at Ciaran's sly smile. "You set this up, didn't you?"

Ciaran shrugged nonchalantly and sat back. "The first part of the day was everything you wanted to do. The second part is everything I want to do for you. You're okay with that?"

Chris smiled back. *"Oui."*

They walked around Sorbonne University until they found the Faculty of Arts and Humanities building. Because it was a school day, so many people were going in and out, and they blended right in. Chris had no idea how Ciaran knew where to go, but he followed others to the lower level and stopped at a doorway that said Facilities Closet in French. He simply turned the knob three times and opened the door, pulling Chris with him into what appeared to be a janitorial room until he stepped over the threshold.

The room simply disappeared, and they were in a room with many doors along the side that others were going in and out of. They stood in a twenty-foot-wide hallway that had one large sliding door that opened as people came close to it. Ciaran and Chris walked through and entered a cavernous domelike room that had paintings on the ceiling, resembling the Sistine Chapel.

"Whoa," Chris said softly, but heard his voice echoing in the room. That made the three receptionists at the circular desk look up at them.

Ciaran stepped forward. "*Bonjour.* English? I don't speak French that well."

"Yes, English is fine," the one on the right said. "How may I help you?"

"I'm Ciaran Beals from the Dragon Reservation of Albania, and this is Christopher Jennings, my partner. We are here to visit Dr. Augustin Gambon." He placed his *dulé* on the counter.

The receptionist in the middle took it and put it under a scanner. Then he gave it back to Ciaran and looked at Chris.

Chris smiled and held up the back of his hand. "Commoner," he said with a smile.

The last receptionist glanced up, then back down, and continued typing. The other receptionist gave him a smile and nodded. "*Merci.*"

"One moment," the first receptionist said. She breathed words into a paper in French, and it disappeared.

As they waited, the other two receptionists began to talk to each other in French without looking at one another.

"*Ah. Une autre Commoner ordinaire se faisant encore une fois passer pour un mage. Ils nous tueraient tous dans notre sommeil pour prendre notre sang si nous les laissions, tout cela pour le Vis.*"

"*Et ils sont ensemble aussi. Pourquoi les Magi ne voient-ils pas l'importance d'être avec les leurs et n'arrêtent-ils pas de laisser ces cinquièmes Commoner nous infiltrer?*"

"*Chérie, c'est la question et je—*"

"*Tais-toi et arrête ça,*" the first receptionist that helped them scolded the other two. "*Ce genre de discours est la façon dont la guerre a commencé. Donc, à moins que vous ne soyez prêt à mourir pour votre ignorance, taisez-vous et faites votre travail.*"

"*Pardon, Mme Moreau,*" they chorused.

Just then, a paper appeared before the woman. She read it and gave them a smile. "Dr. Gambon is expecting you," she said in English. "Sixth floor, Magi Medicinal Maladies, third door on the left. His name will be on it."

"Thank you," said Ciaran curtly. He knew the others were talking shit about him and Chris, most likely because of the Magi-Commoner relationship. But his French was not that great, so he let it go.

Chris, on the other hand, said, "*Merci,* Mrs. Moreau. *J'apprécie votre aide et votre gentillesse.* And might I say that your red sweater really brings out the blush undertones of the blood underneath your skin. We ordinary Commoners are trained to notice things like that. You know, for the uprising."

The two other receptionists stopped typing and looked at each other, their mouths open. They'd wrongly assumed that since Ciaran did not speak French, Chris did not either.

Mrs. Moreau smiled. "*Merci.*"

Ciaran was thoroughly confused. "What?"

"Nothing," Chris said with a laugh in his voice. "Come, love, we must infiltrate Scholarly now." He pulled Ciaran along to the lift.

***

Dr. Gambon was happy to have some visitors. He spent most of his time in a lab studying infectious diseases and blood-borne pathogens for Magi, so to get a break from that was going to be a fun treat. He'd happily agreed when he'd received the request from Lucinda Chesterfield, and it showed in his big smile toward the two men.

"Come in, come in," he said in English. He moved papers off the stools in front of the metal desk and sat down, too. "So, you have come to find out about your lineage, yes?"

"Well, I already know mine," said Ciaran confidently as they sat down. "My father's side hails from Scotland, and my mother's side is English-bred. Both are Generational Magi, the Beals and the Livingstons."

"Ah, yes, the Beals," Dr. Gambon said in recognition. "One of the oldest living bloodlines of the *Vis* still around. I have always suspected that Beals continue to have many children with other Generational Magi, just so their bloodline remains strong and viral. Yes?"

"I don't know about all that," Ciaran said, defending his family. "I know plenty of Beals that date, marry, and procreate with Commoners. That's not something that is important to my family."

But Dr. Gambon smiled at him. "Not important to your immediate family? Sure. But generationally? No. Mage Beals may marry a Commoner here or there, but not likely. And Magus Beals definitely did not for centuries and probably still do not. Your relationship with Mr. Jennings is, in fact, an outlier. Now," he said, patting his hand, "you ponder on that while I talk with your fiancé here."

He turned to Christopher. "Your arm, sir."

Chris watched Ciaran's face, as he was indeed thinking about his aunts, uncles, and cousins, and stretched out his arm. Dr. Gambon rolled up Chris's sleeve and took the syringe off the table. He began to collect three small vials of blood as he asked Chris about his family, particularly his mother's side of the family, wanting to know exactly which part of Senegal they hailed from and if his grandparents or great-grandparents had migrated from other parts of Africa.

Dr. Gambon continued asking questions as he took the three tubes over to the PCR machine. He inserted one tube, put both hands along the side of the machine, and said, "*Celeri exolvuntur.*" Then he let go. The machine began to whir, spinning the tubes around.

He went over to the table next to the machine and sat in front of the computer screen. "Interesting," he murmured. Then he motioned for them to come over.

The doctor printed the results as he spoke to Chris. "You are 49.9 percent Irish, 33.5 percent Senegalese, specifically Fula, 12.1 percent French and Portuguese, and 4.4 percent unknown."

"Unknown?" said Chris. "What does that mean?"

The doctor explained, "It just means that there is either an ethnic group no longer in existence or that doesn't have a specific name to it that originated most likely in western continental Africa. A small tribe from a small village, if you forgive my verbiage."

"That is interesting," said Chris, nodding.

"That's not the interesting part, Mr. Jennings," he said, pointing to the screen again. "You see this double helix? This is your DNA. I have color-coded the stem cells to sort out what is the baseline and what is extraordinary. It's always yellow for Commoners. In a Magi, this line," he pointed to the horizontal ones, "would light up blue if you had any trace of the *Vis*."

"It's not lighting up blue," said Chris sadly.

"It's not matching up at all," said Dr. Gambon in revelation. "Look closely. Some of these lines are actually dimmer than the yellow they're supposed to be. Even in a Commoner, this would be the exact same shade as the other lines. See here." He turned around on the stool and slid it to the desk on the other side. They followed him to another monitor.

"My system color codes the stem cells so it can pinpoint exactly where the *Vis* is in a person's system." He clicked on a folder on the computer desktop. "This is what regular DNA would look like." In the picture, the entire double helix was yellow. "What your DNA is supposed to look like. And this..."

Dr. Gambon clicked on another file and pulled up the picture. "See, this is the double helix of a full Magi. If I were to take Ciaran's blood, this is what it would look like." They could see that the strands were yellow and all the horizontal lines were blue.

"And this is what it would look like in a Commoner Magi." He switched file pics and showed another DNA strand that was mostly yellow and many of the horizontal lines were blue."

"So," he said, pushing his chair back and turning it around back to the first computer. They again followed him. "Of your 23 pairs of chromosomes, 12 pairs are simply dudded out. Like a fading yellow, which is not in my color scheme at all. Do you see what I see?"

They all saw it. "What does that mean?" Ciaran asked.

"That I'm below human?" Chris said, only partly in jest. "Less than a Commoner."

But Dr. Gambon turned to him. "I simply do not know. You obviously don't have any intellectual disabilities or abnormalities. I assume you don't have a third nipple or an eleventh toe?"

Chris smiled. "Not that I know of."

"Well, there is something in your DNA," he said. "It's not a magical bloodline. But it could be something else. I have a colleague who studies Lycan DNA at Johns Hopkins University. Maybe I can send him your sample—"

"Lycan as in werewolf?!" Chris exclaimed.

"Well, it wouldn't be unheard of, if it was many generations back—"

Chris turned to Ciaran in alarm. Ciaran patted his back. "You're not a werewolf. Relax." He turned back to Dr. Gambon. "Forgive him. He's a little sensitive to these things at the moment."

"Oh. *Pardon.* Honestly, I don't know why your chromosomes are fading; they're just ... different. You aren't a Magi, but you aren't the average Commoner either." The doctor shrugged.

"Well, maybe that's why I can't hear your thoughts yet," said Chris.

"Or maybe your chromosomes are fusing into mine," said Ciaran. "Our souls becoming one."

"*Excusez?*" the doc asked. "Explain, please?"

They explained to him about the *Ardenti.* Dr. Gambon's eyes lit up the whole time at the knowledge that they were experiencing a very rare magical phenomenon. "*Fascinant.* Yes, it could be. Mr. Beals, may I take some blood samples from you as well?"

"Sure." Ciaran held out his arm.

Dr. Gambon took three small vials and repeated the procedure he did with Chris's samples. The DNA showed yellow strands connected by blue ones, as a Magus would be. He gave Ciaran his ancestry results. "Yes, you know your lineage, Mr. Beals. 48.7 percent Scottish, 46.8 English, Wales and Northwestern Europe, 2.2 percent Benin-Fula, 1 percent Baltics, and 1 percent Senegalese—Fula."

"Fula!" Chris and Ciaran chorused excitedly and hugged, laughing against each other.

"The Fula in me recognizes the Fula in you," said Chris in amusement and gave him a small bow.

"All three percent of it," Ciaran said back with a chortle and a bow.

But Dr. Gabon said, "You're laughing, but that might be the case. And now I am even more curious." He put one tube of Chris's sample and one tube of Ciaran's in the same PCR machine. "If we were to hypothetically compound the two DNAs, let's see what happens." He said the incantation and stepped back.

Dr. Gabon went to the computer with Chris and Ciaran right on his heels. They were all speechless as the screen lit up, staring at the slowly spinning DNA strand.

"What does that mean when the whole thing is blue?" Ciaran finally asked.

But Chris felt the hair on his arms stand up at the sight of it, and he knew what it meant. He knew that magic was deep inside of him. Untapped. Hidden. And the magic inside of Ciaran was the key to unlocking it in him through his offspring.

"I... I..." Dr. Gambon stumbled. "That's impossible. My system scans for the *Vis* in the stem cells. The entire DNA could not be all *Vis*. That would mean there is no trace of human DNA."

"Could this be the *Ardenti* showing itself, doctor?" Ciaran asked. "No trace of him or me?"

"Possibly," said the doctor. "But you are human, Mr. Beals. There should still be a mixture of humanity. It's inconceivable—"

Suddenly the PCR machine began to crackle and pop; then smoke came out of the sides of it.

"What the..." The doctor went over to it and opened up the top, filling the room with white smoke. "I'm so sorry; it's fried. I haven't used it this much in one day in a very long time," he said with a chuckle. "Let's take it to another lab."

He picked up the last two blood samples, one from each of them, and they followed the doctor out the door and across the hall to an empty lab. Chris had not said a word, and Ciaran noticed. <You okay?> he asked him internally. All Chris did was nod, watching Dr. Gambon turn on all the lights and systems in the room. They had to wait for all the equipment to boot.

Dr. Gambon entered the samples into another PCR machine and completed the ritual; then he went over to the computer next to it. They waited in anticipation for the double helix to show. But when it did, it was completely yellow.

"Ah," said the doctor, almost in relief. "That makes the most sense. There is only a 50/50 chance of a child having the *Vis* in their system if only one parent has the true blue strand, as we like to say here. And as you can see, the faded yellow is now a solid one, so whatever abnormality you have, Mr. Jennings, will not be passed down to your children."

But Chris was not convinced. "Do it again," he said. "With another blood sample from the two of us."

"Why?" said Ciaran.

Chris could not explain. Something was up. He could feel it. It was like he was playing a game of chicken with someone. Some*thing*. "Just do it." He held out his arm. Ciaran reluctantly held out his arm, too.

So the doctor put another sample in the PCR machine. The second DNA strand showed blue in the middle of the yellow. "Like I hypothesized," he said, "it will either be there or won't be. It really is up to the Fates on whether your child will have the *Vis* in his or her DNA."

Chris shook his head. "It was all blue the first time. You all saw it. That meant something."

"Chris, it was just a fluke—"

"It wasn't!" Chris insisted. "It... It was all blue. Every single strand. Your DNA and mine. Your ancestry and mine. Our children are not just going to be magical. They are going to be powerful."

Ciaran and Chris stared at each other. It was silent until the doctor spoke. "Magical, possibly. Powerful? Well, that will be determined in how well they study and channel their *Vis*, like every other Magi."

They both looked at him, Chris in annoyance, Ciaran in amusement. Ciaran turned Chris's face to him and kissed him. "How about we come back here when it's time, and we'll figure this whole thing out then? But for now, let's celebrate the fact that we're both Fula."

That got a smile out of Christopher.

CHAPTER 15

The Summit

They stayed and visited other departments at Scholarly: Mystical Archology, Ancient Languages and Ruins, and Magical Interface, which was the science behind magic. When they left Scholarly, it was dark out, but it had stopped raining and the clouds were trying to clear up.

Ciaran turned to him and asked again, "Are you okay, Christopher?"

Chris looked down at the paperwork in the manila envelope he held. Dr. Gambon had given them their DNA results and the pictures of their individual double helix. They even obtained one last small vial of blood from each of them so that if they wanted to have it checked at another Scholarly facility, they could. He had everything except the one thing that would prove his gut feeling. No one would believe him, anyway, and it wouldn't happen again. So he once again kept it to himself. Because he knew at some point, it would all come out.

"I'm great, love," Chris said, turning to him. "Put this in my backpack, will you?" Ciaran turned him around and did.

"Eiffel Tower next?" Chris asked. "It will be closing in the next couple of hours."

"Not yet," said Ciaran. "We still have about three hours to kill before closing."

"So what are we going to do to kill time?" Chris asked.

Ciaran took his hand. "Don't worry, love. I always have a plan."

Chris grinned and allowed Ciaran to pull him along.

He led Chris to the Vedettes de Pont Neuf, and they waited on the dock with a few other tourists. "A boat ride?" Chris said with a smile. He could see the boats, big and small, pull up to the edge as people got on and off.

"*Oui*," said Ciaran. "Paris river cruise."

"Christ, you're such a romantic," he said and playfully rolled his eyes. But it was one of the things he enjoyed about Ciaran the most, how thoughtful he was.

Chris fully expected them to be with other patrons. But when it was their turn, it was only the two of them on a canal boat for hire. They climbed aboard and were greeted by the captain and tour guide. He explained that it was a two-hour-and-fifteen-minute evening cruise along the Seine River as they toured Paris again. They were able to see all of the stops they had gone to on foot, such as the Notre Dame Cathedral and the Louvre again, this time lit up. Their private dinner was four courses, and they ate and listened to the guide give a history of Paris.

At 10 p.m., the boat docked, and the men made their way to the Eiffel Tower. They followed the crowd and quietly took pictures underneath the monument before they began to climb the steps to the second level. They took more pictures of the city, and they could see even more clearly why it was called the City of Light.

"It's breathtaking," said Chris. "Simply divine."

"If only we could see it from the top," Ciaran said with a sigh.

"I know," Chris agreed. "The Summit is closed to visitors; I checked. So even if we got here in time, we couldn't go. Plus, with all the walking we've been doing today, I don't think I could walk up sixteen hundred steps."

"What if we didn't have to walk?" Ciaran said as he leaned on the bar in front of him, staring into the sky. "What if we ... flew?"

Chris slowly looked at his boyfriend. "What are you talking about?"

Ciaran smiled and said in Chris's head, <Ted loaned me his double cloak for the night. So if you want, we could head back down, find a corner, cover ourselves, and just ...> Ciaran lifted his head and looked up to the sky. <...go>

Chris laughed out loud. Others turned to look at him, but Ciaran simply looked away.

"What a magnificent human you are," Chris said. "Let's go."

They exited with everyone else, leaving the Eiffel Tower at midnight. But Ciaran pulled Chris into a nearby alleyway and placed his bag on the ground. He pulled out what looked to Chris like a very big Snuggie blanket with four sleeves and two hoods. They wrapped it around themselves and ended up facing each other. Ciaran stepped closer and tied Chris's end with the rope hanging off to his own.

As he did so, Chris asked, "Won't people see us?"

"No," said Ciaran. "The cloak is like a chameleon. It will blend in with the background. And anyway, Commoners don't notice things like this. Because they don't believe in magic." Then he put the hood on Chris's head before he put it on his own.

Ciaran placed Chris's hands around his waist and said, "Whatever you do, don't let go. The cloak will make you feel weightless, but you aren't. If you let go of me or the cloak or if the rope becomes untied somehow, you will fall to your death. Do you understand me?"

"Way to ruin the moment, love," Chris deadpanned.

"Not joking."

Chris moved in even closer and locked his hands together around Ciaran's lower back. "I'll never let you go."

Ciaran smiled. He put one hand on Chris's shoulder and, with the other, he pulled on the golden rope on the inside of the hood. They began to move upward.

"Holy shit," Chris said in fear as his feet left the ground.

"Holy shit? Not Ho. Lee. Shit?" Ciaran teased as they went farther upward.

"No really, this is—Ciaran!" Chris yelled in fear for a different reason.

"Yes, love?" Ciaran said calmly, pulling the rope again, so they moved quicker. "Don't look down; only look at me."

"No, it's not that," said Chris. "You have the trace on you. You can't do magic to travel with me. They will know. And remember what Arslan said."

When Chris and Ciaran had arrived at the Albanian Magi Division for his first monthly probationary check in February, Inspector Arslan did not give Chris a magical tracker, stating, "If those cunts in the UK didn't remember, I'm sure as fuck not going to do their jobs for them." But he'd warned Ciaran not to get reckless, especially with Christopher, and if they kept their noses clean, he could use his discretion to remove the trace from Ciaran by the end of the year.

Ciaran knew that was what Chris was worried about. But he shook his head as they rose above the buildings. "I'm not using my *Vis*. I'm using a magical object. And you don't have a trace. So the only thing that's being tracked right now is that I'm rising in the air." He leaned to the left toward the tower.

"You really thought this through, didn't you?" Chris said in awe.

"Every moment of it. Just so I can show you Paris." He turned Chris around so that he was in front and yanked on the string. They moved quicker.

"Ciaran—"

<*Do you trust me?*> Ciaran asked.

"Literally with my life right now!" Chris said as they flew parallel to the tower and rose above the first level.

<*Then hold on.*>

Ciaran pulled a third time, and they went straight up at a faster pace. Chris put his head on Ciaran's shoulder and closed his eyes, feeling the air blow past him, almost whistling. He did not open them again until they were right below the summit. Ciaran steered them inside the tower into the elevator shaft, then slowed down. They hovered at the elevator door.

Chris opened his eyes. "What now?"

Ciaran put his hand out and touched it. "*Aperta.*" The shaft doors opened, and they stepped into the enclosed glass space.

Chris landed on his feet, saying, "Whoa. The ground feels weird now."

Ciaran untied the ropes, and they both wiggled out of the cloak. They could hear the wind blow fiercely outside, but they were protected by the glass.

Ciaran went to close the shaft door and conceal the room from any hidden cameras while Chris went to the window, touching the glass. "Ma Ami, if you could see me now..." he said softly.

Ciaran held him from behind. <*She can.*>

They turned around and kissed. Chris took pictures while Ciaran spread the blanket down and used his *dulé* while saying, *"Temperatus mutare sursum."* The temperature in the air in the enclosed room immediately warmed up.

Chris eventually sat down next to him. "Ci?"

"Yes, love?"

"Eli and Fab called it the Fates bringing them together. I'm beginning to truly believe that. This desire in me to have children has always been there. Meeting and falling in love with you was destiny, and it has only fueled my desire. But I believe that the Fates have brought us together to procreate. When we have children, you'll see. Your Beals bloodline and mine was meant to combine. So the ova has to come from your side of the family. A cousin. Maybe Diana, if she's willing to be a surrogate or donate an egg. It will unlock something in my bloodline. What, I don't know. But it will."

Ciaran turned to him. "I've been meaning to talk to you about that." Chris turned to him, too. "I understand your desire to have a child. And I want a family with you. I don't know about them being all-powerful or unlocking a secret bloodline, but I do know that I want what we talked about under the Motus Willow: brown skin children with red hair. A legacy for us."

Chris could sense the hesitation. "But..." The wind shook the summit hard, as if it were a warning.

"But." Ciaran softly sighed. "I have a feeling that you want to get married in August and find a surrogate in September."

"And?" Chris waited.

Ciaran hesitated again, but said, "And I think we should wait a while."

Chris stared at him. "How long is a while?"

"Four, maybe five years..."

Chris gasped in frustration and annoyance and started to rise away. But Ciaran touched his leg to steady him, needing to explain, needing to get it all out, needing Chris to understand.

"I know this is important to you. But right now, what's important to me is your well-being, your safety, and our relationship. Less than two years ago, you didn't even know magic existed. And now your whole world is turned upside down. Dragons and near-death experiences and this *Ardenti* thing that has us locked and ready to kill or die for the other at any given moment. Can we please, please, just ... take a breath, Christopher? Before we bring life into our chaotic world?"

Logically, Chris knew that what Ciaran was saying wasn't wrong. There was still so much to know and learn. Just last night, he'd discovered that werewolves existed. It made sense for him to fully understand the Magi world and community. And it made even more sense for Chris and Ciaran to have a few years of stability before starting a family.

But selfishly he didn't want to wait. He wanted to be a father first and foremost, something he'd always desired. He also wanted to show everyone that his gut feeling about him having a hidden magical bloodline was right.

"Five years is way too long," Chris negotiated. "I've always seen myself having little ones by the time I was thirty, with or without a partner. You know this. And I'm twenty-eight this year. So yes, I wanted us to get started this year so that by next year we would have our first."

"That's less than a year, and that's too short," said Ciaran. "And I'll still be on probation with the Magi Council. I want to do a lot more research around *Ardenti*. I want to buy the right land, build the right house. Establish our lives together."

Chris huffed. "Two years?"

Ciaran gave him a wry look. "Three? I promise on our third wedding anniversary we can begin looking into it. And I'll shut up about everything and let you handle it all. Just tell me where to deposit my sperm."

Chris cracked a smile. "My sperm. My DNA. Your … cousin or something."

"Bloody hell," Ciaran said and smiled back. "We'll talk to Diana first. When the time comes and not a moment before. She may change her mind about having children or be with child herself by then. And if so, then we'll knock on Alastair's sister Isla's door and kindly request an egg from her uterus or for her to be our surrogate. Or my father's first cousin in Scotland, Uncle Evander, has three daughters. I'm sure they'll be excited to do it for me. According to Sean, they can't wait to meet you."

"Okay," Chris agreed. He came closer and straddled Ciaran's lap as a response. He took the band out of Ciaran's hair so that his long, fiery red mane flowed around his face. He put both hands through it and leaned in close. "On the day of our third wedding anniversary, our first call is to Diana."

"I love you. Thank you," Ciaran said with a nod. "When the time comes, and not a moment before. And I promise I'll be ready. But for now, let's focus on us for the next few years, yeah?"

Chris kissed him hard. "Let's focus on us right this moment."

They began to remove their clothes, one article at a time, kissing and touching. Ciaran reached over and pulled the lube out of his backpack, handing it to Chris.

Chris grinned. "You were prepared for everything."

"And everything has gone to plan," said Ciaran, grabbing a fist full of Chris's kinky curls and tonguing him aggressively.

Chris moaned, and they kissed for a long moment until Chris ached to be inside of him. He spread Ciaran's thighs apart and prepared him, then slowly inserted himself inside. Chris hovered over Ciaran's body and began to move at a steady pace, watching Ciaran's face turn pink as erotic murmurs escaped his lips. They kissed and held each other while the wind shook the top of the Eiffel Tower.

When Chris was ready, he turned the bottom half of Ciaran sideways so that one leg was over the other and thrust into him. His body flushed with heat, and he released.

Chris slowly pulled out and grabbed Ciaran's face to kiss him. "Every time I think I've had the best night of my life with you, you prove me wrong," he said lovingly.

"The night's not over," Ciaran said huskily and kissed him back.

"Yes, because you have to fuck me against that glass wall now."

Ciaran let out a loud laugh. "Your wish is my command."

Chris moved away from Ciaran's mouth and left small bite marks on his broad shoulders. He lifted Ciaran's arm and sniffed, making Ciaran laugh. Ciaran knew between all the walking they did, his deodorant was barely hanging on. But Chris didn't mind at all; the smell of Ciaran's natural body scent always awoke his senses. Chris began to lick him there while stroking Ciaran's cock. There was no more laughter as Ciaran hardened in his hands.

Chris went across Ciaran's body, giving each nipple the attention it deserved, to Ciaran's other armpit and licked him there, too. His tongue swept across Ciaran's hairy stomach, and he promptly began to suck Ciaran's cock. Ciaran moaned loudly, holding onto Chris's hair, pumping upward into his mouth.

"Okay, okay," he said breathlessly. "I'm ready, unless you want me to cum in your mouth..."

Chris chuckled and let him go. Then he turned around and positioned himself on his limbs. Ciaran added lube to Chris's bottom and held onto his waist. He started out slow but quickly picked up speed. Chris began to holler, "Yes! Fuck me! Breed me! Ah!" fueling Ciaran's passion for him. He grabbed Chris's hair again, turning his neck to the side and bit him there hard, making Chris cry out, then smoothed it out with his tongue.

As Chris panted, Ciaran said in his ear, "Do you really want me to fuck you against the glass?"

"Yes, please," Chris moaned.

"It's going to be cold," Ciaran warned.

"You'll keep me warm," said Chris.

"Fuck yeah, I will," said Ciaran, as he slowly pulled out. He stood up and held out his hand.

Chris took it and stood up, happy to be off his knees. Ciaran kissed and pushed him against the glass. It was indeed chilly, but Ciaran did not give him much time to complain, shoving his tongue into Chris's mouth again. Chris kissed him back just as hard. He turned Chris around, and Chris yelped at the feel of the freezing glass against his cock. He arched his back for Ciaran, but also to remove his skin from the cold.

Ciaran added more lube and slammed into Chris again and again. Chris laid one palm against the glass and the other slowly stroked his cock. He held steady as Ciaran jackhammered into him, this time Ciaran yelling with every thrust, "Yeah! Fuck! Yes! Yes! Fuck!"

Ciaran felt it coming. He turned Chris's neck to the other side and clamped down with his teeth as he began to cum. Chris felt Ciaran filling him up and began to tug on himself at warp speed. As Ciaran's orgasm ended, Chris's rose. He choked out a moan and came on the glass wall.

While his cock retracted, Ciaran wrapped both hands around Chris, squeezing him tight, nibbling his neck. Chris put one hand on Ciaran's arm around his midsection, and with the other, he reached back and touched Ciaran's leg. They stood there naked and in silence, looking down at the lights of Paris with the heat of their bodies still blazing against the other.

When Ted came to pick them up the next morning from the station, he immediately noticed the large bite marks on Chris's neck and the smaller bite marks on Ciaran's shoulder.

"*Bonjour.* Did you get into a row with werewolves and vampires yesterday?" he asked with a smile on his face. He began driving toward Maison-de-Charme.

Chris grinned and kissed Ciaran's neck. Ciaran was also grinning, but he then said, "Speaking of werewolves, I'm going to take Zach's head off when I see him tonight for what he did to Chris."

Ted sighed in response.

CHAPTER 16

Emotional

The Musée Historique des Magi Gérard Bruguière was bursting with magic. As soon as they entered the ballroom, they were met with shimmering stars floating above and glitter raining down like snowflakes that disappeared when they touched fabric, the same kind that was in the envelopes. Chris and Ciaran wore black tuxedos and bow ties, but upon entrance, they were all given a dark blue Magi cloak with different shaped red circles on it.

Chris turned to Ciaran as he put it on, but Ciaran already answered him, "No, this one doesn't fly." Chris pouted, feigning disappointment.

A champagne glass floated up to Chris. He took it from thin air. "Thank you," he said to no one and drank.

There was a live band with a singer turning out melodies from the mid-century. Many couples were already on the dancefloor. Chris and Ciaran walked through the crowd, greeting fellow guests. But every time Ciaran introduced himself, he was met with more questions about his work on the Dragon Reserve and his thoughts on Magi-Commoner relations. He quickly realized that Jean-Paul must have been touting his name as a Scholarly official.

Chris saved him a few times by coming over with a plate of food or pulling him to the dancefloor to pretend to waltz or to explore the rest of the museum, learning the history of the founders of Maison-de-Charme, which Ciaran was grateful for.

Ted and Elodie were standing beside Ciaran and Chris when the stars above stopped twinkling. Suddenly the red circles on the cloaks began to spin, and white light beamed from them, brightening up the space. People around them began to clap, and they realized that Fabian and Elinore had entered the room. The older couple had on similar cloaks, but the colors were reversed: red with blue circles.

The band began to play "That Old Black Magic" by Glenn Miller as they slowly walked to the dancefloor and the crowd clapped for them. Eli wrapped her arms around her husband, and they danced. Suddenly they began to rise, hovering about ten feet off the ground, thanks to Fabian's cloak. Loud booms began over the museum. Through the high glass ceiling, they watched fireworks burst over their heads as the couple slowly spun in the air. The crowd clapped and cheered again. When the song was over, Fab and Eli made their way back down to the floor.

"Thank you for celebrating eighty years of love and family with us," said Eli in a loud and enhanced voice, without a microphone. In French, she thanked their guests, prominent members of the community, and dignitaries from other countries, naming Minister Ciaran Beals from the UK Scholarly Bureau as one of them.

"Christ," Ciaran muttered under his breath and took another sip of wine, smiling at those who smiled at him.

Chris chuckled. "I'm going to start calling you 'Minister' in bed."

Ciaran raised his eyes in thoughtfulness. "Okay, that might work." They giggled together.

Once the acknowledgments were done, the starlights above came back, and the silver glitter began to fall again. "That was magical," said Chris as the band started up with a new song. "Can we do that at our wedding?"

"Sure, as soon as you figure out a way to explain us floating in the air to your side of the family and your friends, we will," Ciaran deadpanned. Chris chuckled.

Jean-Paul walked over and interrupted them. "Ciaran, I'd like to introduce you to our gaming minister, Max Trémaux. He has some questions about your dragon reservation. Come." Ciaran put a smile on his face and followed Elodie's father a few feet away.

"That was just divine, wasn't it?" Elodie said, as she turned to Ted. She kissed him first. "We should get married again."

"I'd marry you every week if I could, El," Ted said back, pulling her closer. They kissed again.

"You should want to marry me every day," she said smugly.

"You two are going to be with child again before the night is over, innit?" Chris said with a smile.

Ted was about to respond when suddenly Elodie gasped, looking beyond him. *"Mon clair de lune!"* Then she ran up to the man who was near the door.

"My moon?" Chris asked. "Who's that?"

Ted smiled. "You don't recognize him?"

Chris looked at him like he was insane. He knew a total of ten people there, and all were Elodie's family. He glanced back at the clean-shaven man with soft, long brown hair slicked back and tied in a ponytail at the base of his neck.

Chris watched him and Elodie hug tightly. She kissed both his cheeks and hugged him again, talking in fast French.

"Why would I?" Chris asked. But Ted did not answer as they came closer.

Elodie held the man's hand and walked him over to Ted and Chris. "Christopher, this is my baby brother, Zacharie. Zach, this is the Frenchman I wrote to you about. The newest Beals and my new best friend." She beamed excitedly.

Chris stared at him, not speaking. He looked nothing like the beast who had attacked him two days before. Except his blue eyes with a yellow tint around the iris continued to be shifty. Cold.

Zach held out his hand with a friendly smile. "Very nice to meet you, Christopher. My sister thinks the world of you."

Chris did not take it. "I feel like we've met before," he deadpanned.

"Have we?" he said, keeping up the smile. Zach graciously closed his hand and touched the center of his black suit with the silk lapels.

Ted shook his head and rolled his eyes. "Elodie, love, do you mind refreshing my drink?" He handed her his drink before she could respond.

She looked at him curiously, but he was staring at Zach, while Zach was staring at Chris. "What is wrong? What happened?"

"Elodie," Ted said again. He raised one eyebrow at her.

She sighed and looked at her brother. *"Qu'as-tu fait, Zach?"*

"Elodie," Ted said again, more sharply.

"Fine," she snipped. "No fighting. Please. This is a cultured event. *Faites preuve de dignité et de décorum pour une fois.*" She walked away with Ted's glass.

"Sooo..." Zach drawled out with a sly smile. "A Commoner in M—"

But Ted cut him off. "If Ciaran sees you, he will kill you for what you did. Walk away from Chris. Now."

Zach stopped smiling and looked at Ted. "I'm not afraid of him or you, Ted. I do what I want. I go where I want. And I take what I want."

"You know the last time you made that speech at Teddy's christening, when you tried to have a go at Ainsley, I believe it was Shane who crashed a champagne bottle over your head," said Ted. "You want to try it again with another Beals? Walk. Away."

"I just wanted to officially see what the big deal was about this one." He threw a thumb at Chris without looking at him. "He smells..." Zach took a long exaggerated sniff, "mundane."

Ted looked over his head and saw Ciaran had noticed and was walking over to them briskly. "Last chance," he said to Zach.

"Ah yes, I thought I smelled dragon shit," he said without turning around. "Hello, Ciaran."

Ciaran walked up to Zach and got directly in his face, his own mouth set in a scowl. "I should kill you where you stand for what you did."

Zach smiled at him, but this time it was more of a grimace. "I could tear your heart out in a blink of an eye."

"Yeah?" Ciaran cocked his head to the side. "Try it, you prick."

"Ciaran," Chris said softly, trying to get his attention. He could feel how angry Ciaran was. The rage was stewing inside of him the way it was stewing inside of Ciaran. "Calm down."

"Yes," Zach drawled out. "Listen to your ... mate."

"You stay the fuck away from Christopher," Ciaran said dangerously. "You don't speak to him, you don't go near him, you don't even look—"

Zach glanced at Chris. Chris felt it inside, the rage that licked up Ciaran's spine and exploded before Ciaran snapped.

"HEY!" Ciaran growled. He grabbed Zach by his suit jacket and pushed him back a few steps into the nearest table. "You. Don't. Look. At. Him."

Zach grabbed him back, but Ciaran was angrier and pushed him again, this time moving the table a few inches. People noticed their scuffle. Ted ran up and reached across Ciaran's chest to hold him back. "Let him go, little brother," said Ted calmly.

Elodie ran over, seeing the commotion. "Stop this!" she said, practically stomping her foot. "You are ruining the event of the season!"

Ted said again, "Let him go. Go take a walk, Ciaran. A long one." Ciaran did not let go. "Ciaran—"

Ciaran released him with a final push. "You heard what I said, you filthy mongrel. You ever put your paws on him again, and I will fucking kill you." He walked away and out of the museum through the side door.

Zach watched him walk off, then turned to the other two men who were scowling at him. He threw both palms out in faux surrender. "No harm the other night. I was just having some fun, *mesdemoiselles*."

Chris could still feel Ciaran's anger, and it overpowered his original fear of the man. He walked up two steps and punched Zack in the face, sending him into the same table. Zack's head flew back, and his nose burst in blood. Elodie shrieked.

"Having fun now?" Chris snarled at him. He turned his back on the wolf and walked out the same door Ciaran left from, not waiting for the aftermath.

The air was cooler out there, which Chris was grateful for. But Ciaran was nowhere to be found. "Ciaran?" Chris called out. No response. "God, I wish I could talk to you telepathically," he said to himself. "Ciaran!" he yelled. "Talk to me! Please."

<Come toward the oak tree,> Ciaran said in his mind. *<The one on the second hill. I'm here.>*

Chris did as he was instructed, walking over the first hill, down a small slope, then to the next hill. He could see Ciaran's figure on the far side, looking out into the rolling hills. Chris silently sat down next to him.

"I could have killed him," Ciaran said in a hollow voice.

"I know," Chris said back. "I can literally feel the rage inside of you."

"And I felt the fear in you again," Ciaran said back. "It made me angrier."

"You really were ready to kill a man for me," Chris said.

"I would. Don't forget who I used to be," Ciaran said seriously. "A mercenary for the Magi Council, and a deadly one. If a person ever harmed you or tried to separate us, it would be the last thing they ever did."

"Christ, Ciaran," Chris said, wide-eyed. "You mean that. I felt that in the very core of my being. As if it was my own thought and feeling."

Ciaran nodded. "The *Ardenti* is getting stronger. Soon we won't be able to distinguish our feelings from the other."

"It's a scary thought," said Chris, staring into the night sky.

"Yeah. It is."

After a moment of silence, Chris said, "Ciaran?"

"Yeah?"

"You're still pent up. And aroused."

Ciaran couldn't help but to chuckle. "It's just the adrenaline. It will wear off."

"But now it's making me aroused."

Ciaran slowly turned to him. "So let's burn off some of this passion."

They moved at the same time, their lips crashing into each other, throwing off their cloaks to spread in the grass. Before he could think about what he was doing, Ciaran took Chris's neck and pushed his face into his lap. Chris did not hesitate; he popped Ciaran's pants button and zipped them down. He thought to pull it out through the hole in his briefs but then flipped over to kneel in front of Ciaran and helped him pull down his pants and underwear all the way off.

Ciaran grabbed Chris's pants too and did the same. Then he turned Chris on his side and flipped downward. Chris got the hint, pulling Ciaran's waist closer to him. Greedily, they sucked and stroked each other. Chris moaned with Ciaran's large cock in his mouth, and Ciaran deep-throated as he fondled Chris's balls. Ciaran came first, having to pause with Chris's cockhead on his tongue as his midsection froze and his testicles emptied. Chris's mouth filling up with the essence of his lover was enough for his eyes to roll back, and he returned the favor, cumming in Ciaran's throat.

Chris came up for air first, gasping and lying on his back in the grass, his genitals plopping out of Ciaran's mouth. His mind was swirling, drowning in feelings that he could not tell which were his and which were Ciaran's. Ciaran turned on his back and put his hands behind his head, also feeling Chris's emotions. They lay there in the grass, staring at the stars side by side with suit jackets, bow ties, and no pants.

Chris broke the silence again. "I'm starting to think you're right."

"About?"

"Taking the time to learn more about us as a couple. This *Ardenti*, it's ... intense. Feeling each other's emotions so strongly is so insane."

"Yeah. And not just that. It's the living for each other. Dying together," Ciaran said softly. "If you die, I die, Christopher."

"If you die, I die," Chris repeated softly. "I think a part of me always knew that. From the time you almost died with the chimera. I told you I felt that way, and you thought it was just my dark cloud talking. But no. It's my soul talking. If I die, you die, too."

"It's a scary thought indeed, but I'm not afraid of it," said Ciaran. "How intense things will get between us. Our souls becoming one. I want to understand it, but I'm not afraid of it."

"I'm not afraid either. It almost brings me comfort to know that I will never be alone in this life," said Chris.

Ciaran flipped upward until he was next to Chris. He lay on his side and gently touched Chris's face, turning it toward him. "You will never be alone in this life," said Ciaran.

Chris turned on his side to face him. They lay there staring at each other instead of the night sky in silence.

CHAPTER 17

Minister Duties

Ciaran made sure Christopher was sound asleep from his overnight shift before he Wisp'd to the woods for his Saturday morning workday at the Reserve. He stepped in and observed the warmth of the sunshine while making his way to his office. He no longer had to go to the locker room but poked his head inside anyway to see the schedule. He was happy to see that Vlad was working, too. Ciaran went upstairs to his office.

As Ciaran was taking off his outerwear to put on his coveralls, the door swung open, and Dale was standing there with a package in his hand. "Good. You're in."

Ciaran turned around. "Good thing I wasn't naked."

"I don't give a toss about your balls, Ciaran," Dale said. "You must have mistaken me for your cocksucker." He put a manila envelope on his desk. "Since you're a Scholarly official now, this is yours, *Minister*."

"Dale, it was like for twenty minutes so I could give Chris The Oath," Ciaran said. But he lifted up the envelope and pulled out the memo on top of a stack of papers held together by a large binder clip. Ciaran read it with his eyes scrunched in. "Seriously?"

"Yes. You're going to help the town of Gullfelt create a dragon reservation for the dragons living in the Torngat Mountains. Help them set up their perimeter. Teach them how to interact with dragons safely. Educate, monitor, write up, and submit your report."

"Submit to who?" Ciaran asked. "And where the hell are the Torngat Mountains?"

"Newfoundland and Labrador."

Ciaran double blinked. "And where the fuck is that?"

"Canada. Think above Nova Scotia."

"Above Nova Scotia?!" Ciaran exclaimed. "For how long? I'm getting married in three months, Dale."

"That's why I told them you can do it in sixty days," Dale said with a shrug.

"You're joking," said Ciaran. "I can't single-handedly create a dragon reservation in sixty days."

"You're not creating anything," said Dale. "The town at the bottom of the mountain has been the gatekeeper for the dragons there for centuries. They know what to do. Now the Canadian Magi Council, the CMC, wants it to be a legitimate reservation, so they need someone to give them official training and a stamp of approval. And I'm sure as fuck not going to Newfoundland. It's all yours, *Minister*."

"And why can't the Canadians do it themselves?" Ciaran asked. "Surely they have Dragonologists there?"

"Actually, they don't," Dale said. "North America doesn't have any official dragon reservations, so it's not part of their Campus curriculum. This would be the first of its kind. And the terrain is similar to what we have here, albeit much colder. They requested the assistance of our Magi Council.

Your cousin, Alastair Beals, recommended you to oversee the operation, *Minister*."

"Bloody hell, Alastair." Ciaran groaned.

"Bet you'd like to thank him yourself, huh?" Dale said with a smile. "Because to answer your other question, you aren't single-handedly doing it. He's going with you. And so is Felix; I already told him. He's going to train their Novo while you train whoever they have up there monitoring the dragons. I assume the constables. And to answer your first question, your report gets sent to your boss, Lucinda. She's expecting a full write-up upon your return by the last week of July, *Minister*."

"Oh, fuck off with that minister shit!" Ciaran finally said with an attitude. Dale chuckled as Ciaran shook his head. "Chris is going to lose his shit."

"He'll be fine," Dale said dismissively. "You'll be back in time for your precious tie-bind."

"No, you don't understand... *ugh*." Ciaran groaned again. "I can't be away from him for sixty days. I literally ... *can't*."

Dale watched him for a moment. "Just take him with you."

Ciaran looked up. "Can I?"

"He's one of us now," Dale reminded him. "As he liked to remind me while hanging upside down by his knickers."

"He is, isn't he?" Ciaran said, and a smile slowly formed on his face.

Dale pointed a finger at Ciaran. "But keep him in the town and away from the dragons. You're already on thin ice with the Council, in England and here in Albania."

"You know I'll keep him safe, Dale. I'll protect him with my life."

"Good. Have a great day, *Minister*." Dale walked out just as briskly, ignoring Ciaran's scowl.

Then Ciaran chuckled to himself. "Chris is going to love this mission."

———————

But Chris surprised him by saying, "I can't just pack up and go for two months, Ciaran. I already took off the month of August for our wedding and honeymoon." Chris shook his head in disbelief.

"But I have to go, Christopher," Ciaran implored. "I can't turn this down because there is no one else to do it, except Bruno. And I'm sure as fuck not letting Bruno set up a dragon reservation. So, are you going to be okay with us being apart for two months?"

Chris looked away. "You know I won't be."

"Then," Ciaran said, getting closer. "Come with me."

"Is this what it's going to be like?" Chris asked. "Either I go with you on dangerous missions, or I feel how in danger you are from millions of miles away?"

Ciaran touched Chris's cheek. <Remember what Eli and Fab said,> Ciaran told him in his head. <One day we'll be able to communicate no matter how far apart we are. But until that day...>

Chris sighed. "Okay. I'll work it out with Bergina."

"Excellent!" Ciaran said happily. "It will be like our honeymoon before the wedding. We're going to have a great time."

Chris agreed. "Maybe hanging out with dragons all summer wouldn't be a bad thing."

Ciaran gave him a stern look. "You will not be hanging out with dragons."

"What?" Chris cried.

Ciaran shook his head. "No."

"You're dragging me to no-man's-land, and I don't get to hang out with dragons?!"

"No, Christopher," Ciaran said, folding his arms across his chest.

"C'mon. Will I at least get to touch one, like I did with Betta?"

"No."

"Can I get close to one?"

"No."

"Will I see one in the far-off distance at least?"

"Maybe."

Chris grinned. Ciaran grinned back.

———

Chris opened his eyes. The sun was streaming right through Ciaran's curtain, brighter than usual. Ciaran was lying on his stomach, snoring away with Chris's arm across his back. He reached up and caressed the nape of Ciaran's neck to wake him.

Ciaran groaned. "Five more minutes, Mum."

Chris chuckled. "We have to get up, love. We have a long flight ahead of us."

"*Too right,*" a posh voice called out in the room.

Both Chris and Ciaran sat up startled. A translucent, silver possum was pacing at the bottom the bed. "Bloody hell, Alastair!" Ciaran yelled, pulling the covers as if he could see them.

"*Now that you are awake, can we please get going?*" the Amina said in his cousin's voice. "*There isn't a moment to waste.*" The possum promptly walked out through the bedroom door.

Ciaran plopped back onto the bed. Chris chuckled and hopped out of bed. "Not a moment to waste!" he said, mimicking Alastair's voice and heading to the shower.

Alastair was downstairs in front of the SUV in a white long-sleeve crewneck shirt, black jeans, a black form-fitted hat, and shades. He held up a cupholder with two coffee cups in one hand and his own coffee in the other.

"Well, look at you, Alastair, looking just like us regular blokes out here," Chris teased as he took both cups, handing one to Ciaran. The driver came out of the car and rolled their suitcases to add them to the trunk.

"Good morning, Ranger Jennings," Alastair said. "And before we begin this excursion, may I say how highly inappropriate it is that you are accompanying your partner on this sensitive and confidential work assignment. As a Senior Dragonologist and Minister of Scholarly, Ciaran will be called away at various times to complete important work for his department, and you simply cannot include yourself in missions that, at best, you become a distraction, and, at worst, could be killed."

Ciaran was about to scold his older cousin when Chris lifted up his hand to stop him. Chris placed that same hand on Alastair's shoulder. "Before these two months are over, I'm going to make sure you get some pussy," Chris said with a straight face.

Ciaran snickered. Alastair huffed and straightened out the glasses on his face, turned around, and entered the passenger side, shutting the door.

Chris opened up the back door and held it for Ciaran. "Shall we?"

"There isn't a moment to waste," Ciaran said. He gave Chris a kiss before he entered in.

As expected, the alarm went off when Chris and Alastair entered the Reserve. But Ciaran had already sent his *Amina* ahead of him, letting the day crew know they were on their way, so there was no flurry of men at the entrance. Just Dale who grumpily turned it off before muttering to himself back up the small hill, and a few of their friends to see them off and wish them well on their mission.

Felix met them in the meadow next to the Flyer. He gave them both handshakes, and they said their goodbyes to Vlad, Tommy, Khalid, and Bruno while Alastair made Silas go through all his safety checks, much to his annoyance, and double-checked to make sure they had two weeks' worth of food in case of emergencies.

Once they entered, Felix immediately went to the far back seat and spread out with his laptop, books, and headphones while Chris and Ciaran found seats in the middle of the small aircraft right next to each other. Chris brought a pile of fantasy novels to share with Ciaran, but Ciaran grabbed an eye mask immediately as they rose in the air and leaned his chair back. Alastair pulled out a huge binder and began to read, making notes in the margins.

After a seventeen-hour, mostly quiet, flight with Alastair in his Canadian Magi laws binder, Felix with headphones in his ears watching movies and sleeping, and Chris and Ciaran keeping each other occupied, they landed in a valley in Newfoundland, Canada.

Alastair stood up and gave out commands and coats. "Now listen carefully," he began. "We are here on official council business. We represent the Magi Council of Europe, so please act accordingly. Especially you, Commoner Ranger Jennings, since you have no official business here."

Chris threw up his hands in faux surprise. "I have official business," he said. "I'm here to keep Ciaran ... happy."

Ciaran grinned and let out a low snort. But Alastair was not amused. "I'm serious here. No solicitous or rude behavior. No sexually explicit activities, no use of illegal drugs, magical or common, and if there is an altercation brewing between you and any one of the townsmen, you come to me and let me handle it with the government officials of Gullfelt. Is that understood?"

No one responded. Chris had a smirk on his face because he'd brought a few joints with Sean's marijuana strain with him. Felix was frowning at the "no sex" part of his speech. Ciaran was indifferent to Alastair's rules.

Alastair continued, "It's a ten-kilometer trek from here into White Fields. The small town of Gullfelt is located right at the base of the Torngat Mountains. The town is expecting us, so please, make haste. There isn't a moment to waste. It is approximately 16 degrees Celsius, so dress in layers. The nights are colder. I hope you packed appropriately." He turned around and began to put on his hiking boots.

"Sure thing, Papa," Chris said and put on his coat.

Together, they stepped off the Flyer onto the rocky road and into the bright sun. "It's so beautiful," Chris said in awe, looking around.

"And there is nothing magical about it," said Ciaran. "It was created just like this."

Their backdrop was clear blue skies over miles of green hills and pine trees with snowcapped mountains in the far distance. They were in a valley, and a river of blue water ran the length of it alongside a path. Chris walked over to it and knelt down to put his hand in the water. It was ice cold. He cupped his hands and grabbed some to drink. It was just as satisfying as it looked.

He stood up and turned to them. "I think I'm going to like it here."

"Yes, yes, beautiful," said Alastair as he held up his compass. "Make haste." He started walking briskly. "Not a moment to waste."

"I swear to Christ I'm going to curse that line," Felix muttered, staring at the back of Alastair's cap.

Ciaran chuckled. He adjusted his backpack and followed behind Felix. "What about our luggage?" Chris asked.

"Silas is going to wait here until we send for it," said Ciaran. "When it disappears from him, that's how he knows we made it safe, and he can head home."

"Oh." Chris looked up and waved at Silas, who waved back.

They walked for over an hour through the valley, with Chris taking pictures of the grassy lanes, crystal lakes, cliffsides, and mountaintops. At the end of the valley, they continued on the dirt path that was on the outskirts of a cliff. He noticed a sprinkle of hikers and waved to them, and they gave him a friendly wave back. They passed other secluded homes, some along the river, some on the cliffs, and one interesting-looking structure like a boathouse, but it was dark and the windows were boarded up.

Because he was paying attention, Chris was the first one who saw it. "Look." Chris pointed toward the right as the rocky path became smoother. "Gullfelt, right?"

"Oh, no," Alastair said, stopping abruptly.

"I know. This is not good," Ciaran said behind him.

"What?" Chris asked.

"We don't feel it," said Felix.

"Feel what?" Chris asked, bewildered. "I don't feel anything."

"That's the point, Chris," said Ciaran. "It's a Magi town with absolutely no enchantments or wards or spells or repellent for Commoners or other Magi."

"Precisely," said Alastair. "Absolutely anyone could walk into the town and cause havoc."

"Which means anyone could walk into the mountains, too," said Felix. "They need our help with a lot more than the Reserve. It's like they learned nothing from the first time around."

"The first time?" Chris and Ciaran said together.

Alastair looked exasperated. "Clearly, you did not read the three-hundred-page brief I sent to the Ringmaster. As a minister, it is your duty to—"

"Obviously, I didn't read it." Ciaran cut him off in exasperation. "Because briefings are no more than thirty pages, not three hundred. Now one of you tell me what I missed?"

Alastair turned to him. "During the war, Gullfelt was under siege by a group of *Caerulus Veneficus*. They posed as Magi officials—because some of them actually were—sent to protect the town, but they enslaved them instead for two reasons: the dragons in the mountains and the gold in the fields. You see, they couldn't get to the DRA; obviously, you know they tried. They couldn't get to any of the other Reserves in the UK, Eurasia, or South America. But they did get to this area, and ... it was terrible, to say the least. They went from a town of over a thousand residents to less than five hundred. When the war ended, the CV's were either captured or disappeared. Gullfelt spent the last couple of years regrouping as a town, and being able to protect the dragons in the mountains is an important part of that."

"Sounds like they are going to need to protect themselves, too," Ciaran said.

"Too right," Felix said with a sigh. "Come on, let's see what we're getting ourselves into."

CHAPTER 18

Gullfelt

The four men turned onto the paved road and walked into town. People smiled and waved hello as they passed by the shops and parks, making their way to the address given to Alastair. Not a car was in sight; people walked or Wisp'd everywhere. There were single-family homes right next to each other, and every house was a different color. But one thing was glaringly obvious about their quaint town.

"What's with all the pussies?" Chris said out loud.

A fluffy gold and white Norwegian Forest cat came up and rubbed his leg. Chris bent down to pet it, and another white and gray tabby came over for rubbing, too. Then a third cat, a Maine Coon. Every shop, home, and building had at least two to four cats milling around it. More cats lay on the sidewalk and in the street.

Alastair sighed loudly as he waved to another townsman. "You really need to read the briefing I sent over."

Ciaran rolled his eyes as Felix answered him. "One of the warlocks that enslaved this town was a trickster. If someone stepped out of line or tried to fight back, the punishment would be a transformation into a cat and then tossed into mountains. Some found their way home, but not all."

"Oh. Is that what Graham meant when he asked me once about whether I turned Chris into a cat?" Ciaran asked. "Interesting."

Chris chuckled as he officially gave up and sat on the ground as a fourth cat came over for petting.

"You would have known that if you'd read the brief—" Alastair began to scold again.

Suddenly an older man Wisp'd in front of them. "Minister Beals! I'm so glad that you made it. And just in time for dinner."

Alastair walked quickly ahead. "Good to meet you, Mayor Hugo Dubois." They shook hands. Then Alastair introduced everyone else. "This is Minister Ciaran A. Beals of the Dragon Reservation of Albania; the dragon reservation's Novo, Felicio L. Montenegro; and Minister Beals's fiancé, Commoner and Forest Ranger Christopher M. Jennings."

They all looked at Alastair like he was crazy and reintroduced themselves.

"Right. I'm Ciaran," he said, raising his hand for a shake.

"Felix," he said, raising his hand as a wave.

"Just Chris," he said with a smile from the ground.

Mayor Dubois gave them a friendly smile and shook their hands. "The whole town is excited that you're here. Welcome, welcome!" He began walking and talking. Chris reluctantly got up and followed them. "You must be exhausted from your trip. And don't worry, we've set you up with your extremely distant cousin on your father's side, Mrs. Melodie Beals. She even has dinner ready for you."

Alastair was confused. "But isn't she—"

"Not without help, of course," Mayor Dubois said. "But I would love for you to meet your security team. Starting with—ah, here is Inspector Neal now."

They all watched a round and very fluffy Norwegian Forest cat, this one gray, black, and white, trot its way down the steps of the police station and stop in front of them.

"You've got to be joking," said Felix first.

"I promise you, I am not," said the mayor. "Deputy Chief Inspector Neal was the leader of this community for twenty years before those bad Magi men took over. He protected several of our people, and our felines, by leading them out of the mountains safely. He deserves all our respect."

The cat sat up in pride. Ciaran bent down and petted the chief's head. The cat purred. He stood up. "Lead the way, Inspector."

The cat let out a short meow, turned around, and headed up the steps. The others followed. He went through the cat flap as everyone else used the door.

The police station had one large desk in front, several desks behind it, and a few offices toward the back. The Magi constables were loudly talking about hockey teams, some sitting on desks, some sitting in chairs with their feet up. Chris noted that they had their *rodulés* on one side of their tool belt, but the gun holster was empty. A cage in the back housed the firearms, and it looked like it had never been used. The head cat constable jumped on the front desk and meowed loudly. The officers looked up and began to straighten themselves up at the sight of company.

"Meet the Magi Newfoundland Constabulary of Canada," said the mayor proudly. "M.a.N.C.o.C."

Chris opened his mouth. *<Don't even...>* Ciaran said in his head. Chris slowly shut it.

Alastair did not miss a beat. "It's wonderful to meet you all. Outside of Deputy Chief Inspector Neal, who else should we direct our inquiries to?"

"Sergeant Jonathan Hinkley is our second-in-command and lead detective," said the mayor as Inspector Neal hopped down and trotted to a burly man sitting on the windowsill drinking coffee. "Of course, Gullfelt is a quiet town again, so no need for too much investigations happening. We pride ourselves on that."

The man gave them all nods, but did not bother moving from his position. Alastair gestured toward Chris and said, "Christopher Jennings is an officer of the law, a ranger, if you will. It would be good to have him be a part of your team while we're here. I'm sure he would love to keep busy in that way, assisting your constables."

Chris's head snapped toward Alastair and gave him a double blink.

"That would be wonderful," the mayor said. "We will revisit the idea later, but for now, let's let our guests rest up. I will show you to the home. It's just down the street. And if you need me, my office is right next door to the constable station."

"Good day, Constables," said Ciaran. Most greeted him back, but Hinkley looked at him suspiciously before he turned away.

The group left the station, walked down another block toward the end, and stopped at the Victorian home on the corner where a large orange cat was sitting on the ledge. Mayor Dubois walked up to her and rubbed her head. "Your guests have arrived, Mrs. Beals."

She stretched and yawned, then hopped off to go through the cat flap on the bottom of the screen door.

Mayor Dubois said, "You're in great hands with Melodie Beals. We'll regroup in the morning, bright and early, with our informal dragon expert." He went down the porch steps and walked away.

As soon as he was out of earshot, Chris turned to the others. "Okay, mates, are we seriously in the twilight zone right now? The cats? The officers that are about as useful as the staff at the Dunder Mifflin Paper Company? The mayor of Pleasantville? Is this real life?"

"Even for us Magi, this town is a little wonky, but it has charm," said Felix, looking around. He waved to a neighbor across the street, walking with their Emmth.

"Most importantly, we're here to help, not judge," said Ciaran. "And we're here to help them preserve the dragons all on their own. That's the mission." He waved his *dulé* at an empty space on the porch, and their luggage materialized.

"And thank Merlin we are here," Alastair said with a definitive nod. "We'll need to whip this so-called Magi village into shape. It's preposterous. Mulling about like ignorant Commoners. And taking orders from cats is not something that I plan on doing here. It's like the blind leading the blind. We must show these war-torn and badly misshapen magicians how it's done. I will simply have to lead." He nodded again, just as definitively.

"Don't worry, Minister, we all have our sight back now," a woman said as she pushed open the screen door. "They just haven't lost that nice Canadian charm. I'm Luanne Ludlow, but everyone calls me Lulu. Nice to meet you all. Would you like to come in for dinner?"

They heard her words, but Lulu was distracting. Her bright, long, multicolored skirt dragged behind her, and her green bra was covered with a brown fishnet shirt that showed her two belly piercings. Her arms were entirely covered in tattoos from the shoulders to her wrists. Up the side of her neck were scenes of dragons, wild plants, mountains, and vines. All of her fingers had silver rings on them except one, and she had a row of piercings going up both cartilages. Lulu's hair was long and wavy, down to her buttocks, with the top half in a messy bun, her *rodulé* sticking through it, and the sides were shaven down completely on her head. Round glasses were on her face, and her brown eyes blinked from behind them.

"Well?"

"Of course," Alastair said, gathering his composure first. She held the door open wider for him to grab it. "Thank you."

"Welcome," she said. She walked them past the living room and headed up the stairs. Mrs. Beals was stretched out on the couch, watching them curiously. They piled up at the top of the stairs, and Lulu pointed at the first door.

"Single room, Minister," she said to Alastair. She pointed at the second door across the hall. "Another single room for you, Novo," she said to Felix. She motioned toward the door farther down the hall. "Back room for you two," she said, pointing at Chris and Ciaran. "You're the gays, right? Fiancés?"

Ciaran smirked. "We are, in fact, the gays," Chris said with a grin.

"Cool," she said as she made her way to the steps.

"How did you know who was who, Lulu?" Felix asked her.

She stopped on the stairs and looked up. First pointing at Chris. "Gay men love *The Office*. And since you're the only one that mentioned dragons," she said, pointing at Ciaran, "that makes you the Dragonologist with the fiancé partner that was tagging along." She pointed to Alastair. "And you're an elitist fuck, so you're definitely a ministry official. That leaves you," she said to Felix, "as the Novo."

Chris, Ciaran, and Felix grinned, but Alastair took great offense. "Excuse me, I am not elitist," he said with a huff. "I would have you know that my father—"

"Dude, save it," she said, talking loudly over him. She began walking down the steps again.

"Dinner's on the table, fish ball soup and fresh baked bread. If you need anything, I'm right across Kimble Street." She stopped at the bottom of the stairs and looked up again. "Also, don't ever disrespect Mrs. Beals again. That woman is the kindest, bravest person you'd ever meet. And she's even sweeter as an orange tabby. She was supposed to be my mother-in-law, but she sacrificed her human life for me after her son was killed in front of her. So yeah, I take orders from that cat. And so will you."

She left the home without another word, leaving them stunned in the upstairs hallway.

"Well," Alastair said in a huff. "It's no wonder she has a ring on every finger except her left ring one."

"Christ, you're a nob," Felix said in disgust, touching Alastair's shoulder before he disappeared into his room.

Chris and Ciaran did the same, shaking their heads, leaving Alastair in the hallway alone.

CHAPTER 19

Sunflowers

The next morning, Chris woke up to Mrs. Beals lying at the bottom of their bed, watching them. Chris sat up first. He motioned with his hand for her to come closer. She stood up, stretched, and crawled up his body. She leaned on his chest and watched him. Chris scuffed up the top of her head and along the side. Mrs. Beals purred loudly against him.

"You are the sweetest," said Chris. Mrs. Beals reached a paw out and touched his chin. "Do you understand me?" he asked. She let out a soft meow. He grinned.

"Okay, I get it; we'll get you a cat," Ciaran mumbled from his pillow with his eyes still closed.

"What if I want this cat?" he said. "Hmmm? Would you like that, Mrs. Beals? Wanna come back to Albania with us?"

The cat continued to purr loudly. Then she immediately sat up. She walked across Ciaran's back and hopped off the bed. Then she stood in the doorway, expectantly.

"Breakfast?"

"Mew!" she responded.

"Are you seriously talking to the cat?" Ciaran mumbled again.

"Her name is Melodie Beals, and you best remember that if you don't want Lulu to kick your arse." He slapped Ciaran on the butt and climbed out of the bed. Ciaran groaned.

The four men met at the table, gathering porridge from the crock pot on the counter, listening to more of Alastair's rules for their conduct in town. As they were finishing up, the doorbell rang. They watched Mrs. Beals jump off the couch and run to it, then use two paws to shimmy the door open.

"Well, look at that," Felix said in awe.

"That's actually typical feline behavior," Alastair said in a bored fashion.

"And she's a genius cat," said Chris as the door opened and their guest arrived.

Mayor Dubois, with a yellow windbreaker jacket on, greeted Mrs. Beals first, then walked over to the table. "Good morning," he said with a smile. "Are you ready for a hike?"

"Can't wait," Ciaran said as he stood up, eager to get started. Felix and Alastair followed him, and they stepped out onto the porch together, including Chris, still in his pajamas.

However, they were surprised to see Lulu standing there. She was wearing a long-sleeved shirt that rose above her belly button, exposing her jewels and vine tattoos; camouflage army pants; and a yellow jacket. She had a few more yellow jackets in her hand and held them out.

"You?" Alastair said first with his face scrunched in, slowly taking it from her. "The housekeeper?"

"It is I, your grace," she said in a mockingly Old English accent. She bowed, then looked back up. "Would you like me to unwind your royal balls before we venture?"

Chris, Ciaran, and Felix snorted in laughter. Alastair was pissed.

"Lulu is not just Mrs. Beals's caretaker, she is our Novo and our dragon expert," the mayor said. "She didn't tell you?"

"No, she didn't," Ciaran said. He raised his hand to shake hers. "Nice to properly meet you, Novo Lulu." She shook his hand back. Felix did the same. Alastair continued to eye her suspiciously.

"If you have a Novo, then why am I here?" Felix said. "Not that I mind the holiday."

"It was not in the briefing that there was a qualified Novo," said Alastair to him. "So I requested an experienced one for the trip."

"Ah yes, because we're badly bruised, war-torn, and as ignorant as Commoners, so of course we wouldn't have an experienced Novo here. Isn't that correct, oh wise British man?" Lulu deadpanned. Alastair scowled again.

"Lulu is our Novo, but she is also the only one to successfully care for the dragons," said the mayor. "The ones that will let her, at least. She has a base set up a few kilometers up the middle mountain and has a system, such as wearing yellow to blend in with the sunflowers. We're going to Wisp over there."

"No, we're going to Wisp to the base of the mountain," she corrected. "Then walk about three kilometers in to the field of sunflowers. Dragons do not like the Wisp." She looked at Alastair. "Are you going to be able to keep up, Minister? This isn't desk duty."

"I can walk," Alastair gritted through his teeth. "But Wisp'ing is faster, obviously."

"We can't Wisp; it startles them," said Ciaran. "Lulu is correct. It's why we aren't allowed to Wisp at our Reserve.

Now I'm curious why I'm here at all too if you have Lulu. She can certainly teach you all how to manage the dragons."

"That's what I said," she retorted, rolling her eyes.

Mayor Dubois chuckled, nervously. "The CMC wanted to have someone with credentials and expertise to lead the operation."

"No, they wanted someone that was Generational Magi," she said to the mayor. "And I am not."

"So you are an ignorant Commoner," Alastair muttered.

"Alastair," Ciaran scolded him quietly as Lulu narrowed her eyes at him. He knew she heard him, too.

The mayor did not hear. "We love Lulu." He turned to her. "We do." Then he turned back to Ciaran. "Her Magi status from a Commoner family means nothing to us here; she's still a strong, powerful, capable Mage. But there is bureaucracy between the Council and Scholarly, and we had to follow along for the funding and support of our dragon reservation."

"Well, why doesn't she just get her Dragonology degree to prove her worth?" said Alastair, speaking to the mayor but looking at Lulu. "Surely, it wouldn't be that hard for her to pick up a book? You can read, can't you?"

"Alastair!" Ciaran scolded again at his rudeness. But Alastair was through with Lulu's snark and wanted it to be known.

But Lulu gave him a smile. "Tell me, Minister, what is the classification for a sixteen-foot Amphithere type species with a spiked tail, pouched cheeks, but no fire?"

Alastair was flustered. "Well, I... Amphitheres are generally non-threatening, and the short stature alone with no ability to breathe fire would make it a Class A—"

"Errr!!" she said, making a loud buzzing noise. "It's a Class C. Its ability to kill is two ways: with the spiked tail and the pouch, which most likely means it produces poisonous saliva. And you never even asked me about the size and shape of its mouth and teeth."

Alastair looked at his cousin, who nodded in the affirmative. "She's exactly right," Ciaran said. "It's not the type of dragon that classifies them. It's how deadly they can become."

Lulu walked up to Alastair and practically snarled in his face, "Now who looks like an ignorant Commoner?"

Alastair tried to keep his face stoic, but he turned away first. "My apologies," he mumbled.

Lulu's mouth turned up in a sarcastic smile. "You're forgiven."

He turned back to her with a look of bewilderment, but she had already approached Ciaran. "You're with me, Dragon Tamer. Kiss your lover goodbye and let's go."

Chris grinned. Ciaran turned around and kissed him on the lips, then turned back to Lulu. She linked her arms with him, and they walked on, Wisp'ing the few kilometers to the base of the mountains. Chris watched the other three Wisp away too.

He looked down at Mrs. Beals. "It's me and you, love. Let's go clean up breakfast, then take a walk." Mrs. Beals let out a short meow of approval.

The five of them met at the base of the second Torngat mountain and then began hiking the trail up. Ciaran looked up but couldn't see much through the clouds and fog. Felix and Lulu walked ahead, talking amicably, Alastair was in the middle with the mayor, also talking, and Ciaran was silently taking note of the path and the animals along the way. He kept looking up, but there were no dragons in the sky. He thought that was interesting.

They made it to the field and walked through the strips of large sunflowers until they came to a small hut in the middle of it, also yellow with a bright sunflower on top. When they entered, it was much larger than it appeared to be on the outside, expanded by twenty feet by thirty feet. There were five large whiteboards with pictures of the live dragons as well as a colorful drawing and everything from their height, weight, and characteristics to what they eat and when they fly was listed. In the center was a clay model of the three Torngat Mountains with a miniature clay dragon placed where each one lived.

"So five dragons total," Ciaran said, stopping at the first white board. He looked at the drawing of the Western Dragon named Gabbana. "It looks like London."

Felix came over. "You're right," he said. "Brown with hairy skin instead of scales, the same horns and everything."

"He had a twin," said Lulu. "I called them Dolce and Gabbana. They were here for at least a thousand years before anyone disturbed them." She sighed. "The twins were the first dragons those monsters caught, really early on before we knew what they were doing up here, for two whole years. They were inseparable before that, but Dolce was separated from Gabbana, and put on separate mountains. Both were tortured, and experiments ran on them. Trying to see if they could beat them into submission to control them."

"You cannot control a dragon," said Ciaran.

"I know that, and you know that," she said with sadness. "But they tried for many years. One day, I snuck up on his mountain, released Dolce's chains, and helped him escape. He flew away, and I never saw him again."

Felix and Ciaran looked at each other. "Could it be?" Ciaran asked him.

Felix lifted up his *dulé* and said, *"Orbis terrarum."* A translucent globe of the earth appeared in front of them. He followed a makeshift flight plan from the tip of his *dulé*.

"It is possible," Felix said. "A Western Dragon can fly up to 194 mph. And even if he were hurt, half of that would be 97 mph. The trajectory plus wind formation can add an additional 300 mph so without stopping could have him in Albania, which is the closest Dragon Reserve, in a few days."

"Whoa," said Ciaran, following Felix's tip. "No wonder he stayed up on the cliff edge for a week. He wasn't just afraid of humans. He was exhausted."

"I'm sorry," Alastair interjected. "What are we talking about?"

They both turned to him. "London," said Ciaran. "A few months before the war ended, a dragon just like this one showed up at our Reserve. Dale said he looked like he flew all the way from London to get there. That's how he got his name." He turned to Lulu. "But now I'm thinking he flew farther than that."

Her mouth was open in shock. She came closer and touched his arm. "Is he okay now? I've been so worried about him."

Ciaran and Felix exchanged looks again. Ciaran said, "We took care of him. Cleaned up his wounds. Gave him a home. He was happy there, safe, made friends. Trusted at least one human again."

"Was?" she said as tears pooled in her eyes.

"He died in his sleep last year in the spring," said Felix. "We don't know exactly what from, but it was internal. I suspected a slow internal bleed from a turned rib bone. We gave him a grand funeral march, all the bells and whistles. He was a good boy."

"Oh." She wiped a tear that had fallen. "Thank you."

"Of course. That's what we do," said Ciaran, touching her shoulder gently.

"But it also shows that if we need to move the dragons, they can follow that same path to the DRA, correct?" Alastair said, looking at Felix's map still in the air.

Lulu looked horrified. "Why would you do that?!" she exclaimed. "You're here to take my dragons?!"

"Well, if we cannot maintain a Reserve here, they would have to be moved to a better location. Ours," Alastair said factually. Ciaran gave him a hard look.

"You cannot, and you will not move my dragons," Lulu said to Alastair. "This is their home."

"But it is not a reservation," said Alastair. "This is a few stony mountains and a magical hut. You cannot care for them here."

"They can care for themselves."

"What if one of them is hurt or needs food or attention?"

"They are wild animals," she yelled at him. "They lick their own wounds, hunt for their own food, and keep each other company if they want."

"Correct. They are wild animals. And it's our job to secure their future," Alastair argued back. "And the only way to do that is to tame them under our control. Subdue their fire and their deadliest attributes. You obviously do not have the skills to do that here."

"Didn't you just hear your cousin? You cannot control a dragon, you asshole," she snapped. "You cannot subdue them, you cannot contain them, and you cannot medicate them."

Alastair scoffed and turned to his cousin. "Please talk some sense into this woman," he said. "Let her know how we maintain our dragons by giving them medical care, a place to roam freely, play and take flight with them, and we cannot do so without taking away their fire-making abilities."

Lulu turned to Ciaran, wide-eyed again. "You subdue their fire?! You *ride* them?!"

Ciaran hesitated, so Felix answered, talking very gently. "The ones that sleep in the valley and frequent the base camp, yes, to both. Riding is a way of building trust. And subduing their fire was the only way to secure our safety so we could help them. We started doing that about twenty years ago."

She shook her head in disbelief. "You're monsters. All of you."

"Hold on now," said Ciaran. "For what it's worth, I agree with you. We don't try to control them. They can choose not to come into the valley at all and stay in the Verdant Mountains. But we have six that we care for because they choose to be there to be close to us. They trust us."

"Seven now," Felix murmured. "Dory stays with us. So that's three youngsters, four older ones. Another five in the mountains that we never see, except Rehoboth who comes to check on her daughter from time to time."

"So they become your pets," Lulu said nastily. "They can't even take care of their young without you."

"That's not why—" Felix started, but she cut him off, talking over him.

"You ride them like horses. You take away their ability to hunt for themselves, so they have to rely on you for food. You should all be ashamed of yourselves," she snarled at him.

Ciaran shook his head. "It's still their community, their land and mountains. We just make life better for them.

London—Dolce—he lived in the valley, right below our base. And he was happy there being taken care of."

"And for the record," Alastair said, chiming in again, "They are beasts, so should be treated as such."

"What?!" she shrieked. "How dare you?!"

"Dear God, Alastair, can you please just shut up!" Felix snapped at him. "You're making it worse."

"No, I heard all I needed to hear," she said with a hand up. "Leave, all of you. Now."

"Excuse me, Luanne, but we came here with a job to do, and we intend to complete our mission," Alastair said in indignation. "We can't just—"

In a flash, the *dulé* was out of her hair and in her hand. "*Silencio!*" she screamed, pointing her *dulé* at him.

Alastair's mouth continued to move until he realized no sound was coming out. His mouth shut in annoyance.

"Lulu," Ciaran began cautiously.

But she pointed her *dulé* at him next. "I said get the fuck off my mountain and away from my dragons," she snarled. "Now!"

The mayor, who was quietly listening to the exchange, tried to intervene. "Now, now, Lulu, calm down. The CMC needs—"

"Get out!!!" she screamed again. She pointed her *dulé* upward. A lightning bolt came from it and made a hole in the roof. Thunder shook the cabin. "All of you, get out!"

Felix turned around and pulled Alastair's arm through the hut's door. Ciaran followed. The mayor had some words with Lulu, but he walked out after them, out of the meadow and back down the mountain.

CHAPTER 20

Comfort

After reading the first hundred pages of the brief, Chris went outside around noon to find something to do. He knew that Ciaran would not be back until the evening, so exploring the town was an option. Mrs. Beals saw him getting ready to leave the house and trotted over to him.

"Would you like to show me around?" he asked. She gave out a short meow and rubbed her face against his leg. "Alright, let's go."

They walked to the end of the block and turned the corner. As they walked into the main part of Gullfelt, a few cats came over and greeted Mrs. Beals first and then Chris. After a few rubs they continued walking.

Chris stopped at the town square. He looked down and asked, "What's better, Marley's Fish and Chips or Salamander's Bar and Grill?" Mrs. Beals started walking toward Marley's. He gave her a look. "Now you wouldn't be saying that because you have a fish preference, right?"

She circled in the middle of the street and continued walking toward the smaller food shop. "Marley's it is," he murmured.

Chris was not disappointed. He ended up spending the rest of the afternoon there, eating and talking with Marley and his customers. His catfish sandwich with sweet potato chips was possibly the best thing he ever had. And the locals were delightful, greeting him and thanking him for traveling all that way just to help their little old town. Chris explained that it was his fiancé who was the Dragon Tamer, and he was along for the ride, but they continued to thank him anyway.

They also told him stories of the war, how their sheriff's station was almost wiped out, and all the men in town were forced to work in the meadows and mountains digging for gold for the evil warlocks or used as bait for the dragons. So many of them had loved ones that were either killed or turned into a cat and dropped off halfway up the mountains for the dragons' sport.

Despite that, they were optimistic. They cared for their feline loved ones and formed a task force, that Lulu was the head of, to find a way to break the curse.

"Very few have been able to break a hex of this magnitude," Yolanda Grimes, who owned a small boutique, said. Her son sat in her lap, curled up and asleep.

"So I assume *Vis carmina omittere* wasn't working," asked Chris, then immediately regretted joking about something so serious. But others in the small eatery laughed.

"It's blood magic, son," Eugene Jenkins, the town tailor, told him. "A hex created by its owner and only its creator can use it or break it. And the only sure way to break it is to end the life force of the creator's *Vis*."

Chris's eyebrows went up. "You mean death." There were nods all around. "So where is the Magi who created it?" Chris asked.

"Pénitenci," Marley himself said from behind the counter. "Canada's Magi prison. It's on the highest north coast of British Colombia. Very far. Very cold. Theron the Trickster, along with thirty of them, will die in there for what they did."

"Except Rodango, their leader," Mrs. Jenny Cho said. She owned the Chai and Caffe shop across the street from the police station, but had left her daughters Emily and Femy in charge along with her other daughter, Debony, who was a cat that never left the shop. "He escaped. We think Theron somehow got him away, sacrificing himself, being Rodango's second-in-command."

"Okay, but if you all know where the Magi who created it is, why hasn't the CMC done something about it?" Chris asked. "Make him reverse the hex."

"They have tried," someone else said, a woman that Chris never caught the name of. "They pleaded with him, threatened him; nothing has worked. He thinks it's funny that lives were ruined. That whole families have been split apart. My husband does nothing but sit in his chair in our home day and night." She sniffed.

"It's a fate worse than death for some," Eugene said. "The ones that were killed are the lucky ones. We get to stay behind and watch our townsfolk wither away." Eugene's sons were both constables and were killed early on.

"So why doesn't the CMC execute him for his crimes?" Chris asked. "He was the second-in-command and gave orders. He killed, he stole, he kidnapped, he enslaved people, and that's outside of hex. Surely it's enough to convict him and sentence him to death."

The room went quiet. "We're Canadians," said Mrs. Cho. "We don't believe in the death penalty here, love."

Chris nodded. "Okay. I get it. I don't necessarily believe in the death penalty either. But there has to be another way."

"That's why we're so grateful for Lulu," Marley said. "We're so thankful that she stayed in Gullfelt and became our Novo."

"Right now, Lulu is working on an antidote made from Theron's blood, hair, and skin," said Ms. Cho. "And she's training my Emily as a Novo to help her. Every few months, she asks for a feline volunteer, but she hasn't in a while. We're hoping that she's successful the next time she asks."

"Here's to hoping," Chris said.

Chris explored the rest of the town on foot. He glanced through the window of the police station and watched about a dozen constables lazing around, doing nothing. He shook his head and kept going. He found the small post office, the front area for actual post and the back room of pigeons, and talked with Mr. Conners before sending a pigeon with a postcard attached to his sisters.

He stopped at the small church and met the monsignor, Father McClain, and talked with him for a moment about his Catholic faith and the faith of many Magi who believed in a divine power. He believed that their faith was what got the town of Gullfelt through the dark days of enslavement.

He found the market, where Mrs. Beals caught up with him, directing him on what the house needed. And Chris found himself arguing with a cat on which chicken cuts were better and which ice cream flavors to get. Not that anyone in the store noticed or minded. When he tried to pay with the Sagems he had, he was told that it was all covered by the Canadian Magi Council. Chris left a couple of Magi money on the counter anyway.

When Chris and Mrs. Beals returned with the groceries, Ciaran and Felix were sitting on the rocking chairs on the porch, looking solemn. "I didn't expect to see any of you until sunset," he said, dropping the bags at their feet.

"Yeah, well, Minister Arsehole got us kicked off the mountain. Literally," said Felix with a scowl.

"Ah," said Chris, sitting on the top step with his knee up. "Alastair put on that snooty charm, did he?"

"She's never going to trust us," Ciaran muttered, his hand patting his thigh every few moments. "I know how she feels. The dragons are like her children. And we just threatened to either cut her children's hands off or take them away."

"Correction," Felix said. "*We* didn't threaten to do anything. I'm perfectly fine if they continue to be wild and free. I'm just here to give her tips on how to care for them should they need assistance, like she did when the CVs were here."

"Doesn't matter," Ciaran said, looking at the ground. "She sees the three of us as one voice."

"So don't be one voice," said Chris. They both looked at him. "Each of you have a different role to play. Ciaran, you're the Dragon Tamer. You should be the only one going up there with her. I'm sure you can convince her of that. You can report back to Felix if there is anything in particular he needs to know or you need to ask him about dragon health. And if Felix goes, it's just to do that, give her tips on how to care for them. Just because it's Alastair's proposal doesn't mean you're not in charge of this mission.

"Felix, you're a Novo, and you're brilliant. Lulu has been working on a cure for the last four years to end the feline curse. She's training a new Novo, but she could use the help, another brilliant brain. Offer to help her on that. She'll appreciate it. And Alastair... well, he's here to oversee, so he can oversee from this house right here. Or the mayor's office. I'll get him to focus on building up their wards and such. Everyone has a job to do, right?"

Felix and Ciaran looked at each other. "You've got a live one there," said Felix to his friend. "I see you've been punching up."

"Shut up," Ciaran said with a smile. He turned back to Chris. "You're right. Solid advice, mate. Thanks."

"You're welcome."

Felix stood up. "I'm going to go for a walk. Go find dinner. I have a feeling Lulu won't be back any time soon."

"Not until tomorrow," Ciaran agreed. "Maybe the day after that. She's going to stay with her dragons tonight to keep them safe from us." Ciaran sighed.

"Might I suggest Marley's Fish and Chips?" said Chris. "Really great comfort food. Also, stop by Mrs. Cho's chai shop and talk with Emily Cho. She's been helping Lulu with her experiments, and she's Lulu's apprentice Novo."

"Good to know on both accounts," said Felix. He gave them both daps and headed farther into town.

Chris looked up at Ciaran, who still looked crestfallen, staring into the distance. "Rough day at the office, love?" Chris deadpanned.

Ciaran sighed again, looking up at the mountains. "I have to figure out how to get this mission back on track."

"You don't have to figure out anything right now." Chris stood up and held out his hand. "Shut your brain off and come upstairs."

Ciaran took it and stood up, too. He picked up the bags of groceries, and together, they walked into the home. After dropping the bags on the kitchen table, Chris walked him into the house and right upstairs to their bedroom.

Mrs. Beals was on their tail, but Chris stopped her at the door. "Now you know I love you," he said gently to the cat. "But some things we don't need an audience for." She meowed at him and walked away. Chris closed the door on her.

Ciaran smiled. "Okay, yes, I will get you a—"

Chris kissed him, pushing him onto the bed. Ciaran moaned and allowed Chris to take control.

Chris unbuckled his jeans and slipped them off one leg at a time, then went back up, and took off Ciaran's underwear. He put his face in Ciaran's crotch, sniffing deeply first, the smell of him making Chris dizzy with arousal. Then he proceeded to lick up his cock and blow him.

He took his time, making sure Ciaran forgot about the troubles of the day as the blood left his brain and rushed to his midsection. Ciaran ran his hair through Chris's curls and sighed as he came. Chris came off the bed and took off his clothes as Ciaran silently watched. Then he grabbed the lube and lifted Ciaran's thighs to prepare him. Chris pulled the covers over them and pushed inside.

"God, I love you," Ciaran murmured. He wrapped his arms around Chris's hard body, never having felt safer than when he was in Chris's arms.

Chris responded with a kiss and moving inside of Ciaran. Again, he took his time, changing positions twice and adding more lube at times to keep them going. Ciaran kept himself submissive and malleable, having no desire to take charge of anything. And Chris could feel that in him as they kissed, and he licked Ciaran's armpits, all while stroking all his erogenous zones inside and out.

Eventually, Chris did cum with a shudder. He came off Ciaran, but stayed on his stomach. "I love you, too," he murmured back.

Ciaran turned to his stomach, too, and put his head on Chris's back. They watched the colors of the sky light up as the sun set with the mountains as the backdrop. Once the sun went behind the mountains and the northern lights began to swirl in the sky, Chris rose from the bed and went to make Ciaran Tavë Kosi, an Albanian dish and a taste of home.

CHAPTER 21

Ciaran in Charge

As suspected, they did not see Lulu at all that evening. So, right as the sun began to rise, Ciaran put on his yellow windbreaker and Wisp'd to the bottom of the mountain and began to head up the path. Chris was right. Alastair put the debrief together, but he was named lead of operation. And it was time for him to take control of this mission.

He remembered the way from the day before and was fine until he got to the sunflowers. As he made his way through, suddenly he lost the trail underneath him. He stood still for a moment, looking up at the sun to gauge which direction was east and which was west. He knew the hut was on the western part of the sunflower field, so he headed there. After walking straight for twenty minutes, he stopped again. He slowly did a 360 and noticed the flowers all resembled each other. A little too identical. He looked up, and the sun was in the same position.

"Fucking magicians," he heard himself mutter, sounding like Chris. Then he said loudly, "I have a feeling you can hear me, Lulu. It's just me. Let me in, please."

After a moment of silence, he heard her voice call out, "Why would I do that?"

"Because I'm here to help," he said. "I want to learn about them, observe them, teach you how to be a more efficient caretaker to them. That's the only reason I'm here, one Dragon Tamer to another. I don't want to change how you do things. I just want to help you do it better. Will you give me a chance?"

Suddenly the sunflowers behind him parted, making a path. Lulu was standing at the edge of it in front of her hut. He walked toward her. "So I was going in the wrong direction," he said.

"No. You would have been lost in there forever." She turned around, saying, "Let's go, Dragon Tamer."

Lulu allowed Ciaran to spend the day with her, going through each of the whiteboards and learning about the five dragons in the Torngat Mountains. He asked her, "Lulu, I haven't seen any traces of dragons. Why is that?"

She hesitated, then said, "The warlocks pushed many of them farther up or deeper into the mountain terrain. We used to see them all the time. Now they rarely come around, not even to fly over Gullfelt."

"Then how do you have all this information?" Ciaran asked. "These notes aren't from years ago."

"I can get closer," Lulu said simply. "They trust me."

"But how—"

"Do you have pertinent information I can add to these whiteboards or not?" she said, cutting him off. So Ciaran did, writing out other attributes of each of the five dragon types she had listed.

As the sun began to set, they went back down the mountain and Wisp'd to Kimble Street. Lulu said to him, "Sorry about dinner last night. I can whip something up real quick for you all."

But Ciaran shook his head. "No worries about that. Chris is taking care of it tonight. Go clean up and come over in thirty minutes. We're treating you to dinner as a thank you."

She smiled at him. "So the fiancé is gorgeous, supportive, funny, manly, and he cooks, huh?"

"Definitely punching above my weight, innit?" Ciaran said with a smile.

"Am I supposed to know what that means?" Lulu asked in confusion.

Ciaran laughed. "See you in thirty minutes."

He watched her walk across the street. Then he sent a message through his *Amina* all the way to London before he stepped into Mrs. Beals's charming home.

Lulu appeared as the food was hitting the table in jean overalls, a black bra, and no shoes. "It smells amazing in here," she said as she opened the door. They could see the vines traveling across her belly around to her back and wrapping around her arms, disappearing into her other colorful tattoos.

Alastair stared at her as she sat down next to the chair he was about to sit in while the others continued around her.

"It's chicken yassa," said Chris as he put the large steaming bowl in the center of the table. Ciaran was right behind him with a second big bowl of white rice.

"Mmmm... Can't wait," she said excitedly, rubbing her hands together.

"Thanks for helping there, mate," Felix muttered sarcastically to Alastair as he also put steamed carrots on the table right before he sat down next to her.

"Oh," Alastair also muttered as he glanced at Lulu again. "Apologies."

Chris and Ciaran sat across from Alastair, Lulu, and Felix. Mrs. Beals sat on a chair next to Chris and also waited patiently. Chris added warm, wet cat food to the plate for her, and she immediately dug in, not waiting for the humans.

"Before we begin," Ciaran started, "I just want to say how happy I am that we're all here together. My loving and supportive partner..." He gave Chris a soft nod. "One of my best friends and the smartest fucker I've ever met," he said, looking at Felix.

"Cheers," Felix said back with a smile.

"And my brilliant older cousin, who goes out of his way to give me opportunities to prove my potential." He nodded at Alastair. "Thank you."

"Well, I..." Alastair stumbled. "You're welcome."

"And thank you, Luanne, for allowing me into your world today. You are also pretty brilliant. And bad-arse."

She grinned. "And you have lived up to your reputation, Ciaran Beals. I appreciate you."

"And, of course, we cannot forget the lovely Mrs. Beals, who opened up her home to us. You are a true gem." The orange cat paused eating and looked at Ciaran. Chris reached over and stroked her head affectionately.

"I know it's only been a few days," Ciaran said, "But I have a great feeling about this trip. It's going to be life-changing."

Chris squeezed Ciaran's hand, then said, "Let's dig in."

They passed around the bowls and filled their plates with the spicy and savory dish. Felix asked about Lulu's research and experiments to find a counter-curse or anti-dote for the feline hex. Lulu discussed a mixture of elixirs and spells and getting bodily fluids from Theron to run tests on, and Felix went through the historical context of blood magic. Christopher was thoroughly interested in the conversation and chimed in about what he'd learned from the townsfolk. But he was also interested in how Alastair kept glancing directly into Lulu's overalls and the tattoos covering her body.

"And you're training a Novo?" Felix asked Lulu.

"Yes, Emily Cho, the youngest of the Cho daughters. She's smart as a whip and has really great suggestions. So maybe the three of us can get together, and I can show you what I've done so far."

"I'd be honored," said Felix. "Where is your lab?"

"In my basement," she said. "Truthfully, I had been working on it during the war, but I had to keep it a secret. Emily came over one day and caught me. But she's been a great help since then. She called it my hidden lair."

"Well, two heads are better than one," said Felix. "Three, now that you got me. You and Ciaran focus on the dragons while you introduce me to your lab, and we'll see if we can get something going with a cure."

She smiled at him and touched his arm. "I appreciate that, Felix."

Alastair coughed. "Excuse me." Everyone turned to him. "That's not the mission. Felix, you are to report to the Torngat Mountains with Ciaran at once, monitor the dragons' health and well-being, and then report your findings to me. And, Ciaran, you are to train Luanne on how to tame the dragons, keeping them safe. And if not, we remove them. That is the mission."

"Well, Alastair," said Ciaran, expecting his reaction, "Luanne is not a circus monkey that I can train. She's a very experienced, very knowledgeable Dragon Tamer in her own right. So I have decided to change your mission."

Alastair scoffed. "It is not my mission. It is what the CMC expects."

"Because that was your proposed outcomes," said Ciaran. "Chris read it, not me. I'm not reading a three-hundred-page brief that you single-handedly put together with zero input from an actual Dragonologist."

"Well, I—"

"And further," Ciaran said, cutting him off. "The overall mission is to assist Gullfelt in becoming a stronger Magi Community. Your words, Alastair. Felix refocusing on the feline serum will indeed help Gullfelt by bringing their citizens back, becoming a stronger community. So they can stop acting like... what was it you called them?"

"Ignorant Commoners," Chris, Felix, and Lulu chorused.

Alastair raised his chin in indignation. "That is not—"

"And lastly," Ciaran said. "I don't take orders from you, Minister Beals. My true allegiance is to Scholarly, where the DRA falls under. Not the Magi Council of Europe. I've already sent word to Lucinda to tell her of our amended mission and agenda. I expect her stamp of approval by the morning. She trusts my judgment."

Lulu, Chris, and Felix grinned. Alastair glared at his cousin. "You went behind my back?" he said in resentment. "You went over my head?"

"Can you do that, Ciaran?" asked Chris. "Is it physically possible to go over one's head and also behind their back?"

"Anatomically it is," Felix jumped in. He started doing hand motions. "You would have to stand directly in front of said person, walk around to position yourself behind them, thus going behind their back. And then hop at a horizontal projection to travel precisely above the cranium, thus landing at the point of entry in front of the subject. Also known as, over one's head."

Chris tried hard to keep a straight face. "Thank you, Novo Montenegro. You truly are the smartest fucker that I've ever met as well."

"Why thank you, Ranger Jennings," Felix said with a smile, raising his glass. "Cheers." Chris toasted him.

Alastair huffed. "I'm glad you all are having a nice hearty-har-har, but the fact is the Canadian Magi Council deemed Luanne Ludlow unqualified and must be monitored until she has our approval. And by the looks of her attire, we all have our work cut out for us. So despite your underhanded betrayal, Ciaran, I must continue to pull rank and do what we set out to do here."

Before Ciaran could respond, Lulu turned to him. "What's wrong with my outfit, Minister Buttface?"

Chris snorted. Felix laughed and put another spoonful in his mouth. Ciaran smiled.

Alastair scoffed. "Did you forget your shoes? And your *shirt*?" he asked.

Lulu stared at him. "Why? Is the shape of my tits in this silk bra bothering you? Would you like to inspect them yourself? You know, for your full approval. And they are a handful."

Chris laughed out loud. Felix snorted. Ciaran smiled.

"Must you be so crass?" Alastair said with an attitude, peering at her over his glasses.

She pushed her glasses down to the tip of her nose and mimicked his peering. "Yes. Must you be so posh, you elitist fuck?"

"I am not elitist or posh. I simply carry myself with dignity, respect, and decorum. Three things you know nothing about."

"Hey!" Ciaran said to his cousin.

"Well, it's true," said Alastair. "I mean, who comes into a home full of men wearing…" he waved his arms in front of her, "that?"

"There is nothing wrong with what she's wearing," said Chris.

"It's how she wants to express herself, you prick," Felix yelled at him, too.

"I'm not trying to be rude, I'm just—" Alastair started.

"Oh, now, you're not trying to be rude?" Ciaran said sarcastically.

"It's fine," Lulu said, standing up before they continued arguing. "Thank you for the amazing dinner, Christopher. And for the lovely company, Felix."

"You're welcome," Chris said at the same time Felix said, "Anytime."

"And Ciaran," she said, as she reached her hand into her overalls behind her to unhook her bra. "Thank you for being you. I've always had a thing for Beals men. It's a shame that Chris has your heart." She winked at Chris. "I'll see you in the morning. I have another space to show you, where I watch the dragons freely. But I have one rule and one only."

Lulu slipped the bra off her shoulders, slid it off from inside her overalls, and put it to her mouth to whisper an incantation. "That this nob—you call dicks 'nobs,' correct?"

Ciaran tried hard to contain his smirk. "That is correct."

"That this nob never, ever, sets foot on my mountain again." She dropped the bra onto Alastair's head with the strap landing on his plate. "Deal?"

Ciaran nodded. "You have my word on that."

"Thank you. Felix?" She turned to him.

"Yes, Lulu," he said with a straight face, looking into her eyes, willing himself not to look down.

"Walk me home? And stay a while. I'll show you to my ... lair."

"It would be my pleasure." He stood up and smiled at Chris and Ciaran, who grinned back at him. He held out his elbow. "Shall we?"

"You're such a gentleman," she said as they walked through the door.

Alastair sat there, scowling as the door closed behind him. "She is extremely inappropriate," he grumbled.

"Oooh," Chris said mockingly. "Is 'extremely' higher than 'highly' inappropriate? Just, you know, asking for a friend."

"That woman—" But Alastair stopped talking as he reached up to take the bra off his head, and it crumbled into black sand, covering his hair and face and getting into his dish.

Ciaran couldn't hold back anymore. He busted out laughing. Chris started howling in laughter, too.

"You are both children," Alastair said, standing up in a huff. "Grow up!"

But Chris and Ciaran could not stop laughing as Alastair made his way upstairs.

CHAPTER 22

Fire Power

After Ciaran left with Lulu and Felix was poised in Lulu's basement office going over the notes for her anti-feline serum, Chris tired of listening to Alastair complain how "highly inappropriate" it was for them to leave him behind for the second week in a row. He announced that he was going for a walk and left Alastair at the house with Mrs. Beals.

He breathed a sigh of relief as soon as he hit the porch steps. He looked to the right at the mountains in the distance and smiled. Then he walked to the center of town.

Chris walked to the Chai and Caffe shop to say hi to Mrs. Cho and talk with her and Femy for a while. While Mrs. Cho was in the back to get more supplies and Femy was with a customer, a pretty cat that was mostly white with gray patches of fur came to the bottom of the counter and watched him from the corner. Chris motioned with his finger. She did not budge. So he got on the floor and "pssst" at her a few times.

"Come here, cutie," he said to her softly. "I won't hurt you."

The cat slowly came toward him. Chris held his palm out. She sniffed him a few times. Chris moved his other hand out slowly to rub the top of her head. After a long moment, she began to purr.

"Ah, Debony came out," Mrs. Cho said as she put a row of coffee cups on the counter. The cat scurried back behind the counter and disappeared.

"Previous human?" Chris asked as he stood up.

"Hmm. My daughter," she said. "A week before they revealed themselves as enslaving scumbags, she was supposed to leave for college. Obviously, they would not let her go. She tried to escape and got caught. I suppose the trickster turning her into a cat was better than killing her on the spot." She sighed. "But she's sad. Lonely. She used to be my adventurous daughter, but now she never leaves the shop."

Chris touched her hand on the counter in sympathy. "I'm sorry."

"Hmm." She touched his hand back. "Gullfelt is surviving."

"Yeah, I can see that," said Chris as he looked out the window at the police station. He shook his head, thinking of how useless they appeared to be. Then he made a decision.

Chris said, "I'll see you later, Mrs. Cho, Femy. And Debony, you too!" Chris left the tea shop and went to the station.

He opened up the glass doors and stepped inside. The same twelve or so officers were there, talking, laughing, playing on their phones, doing nothing. Deputy Chief Inspector Neal was sitting on top of the front desk, grooming himself.

Chris shook his head and said loudly, "So this is the great Man-Cock."

They all stopped and looked at him. Even Inspector Neal paused licking his back leg.

Sergeant Hinkley was the first to stand up. "You've come to make fun of our name, Commoner?"

"No, I've come to find out what you're doing about security in this Magi town," he said. "Because from where I'm standing, your officers are either bored or lazy, your townsfolk are depressed and sitting ducks for another attack, and your magical defenses are shite."

"Now hold on there," another officer said, standing up. "What do you know about magical defenses? You're a Commoner."

"I know that I lived in Albania my entire life, played in those same woods as a boy, worked in them as a man, and I never once got close to the Dragon Reservation of Albania because of their wards, spells, and incantations. And even after I met Ciaran, it was only after he put an aversion on me to block the wards that I was able to get near it. That's what I know about magical defenses and how they actually work.

"Also, I'm an officer of the law," Chris retorted. "What are *you*?"

"I'm Constable Broock," he said. "And I lost my entire family to the war. My wife. My adult sons. I fought and bled and almost died. I protect this town with my life. Don't you dare come in here and judge me."

"I'm not judging you, Constable Broock," Chris said. "And I'm sorry for your loss. But isn't that all the more reason to ensure it never happens again?"

"It won't," Hinkley said casually, sitting back down and leaning back in his chair. "The bad men are all gone now. We're fine."

"Are you?" Chris challenged him.

He pulled out his gun from his holster, aimed, and shot the lamp on Hinkley's desk. The bulb burst, sending glass everywhere. Hinkley fell backward in his chair. The three officers around it ran for cover. Three more stepped forward, pointing their *dulés* at Chris.

"You want to die here today, Commoner?" an older officer growled at him.

"No. I just wanted to show you something." Chris calmly lowered his gun. "A Commoner like me could walk into your town, into your police station, and kill any one of you. Want to know why?" he said, looking around. "Because you can still die like men. And if you don't begin to protect yourself, you will die like men."

Hinkley stood up and wiped down his shirt. "A Commoner like you could never kill any one of us. Commoners are beneath Magi. Or have you not observed your third-class status in our world?"

"Third class?" Chris asked in confusion. "Who are the second-class Magi?"

"Yes, third class. You're the scum right below the Commoner Magi. The lizard hybrids I like to call them." A few officers snickered.

Chris scoffed. "You're a real prejudiced arsehole, Hinkley." He holstered his weapon. "Any one of you non-prejudiced arseholes who wants to do a little target practice, meet me in the meadow right outside the edge of town with the guns from your armory at 9 a.m. Let's really start to protect this town."

He turned to the cat, who was still eyeing him suspiciously. "Good day, Deputy Inspector Neal," he said with a nod.

Chris walked back out of the police station, knowing that *rodulés* were still pointed at his back.

"How did Mrs. Beals become a cat?" Ciaran asked as they walked up the narrow, stoney path in a single file, almost in a vertical way. They had bypassed the sunflower meadow that morning and kept going up the mountain, at Lulu's request. "You said she saved your life?"

Lulu sighed. "The day we buried Jasper, her son, Theron had the nerve to come to the funeral. I lost it. I ran up and started wailing on him, punching, biting, scratching. They pulled me off him, and the trickster pulled out his *dulé*. We all knew what that meant. I would have been turned into a cat and tossed into the mountains. But Melodie screamed, 'Not my daughter!' and jumped in front of me just in time. The hex hit her instead of me."

She looked at Ciaran with sad eyes. "That was the last words she ever uttered. She called me her daughter. And Jasper and I weren't even married."

"I'm so sorry, Lulu," said Ciaran. "That must have been awful."

"It was," she said. "They tossed her into the mountains. I was devastated and hid in her home, thinking I was next. A week later she came back, scratching at the door. I don't know how she made it through. Maybe it was her color? She was able to blend in with the sunflowers, I guess. But she found her way home. I hid her in the house for three years. That's why she likes to be outside so much now. Because she couldn't before."

He was about to respond, but she stopped walking and said, "Stand still as stone. And look up." Ciaran did.

They watched a green dragon with a dinosaur-like beak mount an edge of the cliff directly above them. He sniffed around. Neither of them moved a muscle as another dark gray dragon with a red belly and a long, spiked tail came flying around him. The green one let out a small cry and spread his fifteen-foot-long wings. He pushed himself off the edge with his clawed feet and flew into the air. The gray one flew in a circle for a moment, then went higher into the clouds, and the green one followed.

"They're both so beautiful," Ciaran breathed out.

"Willard, the green one, is a Wyver/Ptero mix," said Daisy. "Dressa, the Krekardron, keeps to herself mostly and loves the highest peak of the mountains. She knows when I'm here, though, and she'll come closer."

"She looked a little like Malik. But Malik is more scaly than spiky. Probably because he's still so young. That dragon you have here is at least a hundred years old."

"And Malik is?"

"Malik is also a Krekardron. Small face, two short front legs, large wings, spiked tail. Which means Dressa's fire range is probably long too."

"It is," Lulu said as she continued to walk. They made it to the ledge and saw the entrance of the cave that the Wyver came out of. "But Dressa is the kinder one. She rarely breathes fire because she doesn't need to. The others leave her alone. Her and Willard are friends and play together."

Ciaran nodded. "Krekardrons only need one friend."

They continued walking to another ledge that resembled the meadow below but without sunflowers. Three cats came up to her and meowed and purred around her leg. They followed her to the opening of a smaller cave that had a yellow painted rock against it.

She pointed her *dulé* and said, "*Labi.*" The rock rolled to the side, and they entered the stone lair.

It was smaller than the shack, round and just about six feet tall, so Ciaran had to crouch a little. There were little openings in the rock where they could see out. A stone table sat in the middle, and a bed was in the corner of the room.

"I created it as a refuge for the town cats," she said as the cats followed her inside. "There is a sound that you can't hear. It's a high-pitched frequency. If they made it here, I kept them safe and brought them down one by one."

"So you were the one that led them out during the war," Ciaran said. "The mayor told us that Inspector Neal led them out."

She shrugged. "Gregg Neal was the first one I found. He was hiding in this cave. Once I showed him the way, he showed the others. And then I did this." Lulu pointed her *dulé* upward and said, *"Pellucentia."*

Suddenly the walls became translucent and disappeared, as if they were right outside. But Ciaran knew better. He touched above him, and the rock was still solid, just see-through. "Pretty wicked."

"Don't worry, they can't see us," she said. "It was how I was able to see what they were doing up here, monitor, track them, be able to fill my whiteboards. Now I just come here to watch, learn, and take notes."

Lulu walked to the edge and motioned for Ciaran to come closer. "The drakes come out earlier in the day. Every day, they walk through this small rocky path from their burrow to another area where they search for food. Here they come now. I named them Thor and Hera."

Together, they watched two brown, muscular, spiky dragons with very small wings not made to fly slowly walking single file through the trench.

"I've never seen drakes in the flesh before," said Ciaran, in awe. "They're native to North America."

"Thor is the dark brown one, the male. Hera is the light brown one," said Lulu. "They have a family back there. Only Thor and Hera leave to hunt. They eat first, then come back with carcasses of caribou, bobcats, even seals. In a few hours, you'll see."

Ciaran turned to her. "How many children?"

"Three so far. And an older female drake. I call her Gaia. So six drakes all together. But you'll never see them. Only Thor and Hera leave their burrow ever since the CVs killed Zeus, her partner."

"So you have more than five dragons up here?" Ciaran said with a sly smile.

She hesitated. "You can't tell anyone."

"I won't. But you need to bring a few people up here to help you monitor them, Lulu. And you have to track them, officially."

She shook her head. "They only trust me."

"And as the Lead Dragon Tamer, you can get them to trust others. If they trust you, they will trust who you trust."

"I don't know if—" She was cut off by a loud roar.

They both looked up. A long-necked, twenty-nine-foot-long dragon with six legs and two enormous wings was flying directly above them. Ciaran followed it to the other side to stare at it. "Whoa. That is definitely London's twin." He watched it fly to the mountain edge across from them and land gracefully. He put his snout in the air and sniffed.

Ciaran took out his cell phone and snapped a picture. "The boys back home are not gonna believe this."

He turned around, and Lulu was writing in her notebook. "I document their wake-up times, eating, sleeping, exercise. If something is out of the ordinary, I document that, too. Gabbana doesn't normally come this close. Neither does Willard. They know I'm here. But they're catching your scent, too."

"Indeed." Ciaran turned to her. "Is there something of yours here that I can wear? Something with your scent on it?"

Lulu looked at him in amusement. "My shirts are a little too small for you."

Ciaran grinned. "Maybe. But..." He looked around and saw the bed had an orange throw blanket on it. "Do you use this often?" He brought it to his nose to sniff.

"I do, especially during the winter months when I sleep up here."

Ciaran wrapped it around his waist like a long skirt. Lulu giggled. "You look smashing. That's an English slang word, right?"

"It is." Ciaran laughed. "Can't wait to learn American slang from you, too. Dead in the arse."

Lulu grinned. "It's 'dead ass.' And never say that again."

Ciaran laughed again. He grabbed the scarf also on the bed and wrapped it around his head. "Let's go find your Wyver."

At dusk, they made their way out of the cave. Lulu rolled the stone back with her *dulé* and stuck it through her hair. They began walking through the meadow to the ledge, side by side. "It's actually pretty cool how much you know about all types of dragons," she said. "Like, I had no idea that drakes could also breathe ice, along with their fire."

"Well, you wouldn't have known that; it's not something they use often, especially not in this part of the world," said Ciaran. "They originate from Greenland and were first spotted in what is now called Nunavut as early as the ninth century."

"Then how did they get here in the Americas?" asked Lulu. "They go as far down as the caves of the Grand Canyon as far as I know."

"Who knows?" said Ciaran. "Migration. Trafficking. But—"

Ciaran felt a chill go through him and stopped walking. He looked up with his hand over his eyes, shielding the sun. "What?" Lulu asked curiously.

But he didn't respond. Something was coming, fast and furious.

Before she could ask again, she, too, felt it, the wind behind them. They both turned around and watched the serpentlike, green and gold-feathered dragon with large wings swoop down and land about twenty feet in front of them. The right eye was completely damaged, but it could see fine through its left eye. And that eye was trained on Ciaran.

Lulu gasped and yelled, "NO!" pushing Ciaran back and jumping in front of him. She held out her hand and said, "Hunaphu, stop!"

The dragon roared at her and slithered in a circle, flipping its venomous tongue at her. Ciaran's mouth dropped. "That's impossible. Quetzalcoatls are extinct. Like over three thousand years extinct. So extinct they are considered myths. Mayan gods."

"Well, sorry to break it to you," she yelled over another loud, angry roar, "but Hunaphu has been here since before this land was ever inhabited. It's his mountains. And he is the god on these mountains."

Ciaran watched as she carefully moved forward, circling the dragon, talking to it. "Hunaphu, he's a friend. I promise. Don't attack. Don't—" The dragon snapped his two teeth at her and flicked his tongue in her direction again. Lulu yelped and jumped back. "Hunaphu! Stop!" The dragon growled again, keeping its eye on Ciaran.

Ciaran very slowly zipped down the yellow jacket and dropped it on the ground. Then he took off his t-shirt. "Lulu."

"I got this, Ciaran," she yelled behind her. "Just don't move, okay?"

"Listen to me very carefully…"

"Ciaran—"

"Shut up and listen, woman!" Ciaran snapped. "You may know *this* dragon, but I know dragons. If you don't do what I tell you to do, neither of us is getting off this mountain alive." He balled up his t-shirt and tossed it at her feet. "You're agitating him. Challenging him. Commanding him. You need to stop doing that. Remember that you cannot control him. He is in total control."

"Okay," she said shakily.

"Take my shirt and rub it against your face and jacket; then hold it tightly in your hand. Then stop circling him. But don't stop abruptly, or he will attack. Slow down, keep talking to him like he's a friend. Keep the fear out of your voice. Get him to trust you like he's always done. Because right now, you're standing between him and his adversary. And that makes you an enemy, too. Be his ally."

"Hunaphu," she said gently, and she reached down for the t-shirt. "I know you're afraid, but I need you to listen to me. I've never harmed you. And I'm not here to harm you now. And neither will Ciaran. See?"

She slowed down, rubbing the shirt on her face, neck, and then in a circle on the center of her jacket. The dragon watched her as she stopped walking. Then she held both hands straight out in a "T" pose, a move she would do when she saw him, and he would slither around her.

"See?" Lulu said again. He began to circle her, watching her, his attention no longer on Ciaran. "Hunaphu, I see you, baby boy. I see you."

After one lap around her, he brought his enormous head up to her. She slowly knelt on the grass. Hunaphu laid his head down, his feathery crown big and wide. His tail was closest to Ciaran, also feathery. Ciaran got a good look at him, as he also knelt to the ground, mimicking her. While Lulu continued to talk and distract him, Ciaran took out his phone and snapped a picture of the thirty-foot-long serpent dragon. Then he very gently nicked a feather and put it down his pants. He sat on the grass and watched the dragon soften to her.

Lulu reached out and touched him right underneath his chin with Ciaran's t-shirt in her hand. "He hasn't come down in years. He killed a few of the CV when they first arrived, but then they had this cannon contraption that nearly killed him, took out the right side of his face, left him half blind. After they were disbanded, I had to regain his trust. That's why I can't let anyone else up on the mountain. Not this high up. So you see?"

Ciaran didn't answer. He watched Hunaphu grunt softly at her feet as she continued to rub his t-shirt along the dragon's mouth.

"He knows your scent now," said Lulu. "Do you want to come closer? Meet him?"

"Absolutely fucking not."

Lulu turned around and grinned. Ciaran did not. She turned back and caressed him with both hands. "It's okay, Hunaphu. He's with me, and we're leaving now. No worries at all."

The dragon nipped the t-shirt from her hand and then slithered around her toward Ciaran. Ciaran did not move as it circled him once, all thirty feet of him, and slid off the ledge. Hunaphu let out a soft roar this time, stretched his wings, and flew away with Ciaran's t-shirt.

As soon as its feathery tail lifted in the air, Ciaran lay in the grass and covered his face with both hands. "Ho. Lee. Shit," he said, sounding like his partner.

"Are you okay?" she asked, coming closer.

He looked up at her from the ground. "How the fuck could you not tell me that you have one of the oldest and deadliest dragons in the history of the magical world here?"

"Because I didn't want you to take him away," she said. "Or kill him. Scholarly would trap him, experiment on him, then put him to sleep, and I can't have that. Please don't tell them. Honestly, that's the fifth time I've actually seen him up close in all the years I've lived here. He doesn't bother anyone, not even the other dragons. He's a good boy."

Ciaran sat up and shook his head in disbelief. "Good boy?! There isn't even a class designation for that beast. It will kill us all in an instant. You're insane."

"No more than you," she said back. "You ride these beasts. I could never." She held out her hand to help him up. "And have you ever met a sane dragon protector? We're all insane to do what we do."

Ciaran thought of Dale, who should be certifiable, and the other Tamers on the Reserve. He thought of young Malechi who he'd met a few years ago, all of sixteen and ready to die for his dragon Malik. He thought of himself at a young age. And him now.

He took her hand and hoisted himself up. "We're all mad, sure." He put his jacket on, and they began to walk down the stony path together. "But this is really dangerous."

"Promise you won't tell?" she pleaded again softly.

"I'll leave the Quetzalcoatl out of my report," he said. "But again, you need help. You can't be the town Novo and the only Dragon Tamer. I'll have Felix train Emily fully to become the Novo, and we'll see if some of the constables want to become Tamers, too. And you lead this team as the Dragon Ringmaster."

"Okay," she acquiesced with a sigh. "Sorry about your shirt. But, hey, it means you'll be welcome on the mountain without me now because your scent will be everywhere."

"How lucky for me," he deadpanned.

She grinned.

———————

Chris was sitting in one of the rocking chairs as the air shifted and Ciaran and Lulu Wisp'd in front of the home. "I'll check on how Felix is doing and then come over to start dinner," she said.

"I got it covered, Lulu," Chris said to her.

She grinned at him. "God, you really are a dream, aren't you?"

"The best thing that ever happened to Ciaran," said Chris with a smile.

Lulu smiled back. "You sure are." Then she looked at Ciaran. "Oooh, I get it. Punching *above* your weight class. Because he's like, out of your league."

Ciaran grinned, and Chris laughed. "Well done," said Ciaran.

Lulu laughed too and walked across Kimble Street to her home. Ciaran sat on the steps and put his head on the rail, then sighed.

Chris immediately noticed he was shirtless under his yellow jacket and had a feather sticking out of his underwear. "And what did you do today?"

Ciaran shook his head, looking off into the distance. "Got attacked by a mythical dragon that's supposed to be extinct and almost got myself killed."

"Fascinating."

"Indeed. And what did you do today?"

"I threatened, then shot up a police station of magicians, and almost got myself killed."

"Wonderful."

Ciaran looked at Chris. Chris smiled. Ciaran smiled back. "I think I love it here," said Ciaran.

"Best holiday ever," Chris agreed.

CHAPTER 23

Votes and Volleys

Chris and Alastair made their way to the field right outside of town. Alastair used his *dulé* to set up firing posts as twelve officers began walking into the field, with Inspector Neal leading them and a floating trunk of firearms behind them.

"No Sergeant Hinkley?" Alastair asked.

"No, he said he didn't have time to be goofing around with a Brit and a lowlife Commoner filth," said a young blond. "Pinkerton, Browne, and Wallman stayed with him. They were losers anyway. The actual lowlifes of this town." He shook Chris's hand first. "Sorry about what he said about Commoners. We don't all feel that way."

Chris grinned. "What's your name, Constable?"

"Sinclair Roth. Just Roth."

"Nice you meet you, Roth." Chris turned to the rest of them. "Line up. Target practice on one side of the field with me, *rodulé* practice on the other with Alastair. We'll do this for about three hours. We break for lunch, and then Alastair will lead a lesson on safe and subtle wards."

The men split up, with some Wisp'ing with Alastair to the far end of the field. Chris turned to the officers with him, Roth being one of them. "Have you ever fired a gun?"

Most shook their heads no, but one named Wayne Timbrell said loudly, "I have. My father hunted deer and taught me and my sister how to shoot."

Chris put his pistol in Timbrell's hand and said, "Show me."

Timbrell turned to the firing post, unlocked the safety, and aimed. He shot three times, and the third bullet hit the glass. The others behind him clapped. Chris smiled at him. "You'll be my right-hand man, Constable Timbrell."

"Yes, sir," he said seriously.

Together, they showed the others gun safety first and then how to aim. Chris only had them use regular pistols; the shotguns and rifles would come later. Roth picked it up the quickest and had the best aim out of the group, next to Timbrell. Chris glanced over at Alastair's group,: they seemed to be doing well, posing in teams with one throwing incantations and the other blocking.

After an hour and a half, Alastair blew a whistle. The officers that were with Chris began to Wisp to Alastair while puffs of smoky black air filled the area as the men with Alastair arrived at Chris's station. Chris asked the same question, and again, most had not, except Timbrell's sister, Anisa, who they simply called Brell. She was not as comfortable with guns as her older brother, but was a skilled dueler.

Broock was part of his second group and informed him that he had been in the Canadian Magi army for a long while as a *Nigri Veneficus*. He'd been one of the few trying to fight the CVs until they murdered his entire family right in front of him and kept him in chains as a prisoner of war. Chris made Broock his second-in-command.

They continued practicing until Marley appeared. He conjured up a long picnic table and put empty plates down, said an incantation while waving his *dulé*, and food began to appear, from lobster rolls to clam chowder to fish and chips. Chris waved to him, and Marley waved back before he disappeared.

Alastair blew his whistle again, and everyone Wisp'd to the tables, except Chris, who had to walk. When he got there, Alastair made room for him, right next to Inspector Neal. Chris looked around at the officers talking amicably about shooting guns and dueling and smiled to himself. These were not the same bored constables he met two weeks ago, or even the day before. They were animated, energized. He was happy to be a part of that.

A puff of smoke appeared, and Felix sat down, too. "I went to Marley's and heard about the fun happening over here, so I decided to join in."

"How's it going over in Lulu's lair?" Chris asked. He heard Alastair snort, but didn't turn to him.

"She's sharp as whip. I'll give you that," said Felix, as he grabbed a sandwich. "She has blood samples and spit samples, pieces of his skin, nails, hair, anything that has Theron's DNA in it. She has books documenting her tests and experiments. Video recordings. Charts. She created her own spells to counter it. But we're missing something. I need to do some more research on the origins of blood magic, so I'm heading out of town for a few days with Emily. She's taking me down to Scholarly in Nova Scotia to do more research, and I'm going to fill out the recommendation for her to become a Novo with the CMC, officially."

"Emily is the cute one with the golden streaks or the cute cat?" Chris asked in jest.

Felix grinned. "I mean, they're both adorable, but the golden steaks, not the white and gray furry." Chris grinned back.

"Besides her attractiveness," Alastair interjected, "is she qualified to become a Novo? You cannot do an official recommendation unless you have properly vetted her skills and knowledge."

Felix cut his eyes to Alastair. "You do know I'm not stupid, right? Emily is extremely talented. Lulu has taught her a lot about herb properties, healing elixirs, and medicinal incantations. She's ready to take the test, and I'm going to help her pass and support her fully."

"I bet you're going to support her fully," said Chris, still grinning. "An overnight trip? Late night studying? What could possibly go wrong?"

Felix grinned back. "Oh, I'm going to make sure everything goes just right." They giggled together and high-fived each other.

"Ahem, excuse me, Novo Felix, but we are here on serious ministry business," Alastair chimed in again. "There is absolutely no time or place for fraternizing in these next couple of months. We discussed this on the transport."

Felix looked at him. "I don't know what's wrong with your cock, mate, but if the opportunity presents itself, mine is getting soaked."

Chris laughed out loud with a couple of other constables.

"That's highly inappropriate," Alastair said with disgust. "And we have female officers at the table who do not want to hear of it."

"I grew up with four brothers," said Brell. "I've heard worse."

"Don't worry, doll," Chris said to Alastair with a sly grin. "I didn't forget my promise." Alastair scowled at him and turned away.

"What promise?" Felix asked.

"I told him that before this trip is over, he'll also get his nob soaked."

Felix and the other officers again laughed out loud. Alastair turned beet red and muttered, "Inappropriate."

After lunch, Felix headed back to work in Lulu's basement, and they stayed at the picnic table.

"So," Chris started before Alastair could, "Is there a reason why there are no magical spells or incantations hiding this Magi town? Are there Commoners here?"

"No," said Constable Brell. "No Commoners here. All of us are Magi. Almost all witches, no warlocks, except for Constable Broock. Most of our warlocks were killed or transformed into cats, and the rest of us really aren't the fighting kind."

"We've never had security wards keeping Commoners away for a reason," said Constable Dawson. "We're the only town out this way, so if a hiker is lost or stranded, if they can't get to us, they're doomed."

"Okay, I get that. Canadian nice," said Chris. "But if you're going to keep your town open, then you need to have other safety measures. Because Commoners and Magi can't just waltz into your village and you just not know about it. Put spells on the path leading into town. If not an aversion, an alarm of some sort."

"I've been thinking about that for years, even before the invasion," said Broock. "We have a bell tower at the top of the church, but we never use it. I mentioned it to the mayor once, but he blew me off."

"Well, he won't blow me off," said Alastair haughtily. "I already informed him that we were going to add wards to the town, that it was standard procedure around any kind of Magi wildlife, especially a dragon reservation." Broock nodded at him.

"How would it work?" said Chris. "What was your plan, Constable Broock?"

"Simple," said Broock. "Once someone passed the threshold, the bell would ring. Once for a Magi. Three times for a Commoner."

"I like it," said Chris.

"But you still need an aversion leading to the mountains and surrounding them," said Alastair. "So that no one, Magi or Commoner, can get too close. And station someone out that way. Who lives the closest to the meadow at the base of the mountains?"

"I do," said Roth. "I'm one of the last houses on that main road."

"Then that's your new post," Alastair said simply. "Whenever there is a Commoner in the town, you're on your porch until that Commoner leaves. If one comes out that way, offer them tea or a home-cooked meal, and scurry them back to the center of town.

"And you," Alastair pointed at the oldest constable there, the one who'd asked Chris if he was ready to die. "What's your name?"

"Constable Houser," he said gruffly.

"You look like a friendly old man. You offer them a nice, friendly ride right out of your town within twenty-four hours of their arrival."

"Ha!" said Timbrell. "Nice and friendly are not words we use to describe Houser."

Houser stuck up his middle finger and growled, "Shove it up your ass."

They all laughed. Chris said, "He'll be undercover. You can be an undercover officer, yeah?"

"I can be nice if I want to," he said gruffly. "Molly can offer them tea or a home-cooked meal too."

"See," Chris said, "you can still be friendly Canadians. Just a bit more vigilant."

Nods all around. "Now we just need to get Mayor Dumbass to agree," said Broock.

"I don't agree with this," Mayor Dubois said, shaking his head.

Alastair, Christopher, Broock, Roth, Hauser, and the deputy chief cat were standing in front of the man after explaining the proposed Magi wards. "I think it makes us look uninviting. Like those invaders won."

"I hate to break it to you, Mayor," said Broock, "but they did win. We lost so much. And now we need to protect ourselves from it ever happening again."

Mayor Dubois stood up sharply. "Enough of that cynical talk from you, Bill," he said. He turned to Alastair. "I knew this was coming. I know what the CMC expects. I am okay with wards around the mountain. To protect the Reserve, sure. But not around town. I'm putting my foot down about that."

"You're lucky you got two o' them and not four, you town idiot," Hauser said gruffly. The mayor cut his eyes to the old man, used to his snark. But the cat also meowed loudly at him.

"The people, and the cats, want protection," said Roth. "Just ask them; they'll tell you themselves. No one wants what happened to happen again."

"It's not going to happen again," said the mayor. "Chances are—"

"Statistically," Alastair broke in, "a burglarized home is three times more likely to be burglarized again. Chances are if a group of warlocks thinks your town is vulnerable, especially since they discovered actual gold growing under the sunflower fields and in those mountains, they will come again. And again. You need to protect your town."

"That's just it," said the mayor. "It's my town. And I think my town is doing just fine."

"But it's not," said Chris stonily. "It's not your town. It belongs to the people. And I agree with Roth. Put it to a vote and let the town decide."

The mayor shook his head. "We don't do elections here. That's the way our town has always been."

"Well, maybe that needs to change," said Chris. "Maybe you've been mayor for too long."

"Now see here, you Commoner—" Mayor Dubois began in indignation.

"I agree with Christopher," said Alastair, cutting off his tirade. "The fact that you refuse to listen to your own people on what they believe is best for them, your own officers as well, makes you an ineffective government official. So either you put it to a town vote, and allow the results to dictate whether a) there will, in fact, be wards around the town and b) the type, severity, and measure of the wards, or I will have no choice but to send a report to the Canadian Magi Council on the incompetence of the Mayor of Gullfelt who has selfishly held office for the last decade."

Mayor Dubois was furious. "We don't have a voting system for our 417 residents."

"Don't forget the 98 cats," Roth reminded him. "We need to find a way to include them."

"Well, you're in luck," said Alastair. "I know just how to create one."

By dinner, a letter appeared on every single door in Gullfelt, explaining the proposed amendment of adding magical security wards to the town borders. It would include use of the Catholic Church bell and the order of the bell tolls, creating a response team for when a Commoner was in town, and officially training a small number of constables as warlocks. The first ballot regarding whether there should be wards would go out at 10 a.m. the next day, and if the measure was approved, the second ballot would go out at 1 p.m. The results would be revealed at 4 p.m.

"And what about the cats?" Ciaran said, as Mrs. Beals sat in his lap. "How are they voting?"

"Well, the old-fashioned way, I'm afraid," said Alastair. "While everyone else will get a magical note to appear in front of them, the felines are lining up at the mayor's office and going into a voting booth, one by one. They will press their paw on an inkpad, then add their paw to their yes or no vote. Those votes will have to be tallied individually."

Mrs. Beals stood up on all fours and meowed. They all looked at her. She took a turn on Ciaran's lap and sat back down.

"I assume Mrs. Beals will also be overseeing that part of the project?" said Chris. Debony sat in his lap, purring softly as Chris gently caressed the top of her head. Mrs. Beals was able to convince Debony to follow her back to the house a few days ago. Ms. Cho was grateful to see her daughter actually leave the shop and told Chris to keep her for as long as she wanted.

"And Inspector Neal," said Alastair. "We've already decided that—"

The door burst open, and Lulu ran in holding onto the paper. She looked at Alastair. "Did you do this?"

He stood up and raised his chin. "Indeed, I did. It's high time that—"

She ran up and hugged him, almost knocking off his glasses. Alastair stood there, frozen, with her arms around his neck. "Oh," he said softly.

"Thank you," Lulu said on his shoulder. "The mayor refused to listen to any of us. And now he has to. Thanks to you." She lifted her head, grabbed his face, and gave him a chaste kissed his lips. "You're good for something, Minister."

Alastair nervously adjusted his glasses on his face. "You're welcome, Luanne."

"Hey, I was there, too!" said Chris. "Do I get a kiss, too?" He puckered his lips.

Lulu laughed and came over to him, but she looked at Ciaran first. "Permission to kiss your fiancé?"

"Permission granted," said Ciaran with a smile.

Lulu gave Chris the same chaste kiss and rubbed his curls. She looked around the room and said, "I'm really glad you all are here." She walked up to Alastair, gave him a kiss on the cheek, and left.

Alastair stared at the door upon her departure. When he turned around, the two men and two cats were looking at him. "What?"

"She kissed you, mate," said Ciaran.

"Well, I..." he flustered. "She kissed Christopher as well."

"Nah, I just did that to make you jealous," Chris said with a smile, making Ciaran laugh out loud.

Alastair huffed. "Well, it didn't work," he said, making his way upstairs, forgetting he was in conversation with them.

"It totally did," Ciaran murmured. Chris turned to Ciaran and kissed him, too.

***

As they all expected, both measures passed with exceeding numbers, much to the mayor's chagrin. Alastair and Christopher looked at each other after reading the docket that landed on Mrs. Beals's door at 4 p.m.

"We've got the green light, Minister," said Chris.

"Indeed, Ranger Jennings," said Alastair. "Let's get to work."

CHAPTER 24

Canada Day

Chris had been slowly watching the flags go up around town the last couple of weeks. Canadian flags mostly, but the Newfoundland and Labrador flags, too. During training, he listened to the constables talk excitedly about their upcoming holiday, what costumes they would wear during the parade, what song they would sing or play for Porchfest in the afternoon, and what outfit they would wear to the Gullfelt Gala in the evening. So when he woke up on July 1st, he knew it was going to be a great day.

Ciaran had stayed out half the night with Lulu and crashed next to him before the sun rose. Chris didn't know quite what they did up there, but from Ciaran's discussions with him, it was focused on training Lulu on the ways of Dragonology. "She has raw talent and a heart for this work," he said. "Now I just need to fine-tune her skills and knowledge of the dragons, particularly the ones she has up there."

A few constables joined them, Roth, Broock, Timbrell, Hauser, Hinkley and Pinkerton, and Ciaran was training them on how to be Dragon Tamers to give Lulu some backup. At first she rejected it, then she resisted, then she reluctantly gave in to having the meatheads, as she called them, in her precious space. But only as far as the sunflower field and hut. No one knew of her cave except for Ciaran.

Chris brought his coffee to the rocking chair out front and watched the streets come alive. Enchanted brooms swept the streets clean; then a hose with no one manning it washed the road down. He knew the parade route would take them right past the house, so he was not surprised when chairs started appearing along the sidewalk. Then, barricades started appearing too, keeping folks from crossing the street in the middle of the parade.

He watched Felix, who had also been working all night in Lulu's basement, step outside of her home onto the porch and look around. Suddenly he disappeared and reappeared right next to Chris in a puff of smoke and a huge yawn.

"Morning," Felix said at the end of his sigh.

"Morning," Chris said back. He held out his coffee, but Felix rejected it with a hand wave.

"I'm going to have a cuppa, take a shower, and get some sleep. Or maybe sleep first, then shower. Dunno." Felix yawned again. "We're so close," he said confidently. "Now that we got the samples of bone marrow, it's the closest I've seen to a compound reaction. Mixed with echinacea, it has the same effect of slowing down carcinomatous cells, which in itself is positive because that would mean the feline traits would cease to cultivate, which would also mean it would give space for the Homosaipan provenances to begin to metastasize; but how long that would take is yet to be determined. What I would like to see is a huge reverse course in the magical compound altogether, but that may be too much to ask for at this stage. It has been four years."

He sighed, which turned into another yawn. "Nevertheless, progress."

Chris stared at him blankly. "So the two of you are not fucking over there?"

Felix laughed. "Lulu is amazing in a very weird and quirky way. But no. Emily is…" He sighed with a smile. "More than enough. Besides, the way Lulu and Alastair go at it when they're in the same room, it's best to get out of their way, yeah?"

Chris nodded. "I see what you see."

"Right," Felix said with a nod. "Also, I'm married to the medicine. Can't you tell?"

"Well, Emily is too, innit?" Chris said with a smile.

Felix grinned and did not answer. He patted Chris's shoulder and went inside.

Wisp'ing smoke started appearing all around him as towns-folk found their chairs and sat comfortably along the side-walk, waiting for the parade to begin. Someone came by to hand him a white and red flag as he sat on the porch. Mrs. Beals came out of the house through her flap and stretched.

"Hello, gorgeous," Chris said. She came closer and rubbed his leg. But when he tried to pick her up, she meowed and jumped out of his way, then ran down the porch steps in between the legs of the patrons. "Guess she had somewhere important to be," he muttered.

The town bell rang five times. He watched the people of Gullfelt rise from their seats, and it was silent. Chris stood up too, out of respect. Suddenly there was a series of drums as they began to put their hands over their hearts. He could not tell where the music was coming from; it seemed to vibrate all around him. A voice echoed through the streets beginning the Canadian National Anthem:

"O Canada! Our home and native land! True patriot love thou dost in us command..."

The crowd also began to sing while a thirty-foot Canadian flag floated through the streets. As the final cords of patriotism faded, another instrumental song began to play, and everyone took their seats again. The first exhibit was the Gullfelt High School marching band, which did a wonderful job at playing symphonies followed by pop songs. The cheerleaders from the middle school and the high school were next, dancing to the songs played by the marching band. Exhibits and floats carried on right through the street as vendors walked through the crowds, offering everything from coffee to corn dogs.

The screen door opened, and Ciaran stepped out with Debony right behind him. He sat in the rocking chair next to Chris and promptly took the popcorn bag Chris bought from a vendor from his hands and began popping kernels in his mouth. Debony perched on the porch between the rails to watch the parade.

"I thought you wanted to rest some more?" Chris said, grabbing the bag back. "There's breakfast in the kitchen," he added.

"Who could sleep with all this ruckus out here?" said Ciaran. "I smelled popcorn," he added and took the bag back from him. Chris relented.

They sat outside until noon, eating street food and commentating on the floats. Emily came by looking for Felix, and they directed her upstairs to his room. They spotted most of the constables in their mummers-like costumes, dancing along the streets. Large, stringless balloons with pop culture icons, cartoon figures, and dragons floated above floats.

Ciaran smiled as the large balloon of a Quetzalcoatl floated past them. And Mayor Dubois's convertible passed by with Alastair right next to him, waving to the crowd, making them chuckle.

"Dubois asked me to join them on the float, and I explicitly told him hell no," said Ciaran.

"He asked me too!" said Chris in surprise. "I gave him a similar, kinder version of hell no. I know he just wanted to use Alastair and me to gain favor with the townsfolk, even though he was completely against everything we've been doing here. But Dubois needs to be the most important person in the room."

"Well, Alastair certainly was not going to turn it down," said Ciaran. "His need to be a very important person just so people won't think he's a wanker like his father is deeply ingrained in him."

Chris turned to him. "What about his father?"

"My uncle Harrison was a very unserious man. People think my uncle Malcolm on my mother's side is unserious because of that quirky shop he has, and that he's always creating a new and crazy spell or potion or incantation. But Uncle Malcolm always has the best of intentions. Unlike Harrison, who was always scheming, swindling, trying to get over, and couldn't keep a job because of it. He went from different departments at Scholarly because he kept getting fired. But we later discovered that was done on purpose. His biggest downfall was a long con he was doing with a bunch of registered Commoners right under Scholarly's nose. He was running a local underground pawnshop, stealing magical but damaged artifacts that didn't work properly anymore and selling them to Commoners. It all came out when a Commoner lost his whole arm because a projector machine malfunctioned and the wolf in the movie he was watching came off the screen and bit it clean off."

"Whoa," said Chris, his eyebrows up.

"Yeah. It was really bad. Of course, no one believed the man, but the police investigation led back to the pawnshop, which led to Commoner police officers at my aunt's door. Which sent an alert to our Magi Council, which started the Magi investigation, and it all came out. Harrison was in Claustra for about five years for that," said Ciaran. "A Clause 73 breach."

"I thought it was an automatic ten years?" Chris questioned.

"It is. My father begged for a reduced sentence for his brother-in-law. The Grandminister at the time was also a Generational Magi, so he honored my father's bloodline and reduced it to five. But five years is still a long time."

"It is. How old was Alastair?" Chris asked.

"Young. I was about five or six the last time I saw Uncle Harrison, so Alastair was about nine years old. Aunt Elspeth told him that he would not be welcomed in her home and broke the tie-bind. She changed her last name back to Beals and made Alastair and Isla Beals, too, so they would no longer be associated with him. So when he came out, he simply didn't have a home to go to. He met up with his old Commoner friends and left England when Alastair was about fourteen. Last we heard, he was working as a mechanic somewhere in the Americas, married a Commoner wife, and had Commoner children. He has had no contact with his ex-wife or children since then, or anyone in the Magi Community."

"Oh, wow..." Chris looked at the back of Alastair's hair as he sat up straight and continued to wave. "I would have thought Alastair came from a family of aristocrats."

Ciaran chuckled. "Not even close. They struggled a lot. My dad helped his sister out whenever he could, and Alastair spent a lot of dinners and holidays with us. But he grew cold and had a disdain for Commoners for a long time. He was on the wrong side of the war until Shane slapped some sense into him. But his whole life is proving that he is nothing like his swindler, feckless father. That's what drives his ambition."

"Hmmm…" Chris muttered to himself. "I think I'll be nicer to him. Considering he has accepted your relationship with a Commoner."

Ciaran chuckled. "He's actually commented to me how professional and focused you've been with the constables. He admires your leadership and expertise. You know … for a Commoner."

Chris laughed out loud. "That sounds like Alastair."

As the parade began to dwindle down and chairs started disappearing again, Chris went into the house to pull out the keyboard. Ciaran helped him set it up on the porch with his chair and Porchfest bucket. Chris did decline being a part of the parade, but singing and playing music was definitely something he was going to do.

When 2 p.m. rolled around, Chris began to play an old French song. Ciaran, always enamored by Chris's singing voice, sat on the steps and listened. Others came by, listened for a while, threw Sagems in the bucket designated for donations, and moved on to others who were playing music on their porches. The Sagems were to be used for the silent auction at the Gala later on that evening.

Debony moved over to Ciaran and rubbed against his leg. Ciaran absentmindedly picked her up and rubbed her head, and she purred with him. After a couple of songs, Debony went over to Chris and jumped on the piano, wanting his attention.

"Hello, beautiful," he said and rubbed her chin. She walked in a circle, then got comfortable, and stretched out. Chris continued to play and serenade the crowd and the cat.

The front door opened, and Felix walked out with Emily, looking refreshed. But she took one look at the cat and yelled, "Debony! What are you still doing here?" She picked up the cat off the piano. "Femy has been worried about you."

"She's been here with us for weeks," Chris said. "She followed Mrs. Beals over here and never left. Your mum knows where she is."

"And that's surprising because she rarely leaves the chai shop," said Emily, trying to steady her squirming. "How Mrs. Beals convinced her to follow her here—ow!"

Debony had scratched her sister and jumped out of her arms, back onto the piano. Then she slid into Chris's lap and tried to cower there.

"I guess she wants to stay here with me?" said Chris and rubbed her face. The cat purred in appreciation. "Yeah, you do, sweet girl."

Emily was beside herself. "I'll go tell Femy she's still here." She began to walk away, and Felix followed her.

Debony made herself comfortable in Chris's lap again, eventually falling asleep while Chris continued to play and sing songs in French until 5 p.m. when it was time to pack it up. The cat followed them inside the house and sat on the chair by the window. Since the house was empty, the lovers took that opportunity to make love, lay in bed, and talk about nothing in particular. They heard Felix come in, then Alastair, and knew it was time to start getting ready for the Gullfelt Gala.

After his shower, Ciaran went into Chris's suitcase looking for deodorant and pulled out a small cigarette case. He held it up. "Sean?"

"Ah, I forgot about that," Chris said, coming closer. He took it from Ciaran, opened the case, and sniffed it. "Still fresh. Should we partake tonight?"

"Well, it is a holiday," said Ciaran. "After the Gala. The Minister would have a heart attack if we showed up high."

Chris laughed. "Maybe we'll offer it to him too, make him loosen his balls a little."

CHAPTER 25

Acknowledgment

They were casually dressed, Ciaran and Felix in jeans and a dinner jacket, Chris in tan pants with a white shirt and a black jacket and tie to match. It was only Alastair who thought it was best to dress in proper attire. He came down the stairs in a full three-piece dark gray suit, matching vest and tie. He looked at his three companions and shook his head.

"Do you take anything seriously?" he said haughtily. "We represent the Magi Council of Europe, and the three of you look like you're going to a class reunion."

That made Chris laugh. "Have you been to any class reunions, Al?" He opened the door for Ciaran and said, "Shall we, love?"

Ciaran kissed him on the lips as he crossed the threshold. Felix also walked past him, saying, "You're not getting a kiss from me." Chris laughed and slapped Felix's butt hard.

Alastair stepped onto the porch, not even looking at Chris. But all three stopped as they watched Lulu walk down her own porch steps from across the street.

"Best friend mode activated," Chris breathed out.

"Activation granted," Ciaran said back, also staring.

"Ho. Lee. *Shit*." said Chris.

"Holy shit is right," Ciaran agreed.

Lulu wore a short, dark red dress wrapped around black fishnet stockings. The sides of the dress were completely open, revealing her vine and scenery tattoos. Her long hair was flipped to the side to show one shaven side. She had dark makeup outlining her eyes, sans glasses, with ruby-red lips to match her dress and open-toe heels.

"I take back what I said earlier. She's bloody gorgeous," Felix said plainly. "If she lived closer and I really wanted a wife, I would put the moves on her."

"She's alright if you like that type," said Alastair as he swallowed. But he couldn't take his eyes off her either.

Chris was the first to move, going down the steps and walking up to her in the middle of the street. He looked her up and down seductively and whistled as he walked around her touching her bare back. "Lulu, love. If I wasn't already betrothed, I'd be vying to be as close to you as that dress is."

Lulu laughed out loud. "Where do you fall on the Kinsley scale, handsome?"

Chris gave her a sly smile. "I am all things to all people, and right now, I am all yours." He held out his arm. "Fancy a gentleman on your arm for the soiree?"

She looked at him with wide eyes, then back at Ciaran. Ciaran waved his hand at them as if to say, "Go."

"Yes, I would like that." She took his arm, and they walked down the street together.

"Aren't you tired of him flirting with her?" Alastair said with an attitude and a scowl on his face. "That's highly inappropriate for a soon-to-be-married man."

"Chris flirts with everyone," Ciaran said in a bored fashion. "And you're the one that sounds jealous."

"I am not—"

Ciaran turned to his friend and held out his arm. "Felix, be my date?"

"I thought you'd never ask," Felix said with a smile, wrapping his arm around his best friend. They fell in step behind Chris and Lulu.

"Highly inappropriate," Alastair muttered, but he, too, followed them to the banquet hall.

The music was lively, and the drinks were flowing. The entire town was partying, including a section for children under twelve. Cats with bow ties or colorful bows around their necks scurried around the legs of the partygoers. Chris and Ciaran danced with each other and mingled around. The silent auction was a success with Chris auctioning away his old ranger fedora since he had been using the one Ciaran got him for Christmas, and Ciaran giving away one of his sister Diana's aphrodisiac soap bars.

Mostly everyone seemed to be in high spirits at the joyous event, especially when it came time for the special awards being handed out by the mayor. Humans and cats alike were recognized in different categories: everything from Humanitarian to Social Services Advocate. Mrs. Beals won the Hospitality Award for giving the foreigners a place to stay. And it was a nice surprise to see Luanne Ludlow's name called for Woman of the Year, for her extraordinary efforts in finding a cure for the feline curse and protecting the dragons in the mountains.

Lulu graciously accepted, giving a rousing speech about how the feline curse had attempted to rip through the fabric of the strength of the Gullfelt people, but they had risen above their circumstances and come together as a community. She thanked Felix for his assistance with her experiments and his brilliant mind, thanked Ciaran for his quick thinking and skills with the dragons, and even thanked Christopher for lending her a few of his newly trained warlocks to become the Dragon Squad.

They clapped and watched as she took pictures with her plaque and with other mayoral officials. "Hmpf," Chris heard Alastair huff next to him.

"What? She didn't include you in her speech?" Chris said, taking a sip of his liquor.

"Too right," Alastair complained. "As if I wasn't the one that put this whole mission together. She intentionally leaves me out of important parts of this very important mission, and I, for one, am troubled by her childish antics. And I don't see why none of you aren't pulling her aside to scold her, to cajole her to act like a professional Novo, at least with some level of ladylike decorum. You just allow her to carry on as if she is some queen of dragons; well, I will not stand for it any longer. If she expects any semblance of respect at the effort she puts into making Gullfelt great again, then she needs to provide a level of acknowledgment for the work that I, too, have contributed to this society in a short period of time."

Chris continued drinking while listening to Alastair complain about his importance not being valued, thinking about the marijuana joint he had waiting for him. Tonight was definitely the night for it.

"You know," he said loudly, cutting Alastair off, "it's okay if you think she's hot."

Alastair turned bright red. "I do not!"

"Yeah, you do," he said and took another sip.

"I think she is rude and crass and has no concept of what it means to be a respectable lady."

"She's also hot as fuck," Chris said plainly. "And if I wasn't deeply in love with someone else, I would probably want to lick every vine on that fit body of hers. And I think you do, too."

"I—" He stopped and looked at her laughing with someone else, taking a sip of her wine and leaving her red lipstick there. The vines across her torso were visible on her sides and through the deep V dip of the back of her dress.

Alastair huffed again. "Even if I thought she was attractive, I could never. I am here on official business, not to get my ... nob soaked."

Chris busted out laughing. He put his hand on his fiancé's cousin's shoulder. "Well, maybe you should, Alastair."

Alastair huffed. He stole one last glance at Lulu before he turned around and walked away.

* * *

Lulu was having a good night. She went over to the bar and sat on the stool, waiting for the bartender to notice her to top off her wineglass. Then glanced to her left, and Hinkley was staring at her in disgust, visibly drunk. "You look like a whore," he muttered.

Lulu smiled. "But I'm not. You just wish I was. You've been trying to fuck me since my fiancé died. So what does that make you?"

"A weak man," he said. "But I'm not weak anymore. You'll see."

She rolled her eyes and looked away. "Fuck off, Hinkley. You're still a loser."

"You think that pity award makes you a winner? Woman of the year, my ass," Hinkley said with a scoff.

"Excuse me," she said with an attitude, finally looking at him.

"You heard me. You're the real failure. It's unbelievable that they give an award for almost doing something. For failing at something year after year after year."

Alastair, who was coming over to have a civil conversation with Lulu, heard Hinkley's last words. "What is your point, Sergeant Hinkley?" Alastair said before she could answer.

He looked up in confusion about who was talking, then scowled. "My point is that she doesn't belong here," said Hinkley. He stood up. "And you don't either. You're not even from Canada, let alone Gullfelt. Go home, both of you."

"This is my home, you piece of shit," she said back as the bartender placed a fresh glass of red wine in front of her. "And what have you done for this community, huh? Because during the entire war, your stance was to play along to get along."

"I got out of the war alive. Unlike Jasper," he said with a smile. Alastair frowned.

Lulu picked up her wineglass and threw it in his face. "Go to hell."

She got up and began to walk away. Hinkley wiped his face and yelled after her, "And you go back to Los Angeles, you worthless cunt. Oh, but you can't, because you're a lost angel. Not even your filthy Commoner parents will accept you back."

"Fuck you, Hinkley," she screamed at him. "Eat shit and die!"

Others turned to her as she sniffed back tears and ran to the front doors of the ballroom. Hinkley chuckled, sat down, and turned back to the bar.

Alastair said, "If there is anyone in this entire town that has displayed worthless cunt behavior, it's you." He stepped closer. "Don't ever talk to a woman like that in my presence again, or I will be forced to throttle you."

Hinkley scoffed. "That bitch—"

"*Duratus!*" said Alastair, with his *dulé* on Hinkley's back. Hinkley's entire body froze. He touched Hinkley's shoulder. "A little time-out should help you find your manners."

Alastair turned from the bar. He heard Hinkley mumble through his lips, "You'll all pay for this. Soon, really soon, you'll all be begging for my mercy."

Alastair ignored him and left the hall to find Lulu.

He knew she would be headed home, so he started walking in that direction, but he didn't want to Wisp in case he missed her. When he turned the corner, he spotted her with her heels in her hand.

"Luanne?" he called out.

She stopped and turned around. "I saw you leave and…" He came closer; there were tears on her face. "Oh. Sorry. If you would like to be alone—"

But she threw her arms around his neck, and buried her face in his shoulder, sobbing. Alastair wrapped her up in his arms and held her. "There, there," he said, comforting her. "It will be alright."

When she was done, she stepped back and wiped her eyes. "Thanks, Al. I'm okay. You can go back to the gala." She turned around and began walking again.

"Well, hold on there," he said, walking beside her. "A gentleman never lets a lady walk home at night by herself. And … you don't seem okay. So let me take you home."

She sighed and nodded. He held out his hand, and she put her shoes in them. He nodded at her. They walked in silence to her house. When they arrived, instead of going inside, she sat on the steps. He sat next to her awkwardly.

"Hinkley was out of line," said Alastair. "I'm sorry. Regardless of what happened to your love, you belong here."

She turned to him. "I'm not from Canada. Can you tell?"

Alastair scoffed. "Besides the fact that you dress like you're at a punk rock band concert all the time?"

She giggled. "You're funny when you want to be, Minister."

"Well, I've been known to tell a joke from time to time," he said with his chin raised.

"I'm from L.A.," she said. "Los Angeles, California, in case you don't know where that is. It's extremely far from here. My parents were frightened when my *Vis* was activated at age seven and were almost happy to send me away to a Magi boarding school. The States only have four Magi Campuses sanctioned by the United Magi of America. The Campus closest to me was in Portland, Oregon, and I didn't want to go there. The one in Salem, Massachusetts, is the first biggest one, and you have to get recruited for that Campus. The second biggest one is in Houston, Texas, and the one in New Orleans, Louisiana, is the smallest one. I chose to go to the one in New Orleans because they call it NOLA. Even at ten, I knew I was never going back to L.A."

Alastair smiled. "Cheeky."

She grinned too. "That's where I met Jasper. There is one actual Campus in all of Canada, in Alberta, but most kids here don't go at all; Canadians homeschooled their Magi children on learning how to control their *Vis* and attend regular schools. But Jasper also wanted to be in the States. So he ended up at the NoLa Campus. Jasper was my best friend and the complete opposite of me. Kind of nerdy like you, but beefy like Ciaran, with strawberry-blond hair and freckles and the biggest smile and kindest heart. But we didn't fall in love until our last year when we were seventeen. We did our one year of service separately, me in the States becoming a Novo, him in Alberta in the army, but we stayed in contact. Then he came back to New Orleans and asked me to marry him. I said yes, packed up all my things, and came with him to this small town, just to be with him."

She sighed. "We never did the tie-bind. Jasper was the one who discovered that they weren't Canadian Magi officials like they said they were. Melodie begged him not to, but he confronted the leader, Rodango. And Rodango raised his *dulé* and just ... killed him. Right in the middle of this street in broad daylight on a Thursday. It was over in an instant. They didn't pretend anymore after that. They sealed up the town and kept us prisoners for three years. When word got to us that Talindra was gone, thanks to you Brits, more than half the warlocks split in fear. That gave the CMC a chance to clean house, town by town. Gullfelt was one of the last ones to be saved.

"I should have left four years ago. I should have went back home to my family in L.A. or back to NoLa. But Gullfelt needed a Novo since the last one was turned into a cat and tossed into the mountains. And Mrs. Beals lost her son. Her only son. So I stayed to take care of her. Like she took care of me."

"And everyone here is so grateful that you stayed, Luanne. You've done a brilliant job as their Novo, creating tonics and medicinal solutions for the people and the cats, leading the task force. And the dragons, my God woman, you're amazing. Thank the stars that you stayed. You are truly a remarkable young woman, Lulu."

She turned to him again, staring into his eyes. Alastair found himself staring right back as he spoke again. "I'm sorry I didn't give you any credit at first for your resilience, your intelligence, your aptitude. You are brilliant. And... and hauntingly beautiful."

Lulu moved closer. Closer. Closer until her lips touched his. She pulled back and took his glasses off his face, placing them on the steps, and kissed him again. Alastair kissed her back, gently touching her face.

They kissed for a while until she said, "Do you want to come inside, Minister Beals?"

Alastair knew it would be highly inappropriate. And yet he nodded anyway. She stood up and reached her hand out. He took her hand, and she led him inside her home.

Chris wasted no time upon arriving at the house, grabbing the case with the joints, not caring if Alastair caught them. He lit one and sat on the couch. Ciaran sat next to him and took it from his hand. He took a puff. Chris snatched it back from Ciaran, kissing his lips first before he took a pull. They silently smoked together.

The door opened, and Felix came in. He sat on the chair opposite the couch. "Gentlemen." He held his hand out.

Chris gave the joint to him. "I thought you were staying with Emily tonight?"

Felix held it in for five seconds before he breathed out the smoke and passed it to Ciaran. "I really like Emily; I do. She's a fucking alley cat in the sack. But she's looking for a longer-term commitment. And I'd rather not lead her on. So I sent her home tonight."

Ciaran nodded. "Good man." He puffed and passed it to Chris. "Speaking of leading people on, anyone seen Minister Beals?"

"I saw him walk out after Lulu after Hinkley said some nasty shit to her," said Chris. "He's probably across the street still comforting her."

"Oh, yeah," said Felix. "Alastair put a hex on Hinkley, so when I left the gala, he was still sitting at the bar, his face over his glass. And not one person ended the hex." He chuckled as he picked up another joint, since the first one was almost done, and lit it with a flick of his wrist. "His back is going to be shit in the morning."

They all chuckled. "Anyway, now I need to focus, justify my job somehow," said Felix. "Because I came here to train a Novo who is already a Novo, and I'm not a Dragon Tamer, so I can't help the Dragon Squad, and I'm not a warlock or ranger, so the tactical training with the constables is left to Chris and Alastair. So I must figure this out for Lulu to feel better about my existence. Especially now that she acknowledged my help."

"You're smart enough. You can do it," said Chris.

"I don't know… nobody has been able to figure out how blood magic works, really," said Felix with a sigh. He took a couple more puffs.

"I mean, what, you dip your *dulé* in your blood, say a little incantation that you created, and *voilà*. Your own personal magical bond," said Chris. "So reverse that shit."

Felix shook his head. "But it's not that simple. You also have to mean it, be serious about it. So maybe it's not just blood, maybe it's brain matter."

"Yes, it has to be intentional," said Ciaran with his hand out. "Bonding. Like the *Ardenti*. Love magic is just as powerful as blood magic. But both are connected to our genetics, but also maybe our soul. That's why there is only one guaranteed way to end a love magic or blood magic spell. When the soul dies, so does the hex."

"Well, you can't get pieces of the soul, but how many ways can you get DNA?" said Chris.

"She went through it all, my friend," Felix said with another puff, then passed it to Ciaran. "Blood, obviously. Skin. Hair. Nails. Saliva. Emily and I even got the bone marrow when we took that trip. No major changes in the serum."

"Sperm?" Chris asked.

All three men chuckled. "I don't think she's asked for that," said Felix with a face. "Plus, he'd have too much fun extracting it, and we can't have that."

Chris laughed. "Is there a magical way to extract sperm?"

"Sure is," said Felix. "But it's more science than magic. They put you in a room, and you go through a VR simulation as if you're actually having sex with someone. It's more efficient and cleaner than wanking off."

"How do you know that, Felix?" Ciaran asked, always in awe of Felix's knowledge.

"Well, while you Magi mercenaries were off bringing down bad warlocks and fighting battles, us Novos were trained differently, in the ways of biochemical warfare. But we got to peek at other things Scholarly was doing, like IVF and genetic cleansing for Generational Magi."

"Creepy but cool," Chris said with a smile. "IVF is how Ciaran and I are having children."

"Is it?" Felix asked in surprise.

"Of course. We're absolutely using my sperm, my DNA. I got magic in there. You'll see," Chris said confidently, snatching the joint from Ciaran.

Ciaran laughed. "Sure you do."

"Mock me if you want," Chris said, "But you'll be shocked and appalled when our children have the *Vis*, and it has nothing to do with you, and everything to do with my stem cells."

"I'm pretty sure it will be the Beals Mage that we use for egg donation that will account for the *Vis*," said Ciaran.

"You really don't see it yet, do you?" said Chris. He took a few puffs. "But mark my words: My stem cells alone will have all the power."

Ciaran chuckled, and so did Felix. But then Felix's eyes went wide, and he sat up and gasped loudly. "Stem cells!"

They both looked at him as he jumped up and began pacing and talking. "The *Vis*, the magic. Every cell in a person's body has the same hereditary material, so the deoxyribonucleic acid is the double helix that carries genetic instructions for the development, but each proponent is a carrier of the DNA and not the genetic material itself. If we could separate the polymer and extract the material at its core, then transvent the potion as an antiserum using said polymer, it just might work!"

Ciaran and Chris stared at him, his joint midair. Felix stopped walking and yelled, "Don't you see?! The stem cells!"

They continued to stare at him blankly.

"Ugh!" he screamed again. He pointed at Chris. "I could kiss you, mate."

He ran out the door without another word, running across the street, banging on Lulu's door; then he let himself in and went to the basement.

Chris and Ciaran looked at each other and laughed.

Chris was sitting out front watching the sunrise with a cup of coffee in his hand. He heard a door creak open and looked in the direction of Lulu's home. He watched the door open wider, and Alastair gingerly step out, then turn around to give Lulu a long, lingering kiss. She closed the door behind him. He stepped farther onto the porch, searching for something, then picked up his glasses, and put them on his face.

He stepped down onto the sidewalk, looked out into the sunrise, and smiled. Then he turned his head and saw Chris. Chris smiled. Alastair frowned.

Alastair walked back across Kimble Street with his chin up and up the porch steps. As he opened the screen door, he heard Chris say, "I see I met my promise."

"Come again?" Alastair said.

"I told you that you were going to get you some pussy before this trip is over."

He paused and looked over at Chris's smirking face. Alastair turned around and walked into the house with his head held high.

CHAPTER 26

A Telepathy Thing

Ciaran woke up before the sun rose. He wanted to get going early: Lulu had slept out there. He planned to meet up with her and go farther up the mountains and see if he could get a tracker on Hunaphu. He started to rise and heard Chris sigh in his sleep. Ciaran looked over and saw that Chris was naked beside him, not even in underwear. He didn't remember Chris taking them off in the middle of the night, but it was one of the hottest nights since they had been in Gullfelt.

Chris's body was emitting heat. Ciaran absentmindedly touched his skin. He instantly felt that same heat flash through his own body, and it wasn't from the weather. He wondered what Chris was dreaming about. He closed his eyes and tried to enter Chris's mind. After a long moment, it flashed in his mind: He and Chris lying side by side in the grass in Maison-de-Charme, staring at each other. *You will never be alone in this life*, Ciaran was saying to him in his dream.

Ciaran sighed, realizing that Chris had sighed too, at the same time. He began talking to him. *<I remember the first time we made love... Do you remember?>*

Chris did not respond. He could hear Ciaran in his sleep, but somehow it was still a dream.

<I remember looking at your body and thinking to myself how incredibly attracted I was to the shape of your pecs, your flushed-out abs. The curve of the muscles in your arms. The bones that jutted right below your neck...>

Ciaran leaned over and kissed his collarbone. Then he trailed his tongue from there to his left pec. Chris didn't stir. He was still deep in his sleep, but the dream changed for him; it became a sexual one. Ciaran moved his face down to Chris's crotch, which was even hotter, even though his penis was lax. Ciaran kept talking as he waved his hand to the nightstand to make the lube float over.

<I remember looking into your eyes when you were beneath me. The hunger. The fire. You wanted me inside of you so badly. Your body was so warm and inviting. But do you know what I remember the most, Christopher?>

Ciaran gently lifted Christopher's balls, and extremely slowly, very gently inserted two lube-soaked fingers into his anus.

<I remember the heat.>

Chris pulled in a long gasp and let out a low moan as he exhaled. His body was more awake than his mind was, but Chris was definitely up. He lifted up his legs and let his knees fall to the side, as Ciaran curved his fingers upward to stroke his prostate.

<I remember how incredibly hot it was, being inside of you. My cock felt like it was wrapped in a warm, wet blanket. You stopped me a few times from going all the way in. Do you remember that, Chris? You weren't used to my cock size yet.>

Chris let out another low moan in response.

<*But, after our first date at Nemo's... you remember that right? When I...*>

Ciaran used his other hand to lift up Chris's cock and sucked it.

Chris let out a guttural moan, fully awake now. "Ciaran... Oh, my god..." Ciaran continued to suck and stroke while communicating inside Chris's brain.

<*I was such a novice that night. But I wanted that heat. I wanted to feel your cock in my mouth. I wanted to taste that intoxicating scent between your cheeks. I wanted to bury myself inside of you and never... never... never... stop. The way I thrust into you. The way I rode your body. So hot... like a fire burning in you. A fire for me.*>

"Ciaran..." Chris moaned out loud again. He began to reach down and run his hands through Ciaran's hair.

But Ciaran looked up and said, "*Indocillis* wrists."

Chris's hands immediately went up above his head, connecting at the wrists. Chris could not move them.

"Kiiiiii... raaaaan..." Chris moaned loudly.

They heard footsteps pass their room door. "Did you soundproof the room?" Chris asked desperately, squirming underneath him.

Ciaran leaned over and dragged his tongue along the side of Chris's body, from his hipbone, past his ribs, across his hairy armpits, up to Chris's elbow, all while stroking his prostate. He kissed down his arm and shoulder until he made it to Chris's lips. Chris still had not opened his eyes.

Ciaran gave him a chaste kiss and answered him, <*No.*>

He kissed down the center of Chris's body, positioning himself between Chris's legs, saying to him, <*I'm going to make you cum hard first. Then I'm going to ride your body until the sun rises. And the whole town of Gullfelt is going to hear you.*>

"Ho. Lee. Shit," Chris said out loud. Then he let out a moan again as Ciaran stroked him internally and sucked him externally.

The fact that Chris could not move his hands made it worse. Or better. If Chris was warm to the touch before, Ciaran was setting his body on fire. He tried desperately to be quiet. But Ciaran continued to add more and more lube, making Chris's insides ridiculously wet and Ciaran's fingers travel smoothly over the bundle of nerves. And Ciaran kept spitting on his cock and stroking him with his other hand. And Ciaran was giving him nice, strong sucks. And Ciaran was talking in his head, giving him images of the first time they made love. And the second. And the third…

<Remember when we were in my bed, and I rolled you over, and you rode my cock? You were trembling, your body so hot, desperate to cum. Remember when I made you cum again. And again. And again.>

"Oh, my god uuuuugh…" Chris moaned out.

<Remember you kept saying to me, "I can't." But I told you could. And you did. My cock made you cum once… twice… three times… four, I think. Do you remember, Christopher?>

"Jesus fucking Christ, Ciaran!" he yelled out.

<Sounds like you're ready. You're ready, love? Come hard for me, okay? Cream in my mouth.>

Ciaran moved his hand and deep-throated Chris over and over again, still stroking his prostate. Chris let out another loud guttural moan. His waist shook as he came in Ciaran's mouth.

Ciaran held it, waiting for Chris to stop shaking. Chris finally opened his eyes and smiled, still breathless. Ciaran cupped his hand below his face and looked at Chris while he spit cum and saliva into his palm. Then he reached down and stroked himself with it.

Chris's body flushed with heat at the sight of Ciaran using his cum as lube. Ciaran moved closer and inserted himself inside of Chris, making Chris moan loudly again. Ciaran's nine-inch cock was ten times better than his strong fingers. Ciaran laid his body on top of Chris and began to move.

"Let me hold you, love," Chris moaned. "Let me hold you."

Ciaran pulled Chris's hands toward his face, thought of the incantation, and blew on his wrists. They were immediately released. Chris held onto Ciaran as Ciaran did what he said he was going to do: make love to him until the room began to lighten with the rays of the sun, with the headboard banging against the wall, and the coils of the mattress squeaking under their weight. Every time Ciaran felt his orgasm begin to rise he consciously slowed down. But after a while, he lost the battle, as he lost himself in Chris's arms and the heat of him. His body shook violently, and he unexpectedly began to cum, letting out his own guttural moan. Chris felt every spurt deep inside of him, and he found himself moaning with Ciaran.

Ciaran slowly pulled out but did not move from lying on top of Chris. Chris didn't mind at all, wanting to hold on to him forever.

"I have to get going," Ciaran said eventually.

"I know," Chris said with a sigh.

"But I'm so addicted to you," said Ciaran, kissing his sweaty skin.

"Well, it's a good thing that we're going to be together forever then," said Chris.

Ciaran looked into Chris's face. "And three days after that."

Chris took his face in his hands. "I love you, Ciaran Beals. So much."

Ciaran smiled. "Well, then. It's a good thing we're going to be together forever."

Chris grinned.

———◆———

After a hot shower, Ciaran and Chris came downstairs together, holding hands. Felix and Alastair were sitting in the dining room, drinking tea and having toast and jam. They both looked up at them, Alastair frowning, Felix shaking his head with a smirk.

Ciaran and Chris looked at each other with a smile, then at the men at the table. "Sorry," they chorused. Alastair huffed, and Felix continued smiling. Neither man believed they were actually sorry.

After breakfast, Chris walked Ciaran out onto the porch. Ciaran turned around and pushed Chris's body against the wall and kissed him passionately, pulling on his full lips with his own. He kissed Chris's cheeks and neck profusely, making him laugh, before he stepped away.

"God, you make me feel like a giddy schoolgirl," said Chris.

Ciaran turned around on the pavement. "That's how it's supposed to be, innit?" He touched two fingers to his lips and blew Chris a kiss.

<*Love you,*> he said in Chris's mind and Wisp'd on the spot.

Chris watched the smoke disappear as quickly as it arrived. He gently touched his chest to slow down the pounding of his heartbeat, so full of love for his mate.

———◆———

Chris walked through the five constables as they shot off their arrows. Roth was a little off, so he paused there. "It's your form," said Chris, seeing the frustration in the younger man's eyes. "Your hands have to be steady, but so do your arms. Even though you're holding the bow with your non-dominant hand, it still needs to be aligned."

"I'm better at dueling. And firearms, apparently."

"Yes, but it's another tactic for protection," said Chris. "And you signed up for this."

"Brell was doing it, so I wanted to be here too," he said quietly, looking over at the blonde who seemed to be doing just fine.

Chris looked over at her, then back at Roth. "Well, well, well, Sinclair. Following your heart seems to have led you down an unwanted path." Then he whispered, "Or maybe you're following something else?"

Roth chuckled. "It's how I signed up for constable duty, too. Just to get her to notice me."

Brell hit a target, then looked around. She and Roth caught eyes. She smiled, and he smiled back before she began to load it again. Chris turned back to him. "She's noticing you now."

Roth blushed. He set his arrow again. Chris watched him follow through, and it went closer to the mark. He grinned.

Chris walked around Broock, Brell, Hauser, and Dawson again, giving instruction, until the timer went off. They all turned to him.

"You did great for our first real archery lesson," he said. "Remember that weight has to be distributed evenly. From your stance to the way you hold your bow."

He walked over to Roth and held his hand out. Roth gave him his bow. Chris turned toward the bullseye and spoke as he directed.

"Watch my feet. Make sure they are parallel with each other. And when you nock your bow...."

Suddenly, Chris felt a heavy dull pain in the back of his head. His eyes crossed, and he went dizzy. The officers watched Chris fall face forward onto the ground and lie still.

———◆———

<Christopher... Can you hear me... God, I don't know if this works yet... But if it does... Chris, I need you to hear me...>

Chris whispered, "I hear you, Ciaran."

"He's awake!" someone yelled.

Chris opened up his eyes. There were two cats and eight people standing over him: the five constables he had been with, Alastair, Felix, and Mayor Dubois. Felix was patting his head with a white cloth.

"What happened?" he asked groggily.

"You passed out. You were talking, and you just passed out," said Brell in worry.

"And we couldn't wake you," said Felix. "It's been hours."

"Hours?!" Chris sat up. He was in the back room at the police station. He looked out the window at the lateness of the sun. "Where's Ciaran?"

Alastair looked at him curiously. "He should be on his way back with Lulu by now."

Chris shook his head furiously. "No, he's not. Something happened to him."

"What do you mean?" Felix asked in alarm.

"Just what I said," Chris said, getting off the couch and stepping over the deputy chief cat. "He's..." Chris closed his eyes and did a body scan. "He's hurt. Someone bashed him on the head with something heavy. Probably a rock. He just came to. He's ... confused. He doesn't know where he is."

"What are you talking about?" the mayor said.

But Chris shushed him as Ciaran talked in his head again. *<If this Ardenti shit is real, then you should have been knocked out when I was knocked out, Chris, and woke up when I did... God, I hope you can hear me... They took me and Lulu. I don't know where we are. It's dark here. Blacked-out windows...>*

Chris opened his eyes and stumbled to the nearest desk; his head was still hurting where Ciaran had been hit. He grabbed a piece of paper and leaned on the table, writing things down, muttering, "Dark... Blacked-out windows... Can hear the river... Smell the swamp... What else, Ciaran, what else??"

"What is he doing?" Dawson asked.

"I..." Alastair began, but then he walked over to Chris. "The *Ardenti?*"

Chris nodded with his eyes closed. "What else, Ciaran, talk to me..."

"What happened?" Alastair asked.

"I don't know..." said Chris in tears, opening his eyes again. "Someone took him and Lulu. He just said they; he doesn't know who they are. He was giving me information on what he was seeing and hearing. Then he went quiet."

Alastair became fearful. "Is he alive?" he breathed out. "Is my cousin alive, Christopher?" he asked with more force.

Christopher slid to the ground and sat on his legs. "Yes. He's alive. Because if he wasn't, I'd be dead too."

The room went quiet. "Is this a telepathy thing?" asked Dawson in a whisper to Felix. "I thought that only worked if you're in the same room with the person."

Alastair looked up sharply. "No time to explain the how. We have to go to the hut. Look for clues. Ciaran and Luanne have been kidnapped." He grabbed the walkie off the desk in front of him and another off the next one. He gave it to

Chris. "Let me know if he says anything else." He turned to the others. "Let's go, now."

The five constables, Alastair, and Felix began gathering their gear and walking toward the front glass doors. But Chris yelled out, "Waaaaait!" They paused.

<Christopher... You're not going to believe who's standing in front of me. Or maybe ... you will.>

CHAPTER 27

Down by the Riverside

"I'm sorry it's come to this," Sergeant Hinkley said as he pulled up a chair and sat in front of Ciaran.

The side of Ciaran's face had blood running down it, matting with his red hair. His hands and feet were tied behind him with twine rope connected to the chair he was on. He stared at the second-in-command with distaste, muttering an incantation. But as he suspected, the ropes were bonded by magic.

"I know you didn't think it was going to be that easy," Hinkley mused, watching him. "You cannot magic your way out of these ropes. Scissors might do the trick, but your Commoner boyfriend isn't around to help you. In fact, he has no idea where you are."

"What is this about, Hinkley? The dragons? You want power and control over Gullfelt?"

"I don't give a shit about those beasts or Gullfelt," said Hinkley. "It has and will always be about the gold. And you're in my way."

"You're a sorry sack of shit, aren't you?" Ciaran said. "Selling out your own town. And for what? Who put you up to this?"

Hinkley smiled at him, but it was more like a snarl. "What you don't understand is that the gold in these mountains is worth something. The fact that we allowed others to come in and steal it when we were sitting on it the whole time is astonishing to me. Our little town could have been the richest in all of the Americas. But that idiot mayor of ours wouldn't listen to reason. He was preserving a way of life that was no longer feasible. Not after the war. So I made a deal with them. They can have the dragons and the town. Take them away, kill them, I really don't care. Mayor Dubois will understand once he sees how profitable we've become. And I get filthy rich."

"The mayor called the CMC for assistance with the dragons," said Ciaran. "He's never going to go for your stupid proposal to kill them all."

"He will," said Hinkley, "And if he doesn't, we'll kill him and put someone else in his place. Your team made that possible, putting elections back on the table for Gullfelt. Either way, we don't need you here."

"You're an idiot," Ciaran said simply. "You're a fucking idiot, and you're never going to get away with this."

"Oh, Dragon Tamer," he said condescendingly. "We already have. You're done. And all that is standing in our way is the dragons. They are supposed to be untamable. You were supposed to be reporting that it is best for the dragons to be killed or taken to your Reserve, rather than building a reservation here. You and Lulu are ruining everything. So you both have to go."

"So what do you plan on doing?" said Ciaran. "Slit our throats and throw our bodies in the river? Because I think the Canadian and European Magi ministries might notice our disappearance."

"No, that wouldn't be wise," said Hinkley. "We're going to burn your bodies and leave them in the field of sunflowers. That's how we show the mayor and CMC how dangerous it all is. Your own cousin's response will be to kill the dragons or capture them and send them somewhere else. Then our work in the mountains can continue."

"So, what are you waiting for?"

"For the right time," he said simply. He stood up and began to walk out of the room.

"You mean for your orders," Ciaran called after him. "Because, as I rightly deduced, you are not in charge, Hinkley. So who is it? Who are you answering to?" Hinkley didn't respond. "Because we both know you don't have it in you to run an operation like this. Like I said, you're stupid."

The sergeant turned back around. "I never liked you or that Commoner filth of yours that you brought here. And I'll be glad to see you dead and him crying like the bitch he is." Hinkley walked out of the room and closed the door, putting Ciaran in complete darkness again.

<If I get out of here alive, Christopher, I'm going to kill him with my bare hands,> he said darkly. *<And I know you can feel how much I mean that shit.>*

After Chris told them about Hinkley, they all went with the constables up the mountain, wearing yellow rain jackets. Inspector Neal and Mrs. Beals joined them, too. When they got to the field of sunflowers, they knew something was wrong. A huge section of it was already blackened, as if it was burned. But it was Felix who confirmed, "That's not actual dragon fire. That's *draconius*, the incantation."

Broock went to the door of the hut and tried to open it, but it was locked tight with Lulu's spell. "Whatever happened, it happened before they got inside," he confirmed.

"What is Hinkley up to?" Alastair murmured to himself.

"It's my fault," Dawson blurted out. They all turned to him. "He's been asking me about the Dragon Squad, and I've told him what we're doing, tracking and learning about the dragons. I just thought—"

"You did nothing wrong," said Broock. "Hinkley and Pinkerton cornered me, too, and I told them. It wasn't a secret; they've been up here with us before. And he's our lead inspector, so if he asked, we tell him. We didn't know."

"Hey, guys," Brell called out. They went over to where she was by the door of the hut. "Is it me, or does this look a little too neat? No footprints or anything, as if no one had ever been here. Like," she lit the end of her *dulé* and pointed it down, "does it look like drag marks that someone tried to cover up?"

Chris knelt down. "Good eye, Brell," he praised her. "I think you're right. I think this whole area is staged to look like some terrible accident." He looked up at Alastair. "That's what he's up to. He's going to try to make their deaths look like a dragon death."

It was quiet. Suddenly the deputy chief let out a loud meow. They all ran to where he was. Inspector Neal was circling a large rock with blood on it.

Chris could smell it. He didn't need to get close to recognize it. The same scent that had been filling his senses since the day he picked up Ciaran's tank top off the table in the Tank and put it to his nose almost two years ago. "It's Ciaran's blood," he breathed out.

Chris inhaled and exhaled, trying to control his fears as the colors in the sky showed the lateness of the day. Then he heard Ciaran say, <I can feel your worry. You know I'm not back. Or you found something. You know something is wrong. You can hear me, Chris, can't you? You can feel me too.>

Chris turned around to them. "Start searching along the river. Every single house," he commanded. "We're looking for one with blacked-out windows. Keep your *dulé* on your dominant side and your gun on the other. Be ready for anything."

They headed back to the police station, and each grabbed a firearm. Timbrell, who was alerted by his sister, was already there. Alastair instructed him to take the lead, gathering the other constables and searching every house, building, and corner of Gullfelt while they searched the river leading to the town.

At the edge of town, Alastair split them into twos: Chris and Constable Broock, Felix and Constable Dawson, Constables Brell and Roth, and Alastair with Constable Hauser. Inspector Neal and Mrs. Beals sped along ahead of them, trying to catch Ciaran's and Lulu's scents. Half of them Wisp'd to the other side of the river, while Chris and the others started walking along the riverbank. The sun had completely set, so all the Magi had light emanating from their *dulés* while Chris carried his phone with the flashlight on. He and Broock were behind everyone else, looking for the clues Ciaran gave him. An hour in, he heard Ciaran say, <You're too calm. What are you doing, mate?>

"I'm not calm, Ciaran, I'm focused," he said out loud.

<I wish you could give me a sign that you hear me. I have no idea if this is working.>

Chris stopped and looked around. Broock asked, "What happened? Did he say something again?"

Chris found what he was looking for. He bent down and put his left hand on the ground, with his fingers spread out. He picked up a smooth rock and smashed his pinky finger. Then he hollered in pain, grabbing it, and falling to the ground.

"What the hell did you do that for?!" Broock yelled at him.

"Ciaran needed to know that we're coming for him," Chris said in between his tears, rocking back and forth.

"Did it work? Because if not—"

"Shhhh… I'm listening," he said with his eyes closed, still holding onto his left hand.

<You're bloody brilliant mate,> Ciaran said in his head with a chuckle. *<Message received loud and clear. And hope your pinky is okay.>*

"Yeah," Chris said with a smile. "He got my message. Let's keep going."

Almost another hour later, Chris's walkie croaked, and it was Dawson's voice. "I think I found it. Or rather, where it's supposed to be."

"Where are you?" Chris said into the walkie. He stopped walking.

"On the west side of the river. There used to be a shack over here. And now it's gone."

Brell croaked in, "Roth and I are on the east side. How far down?"

"About six kilometers from Gullfelt," said Dawson.

Roth took the walkie from Brell. "I know that shack there. I know who used to live in it before they abandoned it during the war. It literally disappeared?"

"Or it's concealed," said Alastair.

Chris turned to Broock. "I remember there was an old shack when we were walking to Gullfelt that first day. I know exactly where it is. Or where it should be. But we're on the east side, too."

"Brell and I came to the west side," said Roth. "We'll Wisp to your location, Dawson."

"Wait," said Chris into the walkie. "Let Dawson and Felix go on their own. If it's the place where they're holding Ciaran and Lulu, we don't want to spook them by showing up all together."

"Heard, boss," Dawson said in the walkie.

Dawson began to get closer to the large dock that the building used to be on. The dock was completely empty, as if someone had picked up the boathouse and moved it. Felix kept watch as Dawson inched closer. But Ciaran's voice rang between Chris's ears.

<Chris, if that's you, hide now! They know you're out there!>

Chris whispered into the walkie, "Dawson, Felix, hide! Ciaran said they know you're out there."

Felix dropped completely to the ground. Dawson grabbed onto the nearest tree, wrapped his arms around it, and said, "Miscere me." He began to blend and camouflage with the brown bark.

Dawson held on tightly and did not move. He watched a door appear out of thin air at the base of the dock and three men step out with their dulés raised. They looked around before they stepped off the dock. One was close to Dawson, who had to stop breathing for a moment.

"Maybe it was a deer," Constable Wallman said.

"Yes. Maybe," said Constable Browne.

"Come on. Rodango should be here any minute," Constable Pinkerton said. They went back inside, and the door disappeared.

Dawson peeled himself off the tree and whispered what he saw and heard into the walkie. "I don't know how we're getting in without being noticed," he whispered.

"We'll find a way," said Chris. "We'll look for a sign. In the meantime, everyone make your way to where Dawson is. I'll get there, eventually." He turned to Broock. "You too. You'll be needed over there."

"It will take you an hour to get over there," said Broock.

Before he could respond, a cloud of smoke appeared, and Alastair stepped out of it. "Grab my arm, Christopher."

Chris looked at him like he was crazy. "We can't, Alastair. That's literally why Ciaran almost spent five years in Claustra. You were there for that, remember?"

"Do you want to go or not?" Alastair snapped.

"Yes."

"Then shut up and take my arm, Christopher," Alastair said again. "You remember exactly where it is?" Chris nodded with wide eyes. "Close your eyes and visualize it. Remember where you were when you saw it?"

Chris closed his eyes. "Yes." He grabbed Alastair's arm.

"Good. Don't lose that image. It will be you guiding me."

"Wha—"

But he was cut off by the sound of rushing wind; then the air changed around him to all black.

When he opened up his eyes, he was on the road to Gullfelt about a hundred yards away from the dock where the house should have been. "Yes. This is where I was when I saw it first."

"Excellent," said Alastair. "We'll go through the trees. Stay low."

After walking a few yards, Chris pointed to the smoke mounds. "I see the others," Chris whispered.

But as soon as they approached the constables, a big cloud of smoke appeared, making them all crouch and fall to the ground. Four men in regular clothing and one in a long white cloak stepped out of it.

"That's Rodango," Broock growled. "I can't believe that motherfucker had the nerve to come back." His mouth set in a scowl.

Chris put his hand on Broock's shoulder. "You'll get your chance. We all will."

"So what's the plan?" Dawson whispered as the door appeared again, then opened. Pinkerton stepped out to greet them.

"I guess we—"

But he was cut off by a ball of orange fur that came from behind them and ran up to the men.

"Was that Mrs. Beals?" Dawson asked, bewildered.

"What is she doing?" Alastair asked.

They all watched Mrs. Beals begin to hiss and attack Rodango. She managed to dig her nails into his leg. He howled and flung her off. Inspector Neal also ran ahead and bit a warlock. One of Rodango's men pulled out his *dulé*, but Mrs. Beals had already run inside the house, past Pinkerton at the door.

"Fucking cats," Rodango complained. "I blame Theron for that." He stepped onto the dock. "One ran inside. Someone find it and kill it, and find and kill the other one. I have work to do," he said as he stepped through the doorway. The door closed and disappeared at the same time. The one guard left out there started walking in the direction that Inspector Neal went.

"Oh, no, you don't," Brell growled. "Not my deputy chief inspector."

Before anyone could respond, she took off after the guard. They could hear the spells and see the lights being thrown around them. Suddenly Brell yelled, *"Emarcesco!"*

They heard nothing else but her footsteps crunching on the grass. She plopped down next to them with a smug smile on her face. "What did you do?" Roth asked her.

"I simply changed the rules of the game and shrunk him," she said with a smile. "Now instead of him chasing Neal, Neal is chasing him. And Inspector Neal will catch that sonofabitch." Roth gave her a high-five.

"Now what do we do?" Broock asked Chris.

But it was Alastair who said, "I have a feeling that Mrs. Beals will give us a sign. And when she does, be ready."

CHAPTER 28

Either Us or Them

Ciaran heard footsteps in the hallway, then the door opened, and brightness flooded the room. Once his eyes adjusted, he stared at the gray-haired man with black eyes that eyed him impassively. Hinkley was right behind him.

"So you're the Dragon Tamer?" the old man said softly. "The great white hope that came to save them all?"

"And you're the arsehole in charge," said Ciaran. "You'll never get near those dragons. Mark my word on that," Through his peripheral vision, he saw a ball of orange fur run past the doorway. He kept his eyes on the warlock before him.

"Oh, I will," said Rodango. "If I have to kill every last man, woman, and child in that town, I will. I should have done it the first time. In fact, that is the plan, to burn down the entire village, taking as many lives as possible, including that idiot mayor. So don't worry, you'll have company in death."

"Jonathan Hinkley will die before I do," Ciaran said viscerally. He looked at the other man. "So you better kill me now because if you don't, I'm going to kill you myself, Sergeant. And that's a promise."

Hinkley raised his *dulé* and moved forward, but Rodango held up his hand to stop him. "Don't worry, Jonathan, you'll get your turn." He turned around saying, "Now where is that Novo bitch?"

"Hey!" Ciaran called out. Rodango turned back to him. "Why don't you take these ropes off me and show me what you're made of, yeah? Instead of going after a simple girl. Are you that much of a cunt?"

Rodango walked up to Ciaran and touched his face with the tip of his *dulé*. He burned a scar from his eyebrow down his cheek. Ciaran hollered.

"Oh, don't worry," he said softly. "You're the dragon I'm going to tame next." He removed his *dulé*, and the pain stopped.

Ciaran glared at him. As they began to leave the room again, Ciaran called out, "You're going to die today. One of you, both of you, I don't care. Just know that one of you will not see the sun rise."

They both turned around, but it was Sergeant Hinkley who said, "Not likely." He smiled before he closed the door.

Ciaran was once again flooded in darkness as blood ran down the other side of his face. Suddenly two glowing eyes came out of the corner of the room. He heard a soft meow. Ciaran sighed in relief. "I thought that was you, Melodie. I got his attention enough for you to be in here with me, didn't I?"

Of course, the cat did not give him a verbal response. Instead, he felt her fur on the back of his hand as she began to chew the ropes. They both could hear Lulu in the next room cursing them out.

"…sick sonofabitch," Lulu was snarling at him. "I should have known it was you that was really behind it all. That asshole behind you has no brain cells."

"Ah, yes," Rodango drawled. "That United States charm of yours has not changed, has it?"

"Fuck you, you limp-dicked, shit-eating, pussy ass bitch," Lulu said back. "How's that for American charm?"

Once his hands were free, Ciaran and Mrs. Beals together began working on the rope around his ankles.

"Aren't you the one whose fiancé I killed?" Rodango was saying. "What was his name? Jasper the Joker?"

"Why don't you take these ropes off me, hand me back my *dulé*, and I'll remind you personally who I am, you sick fuck."

Mrs. Beals's teeth were faster than Ciaran's hands, getting one leg free. They worked together on the other one.

"Now, why would I do that?" Rodango said. "This is all part of my plan. The only way to gain access to the dragons is to get rid of you."

"Kidnapping and killing me isn't going to stop the CMC from building a Reserve you morons!" she yelled.

"It will if they believe it to be unsafe," said Rodango. "If one of those Class C or D dragons were to suddenly burn you and the entire village down, no one would be foolish enough to go up there again."

Ciaran jumped up, finally free. "I would kiss you if I could, cousin," he said to the cat. He immediately tried to Wisp but nothing happened. "Fuck!" he whispered to himself.

"I'll burn for a moment, but you're going to burn in hell for all eternity," Lulu spat at him. "You and that bitch boy behind you."

Rodango raised up his *dulé*. "Fair. But you'll still burn first."

Lulu squeezed her eyes shut, ready for impact, but instead she felt wind as the door burst open. "Hey, you limp-dicked, shit-eating, pussy ass bitch!" Ciaran yelled. He raised his hand and yelled, *"Quad Electra Maxima!"*

Both Rodango and Hinkley were blasted to the wall on the left side of the room. Ciaran was about to go into the room, but a spell whizzed past his head. He turned and saw Constable Pinkerton shooting spells off with his *dulé*, so Ciaran ran down the hall instead. Hinkley growled in anger and ran after him.

———

Outside, the force of Ciaran's spell was so great it rocked the dock and the water behind them. "The fuck was that?" Roth asked, bewildered.

"Go time," said Chris, and he began to run toward the dock, feeling Ciaran's adrenaline.

The door appeared as soon as he got there, a dim light flooding the trees around them. And suddenly his fiancé was standing there in front of an open door floating on the dock.

"Chris!" Ciaran yelled first, having never been so happy to see him.

"Ciaran!" Chris yelled back.

They began to run toward each other. But a bright yellow light flashed behind him, and Ciaran was hit in the back. He stumbled out, his eyes rolling back, then closed, and he fell into Chris's arms like a heavy sack of coal. Ciaran did not move again.

"Oh, no, no, no!" Chris cried frantically, holding on as Ciaran sagged against him.

He looked up, and Hinkley was standing there with a smile. Chris held onto Ciaran as the rest of the constables all ran toward the open doorway. Hinkley ran back inside.

Alastair and Felix came over to him as Chris lowered Ciaran's body to the ground. Felix ran his *dulé* over him and checked his vitals. "He's alive. He has a heartbeat, thank God. But it's some kind of knockout hex. It's more like he's sleeping, like he took too much Sleeping Beauty powder." Felix pointed his *dulé* and said, *"Vis carmina omittere."* Nothing happened. "This is really odd."

"Will he be okay?" Chris asked in fear.

"I... I think so..." Felix said hesitantly. "Give him a few hours to see if he will wake up on his own. If not..." Felix looked up. "I'm sure we'll figure out the counter-curse," he said confidently.

"Good." Chris stood up. "Stay with him, Felix. I'm going in."

"Are you mad?" Alastair scolded. "You're going to get yourself killed. You are not a magician; you're a Commoner!"

"I'm so sick of people calling me that, as if I'm an invalid," Chris said and unholstered his gun. "I don't need to have magic. I just need to be better, quicker, smarter than them. I think I can manage that."

Chris walked inside with his gun poised. Alastair followed, but he pushed Chris against the nearest wall. "Stay here," he said, hearing the fighting intensify on the second level. "I'm going to go up and see what's happening. Don't let anyone pass you."

But when he tried to Wisp, he realized that he couldn't. "Bullocks, they blocked Wisp'ing," he told Chris. "But no matter, that means they can't Wisp either."

Alastair turned to the front door and pointed his *dulé.* *"Continentiam arca."*

The door slammed shut. Black streaks hit the door and then spread quickly up the walls. Before Chris could ask, Alastair said, "An incantation to seal up the whole house.

No one is getting in or out. It's either us or them. And I swear on my father's life, wherever that arsehole is, for what they did to my cousin and my girl, it will be them."

Alastair started going up the stairs two at a time and joined the dueling in the hallway.

Chris was quieter as he went up the stairs. He stayed out of sight, then snuck into the nearest room, stood behind the wall, and crouched. Someone ran right in front of him. He fired his gun and shot the man in the thigh. He howled in pain as he fell to the ground.

Dawson cried out, *"Indocillis."* Pinkerton was instantly bound with invisible ropes. Dawson came over and looked at Chris. "Thanks, my guy." Then he ducked as another orange streak of a spell went past his head. He turned around and returned spells.

Chris slipped out of the room and poked his head around the corner into another hallway. Broock was in an intense fistfight with a warlock while Alastair dueled farther down the hall with a third one. Chris had to aim carefully not to hit Broock, who had the upper hand in his fight, but managed to get the other warlock in the shoulder. As the man screamed, Broock knocked him out with a punch. Chris turned to the other fight and fired again, this time shooting the one with Alastair in the buttocks. He went down quickly, and Alastair immobilized him as well.

Chris grinned when Alastair looked up and gave him a thumbs up. "Nice job, cousin," he called out.

"Alastair!!" he heard Lulu scream. Alastair turned around and ran to the nearest room to untie her.

Broock was still in the hallway with the other man, continuously punching him, but the man was already unconscious. Chris took his free hand and grabbed Broock's arm before he did any more damage. "Hey, mate, it's over," Chris said.

Broock looked up with his eyes pooled. "His name is Stenton. He killed my son. I remember his face."

"And now he will always remember yours," Chris said. "Bind him." Broock looked down at his bloodied knuckles and nodded. He found his *dulé* and spell-bound the unconscious and bloody man.

"Where are the others?" Chris asked.

"Last door on the left," said Broock, wiping his face with his arm to avoid the blood on his hands.

Chris went toward the room where Brell and Roth were dueling Wallman and another one of Rodango's men. But before he reached the door, Browne came running out of another room from Houser, who was yelling obscenities at him, heading to the staircase and coming face to face with Chris. The constable raised his *dulé,* and Chris immediately ducked and rolled away, the spell missing him; Chris then fired his gun twice, once into each leg. Constable Browne went down like a ton of bricks, hollering. Brell and Roth both came running out of the room.

Houser bound him as Roth said, "That was awesome, dude."

"Who the fuck is this Commoner?" Chris heard from behind him. Chris turned around and saw an older warlock, wearing all white. "Never mind," he sneered. "I don't care." He raised his *rodulé.*

But before he could speak, Houser, Brell, Roth, and Dawson yelled, *"OBEX!"*

The shield around Chris was so forceful it knocked Rodango back and sideways into a wall, and his *dulé* went flying from his hand.

Alastair yelled from behind them, *"Indocillis,"* from the other end of the hallway, pointing his *dulé* at the barely conscious warlock. Chris felt the spell pass his shoulder, and Rodango was immediately bound in invisible ropes. *"Sito rodulé,"* Alastair called. Rodango's *dulé* came flying from the corner of the hall near the steps and into Alastair's arms. He pointed both wands as he came closer.

"Personalis carcerem." A white cylinder shield surrounded him. Rodango stared at Alastair with hateful eyes as he towered over him.

"You're an idiot for coming here again, Former Minister Octavious Rodango Mansour," said Alastair. "On behalf of the Canadian Ministry Council in conjunction with the Magi Council of Europe, I hereby place you under arrest and confinement. Indefinitely. You will stand trial for all the atrocities you committed and spend the rest of your life in a Magi prison."

"Noooo!" Lulu screamed.

She pushed past the other officers, snatched Chris's gun out of his hand, and raised it at Rodango. "He killed Jasper. He doesn't get to live."

But Alastair stood in front of her, raising his hands. "No."

"Get the fuck out of my way, Alastair!" she screamed at him, pointing the gun at him.

"This will not bring back Jasper, Luanne," he said calmly. "This will only bring you nightmares." He stepped closer until the gun was against his own chest. "I won't let you do this, Lulu. Not for him, but for you."

Her hand was shaking, and tears fell out of her eyes. Mrs. Beals floated around her feet and meowed loudly again and again as if she too were pleading with Lulu. Alastair put one hand on the gun and slowly took it from her. Lulu burst into sobs and fell against Alastair's chest. Alastair handed the gun back to Chris and held her with both arms. Chris took it but held it at his side.

Broock looked down at his bloodied hands, then back up. "I know how you feel, Lulu. But they will get what is owed to them. Some things are worse than death."

Broock's words kicked something inside Chris's brain. "Ciaran," he said out loud and then looked around. "Where's Hinkley?"

They looked at each other. "No one has seen him," Dawson said.

"We have to find him," Chris muttered. "Before he gets out."

Alastair shook his head. "He can't, remember? I sealed up the house." He turned around. "Broock, Dawson, Houser, and Brell, stay with our prisoners. Roth, come with me and Chris since you're familiar with this place. Let's go find that arsehole."

Chris, Roth, and Alastair started downstairs and searched every room, then upstairs. At the end of the hall, Roth looked up. "That's the attic," he said and pulled on the string.

The latch opened, and a staircase began to unfold itself. Alastair went up first with his *dulé* out with Chris next, then Roth. The room was quiet, but the window was open. They began to search the room when a bright yellow spell came out from the corner of the room, missing Chris by an inch.

Roth and Alistair both yelled two separate incantations in the direction of the spell. Hinkley groaned and fell backward into a box of old toys. All three ran up. "Drop the *dulé*, or we'll drop you," said Roth.

Hinkley looked up to see two *dulés* and a gun pointed at him. He raised his hands. "Shouldn't you be out there saying your goodbye to your forever sleeping boyfriend?"

"What do you mean?" Chris asked, his eyebrows raised.

Hinkley chuckled as he stood up and raised his hands again. "I call it *Dormiens cortuum*," said Hinkley with a smile.

Alastair gasped. "A sleeping heart?"

"An eternal sleeping heart. Do you like it? Anything to stop his smug ass from talking."

Chris's heart dropped. "Sleeping heart? What does that mean?" He looked at Alastair, then back at Hinkley. "What did you do to Ciaran?" Chris growled.

"An incantation of my own," he said. "And just like the felines of Gullfelt, no one can wake him but me."

"Blood magic," Chris said stonily. Hinkley smiled.

Alastair pressed the *dulé* against his neck. "You will reverse the curse on him," Alastair snarled.

"I said no one but me could wake him," said Hinkley, standing up. "I didn't say I *would*. No, I think I'll leave him like that. He's better when he's not talking."

"You can't leave him in that state," yelled Roth.

"Why not? The CMC will never execute us. So I'll live out my days in a cell, and Ciaran will outlive the rest of you in his forever nightmare of darkness and loneliness."

"I won't allow you to do that him," Alastair yelled, poking him again. "Wake him!"

"Fuck him," Hinkley said back.

Chris stepped forward and put the gun against Hinkley's temple. "You take that spell off him, or so help me God, I will put a bullet in your head right here and right now."

"You wouldn't dare," Hinkley said with a smirk. "I heard you down there with the Novo. You bleeding heart ministers are all the same."

Chris cocked the gun and placed it back against Hinkley's head. "That was Alastair talking, not me. I'm not Canadian. And I'm not a minister. I'm a black Irish that will do anything for Ciaran. Now, can you wake him or not?"

He sighed as if he was bored. "I would need my *rodulé*."

Chris picked it up. Hinkley held his hand out, but Chris would not hand it to him. "Uh-Uh. Let's go."

They all marched down the steps, Roth leading, Chris next, then Hinkley, and Alastair, holding the *dulé* at Hinkley's neck. The other constables watched them walk through the hall and past Rodango who was alert and sitting up in his invisible cell. He smiled at Hinkley. Hinkley smiled back.

"Keep moving," Alastair said, poking him again.

They made it down the last set of steps to the front door. Roth opened the door and tried to step out, but he hit an invisible wall. They could see that Felix had Ciaran lying flat on his back at the base of the dock. Alastair walked in front of him and stopped Hinkley at the doorway and pushed him a foot back.

"What are you doing?" Chris snapped. "Let him out. He needs to—"

"The moment I cross the barrier, the spell is broken and Hinkley can Wisp away. But *Dulé* works there too, so thanks." said Alastair. "And that is not happening. No. He can break the spell from here."

"You are the smart one," Hinkley said. He turned to Chris. "I lied. I can't wake him," he said with a shrug. "There is no counter-incantation because I never created one. It's tied with blood magic, like you said, just like the cats. The Dragon Tamer will be sleeping forever. I just wanted to step out of this shack so I could get away."

He held his wrists out. "You can bind me like the rest now and take me to Pénitenci," he said in a bored fashion.

Chaos ensued. Alastair grabbed him by his collar and pushed him against the wall. Roth started yelling, demanding that Hinkley take off the spell, not believing him. Mrs. Beals hissed and started scratching his leg, making Hinkley jump around.

Chris stood there, staring at Ciaran's body on the ground right outside the doorway, with Deputy Chief Inspector Neal perched next to him. He closed his eyes and tried to feel what Ciaran felt, tried to mold their minds to see what Ciaran saw. But there was nothing. Chris felt no one there. No one in his head. No one in his heart. Ciaran was alive and wasn't in pain, which was why Chris was alive and wasn't in pain. But it also meant that Ciaran's soul, while alive, was trapped too. Which meant Chris had no soul to cling to. Nothing to live for. Nothing to die for.

You will never be alone in this life, Ciaran had told him in France. For the first time since colliding with Ciaran Beals on that fateful night in the woods, he felt utterly alone.

He wasn't sad. It was emptiness he felt. The same emptiness that Ciaran was experiencing. The emptiness that Ciaran would feel forever and would eventually send Chris into despair.

Chris felt someone touch his shoulder. "It's okay," he heard Lulu say. "We will find another way to break the spell."

"I know you will, Lulu," Chris said, opening up his eyes. He looked at Hinkley's smug face. "But there is only one guaranteed way to sever a blood magic spell. When the *Vis* of the creator dies, so does the hex."

Everyone turned to Chris as Alastair let Hinkley go. But Hinkley's eyes widened in faux surprise.

"What, Commoner?" Hinkley spat out. "You think you're going to be the one to kill—"

Chris raised his gun and shot Sergeant Jonathan Hinkley in the center of his forehead. The gunshot echoed, and then there was silence.

Hinkley's body fell against Alastair, who tripped over the threshold, breaking the containment spell, and landed with a thud on his back onto the dock. Alastair quickly pushed Hinkley off him and stood up with bewilderment in his eyes. Lulu, Roth, Felix, and Alastair stared at Chris in shock. Only Mrs. Beals came over and purred around his legs with her tail up.

Suddenly, Ciaran gasped loudly and sat up, touching his chest.

Chris ran over to him, jumping over Hinkley's lifeless body. He knelt down and grabbed his face. "Ciaran?" he breathed out, wide-eyed and fearful.

Ciaran nodded and kept gasping as if he were gathering all the air around him. Chris fell against Ciaran's chest, burst into tears, and began to sob.

"I'm okay, Chris, I'm okay," he said between trying to breathe steadily.

Chris could not stop shaking and crying as all of his feelings, and Ciaran's fear and confusion, came crashing down on him.

"What happened?" Ciaran said. But Chris could not answer, crying so hard against his chest. He looked around at all the faces. "Who did it? Who cast the spell on me?"

"Hinkley," Felix said, his mouth still partially open.

"Oh, of course, that arsehole," Ciaran said in disgust. "Did you catch him?" Alastair stepped to the right and looked at the man lying on the dock, blood surrounding the hole in his head, his eyes wide, his mouth still open in shock.

Ciaran's eyes widened. "Wha…" He knew that was a mortal wound, not a magical one. Ciaran stared, and it took him a second to figure it out. "Blood magic?" he breathed out.

"Yes," Alastair answered.

Ciaran's senses were awakening. He began to feel Chris. His terror. His guilt. His shame. And he understood. "Oh. He tried to separate Chris and me. Forever."

Ciaran closed his eyes and saw it through Chris's mind. He watched Chris raise his gun and fire, Hinkley go down, falling against his cousin, and a moment later, Ciaran's body rising up. Ciaran opened his eyes as Chris clung to him. He held Chris tighter.

"Hey," Ciaran said softly, rubbing his back. "It's okay now. I'm okay. And you did the right thing." He lifted Chris's face off his chest, held his cheeks, and put their foreheads together. "Remember our oath to each other. I would have done the same thing, no hesitation. You know that, right?"

Chris choked out another sob. He nodded against him.

"So no regrets, okay?" Ciaran said.

Chris nodded again. "Okay," he squeaked out, tears falling out of his eyes, still trembling.

<I knew you would find me, love,> Ciaran said in his head. *<And I knew you would save me. You saved my life. You saved our soul.>* They gripped each other again. *<I will love you forever, Christopher…>*

Chris swallowed and sniffed. "…and three days …three days after that."

Ciaran wrapped his arms around Chris, and Chris buried his face in Ciaran's neck. His sobbing subsided, soothed by Ciaran's strength and love.

"What do we do with the body?" Roth asked.

Alastair turned away from Chris and Ciaran for a moment, overwhelmed by their love for each other. "Let the CMC handle it." He reached out for Lulu's hand. She stepped over Hinkley's body, too, without looking down, and took it. "I'm taking my lady home."

Ciaran looked up at Alastair who gave him a nod. Then he Wisp'd with Lulu on the spot.

CHAPTER 29

Guilt

The doorbell rang. Ciaran came from the kitchen to open it. He looked at the five faces staring at him and sighed. "Good morning, Constables."

"Good morning," they chorused.

"How is he today?" Roth asked first, uncertainty in his voice.

Ciaran leaned on the doorway. "He's ... still processing."

"Oh," said Roth sadly.

"Can we see him?" Timbrell said hopefully. "I know you said he doesn't want any visitors—"

"He still doesn't," said Ciaran.

"But maybe we could cheer him up," said Dawson, just as hopefully. "You know, get him talking about other things."

"Not that you haven't been," said Brell gently. "I'm sure you, as his partner, are doing your best to support him."

"I don't think anything will help right now," said Ciaran. "Except time. So let's give him a little more time, yeah?"

"But you're leaving in a week," said Roth. "Will we get to say goodbye?"

"Of course you will. I'll make sure of it," said Ciaran with a nod. "I'm going to go check on him, so if you will excuse me."

They all looked pitiful as Ciaran began to close the door. But Broock put his foot in the doorway. "Ciaran. You and I are cut from the same cloth. I was a mercenary for the council here, just like you were across the pond. I know what it feels like to take a life. Several lives. I'm sure you do, too."

Ciaran slowly opened the door. "I do."

"Well, then, you know, like I know, that the first time is always the hardest. The nightmares are never ending. The belief that you are capable of doing something like that... It haunts you."

Ciaran sighed. "Constable Broock—"

"Just listen, son," he said. "Tell him that he didn't do anything wrong."

"I've tried that."

"But get him to listen," he said with urgency. "Because Ranger Jennings didn't just save you that night. He saved our town from going through it all over again, or worse. He saved all of us from certain death. So tell him that he may think he did a bad thing, a selfish thing, and an evil thing. But to the Magi Community of Gullfelt, he's our hero. And we owe him a big thanks. Tell him that."

Ciaran nodded. "I'll tell him."

"Thank you." Broock stepped back. Ciaran nodded and closed the door.

Ciaran had spent the last few days giving Chris his space, hugging him at times, forehead kisses other times. Reaching out for him in the middle of the night when Chris would wake up with a start, reliving that fateful moment. And every morning he would ask, "Do you want to talk about it?" To only be met with Chris's silence.

He leaned against the front door and looked at the staircase for a while. Then he began to climb.

———————

Chris was sitting in the armchair by the window with Debony in his lap. He was monotonously petting her while staring into the rolling green hills and the mountains. The cat was purring in reassurance, but it didn't matter. Chris had never felt so low in his life. A part of him wanted to take it back, lifting the gun and shooting Hinkley. But the biggest part of him didn't because that would have meant he and Ciaran would have been separated forever. That thought alone sent a rage through him, and he was glad he broke the spell, even if Hinkley had to die for that to happen. Then just as quickly the guilt washed over him for what he'd done.

The cycle continued for him: the shame, the anger, the indifference, then the guilt for the indifference, leading back to the shame. Chris felt himself going under slowly, not eating or sleeping. Because every time he closed his eyes, he saw himself raise the gun, shoot, and Hinkley go down.

He could have waited. Felix would have figured it out. *He should have waited*, a voice told him over and over again. But everything in him told him that the *Ardenti* would have been severed. If Ciaran's soul was frozen in a state of perpetual sleep, the soul-bind between them would not have survived that. *He might as well have shot himself instead if he was going to leave Ciaran like that*, the other voice said. Chris didn't know which one was right. Maybe they both were. Maybe neither.

Chris heard the door creak open but didn't look up. Ciaran placed a cup of tea on the windowsill in front of him.

"The constables came by again," Ciaran said softly. "They're really worried about you."

"Yeah? Me too," Chris said quietly.

"Do you want to talk about it?" Ciaran asked expectantly. Chris sighed and didn't answer. Also expectedly.

"Broock wanted me to tell you something," Ciaran started. Chris did not respond, but Ciaran told him anyway. "He wanted me to tell you that what you did wasn't wrong or selfish. That your actions saved the whole town of Gullfelt, not just me. And everyone here is grateful to you."

Chris let out a long sigh as a tear fell. He wiped it away and looked up. "But you know that's not true. I didn't have to kill him. We'd already subdued the others. I ended his life because I couldn't bear the thought of being separated from you. I wasn't thinking of anyone else but myself."

"And so what if you were," said Ciaran. "You're still a good man, Christopher. A good man with a good heart and not an evil bone in your body. The fact that it's tearing you up inside shows how good a heart you have. You have to see that."

Another tear fell. Chris didn't bother wiping it away. He turned to the window again. "All I see is me firing and Hinkley falling. Like a never-ending loop in my head."

Ciaran sighed. He had been thinking it all week, waiting for the right moment, and he decided to say it out loud. "So let me take it away."

Chris turned to him slowly. "What do you mean?"

"I mean..." He reached into his back pocket and pulled out his *dulé*. "I can *abscondo* the memory from you right now. That specific memory. Would you want that?"

"I..." Chris's eyebrows scrunched up. "Why would you do that?"

"Because I can't stand to see you in so much pain, so much grief for a man that thought so little of you, of us, of anyone in this entire town. I can conceal it from you so it would never haunt you again."

"So I wouldn't remember at all?"

"If that's what you want," said Ciaran. "I could conceal the whole memory, from the time you came down the stairs to the moment I woke up. Or I could cloud the actual moment that it happened. Or I could make it so you never remember the entire incident. Your choice."

"But everyone else here would," said Chris. "I won't remember, but I would know something was off by the way they treated me."

"We're flying home next week, Chris," he reminded him. "The only people that would know are me, Felix, and Alastair. And the three of us have already made a pact to never bring it up to you. I can keep it out of the report so it doesn't become a matter of public record. And you can be released from your grief. If you say yes, I can do it right now."

Chris stared at him. He opened his mouth to say yes. But then he closed it. Chris closed his eyes and saw it again: His hand raised with the gun, and Hinkley falling. He took a deep breath and forced himself to see past Hinkley's fallen body and Ciaran's rising one. Chris slowly let it out and looked at Ciaran again.

"No," he said. "I have to live with what I've done."

"Chris—"

Christopher cut him off. "Grace said magic doesn't solve all of life's problems. That sometimes you have to feel human. So as much and as badly as I want you to, no. I have to feel all these human emotions: the guilt, the shame, all of it. I'm not grieving Jonathan Hinkley. He was an evil man who had evil intentions. I am grieving the person I was before I took a life. I have to fight through this dark cloud to make it to the other side. And I have to accept the consequences of my actions. I know that a Commoner killing a Magi has a dire penalty, so I am ready to face whatever charges—"

It was Ciaran's turn to cut him off. "There will be no consequences, Christopher, because again, you did nothing wrong. Lulu, Alastair, Felix, and all the constables were already interviewed by the Canadian Magi Council and explained what happened. And I told them what Rodango told me, that their intention was to burn the entire town to the ground and blame it on the dragons, all with Hinkley's help. If Hinkley had escaped, there is no telling what he would have done. He knew all of the town's new wards. Everyone here vouched for you, that you were on the right side of the law. Because you were, Christopher. You were."

Chris nodded. "Then make sure you add it to your report to the Magi Council of Europe. All of it. And let the chips fall where they may."

Ciaran was about to protest, but then he nodded. "Like I said, you're a good man, Christopher Jennings. And I'm going to be damn proud to call you my spouse next month."

Chris gave a small smile, but then he turned away again. "Hey," said Ciaran. "If you really want to fight through the dark cloud that is trying to take you under—and me by the way, I can feel it trying to take me under with you—then let's step out of this room and go somewhere. Somewhere that will bring you joy."

"Where?"

Ciaran smiled. "Wanna see some dragons?"

Chris and Ciaran stepped out in yellow jackets, while most people were inside having dinner, and Debony followed them. They looked over at Lulu's place through her front window, where Alastair and Felix were talking and laughing. They both watched Lulu lean over and give Alastair a kiss. He smiled at her. That made Chris smile a little. He was happy for them. Ciaran tugged his hand.

They walked through the meadow and up the rocky mountain, through the sunflower field, and past the sunflower shack. They walked until they came to a ledge and climbed above it, facing a big, yellow boulder. Ciaran waved his *rodulé,* and the stone moved. They went inside, and it rolled back to close them in.

"Lucerna," said Ciaran. Mini light bulbs along the stone walls began to glow.

"What is this place?" Chris said, looking around. He stopped at the model of the Torngat Mountains on the stone platform in the middle of the room. Some miniature dragons were lying around; others were roaming.

Ciaran began to explain as he pointed. "That's the family of drakes. There is a mama drake, a papa drake, and three young drakes. Oh, and a grandma drake. Grandma and the babies never come out of the burrow."

He pointed to the other mountain, where two dragons were sleeping in the setting sun. "That's Sherry and Berry, the Knucker sisters. I've only seen them once; they are basically serpents with small wings that don't fly." He pointed again. "And that's Gabbana. London's brother."

Chris looked up. "What? Your London that passed away?"

"The very same," Ciaran said with a nod. He explained their theory of how London, whose true name was Dolce, came to them.

Ciaran continued pointing out the other dragons on the mountain, Willard the Wyver, Dessa the Krekradron, and Hunaphu the Quetzalcoatl, which was supposed to be extinct. When he was done, Chris looked at him with love. "Thanks for bringing me here," said Chris. "This is amazing."

"Oh, it's far from over." Ciaran pointed his *dulé* above and said, "*Pellucentia.*"

The cave became translucent, the rocky ceiling and walls disappearing. Chris was in awe. "What the fuuuuck…" he said, straining his neck and looking up into the open sky.

Ciaran turned him toward the west. "See the twins on the ledge?" Chris nodded. "Now look at the display."

Chris looked at the model and the dragons, who were also on the ledge lying the same way. "It's a live model. How did she do that?"

"Magic," Ciaran said with a smile.

Chris grinned. The first real grin in a week.

"We've been tracking the dragons," Ciaran explained. "Hauser, Roth, Dawson, and the Timbrell siblings have been helping us. That's how they became the Dragon Squad. We've been leaving food around for them to digest with a magical serum, the same one we use on the Reserve to track our dragons. So we know where they are at all times. But more importantly, we know their vitals. So that if any of them were hurt or in distress, Lulu or one of the others in the Dragon Squad could help them. And we're officially naming it the Canadian Dragon Preservation. Lulu said it's not a reservation; that we're preserving their way of life here, and I could not agree more."

"The CDP. I like it." Chris nodded. "This mission was a success. You've done great work here, Minister Beals. You should be very proud of yourself because I'm so proud of you." Ciaran smiled and kissed him as a thank you.

Chris knew he could not leave the cave, but being able to see them was enough. He watched in awe as Willard flew over their heads and the drakes walked past the cave so close that if there was no stone wall between them, they would have been in trouble. Ciaran tracked vitals in Lulu's notebooks while Chris went from side to side, watching them. They stayed there all evening, talking about dragons.

Eventually, they lay on the double-size bed, their feet hanging over, buried in Lulu's orange blanket, and watched the dragons fly into the northern lights looking for food, with Debony lying on Ciaran's chest, curled up and asleep. And Chris realized he had not thought about the incident the whole time they were there.

Chris kissed Ciaran's cheek. "Thank you for this, love. I'll be proud to call you my spouse next month, too."

Ciaran looked at him and could feel his emotions. And for once, it wasn't sadness. <I love you,> he said in his head.

Chris snuggled closer. "I love you, too," he said, feeling himself begin to yawn. They watched the outline of Hunaphu high in the air as his eyes started to close. "Ciaran?"

"Yes, love?"

"Do you think I'll ever ride a dragon?"

Ciaran smiled, but he didn't answer. He kissed Chris's head and whispered, "*Somnum.*"

Chris immediately fell into a deep sleep. Ciaran closed his eyes and gave Chris images of flying on Betta, their dragon.

Chris rose that Sunday morning and got dressed. It was the first time all week he wore something other than pajamas. Ciaran looked at him and then silently began to get ready for the day, too. Together, they made their way down the steps and out of the house. The streets of Gullfelt were mostly quiet, but those who did see Chris waved and greeted him. Chris smiled and waved back. He held Ciaran's hand tightly, and they made their way to the church.

They thought since they were arriving at least ten minutes after Mass had begun, no one would make a big deal of their presence. But that didn't matter. As they entered through the double doors, all heads turned to them. The parishioners stopped singing, and the organist stopped playing. There was silence.

Chris swallowed hard as everyone looked at him. He didn't know who started it, but someone began to clap. Then they all stood up and clapped. And soon it was thunderous in the echoes of the church's high ceilings.

Tears began to fall from his eyes as he was suddenly surrounded by hugs and thank you's and well wishes. Eventually, the monsignor asked everyone to take their seats so Mass could continue. But he motioned for Chris and Ciaran to sit in the front pew, which they did. Afterward, Ciaran left Chris with the priest for his confessional and absolution while he went for a walk through the sunflower meadow.

CHAPTER 30

A Gullfelt Goodbye

The four men watched their suitcases disappear from the front porch and knew it was time. They stood up and put on their backpacks, ready to trek back down to the valley where Silas was waiting in the Flyer. Alastair and Lulu held hands, as did Chris and Ciaran. Felix commented on how highly inappropriate it was that everyone was paired up but him, so the orange cat walked beside him instead.

As they made their way through the town, they were stopped every few feet by someone else wanting to say goodbye and give them gifts. Marley came over with bags of food for their trip. Mrs. Cho gave them hand-quilted blankets. Mayor Dubois gave Alastair a plaque with a key to the city. Emily gave Felix a wet, sloppy goodbye kiss. Even the cats came around to purr and rub at their legs and feet.

When they passed the lamppost that signified the edge of town, the bells above the Catholic Church began to chime, three single chimes and then a series of three. Alastair and Chris looked at each other and grinned in satisfaction. Suddenly the first volley of the 21-gun salute began. They looked into the meadow where Chris held practice right outside of town, and the constables fired in unison, as Chris had taught them. They stood and watched in awe, humbled by the honor given to them. At the last volley, the sky burst with colors that came together to form a hundred-foot-long dragon. The dragon roared loudly and flew around and around, then high into the air as it disappeared.

"I will never get enough of this," said Chris in awe.

"That was pretty spectacular, even for us Magi," Felix confirmed.

By that time the constables had walked over. "Thank you," Broock said, shaking Chris's hand. "You saved our town in more ways than one."

Chris felt a twinge of guilt, but he nodded. "You're welcome," said Chris. "The constables are in good hands with you leading them, Deputy Inspector Broock."

The Timbrell siblings both hugged him, vowing to see them in Albania for the wedding.

Alastair turned to Luanne. "I guess this is as far as we go."

Lulu kissed Alastair. "Say you'll come back to me, Minister." She took off her colorful headscarf and wrapped it around his neck. "Say you'll see me again."

"I wish I could Wisp you to London with me right now," he said back, holding her closer.

"I wish you could, too. But they need me here. My work is here."

"And my work is there," he said. They kissed again. "Well, for now."

"I'm so close to a cure for the felines. An elixir made of Theron's stem cells. It needs to sit for a full moon cycle, but I think this one is going to work."

"It will work," said Felix. "The full transformation will probably take a year, but it will work, I promise you that."

Lulu hugged him, too. Then she hugged Chris and Ciaran and went back to holding onto Alastair. Eventually, she stepped back with tears in her eyes and waved them off.

Suddenly Debony ran through the legs of the crowd and up to Chris. Emily chased after her, yelling, "What are you doing?!" She picked up the cat, but the cat scratched her and jumped out of her arms.

Mrs. Cho came forward too and called to her cat daughter. "Debony!"

But Debony moved closer to Chris and Ciaran. Ciaran picked her up, and she did not resist until he brought her over to her mother and sisters. Debony began to squirm in his arms, not wanting to be passed over.

Mrs. Cho threw up her hands. "I don't know what to do. She spent four years never leaving the shop. And now she simply won't come home and stay home."

"It's like she's trying to escape," said Femy. "And I don't blame her. Her life sucks here."

Ciaran looked down at Mrs. Beals purring against his leg. Then back up. "I think Mrs. Beals wants her to go with us. She practically brought Debony over to us, and she hasn't left us since."

"We can't take her daughter, Ciaran," said Chris. "As much as I would love to take this cute little face with us," he added, nuzzling his nose against her face as she clung to Ciaran.

"Maybe you should," Mrs. Cho said seriously. Chris, Ciaran, and Emily all looked at the small woman in surprise. "She was supposed to go to the University of British Colombia when she was turned. She was going to study music, go to London and Paris, see the world. And she's just been a sad, depressed, lonely cat. So maybe you should take her and show her the world."

"But..." Chris glanced at Lulu. "The serum. She has to be here to get turned back."

Femy shrugged helplessly. "Then bring her back if she wants to come back. But until then, I agree with my mom. She never wanted to be here anyway. It's not like she interacts with anyone in the town, human or cat. She never even left the shop before you came."

Mrs. Cho touched Chris's arm with affection. "I know she'll be in good hands with you. Take her. Take care of my daughter."

Chris hugged her tightly. Then he bent down and motioned for Mrs. Beals to come to him. She did and rubbed against his knees, and he stroked her fur. "You sly little pussy, you. You knew what you were doing when you brought her to me, didn't you?" The cat blinked at him. Chris was sure it was more of a one-eyed blink—a wink. "Gonna miss you the most, Melodie Beals."

He stood up and held out his hands. The cat hopped from Ciaran to Chris, equally as happy. Ciaran hugged them goodbye once more. The four men began to walk down the stony road. When they got far enough, they turned back and waved one last time. Debony jumped out of Chris's arms and began walking ahead of them.

After about twenty minutes, Felix said, "You know, you could just pick up the cat, and we can Wisp."

"We can't," said Ciaran. "We have Chris with us."

"So? It's not like you both haven't done it with Chris already," said Felix with an attitude.

Ciaran looked around in confusion. "What do you mean 'you both?'"

"Oh yes, we didn't tell you," said Chris. "Alastair broke the law." He grinned happily at the posh man.

Alastair squeaked a noise in surprise. "I was... it was in the heat of the moment. And we were on official business. We had to get to you and Lulu, and fast."

"So you broke the law to do it," said Chris smugly.

"Well... okay, yes... but... I... I..."

"It's fine, Minister Beals," said Ciaran with a smile. "It won't be written in any report."

"Well, I'll have to report it to the Grandminister anyway," he muttered.

"No, you don't," said Chris. "Just like you don't have to report to the Grandminister how you fucked the town Novo while on official business."

Alastair went completely red and gasped. "That is—"

"Highly inappropriate?" teased Chris. "Classified? For the Johnson-Wanker files only?" Ciaran and Felix burst into laughter.

"Okay, enough of this talk," said Alastair, raising his chin.

"Hey, there is nothing wrong with it," said Chris. "We're all leaving the Americas sexually satisfied. I mean, Emily and Felix had a lot of late nights at Lulu's house, testing out their own serum."

Felix laughed out loud. "Good one, mate."

"And you know Ciaran and I fucked at least—"

"Leave me out of this," said Ciaran, amused.

"Exactly," said Alastair. "Show some decorum. And respect for Luanne's privacy."

"I'm sure you showed Luanne's privates a lot of respect," said Chris with a straight face.

Alastair flushed red again. "I'm warning you to—"

But Chris interjected, "Not talk about how you got your nob soaked again, and again, again, again—"

Alastair lunged for him. Chris jumped out of his way, laughing. Alastair gave chase, but Chris was faster, with

Debony running alongside him. So Alastair Wisp'd in front of him, startling him. Chris tripped over the cat, who hissed angrily at him. He fell to the ground laughing, but then kicked his foot out and made Alastair fall down, too. By the time Ciaran and Felix caught up, they were standing together and laughing with their arms around each other.

"So now that you got all that out of your system, can we Wisp?" said Felix.

"It's a beautiful day, Felicio," said Chris with a broad smile. "Let's enjoy the walk."

<hr />

When they arrived at the Flyer, Silas was standing out front. "Need to do another safety check, Minister?" he said, trying really hard not to roll his eyes.

"No, that would be fine, Mr. Silas," said Alastair. "I trust you and this vessel."

Silas gave him a look of surprise as he entered the Flyer. Chris said quietly, "Yeah, he got some. It really mellows a bloke like him out."

"I heard that!" said Alastair haughtily.

They laughed, and Silas gave Chris a dap of approval. Within moments, the Flyer was in the air, headed back to Europe. Debony sat in Chris's lap and stood tall to see out the small window. Chris was smiling as he too looked at the rolling green hills and snow-capped mountains.

"You're in a good mood," Ciaran commentated.

"Yeah. Feeling much better today. I think I need to get home. See my family. Walk my woods, maybe hang under our tree for a little bit. And get myself ready for our wedding in ten days."

Ciaran patted his hand. "Good. Then it's a good time to tell you that we're celibate from this moment on until our wedding night."

Chris snapped his head to Ciaran. "You're joking. Tell me you're taking the mickey out of me right now."

Ciaran shook his head slowly. "You need some time. Spend time with your family. Spend time at church. Focus on getting back to you."

"I can focus on my spiritual and sexual health at the same time, you know."

"I know," said Ciaran. "So maybe now it's me looking for a little mystery."

Chris narrowed his eyes. "So this is because I said I won't move in?"

Ciaran patted his leg again. "This is because I understand now what you meant. We're starting our lives together. Let's seal our tie-bind officially by consummating our marriage."

"Seriously, Ciaran?"

"Seriously."

"So you're not going to sleep in the bed with me?" Chris said incredulously.

"We'll still sleep in the same bed," said Ciaran. "We just won't be having sex in it."

Chris shook his head skeptically. "There is no way you're holding out if you're in the same bed with me. Not with our souls burning for each other."

Ciaran gave him a look. "My soul will be fine. And so will yours." Ciaran squeezed his leg. "Plus, I want you to heal properly from all that transpired. And not hide behind sex because that's easy for you. It's only two weeks. We can do it."

Chris sat back and was thoughtful. "You better fuck me on our wedding night. All night. I want that magical bar of soap that Diana makes and to get sexually drunk with you."

Ciaran laughed loudly. "I'll make sure she sends it over as a wedding gift."

CHAPTER 31

Chuffed

Clarissa drove with Ted and Grace, while Ciaran and Chris hopped in the car with Charity. It was the day before the wedding, and it was all hands on deck for the preparations. Ciaran was quietly watching the trees pass by, but Chris was all over the place. Even if they couldn't feel each other's feelings, Chris's bouncing leg next to Ciaran told him all he needed to know about how that day was going to go.

Ciaran had stuck to his no-sex rule that he made with Chris about two weeks ago, much to Chris's annoyance. He had freaked out at first and tried the whole first week to trap Ciaran into reneging on his rule. But Ciaran would just immediately leave and then refuse to come over if Chris didn't stop trying to mount him.

"Why are we doing this again?" Chris would ask every time.

And Ciaran would respond, "For the same reason you wouldn't move in with me right away. You are right. There is something sacred about the wedding night. Consummating things with you just feels right." Then Chris would huff and roll his eyes. But after the first week, he actively stopped trying, mostly because Ciaran's parents arrived and they barely saw each other, and Ciaran had to finish up his report on the mission to Gullfelt.

But today was the busiest day. They were scheduled to do a rehearsal breakfast with just the six of the wedding party, then head to the venue for the wedding rehearsal. Afterward, the men were heading to the Atrium in a car service that they hired for the day, mostly for Chris since Ciaran couldn't Wisp with him. Chris was going back home later that evening while Ciaran stayed at the hotel where their wedding night would be spent. Ciaran was partying with his brothers and friends while Chris celebrated his bachelor party at Nemo's with his friends. They wouldn't see each other again until the wedding.

Chris had woken up that morning with lots of energy. He couldn't tell if it was nerves or excitement, but either way, he couldn't help it. He was loud and boisterous at breakfast, physically jumpy and couldn't sit still, making jokes, some inappropriate. Clarissa kept sending him warning looks, but he ignored all of them. Ted grinned in his cup of tea, while Grace kept asking if he was feeling all right.

Ciaran said nothing. Out loud, at least.

After the third joke about milking at the table, Ciaran turned to him. *<Do you really plan to be like this all day?>* Ciaran asked.

Chris turned to him. "Yes!" he said loudly. Ciaran shook his head and sipped his tea.

When they turned from the road onto the dirt path into the forest, Chris was in awe. "It's wider, innit?"

"Yes," Charity said at the wheel. "Grace and a few other witches widened the path so that cars can drive up through the woods into the clearing. They'd cleared away about twenty thousand square feet of brush to reveal a grassy flat clearing and set up the three thousand-square-foot tent earlier in the week. They'd also outlined an area for parking for those who were coming by car and sectioned off a small area for a wedding trailer. The tent would fit about one hundred guests, the front part for the ceremony and the back part for the reception."

"It's perfect," Ciaran said, as they entered the clearing.

Clarissa and Charity parked in the makeshift parking lot of gravel, and they all stepped out of their vehicles. The forty-by eighty-foot clear-paneled tent overlooked the valley below and the mountains behind. It was the first Ciaran had seen of any of it.

"That's the Verdant Mountains," said Ciaran, using his hand as a visor over his eyes.

"The reservation is there, right?" Charity said. "Chris said it would be perfect for you."

He turned to say something to Chris, but Chris was busy running after a stray fairy, hopping up and trying to catch it. The fairy was also having fun getting just out of reach, only to lower itself again.

"What is going on with him?" Clarissa said with a scowl. "He's not taking anything serious today."

Ciaran watched him; then he closed his eyes for a moment. "He's happy. He's so ridiculously happy that this day has finally come." Ciaran opened his eyes again with a smile on his face. "His dark cloud is completely gone."

Clarissa looked at Ciaran, then at Chris, and then back at Ciaran. "Well, he's going to be your problem then, since you're sharing a body now." She walked toward the tent as Charity followed while giggling.

"A soul," Ciaran called out. "We're not becoming one body. We're becoming one soul."

"Well, whatever, get him," she scolded Ciaran as she flipped back the plastic door.

Ciaran looked at Chris jumping high with his arms outstretched and laughing, and the fairy was also squeaking in laughter every time he missed. It was pure joy. He allowed his fiancé another couple of minutes before he gently coaxed him to the tent.

Chris and Ciaran walked through the entrance thinking it would have furniture but inside was empty of chairs. The floor was sectioned off by two pathways, one horizontal and one vertical, that met at a circle in the middle where the officiant was waiting. The four others were standing there, waiting impatiently as well.

"Ah, the men are here now. I am Magus Phineas Abernathy," the tall, thin man in red robes introduced himself. "Let us begin." They could tell he was all business as he began to point. "My understanding is that you are coming from separate entrances, correct?"

"I think we're flying in on cloaks, sir," said Chris jokingly. Abernathy was not amused. Ciaran elbowed him softly.

Charity scoffed at her brother. "Don't mind him, I think someone slipped vodka in his orange juice this morning. Yes. They are walking in from different angles."

Charity arranged Chris, Ciaran, and Ted, and they practiced walking in from separate corners of the room and into the center where they would meet at the circle. Ted reminded her not to walk into the circle at all, but to stand outside of it.

However, Chris danced his way in, dragging Clarissa along in his arm, and then jumped inside the circle to meet Ciaran with a goofy grin on his face, accidentally pulling her in, too. She scoffed and yanked her hand free of him and went to stand where her seat would be. Ted shook his head in defeat.

Ciaran also shook his head, but smirked. "Are you going to be like this all day?"

"Didn't you ask me that already?" Chris said with a smile.

Abernathy stated loudly, getting everyone's attention, "I am going to say words; then you're going to say your vows. Who is first?"

Chris yelled, "MEEEEE!" raising his hand. Then he cackled.

Ted whispered to him, "Seriously, mate, did you smoke Sean's weed this morning?" Which only made Chris laugh harder.

"I'm just chuffed, I'm excited, I'M BUZZING!" Chris bellowed. Then he grabbed Ciaran's face and gave him a sloppy kiss on the mouth. Ciaran laughed and kissed him back before he let go.

"Christopher!" Clarissa scolded with a foot stomp.

The officiant was still not amused. "Can you please wait until the time calls for it?" he said sternly.

Chris stepped back from Ciaran, still smiling. "I'm good now."

The officiant began again. "Christopher will go first, say his vows. Please keep it under two minutes. Then Ciaran says his vows, under two minutes. The rings are exchanged. Best man, you hand your ring over to your brother, your left hand over to his right hand, as Chris, you extend your left to receive your ring. Best woman, you will do the same, ring in your left hand to put in Chris's right hand while Ciaran, your left hand is extended to receive your ring. Left to right for the party, right to left for the grooms. Does everyone understand?"

The four of them practiced the hand movements, but of course Chris kept switching hands on Ciaran and Charity playfully until Charity slapped his hands. "Ow!" said Chris, pretending to be in pain.

"You better not act like this tomorrow and ruin the wedding I planned." Charity waved a finger at him.

Clarissa was also annoyed. "On my life, Christopher Jennings, if you make a mockery of this ceremony tomorrow..." she warned him.

"I won't, honest," Chris said with a laugh. But no one believed him as his sisters exchanged looks of worry.

"Are you sure he's alright?" Grace asked Clarissa. She, too, was worried. Clarissa shrugged helplessly. Ciaran, on the other hand, secretly adored it, so he continued to say nothing.

Abernathy continued, "I will say words that you will repeat individually and place rings on each other's fingers. That act is for the Commoners. The next stage is the actual Tie-Bind. You will link your right hands on your arms so that your wrists are lined up against each other. Who is the *Servus*? Bondmaker?"

"Charity and I both," said Ted. Ted pulled out two long, thin ropes made of gold and handed one to Charity. "It's supposed to be a Magus or Mage, but I think we can do this together, innit?" He winked at her, and she smiled at him, grateful and humbled to be included in this way.

The officiant said to her, "This will be your task." He showed them how to tie the ropes around the couple to bond them to each other.

As Ted and Charity were practicing the Tie-Bind as instructed, Chris mused, "It's not the first time you've had me all tied up, eh, Ciaran??" He winked at him. "But that invisible rope—"

"Christopher!" Clarissa scolded him again.

Ciaran glanced at his mother's wide-eyed look, and said to Chris, "You know, my mother is right behind you, right?"

Chris's smile faded fast. "Oh shite! I'm so sorry! Shite, I'm sorry, Mrs. Beals. I mean, Grace. Oh shite, I'm sorry for cursing. Shite, I did it again. Shite."

Ciaran moved as close as he could with his hand and wrist tied together with Chris's and said, "Chris, love. You should stop talking. You are talking way too much now. Stop. Talking."

"Oh, it's alright," Grace said. "Christopher is clearly excited for the big day, so I'll pretend that I heard nothing." She smiled at them.

The officiant cleared his throat. "May I continue? Thank you. So, after the thread is tied, I will touch it with my *rodulé* like so, and say, 'By the power vested in me by the Magi Council and the Nation of Albania, you are hereby bonded in matrimony.' The thread will dissolve into you, solidifying the Tie-Bind." He mimicked the movement without touching the thread.

"Could you do it now?" Chris asked.

"Do what?" Abernathy asked.

"Bond us in matrimony."

"Well, technically ... yes," Abernathy said hesitantly.

"Then do it."

"What?" Ciaran looked at him.

"Bond us in matrimony right now," Chris told Abernathy.

"Well, no... I can't just... just..." Abernathy stuttered a bit.

"But you just said you can," Chris reminded him.

"Yes, I can. But I won't."

"Why not?"

"Because that's... it's highly irregular—"

"But you just said you can."

"Yes."

"So do it."

"Christopher!" Clarissa yelled at him, stomping her foot again.

He turned to her. "What? If the man said he could do it, then he should just do it unless he really can't do it, then he should say no he can't instead of—"

"CHRISTOPHER!" his sisters yelled at him in unison.

Ciaran stifled a laugh. "Chris. Stop. Talking."

Abernathy cleared his throat again. "Once the Tie-Bind is complete, you must seal it with a kiss. I'll say the Commoner line of pronouncing you as husbands. And that is the end of the ceremony."

Chris said to Ciaran, "Can we practice the kiss?"

Ciaran chuckled. "No."

"But I want to practice the kiss to get it just right."

Ciaran smiled at him. "We don't need to practice. We'll get it right."

Chris fumed. "Okay, fine."

Ted and Charity removed the golden ropes. But as soon as Ciaran moved to walk past him, Chris swept his leg underneath him, and he fell down. Chris jumped on top of him to lie down and kiss him passionately. Ciaran laughed and returned the kiss.

Clarissa's mouth dropped. "Oh. My. God," she said and walked away.

Charity and Ted laughed and followed her and Grace back out the entrance. The officiant was the last to leave with a scoff. Ciaran played in Chris's thick, curly hair as they kissed. Chris started grinding their bodies together.

Ciaran broke off first and said, "You know my mother is still here."

"No, she isn't. She walked away, shaking her head. They all did."

Ciaran lifted his head to look around, and they were indeed alone. He grabbed Chris's hair and kissed him again. "I love your crazy arse. Do you know that?"

"You better because you're marrying me tomorrow." They kissed again, and Chris started grinding his erection against Ciaran's again.

Ciaran groaned and pushed Chris off him. "You're like a dog in heat."

Chris started laughing and groaned. "Fuuuuuuck! Ciaran!"

"One more day. You'll make it one more day," Ciaran told him. He stood up and helped Chris up. "I'm chuffed too, you know."

That made Chris grin with all his teeth. Ciaran held onto Chris's hand how a father would hold a small child's hand and walked them out.

CHAPTER 32

Stag Do

On the way to lunch at the Atrium in the rented SUV, Chris, once again, tried to get Ciaran to cave. He casually touched Ciaran's thigh and then started to massage up to his groin area. Ciaran laughed and casually moved his hand away back down to his knee. Chris stopped moving, but then in one quick motion threw his leg over Ciaran and mounted him, then covered his thinner mouth with his thicker lips. Ciaran moaned and allowed him to because he knew the ride was a short one.

When the car stopped, Ciaran, without breaking away from their passionate kissing, reached over with one hand and opened the car door, letting the hot sun in.

Chris yelped, "Aaah!" and Ciaran took it as an opportunity to push him off his lap.

"Cool off," said Ciaran, and he exited the vehicle. Chris groaned, adjusted his erection, and followed.

Ted, Sean, Quentin, Alastair, and Rob were already there with Andres, Felix, Tommy, Khalid, Sahid, Vlad, and Alexi. After lunch, they went upstairs to Ciaran's apartment, giving each other haircuts and talking about sex and marriage, the best and worst parts of it. At 5 p.m., they began to get ready to split for their individual bachelor parties. But Ciaran wanted to see Chris off, so he hopped in the SUV with him, sending the others to Wisp to the International Hotel in Korçë without him.

Knowing that Ciaran was a little drunker and a lot more affectionate than earlier, Chris tried one last time. This time, he laid his head on Ciaran's chest and gently rubbed his groin. He managed to pop his pants' button open, zip down his zipper, and pull his cock out before Ciaran fully realized how far Chris had gone.

Ciaran grabbed his head saying, "Chris, nooooo…" but Chris had already put Ciaran in his mouth.

And all he could do was moan. He got stiff very quickly as Chris began sucking on his mushroom-shaped head and managed to get more of him in his mouth. Ciaran closed his eyes, getting lost in the moment, running his hands through Chris's thick curls, realizing how much he loved that Chris had grown his hair out. Chris deep-throated, sucked, and licked Ciaran, bobbing his head up and down, desperate to taste his cum.

Ciaran wanted Chris to stop, but then again he didn't and couldn't find the words either way. When the car stopped in front of the hotel Ciaran's bachelor party was going to be in, Chris kept going, stroking and sucking on him. Ciaran knew his orgasm was coming soon. Since he was already against the door, he used his hand to find the door handle and pulled hard. The door opened, and Ciaran fell backward onto the street, and his dick popped out of Chris's mouth.

"Holy shit!" Ciaran cried, as he grabbed his exposed member and laughed.

"Fuck Ciaran, fuck, fuck!" Chris yelled at him. He crawled out of the car and lay on top of him, also laughing.

A hotel employee came over. "Sirs. Do you need assistance?"

"Yes, I am being sexually harassed!" Ciaran laughed.

"But it's okay because he's going to be my husband tomorrow," Chris explained as he rolled onto his back. Then he yelled loudly, "I'M GETTING MARRIED TOMORROW!"

Ciaran could not stop laughing as their joy and excitement fed off each other. The employee said, "Congratulations, gentlemen. Now please remove yourselves from the pavement." He walked away.

As Ciaran continued to laugh, Chris whispered in his ear, "We're getting married tomorrow."

"I know." Ciaran kissed his face.

Chris sat up first; then Ciaran sat up, pulling up his pants and sitting next to him. They sat side by side and looked at each other, smiling.

"One more day," Ciaran said. "We can make it one more day. Go, see your friends tonight, and meet me in the circle tomorrow."

Chris touched his face. "I'll be the one wearing white."

Ciaran smiled. "How cliché, yet so apt."

They kissed a few more times; then Ciaran stood up and helped Chris back into the car to head home. As it drove away, Chris pulled down the window and yelled, "I fucking love you, Ciaran Beals!"

Ciaran's heart was full. He went upstairs to get ready for his bachelor party.

Chris was instructed to head to Nemo's directly at 9 p.m. When the car arrived, Other Chris, Jaxon, and Zeke met him out front, grinning.

Chris shook his head. "Now I'm worried. What's in there?"

"We figured what better place to end your bachelor whoring days than the bar where it all started for you?" Other Chris answered.

They walked in, and Chris's friends from high school and college were there. But the big surprise was seeing his Uncle Donald from the States with his cousin Dougie. He knew his father would not be there, nor his Uncle Ben, also from the States. He also knew his cousins Ben Jr. and Sam weren't going to make it; their father had a distaste for his sexuality, just like his brother, Collum. But he did not let that bother him. He knew that his Uncle Donald being there meant his Aunt Lacey, his father's sister and late mother's best friend, were going to be there to support him tomorrow. And that was enough.

Suddenly Chris was aware of the twenty half-naked female strippers walking around. Nemo was behind the bar looking surly that there were women in his establishment, but Richard, his partner, was all smiles. Chris's mouth was open as he looked around.

Jaxon came behind him and put his hand on his shoulder. "And what better way to close the door on fucking women altogether than to have your own buffet tonight?" he said and winked.

"I-I … am n-not… not t-touching … these women," Chris stuttered.

Other Chris, who was behind him, said, "Oh, that's okay. But they will touch you." His friends laughed and pushed Chris farther inside.

"More! More! More! More!" his friends encouraged him.

Ciaran groaned, then put the hose of the keg in his mouth again. The twins Khalid and Salid held their *dulés* steady so that the keg was upside down, forcing the alcohol into his throat. Ciaran drank much and pulled it from his lips. His friends cheered.

The room was spinning, and the ball of colorful lights that Andres contributed did not help. He had not been that drunk since the days of Rio de Janeiro with Sean years ago. Ciaran stumbled to the closest chair and sat in it. "I'm going to be canned for my own wedding, innit?"

"Nah," said Sean. "We're witches. We have remedies for that."

"But you will be drunk all night," Quentin said, passing him a rum and coke.

"And we're going to have a little bachelor fun, too," said Ted slyly, as there was a knock at the door.

"What, a female stripper is going to pop out of a cake?" Ciaran asked lazily and sipped his drink.

"Even better!" Sean said excitedly.

"Also highly inappropriate," Alastair said from the stool at the hotel room bar. He was watching everything with disapproval, but deciding to keep his mouth shut. It was Ciaran's day, after all.

Vlad opened the door and laughed; then he stepped back. Ciaran almost spit out his drink at the man in a cowboy vest, pants that barely held anything together except the length of his penis in the front, and cowboy boots, complete with stirrups.

"What the bloody fuck?" Ciaran breathed out.

"Thaaaaat's right!" Ted called out. "Chris got me in touch with his friend Jaxon, who gave me the number of American Rodeo, your favorite male stripper."

Rob clicked on the music. The stripper began dancing around the room, making his way toward Ciaran's stunned face.

Chris woke up with the sunlight streaming through his bedroom window. He was eerily calm. All of the jitters he had yesterday did not find him today, at least not yet. He lay there on his back with his eyes open, thinking about that night, exactly two years ago, of coming face-to-face with a dragon and the Dragon Tamer. He thought about every night after that and everything that had brought him to that day. Meeting Ciaran so unexpectedly completely changed his life. Maybe it was a cosmic force that brought them together. The Fates, Eli and Fab had called it. Whatever it was, Chris was drawn to the red-headed, blue-eyed, rugged man from the moment he laid eyes on him, and it definitely wasn't the magic in his DNA. Christopher fell in love with Ciaran's heart.

Charity softly knocked on his door. "Chrissy? Are you awake?"

Chris moved to the right to give her room on the mattress. "Yeah. Come in."

Charity came in and got in the bed next to him. They lay in silence for a bit. After a while, he said quietly, "I'm getting married today."

"Yes. You are," she said just as quietly.

They were quiet again. Then Charity said, "Do you think Ciaran will still let me do this? Crawl into your bed in the morning?"

Chris smiled. "Sure, if you can make your way to our new home, he'll let you in." They chuckled a little. Then Chris said, "The truth is I'm going to miss this, you know? You jumping in my bed. You've been doing it your whole life, crawling out of your toddler bed into mine."

"Well, anytime you need me to, I'm just a phone call away." Charity moved closer to lay on his shoulder. "I'm really happy for you, Chrissy."

"Thanks. I'm really happy, too." He wrapped his arm around her and pulled his little sister closer.

***

Ciaran slept in and woke up midmorning. He turned onto his back and groaned. The boys kept him up until 4 a.m. drinking, getting a kick out of American Rodeo dancing with a very drunk Ciaran. He had a slight hangover, nothing a little Excoquatur Elixir couldn't cure. He was thankful that the ceremony would not happen until the early evening at dusk.

Chris's face floated into his mind. He wanted to reach out with his mind, but decided not to. He was nervous and excited at the same time about marrying Chris, the absolute love of his life. Even without the *Ardenti*, he had a feeling he would still be in the same place with Christopher two years later. Ciaran had never loved anyone as hard and knew he would never love another again.

But first, more sleep. He looked at the time and rolled back over.

Sean woke up by the banging on his hotel room door, almost forgetting where he was. A pretty and very naked blonde was right next to him. *What was her name again?*

He sat up as the banging continued, took the joint off his dresser, and lit it with a flick of his hand. A bobcat *Amina* came through the door next, which Sean fully expected. It said very sternly in his brother's voice, "*Wake the fuck up.*"

Sean chuckled. He came off the bed and opened the door widely. Ted was about to speak, but then he realized his brother was naked. He balked, "Aaaaah!" He shoved him back into the room and put his hand over his eyes. "Something is seriously wrong with you!" he exclaimed.

Sean laughed, walked over, and grabbed a pair of sweatpants from his suitcase to put them on as Ted stood in the doorway. "It's time to wake Ciaran up."

"Right." Sean nodded. "Be ready in sec."

Ted saw a figure turning in the bed. He sighed and said quietly, "Get rid of her, Sean. Just be present for your brother today, like he always is for you."

Sean clasped his hands and said, "Yes, sensei." He put on a t-shirt and followed Ted out to the next room.

Ted knocked on the door more lightly and said, "Quentin, you awake?"

"Yeah, be out in a sec," Quentin said. He kissed Diana and opened the door. The three men walked to the next room and grabbed Rob, then to the last room in the hall, where Ted knocked.

Alastair answered the door with a bad case of bedhead, although he was fully dressed. "Is it time yet?" he asked.

"Yes, let's go wake Ciaran," Ted said.

Alastair stepped out and tried to close the door, but Sean put his foot in the doorway after noticing some movement. "I'm not the only one that had an overnight guest. Who is she?"

Alastair huffed and opened the door wider. Lulu was on the floor in black exercise tights and a workout bra in the Downward Facing Dog yoga pose, her tattoos across her arms, stomach, and back completely visible. She stood up, smiled at them, and waved. All four men waved at her, their mouths slightly open in shock.

"You'll meet Luanne later. Now can we go?" Alastair said. "We're on a schedule, and there isn't a moment to waste." He pushed Sean back more forcefully and closed the door.

"Somebody has some explaining to do," said Ted as they took the elevator up a few floors, poking his cousin's arm. Alastair turned pink, straightened out his glasses, and ignored him.

They all walked down the hall to the double doors together to Ciaran's suite. Ted had a key card. He counted quietly, "one … two … three!"

He swiped the card, and they all burst into the room and jumped on Ciaran's bed singing, "Ho ho! Hey hey! It's your fucking wedding day! Ho ho! Hey hey! It's your fucking wedding day!"

Ciaran was startled but then groaned and laughed.

"Get up; get up; we got lots to do today before your wedding," Ted said. "Last minute tux alterations, and Mum made me promise to trim your hair just a bit more. Then we all have facials and massages because why should girls have all the fun on their wedding day?"

Ciaran sat up. "I love you, guys. Thank you all. I mean it. You've all been brilliant in the way you've just accepted me, accepted Chris, accepted me and Chris together. I couldn't have asked for a better family and best mates to stand by me."

Sean groaned, "Oh no, no sappy talk, pillow fights instead." He waved his *dulé* so that all the pillows fell on Ciaran.

Ciaran grabbed them and started throwing them back. A pillow fight commenced.

CHAPTER 33

Nighttime Nuptials

Chris was standing in the entranceway on the far side, watching the guests arrive. He still felt calm, as if he were attending a party as a guest, not starring in his own wedding. He saw their friends from Newfoundland had made it and knew Alastair would be happy to see Lulu in her very short and very sparkly dress. Roth and Brell were hand in hand, and Timbrell's date was Emily, but she immediately gravitated to Felix, leaving Timbrell dateless.

He watched the other Dragon Tamers make their way in, looking uncomfortable in suits and ties. The two people that wore them well were Vlad's husband Alexi, whose dark blue, three-piece tux and bow tie were impeccable, and surprisingly Bruno, in a dark green suit, black shirt with a matching green tie. He had a beautiful Albanian woman on his arm with a silk spaghetti-strapped dress in the exact same shade of green.

But his smile quickly faded when the next person to enter the tent was Collum, looking uncomfortable in an obviously new suit.

"Noooo…" Chris frowned and turned to his sisters who were standing behind him, talking to each other. "Which one of you invited him?"

Conversation ceased. Clarissa shifted her foot and looked away. Charity looked at him innocently. "Invite who?" she asked.

Chris's eyes narrowed at both of them. "You two traitorous—"

"Oh, Chrissy," Clarissa started with her hand up. "I brought him here. I brought our papa as my plus one."

He looked at her. "Well, that was underhanded of you, seeing as how I had final approval of the guest list."

"He's your father. And he wanted to be here for you," Clarissa said.

"I doubt that," Chris said. "He wanted to be here, but not his brother and my cousins?"

"That was not his decision," Charity said. "That was Uncle Ben's. And BJ and Sam sent money and gifts, but that was the extent of how they could show their support. You can't blame Papa for what Uncle Ben did. But Papa didn't want to miss this single important event in your life."

"Why now? He's missed every other single important event in my life since Ma Ami died. What makes this different?" Chris asked heatedly.

Charity reached out and touched his arm. "Give him a chance, Chrissy, please? Please?"

Chris closed his eyes and took a deep breath, then exhaled. Ciaran had just arrived; he could feel it. "Whatever," he said to his sisters, walking away from the doorway. He was determined not to let anyone or anything ruin this day for him.

Ciaran and Ted Wisp'd together at the edge of the entrance to the clearing. The sun was hanging low in the sky. His nervousness had reached full peak, and his hands were clammy.

Ted looked at him. "Last chance to run, little brother," he said.

Ciaran smiled a little. "Too late, Ted. My soul's already in." He took a breath and started walking to his side entrance to meet his mother.

Chris took one last look at the sun as it continued to dip, leaving orange, yellows, and pinks stretched across the sky behind the Verdant Mountains. It was time. He expected to feel jitters, but they didn't come. He was ready for his walk.

Ciaran, in contrast, was a ball of nerves. His hands kept shaking, and he had to hold them together to keep them steady. He wanted to know what Chris was thinking, what he was wearing, and if he would like what Ciaran was wearing. He hoped Chris liked the fairies, the same ones from the forest, that would be flying high above them. He wondered if Chris's stomach was in knots like his was. But when he tried to feel him, all he felt was ease. He didn't know what that meant.

The music started. Ted touched his shoulder. "You're ready, little brother?" Ciaran nodded. Ted squeezed his shoulder and started out.

At the other end of the venue, Charity gave her brother one last hug. "I will see you out there." She held her morning glory bouquet tightly before her and started walking.

Ted and Charity walked the L-shaped pathway from different ends and arrived at the circle simultaneously, careful not to step inside. Ted wore black slacks and a metallic-colored shirt, mostly silver with hints of eggplant in it. Charity wore a silver, one-strap, off-the-shoulder, lace evening gown that swooshed and swirled when she moved. Ted winked at her, and Charity smiled at him.

As they timed it perfectly, both Ciaran and Chris followed their respective siblings down the same L-shaped path, Chris with Clarissa, and Ciaran with Grace on their arms. The women were wearing silver lace dresses similar to Charity's. The men hit the bend at the same time and got their first glimpse of one another.

Ciaran smiled slightly upon seeing Chris, his nerves lessening. As promised, Chris wore an ivory white, three-quarter length, high-collared kaftan with silver embroidery from the collar to the V-neck opening. Underneath were white ankle pants and white loafers without socks. His curly brown hair, which he had been growing out, was in loose twists, and the sides were shaved down almost like a mohawk of some sort. His face was completely clean-shaven. Ciaran couldn't see anything but Chris's beautiful face, and he longed to run his fingers through his hair.

Chris took one look at Ciaran, and his stomach jolted at the sight of his ruggedly handsome man. Ciaran wore long white Magi robes that had a trail of white buttons along the side down to his eggplant-colored suede shoes, with a circular design on the fabric that was a light, dusty silver, almost glittery. He had a couple of inches of hair cut off his ponytail, which was pulled back from his face, with a very thin goatee perfectly shaped. Chris could not take his eyes off him.

They met at opposite ends of the circle as their walking companions gave them hugs before heading to their seats. Then the men faced each other again. Slowly, holding each other's gaze, they walked counterclockwise around the circle, a replica of what they had done on the night they first kissed around the table in the Tank, as the last few lines of the French love song "Hymne à l'amour" played. They walked slowly and intentionally until they reached the opposite side of where they came from. Ciaran was impressed that Chris had remembered.

Édith Piaf sang her last chord, and they stepped into the circle of limestone rocks at the same time and faced the officiant.

Chris finally smiled. *Hey*, he mouthed.

Hey, Ciaran mouthed back and smiled at him.

Abernathy began. "Ladies and gentlemen, we are gathered here today, family, friends, and loved ones, to witness the marriage and Tie-Bind of Ciaran Archibald Beals and Christopher Macdougal Jennings. A love affair, a magical affair, a Commoner affair."

Some of Chris's side of the congregation chuckled. The invitation mentioned those three "affairs," and it bemused them to see what they meant by magic and what exactly was a Commoner. When asked of Chris or any of his siblings what the words meant, they were told it was a combination of magical and ordinary, something they describe their relationship as. Knowing Chris's playful nature, they accepted the answer.

Abernathy continued to say some flowery words about love and commitment, but neither Ciaran nor Chris were listening. Ciaran had looked down in the circle and noticed they were standing on a bed of pink petals from the Motus Willow tree, at least an inch thick. He saw that the same petals were sprinkled throughout the floor in between the chairs. He smiled. It was sure to be an emotional wedding the audience was not going to be ready for.

Chris, on the other hand, had looked up hearing scratching above, and it puzzled him. He had to squint a bit, but he saw about forty fairies flying in a circular motion. To the untrained eye, they would look like some kind of colorful butterflies, but Chris knew better. He gave a sideways smile and looked at Ciaran, who was looking down. Chris had two sets of vows in his head and suddenly knew which one he was going to say. Ciaran finally looked up and caught Chris's eye. They grinned at each other.

"Christopher and Ciaran have decided to say their own vows. Christopher, you may begin." Abernathy stepped out of the circle, leaving Chris and Ciaran in it.

Chris took a breath and stepped closer to Ciaran. He opened his mouth to speak, then smiled. He turned to the audience. "Let me tell you who Ciaran is." He began walking around Ciaran in the circle, but turned toward the crowd as if he was telling them a story.

"A couple of months after we met, probably late November, early December, Ciaran and I were on patrol, and we came across a wolf by the side of the road. He had been hit by a car, obviously broken, dying in front of us. Me, being a ranger, my first thought was to put the poor thing out of its misery, call animal control, and be done with it. I pulled out my firearm, and Ciaran stopped me. He knelt down next to him, rubbed its head, and talked softly to him. He raised up, carrying it in his hands, and said to me, 'I'll be right back.' I stayed there waiting for him to return, probably five minutes or so, and when he did, we resumed patrolling.

"I asked him what did he do. He said he brought it to Sarah, who gave it a mixture of nightshade and some tonic that helped him fall into a deep sleep so he could leave this earth in peace. The animals on the Reserve will eat it in the morning. I almost laughed, wanting to throw in a

Circle of Life reference. I said, 'What was the point of all of that?' Ciaran stopped me from walking and looked at me. He said something I will never forget. He said, 'The difference between us humans and animals is our ability to care for other living things in a unique way. If we lose that, our ability to care for one another, to show empathy, feel love for someone or something outside of ourselves to the fullest extent, then who are we?' And I thought to myself, wow. What an amazing human being to even think about life and love in that way. It was the first time it really crossed my mind..."

He turned to face Ciaran, "...that I wanted you to love me like that. Because I too was that broken, wounded animal on the side of the road. I had been through so much by the time that we met. And you cared for me, healed me, breathed new life into me. You showed me the power of Love Magic, of what real love can do when it's pure, right, and truly unconditional.

"My oath to you is to love you, purely, rightly, and truly unconditionally, now and forever. I am your Ruth. Where you go, I will go. Where you stay, I will stay. Your people will be my people. And my soul shall forever belong to you. I'm going to love you forever, Ciaran Beals. Forever, and three days after that." His voice cracked at the end, but he held back tears.

Charity's tears flowed freely as she looked at her sister, remembering the inscription on the rings. Clarissa, whose tears were running down her face as well, smiled and nodded, as they both understood. The place was quiet, save for a few sniffles here and there.

Ciaran could not speak. He remembered the day that held no significance for him, but apparently meant everything to

Chris. The lump in his throat was getting larger, and he was fighting back tears.

Abernathy gave him a gentle reminder. "Ciaran, please state your vows at this time." But Ciaran opened his mouth, and no sound came out.

He was overcome with emotion for Chris and just wanted to hold him. As if Chris could read his mind, he took both of Ciaran's hands and pulled him closer, raised them to his lips to kiss, then let them rest at their sides, not letting go. It was enough for the tears to start trickling out of Ciaran's eyes, and he could not stop himself from crying. He stood there for a few moments as they stared at each other, Ciaran silently weeping. Ciaran's friends and family were shocked that Ciaran was showing so much emotion, which was unlike him. More sniffles from the audience were heard as the people became overcome with emotions themselves, watching their display of love.

Ciaran found his voice. "Christopher Jennings, being with you has changed my life. From the moment I met you, you made me feel things I'd never felt before. You've awakened something in me that I wasn't even aware of its presence. You've pulled me out of my comfort zone in more ways than one and showed me things about myself that I never knew possible. You are the most incredible, selfless, loving, passionate, genuine person I have ever met, and I am so thankful that it's me you've decided to love.

"It's your love that has changed me. I don't even talk this much in one sitting, just ask anyone in this room that knows me." Some in the crowd chuckled at that. "But with you, I am truly free, free to be exactly who I was always meant to be. I am strong and vulnerable. I am calm and fiery. I am dark, and I am light. I am all of you, and I am all of me. You have created me into who I am today, and I have been molded in your image. I am forever convinced that it was my soul that clung to you first.

"You've given me a gift. Your love is that precious gift. My oath to you is that I will never take it for granted. I will honor it, cherish it, nurture it, protect it with my life. And I promise to love you back with the same vigor and passion that you have given me always. I promise to love you…" Ciaran's voice started cracking. "I promise … to love you … forever… Forever and…"

He couldn't continue as his tears started flowing again, and he was close to sobbing. Chris let go of his hands and reached up to Ciaran's neck to pull him close, foreheads touching, and closed his eyes, his own tears flowing down his cheeks. Ciaran held onto Chris's wrists, as Chris held onto Ciaran's head, and he closed his eyes as well, his tears quieted with his touch. They blended together again, letting the full weight of their feelings take over, breathing in sync as one.

Almost all of the attendees had their own tears. Ted's eyes pooled with tears that he was refusing to let fall, continually looking up to keep them in, while Charity was openly weeping, as was Clarissa, snot running down her nose that she had to keep blowing away. Grace, Diana, and Chloé were also openly weeping and holding each others' silver-gloved hands. Even Collum, who was sitting next to his oldest daughter, could not control his emotions. He whispered a soft, "wow" to no one in particular and thought of the love he had for his deceased wife. He realized how much Chris reminded him of her in that moment, and tears fell down his cheek.

After a full minute of silence and sniffles had passed, Ciaran completed his vows. "I promise to love you forever, Christopher, and three days after that."

They did not move, foreheads still touching, and eyes closed. Abernathy very quietly said to Ted and Charity, "The rings."

Chris and Ciaran heard and remembered they were in the middle of their wedding. They opened their eyes, stepping back from each other, but not by much. Chris held out his left hand toward Ciaran and crossed his right hand over it toward Charity to retrieve Ciaran's meteorite wedding band. Ciaran, who had almost forgotten the movement, was again surprised that Chris remembered. Chris saw Ciaran's look of surprise and winked at him, making Ciaran smile again.

Abernathy said, "Please repeat after me; then insert the ring on your partner's hand."

And they repeated the words together, "I vow to honor you, cherish you, protect you, through the good and the bad, through sickness, through health, from this day forth..."

The officiant paused. They both turned to look at him. Abernathy said, "You know, the last part is to say, 'as long as you both shall live.' But I believe you have promised each other longer than that. Forever, was it? And three days?"

The crowd chuckled as they looked at each other and smiled. "Yes," Abernathy continued, "I think we will leave it at, from this day forth."

Chris and Ciaran said again, "From this day forth." Then they slid the rings onto each other's fingers.

"And now, for the binding," Abernathy announced.

Chris and Ciaran folded up their sleeves just enough and grabbed each other so their wrists lined up. Chris stared into Ciaran's blue eyes as Ciaran stared into Chris's brown ones, the last flecks of sunlight making both of their eyes have hints of gold in them. Ted and Charity stepped closer, wrapped the gold threads around their wrists, tied the ends of the strings to the other as they were instructed the day before, and then stepped back out of the circle.

Abernathy took out his *dulé*, which brought more chuckles from the Commoners in the audience. He tapped both wrists as he said, "By the power vested in me by the Magi Council of Europe and the Nation of Albania, you are hereby now bonded in matrimony. *Magicis vinculum ligare Beal et Jennings.*"

The golden threads glowed, shocking Chris along with his friends and family members, and then dissolved into their skin at the wrist. They let go and simultaneously touched their wrists. Chris flexed his wrist; it was still there on the inside, warm and snug. The Commoners were awed and clapped at what they assumed to be a parlor trick and light show.

"You may now seal your bond with a kiss," the officiant told them.

They leaned in and gently touched their lips and immediately felt the same warmth between their lips that was felt in the wrist. It spread quickly throughout both of their bodies, from the crown of their heads down to their toes.

Chris broke the kiss apart first and looked at Ciaran wide-eyed, who was also surprised. "Did you feel that?" he asked.

"Yes, I did," said Ciaran. Then he grabbed Chris's head and kissed him harder.

The audience stood and clapped loudly; some hooted their approval. Ciaran and Chris hugged each other and turned and hugged Ted and Charity interchangeably.

Chris said, "I have no idea what we're supposed to do now!"

Before Ciaran could respond, Ted said, "Head out the way Ciaran came in to the wedding trailer to the right. You have one hour." He winked at them.

Ciaran took Chris's hand and led him through their loved ones who threw dark purple Coleus flower petals at them and headed outside. The sun had already set, so it was dark out there. They saw the trailer and ran for it.

CHAPTER 34

Making Love

The trailer was a lot bigger inside than the one hundred-square-foot trailer looked on the outside. There was a small center table with champagne on ice, popped but recorked, and two glasses. Behind it was a huge four-poster bed with colorful draping, and the nightstand had six different flavors of lubricant.

Ciaran laughed and held one up for Chris to see. "Well, they certainly thought of everything, haven't they?"

Chris shook his head and looked around. "It's like *Arabian Nights* in here."

He moved toward the couch in front of the fireplace as Ciaran moved toward the bed and sat on it. "This is bouncy," Ciaran said, moving his bottom around. He lay back on it and watched Chris examine the pictures on the mantel that were childhood pictures of the two of them.

Ciaran watched him curiously and eventually said quietly to him, "Well, I think it went pretty well."

"Yes. I do too," Chris said. "The wedding was perfect."

"Although I'm expecting never to hear the end of it from my brothers with me blubbering the whole time, crying and all."

Chris looked at Ciaran and smiled. "I don't think so. I can't see them making fun of you for it, not even Sean. That was pretty perfect, too." They held each other's gaze. Then Chris said, "I'm going to sit here for a moment if that is okay." He sat down on the couch facing the fire that had no actual heat coming from it.

Ciaran rose from the bed and went to the champagne. He poured two glasses, walked over to Chris, and handed him one. Chris took it but did not drink.

Ciaran sat next to him. "Are you okay?" he asked.

"Yeah," Chris replied. "I'm just feeling ... a bit overwhelmed at the moment."

"Overwhelmed like, 'This is the greatest day of my life' or like, 'Holy shit, what the bloody fuck did I just do'?" Ciaran asked with a smile.

Chris let a moment pass, then looked at Ciaran, and said, "Would you be offended if I said both?"

"No," Ciaran said automatically. "I want you to always be honest with me about how you feel, no matter what. And for the record, I understand."

Chris looked back at the fire. "Well, it's not exactly 50/50, it's more like 80 percent greatest moment, 20 percent how did I get here. And can I rise to the expectation. Be the loving, devoted ... and faithful husband that you need me to be."

Ciaran understood. "I know you will be faithful, loving, and devoted to me. But I knew who you were when I agreed to marry you. I fully expect you to flirt with every handsome man and beautiful woman that will come across your path. But you'll always come back home to me. I know that because you asked me to marry you. If you didn't think you could, you wouldn't have done it. And that honest part of you is one of the many reasons we're here today. So don't be worried about any of that. Because I'm not."

Chris was quiet for a moment. Then he said, "You'll be happy to know, regardless of both of those feelings of elation and worry, I'm glad it's you. I'm glad my soul chose you."

Ciaran put his glass down on the floor and pulled Chris into a sideways embrace. Chris put his glass on the end table and leaned all the way down until his head was in Ciaran's lap. He played with the buttons on Ciaran's robe while Ciaran ran his fingers through Chris's soft twists, gently rubbing his scalp. They sat that way for a long moment.

Ciaran asked, "Who did this style for you? I really like it. It suits you."

"Charity. I was going to fully twist my hair, but she changed up my style this morning, shaved the sides down." He was quiet for a moment, then said, "I'm thinking of growing it out longer. Locking it like Khalid and Salid."

"That would look brilliant on you," Ciaran said. He continued to play with Chris's hair as Chris stared into the fire. "How was the stag do? Did you enjoy your last night of groping the female body?"

Chris chuckled. "I should have known you set that up."

Ciaran laughed too. "No more than you setting up American Rodeo for me."

Chris laughed again. "Yeah, I knew you would enjoy that."

"Wanker," Ciaran said playfully.

Chris went quiet again, and Ciaran let him sit in his thoughts. He wanted to go into his mind and invade them, feel what he was feeling, but decided not to. Chris deserved his moment of thoughtful privacy and was entitled to his own feelings.

After a while, Chris called his name. "Ciaran?"

"Hmmm?"

"Why me? Why did you choose me?"

Ciaran almost laughed. "Are you joking?"

Chris did not answer. Ciaran slid out of his shoes and lifted Chris off his lap so he could lie sideways on the couch. Chris did the same, sliding out of his shoes and lying next to him, facing the fire as Ciaran draped his arm around his torso. His left hand found Chris's, rings clashing with a small clink against the other, and held it close to Chris's chest.

He said, "After we kissed and everything else that happened that first night, it was all I could think about. I went home and replayed it in my head in the bath, in bed, fell asleep, and dreamed of everything we did. I went to work thinking of it, and Tommy was talking to me about something, and I just wanted him to sod off so I could find a nice quiet corner under a tree and replay it again and again. And I remember thinking, 'What was it about me that made him want to be with me? A complete novice at being with a man, sexually inept, insecure about myself and my feelings, and yet he said he wanted to be with me?'

"I didn't understand it then, but I understand it now. I could have written your vows tonight. The bit where you talked about breathing new life into you. Because you made me feel like that every day, and still do. I never saw myself as choosing you and bringing you into my magical world. I always saw it as you making me a part of yours, you choosing me."

Chris was silent for a long moment again. Then he spoke. "I could have written your vows, too, you know. You changed me, created me into the man I am today. Your love is a gift to me, too."

They lay together, spooning, and were quiet. Then Chris asked, "Do you want to make love now?"

"I thought that's what we were already doing. Making love." Ciaran kissed the back of Chris's head and squeezed his hand. Chris smiled a little and squeezed back. Then Ciaran said, "Thirty more minutes. I'm sure there'll be a ten-minute warning that will alert us."

"Okay."

They continued to lie in silence. After a bit, Chris said, "The fairies were a nice touch. It took me a moment to see them, figure out what it was up there. They were so high up."

"Well, after yesterday, I saw how much fun you had with them. I asked Ted to ask them if they would be a part of the ceremony for you."

"Yes. That was very nice."

"The Motus tree petals were better. Not a dry eye in the house. Your idea, I'm sure," Ciaran said.

Chris squeezed his hand. "It's our tree."

"Indeed." Ciaran squeezed back. More silence ensued. Then Ciaran said, "I saw your dad."

"Yeah, so did I," Chris said bitterly. "He better not say one rude or nasty thing today."

Ciaran said, "I don't think he will. I'm sure he was crying."

He felt Chris tense. "I don't believe it."

"Yes, he was," Ciaran confirmed. "He had looked down for a bit; then I saw him look up and wipe his face."

"It was the Motus petals."

"Or he was emotional seeing his son get married," Ciaran countered.

Chris didn't speak for a long moment. "I don't know what to do about him. The last time I saw him, he told me he didn't give a shite about me or our relationship. Then he just shows up to support us? I don't know what to do with that."

"You don't have to do anything. We will greet him like we will greet all of our guests. Then we'll move on to the next table."

"Right." Chris let a few moments pass and then said softly, "It's nice that he came... I guess... At least one of my parents could be here."

"Your mother is here with us, Chris," said Ciaran. "Our loved ones, especially our ancestors, never leave us. That's what my Nan used to say." Chris squeezed his hand in response, and Ciaran squeezed back.

They were quiet again, Chris watching the roaring fire in thought, Ciaran listening to the sound of Chris's breathing and his heartbeat.

"It's so quiet here," Chris said. "Do you like it here? The area, I mean."

"Yeah. It's nice, secluded, but right off the main road for easy access. It was a good choice for a venue." Chris did not respond. Then Ciaran said, "I think they muffled the trailer, anyway. We should be able to hear noise from the tent. It's not that far off."

Again Chris took a long moment to respond, but then said, "I like that it's quiet. And I knew you would like the view of the mountains surrounded by the forest as the backdrop."

Ciaran smiled. "I did. I really, really did."

They lay together in silence until they heard a small ringing like a dinner bell. They both realized it was the ten-minute warning, but neither of them moved.

Then Chris asked, "How are we getting to the hotel tonight?"

"I wouldn't worry about it," Ciaran said simply.

They didn't speak again until they heard the gong. Chris sat up and made room for Ciaran to sit up, and they put on their shoes in silence. Chris stood up first and reached out for Ciaran's hand. They held hands and walked to the door. Then Chris stopped and turned around. He looked into Ciaran's eyes and pulled him close again to pull in his top lip with his two lips. Ciaran grabbed his face, and they kissed passionately, eagerly. He pushed Chris against the door with his body as Chris wrapped his arms around him.

"We're out of time," Chris said between gasps.

"They can wait a few more minutes," Ciaran told him between kisses.

CHAPTER 35

Flattery

Ted was standing in the doorway, smiling, waiting for them. "Good times?"

"Shut up," Ciaran said.

Ted chuckled. He spoke into his headpiece. "They're coming in."

The three of them waited until the DJ said, "Ladies and gentlemen, please welcome for the first time, Mr. Ciaran Beals and Mr. Christopher Beals."

The newlyweds entered the changed venue to cheers, with Motus Willow and Morning Glory petals thrown on them. Ted directed them down the aisle between the round tables to the raised platform, and they sat down. As soon as they did, their guests were served dinner. On their table was a plethora of fruits and vegetables, cheese, hummus and pita bread, smoked beef, and plantains. They realized how hungry they were and began to taste everything.

Elsie came up with a large bowl. "I have been assigned to your table as I always am," she said happily as she placed the bowl down of thieboudienne. "For your entrée, you have the choice between lamp chops, grilled fish, or goat meat."

They chose their entrées, lamb for Ciaran and fish for Chris, and Elsie went to put their order in. Chris tapped Ciaran as he looked to the left. "The cake."

"Whoa," he said, looking at it. "Well done, Mum."

The cake was three tiers, rectangular with white icing and buttercream in a scalloped design to resemble rolling clouds. The topper was two men facing each other, one yellow and one brown, with the yellow man holding a stick and the brown man holding a gun. That made them laugh.

The lights dimmed slightly, and the projector on the side of the room came to life. A picture of Chris at three years old in Superman pajamas came on the screen, and the crowd cooed, "Aawww." Then another picture of a two-year-old with bright, wavy red hair down to his shoulders with a small broom between his legs, smiling. More "awws."

"Oh, no," Ciaran groaned.

More pictures of them as children came up, then teenagers with their friends. Then there were pictures of them together: A black-and-white aerial photo of the two of them together holding hands across the table. Picture of them celebrating Ciaran's birthday in the club, then Chris's on the boat. Random selfies of the two of them at each other's home and their trip to London at Christmastime. A picture of Ciaran's mugshot when he entered Claustra came up, stone-faced and haggard, and people laughed, including Chris. But the next photo was a mugshot of Chris after he was in a bar fight in college, and Ciaran laughed harder. Pictures of them in Paris at the Cordonnier's ceremony; a few pictures of them in Gullfelt at the Gala.

Chris had a thought as the pictures continued to roll through. He didn't remember seeing a cameraman at the

Cordonnier's anniversary ceremony or the gala in Gullfelt on Canada Day. He waved Charity over. "I don't see anyone taking pictures. Is there a professional photographer?" he asked.

Charity winked at Ciaran before she answered him. "Ted took care of that. There are five invisible cameras and two video recorders floating around. One camera is instructed to follow you two everywhere."

Chris looked around. "Seriously?"

"Seriously. So look up and smile."

"Look up where?" Chris asked, bewildered.

"Anywhere," Ciaran chimed in. "It's trained to find our faces." He leaned in to kiss Chris on the cheek, and Chris grinned. "That one made it in, I'm sure of it."

Chris began to respond when he noticed Sean walking up. Charity also sensed someone behind her and turned around. He smiled. "Hi, I'm Sean. Ciaran's younger brother."

She smiled a sweet smile at him. "I know who you are. You're the one who traveled the world with Ciaran."

He chuckled. "Yeah, that's me. So you know about me, huh?"

She shook her head, still smiling. "No. I don't know anything about you."

"Chris or Ciaran or Ted hasn't mentioned how amazing I am?" Sean grinned. Ciaran rolled his eyes. Chris grimaced.

"I know you're Ted's and Ciaran's little brother. That's it," she said.

"But you want to get to know me, yeah?" he asked smugly.

Charity shook her head again. "No."

"*No?*"

"No."

Sean was a little taken aback. Women didn't typically shut him down. Before he could respond, Diana and

Quentin came around, and Charity had already turned away to introduce herself. Diana and Charity gushed about the emotional wedding they all witnessed, while Quentin congratulated the couple.

"I can't wait to get to know you, Diana," Charity said loudly. "I hear that you're the actual witch in the room. And you're brilliant at it."

Diana giggled. "I'm a practicing Wiccan, and everyone knows it. Obviously I don't use my *Vis* around others, so it's mostly elixirs, crystals, tarot reading, and druid dancing in front of Commoners. You know, I could teach you some simple potions for health, wealth, luck, vitality, libido enhancement, and beauty. Make you the witch in a room full of Commoners, too." Diana squeezed her hand. "Want to be a witch, Charity?"

Charity gasped. "I would love that so much!" she squealed.

"Don't let Clarissa hear you say that," Ciaran joked.

Chris laughed. "She'll have you exorcised by dawn by the first Catholic priest she meets."

Charity ignored them. "Let's do it."

They exchanged numbers, vowing to keep in contact and plan their first lesson. They hugged, and Diana left with Quentin. Charity began to walk away. Sean reached out and gently grabbed her arm. Chris noticed his subtle flirting again while she looked him, surprised.

"You gave Diana a hug. Aren't you going to give me a hug, too?" He began to stroke her arm.

Charity stepped closer to him. She pushed her body against his and said quietly on his lips, "No."

She used two hands to push his chest back, cocked her head to the side, smiled, and then walked away. "It's soon time for your first dance," said Charity over her shoulder.

"Fun," said Chris. "What's the song?"

"Something Ted picked out," was all she said as she glided away in her silver gown.

"Uh-oh," Ciaran said with a frown.

"No frowning in my wedding pics," Chris said to him. But his eyes wandered back over to his brother-in-law. Sean was watching Charity walk away, her bottom swaying in the tight dress.

"Hey!" Chris yelled, slamming his palm on the table.

Sean turned back to them. "Having a good time, gentlemen?" he said.

Chris glared at him. "What the fuck are you doing?"

"What?"

"My *sister?*"

Sean chuckled nervously. "I'm just chatting."

"Are you?" Chris challenged him.

Ciaran cleared his throat, stood up, and held out his hand for Chris. "Time for our first dance, husband."

That brought Chris's attention back to Ciaran, who called him husband for the first time. He smiled. Ciaran smiled back. Chris took his hand, and they walked to the dancefloor together.

They were pleasantly surprised as the first chords of Ed Sheeran's "Best Part of Me" started. They held each other and danced in the middle of the room until the song went off, and the crowd clapped. The song changed to "Magic" by Coldplay, and they continued to hold each other as they sang to each other softly. Ted took Elodie's hand and quietly joined them on the dancefloor.

Charity looked over at Sean, still by the table, watching them. Sean was definitely handsome enough, confident enough, and flirty enough. Making him chase her was the fun part. She went over and took Sean's beer out of his hand. "Come on, Loverboy."

Sean smiled. "I knew you'd—"

She held up her hand to his face. "No talking. Just dancing."

Charity pulled Sean to the dancefloor and allowed Sean to hold her by her waist. Diana and Quentin, Rob and Chloé, and Alastair and Lulu all came to dance as well. Their friends joined in, Alexi and Vlad, Other Chris and Emi, Selma and Andres. Petals started to fall again from the ceiling, giving it a romantic feel. Some of the couples started kissing. Sean took his chance and planted one on Charity's lips. Charity allowed it, then remembered it was the petals, and pulled back. Sean grinned. She slapped him and walked away. Others around them laughed.

"She wants me," he said smugly. He straightened out his jacket and left the dancefloor.

The song ended, and the DJ announced the party beginning and began to play pop songs. Chris and Ciaran walked back to their seats and people watched. They watched the Dragon Tamers flirt with Chris's female college friends who came without dates. They watched Felix and Emily sit in a corner and make out while Alastair introduced Lulu to everyone.

They spotted Dale and Sarah with Chris commenting, "She must have dressed him," making Ciaran laugh, looking at his black suit and yellow shirt. And they watched Sean continuously follow Charity around like a lost puppy and her pretending to be annoyed by the flattery and attention.

"That's going to happen tonight," Ciaran said plainly.

Chris frowned. "Sean and my sis? They can't. Isn't that like incest now?"

Ciaran chuckled. "I don't think so. They aren't blood-related."

"But still..." His frown deepened. "I don't think I want that to happen. It gives me the creeps just thinking of it."

"I don't think we have a say. You know your sister. I know my brother." He pointed. "That's happening. Deal with it now."

Chris rolled his eyes as the DJ announced it was time for speeches. The dancefloor cleared, and Clarissa went up to the mic with a cloak wrapped around her.

"Hello, I'm Clarissa. As the matriarch of the Jennings family, it is my duty to be the first to welcome the Beals into our country, home, and community." The audience clapped. "Ever since he was a child, Chris would jump headfirst into things without thinking. He was all heart, following his gut. When he was about five or six, Chrissy had the bright idea to follow the river and see how far it went. My impulsive idiot brother jumped off the bank and into the river. Just like that, no warning. Ma Ami screamed, and our papa didn't hesitate; he jumped in after him and saved his stupid arse."

The crowd laughed. "Ma Ami grabbed him and screamed, 'What did you do that for?' And he looked at her with those big brown eyes and said, 'I just wanted to see where the river would take me.' Well, Chrissy got the beating of his life right in the middle of the woods next to our favorite tree. Which you have to understand was very rare for Ma Ami to do."

Chris and Ciaran looked at each other, knowing it was the Motus Willow that had enhanced her fear, then her rage.

"But that's Chrissy. That's my brother," she continued. "Always jumping headfirst into things, all heart. I didn't even know there was a Ciaran in his life until one day he says, 'My boyfriend Ciaran is here and staying for Sunday dinner.' And they were already months into their relationship. I was truly the last to know."

"Ahem," Sean called out. "I believe the Beals were the last to know, innit?" All the Beals chuckled.

"Anyway, a few Sunday dinners later, I confronted them. 'What is this? Is this a real thing? Is this going someplace?' And my idiot brother tried to weasel his way out of it. But my now amazing mature brother-in-law said very plainly, 'We're together. And we're exclusive.' And I thought, well, I think Chris got it right this time."

She turned to the table. "Ciaran, I want you to know that you are absolutely the best thing that has ever happened to Chrissy. You keep him grounded. Focused. Driven. Being with you has matured him in ways you'll never understand. I mean, he doesn't even break wind at the dinner table any- more. And if you ever smelled one of Chrissy's bombs, well imagine eating a sheep stew to that."

The crowd laughed. "I have," Ciaran called out, "and it's terrible." The crowd laughed harder.

"Well, I have tried to be the best big sister and role model for my siblings when Ma Ami left us sooner than any of us were ready for. I tried to fill her role as the matriarch of this family." She held back tears.

"You're doing great, Clary," Chris said sincerely.

"Thanks, but I'm officially hanging up my Keeping-Chris-Out-Of-Trouble cape and handing it to Ciaran. I know he can be a pain in the arse, my new brother, but you wanted the job of taking care of Chrissy, you got it." She took off her cloak and threw it at Ciaran. It landed on his face.

"Good luck!" Clarissa yelled and walked away.

The guests hollered in laughter, clapping as Ciaran slowly pulled it off his face, showing a grin.

Grace was next. "You know I had a whole speech planned," she began, "but now I want to say something else after hearing Clarissa talk about Christopher. Because my Ciaran was the complete opposite. He never did anything without thinking it through completely. I remember when Ciaran was about six or seven years old, and I was in the garden listening to Ted try to convince Ciaran and Alastair to build a tree house using dead wood from the cedar tree, and Ciaran gave him a point-by-point lecture about why that would be a stupid and dangerous idea. Ted, true to his impulsive self, built it anyway with Alastair. And Alastair went first, fell off, and broke his wrist. When we got there, Alastair was howling on the ground, and Ted was screaming for help. And there was Ciaran with his arms folded, standing there with all the smugness that a seven-year-old could muster, and said, 'Next time, you'll listen to reason.'"

The audience laughed, and Ciaran grinned again. "And I thought, 'I'm not going to have any trouble out of that one.' Little did I know, ho ho!" she chortled and gave her son a stern look, wagging her finger at both of them. "Ciaran had never done anything foolish or reckless in his entire life until he met Christopher. And the truth was, I didn't like it one bit. I wasn't sure that this was a good match at all. I mean, I would have thought to see Sean's mugshot before I saw my sensible Ciaran."

"Hey!" Sean called out in faux indignation.

"I mean really," Grace kept going, ignoring her youngest son. "Did you see that picture? Look at that picture."

The DJ obliged and pulled Ciaran's mugshot again, hair disturbed, sad eyes, stoic face. Ciaran went red again as everyone chuckled. Chris hugged him.

"My Ciaran went to jail for Chistopher, and I was not happy. But—" She raised her hand to silence everyone. "But I realized something. That maybe, just maybe, my Ciaran was a little too safe, too careful. Overthinking with his head, not enough following his heart. Love is supposed to change you, challenge you, make you uncomfortable, make you better. And I may not have known anything about Chris, but there was one thing that was glaringly obvious. Their love for each other was set in stone, written in the stars. Christopher loves my Ciaran, so deeply, so completely. And that's all I could ask for as a mother.

"When Ciaran started writing letters telling me that he's in love... my Ciaran was talking about feelings! So I knew Christopher was something special. And he is." She gave Christopher a warm smile, and he smiled back. "So while this relationship scares the living shit out of me, still I might add, I am happy to hear that the same way Christopher is loosening up my son, Ciaran is adding some sense into that boy." She turned to them. "So cheers and congratulations on this perfect union. Hopefully, you'll balance each other out so that Chris is a little less idiotic and Ciaran is a little less haughty."

Chris and Ciaran turned red, and everyone laughed, clapped, and cheered. Grace walked over to both of them, and they stood up to give her hugs and kisses.

"We love you, Mum," Chris said.

"And I love you," she said to Christopher sincerely. They hugged again.

Hamish stood up next and took the mic. "Well, Grace, I think you stole my speech," he said, and everyone chuckled. "I might have a little more to say..." He went into his suit pocket and pulled out a stack of colorful index cards. "Let's see here... Ciaran has always been the sensible one... nope, can't say that..." He tossed the first card and thumbed through a few of them, muttering to himself. "Christmas was a hard time... no, you clearly already know that..." He tossed the card. "Ah! Here's one. Ciaran, I found you to be different now that you have found the love of your life," he began to read. "Talking about your feelings with us…" He stopped and looked at his wife. "Well, good heavens, woman, have you left me anything to say?" he scolded playfully. The crowd clapped and laughed.

Chris leaned over and said, "I don't think I knew your dad could be so funny."

"I don't think I knew that either," Ciaran said back.

Hamish pretended to thumb through his cards again, then said, "Fuck it," and tossed them in the air. But as they came down, they suddenly were colorful confetti. The crowd was awed and clapped at his magic trick. He turned to the newlyweds. "Congratulations, son. Well done. Don't screw it up." The crowd gave Hamish a standing ovation, including the husbands.

Hamish went over to them, and Ciaran grabbed him first. "You were brilliant, Dad."

"And you are a brilliant son," he said back. "I could not have been prouder." He hugged Chris too.

Charity went to the mic. "Well, that's a tough act to follow." She pulled out a sheet of paper. "I have a lot to say, but I'm going to keep it short." Then she began to read.

"Chris and Ciaran, I want you to know something. While everyone else in this room was surprised and confused about how your relationship blossomed so quickly, I was not. You see, I actually was here from the beginning. Chris came home one day mentioning that he had a new friend, a guy he met in the woods, a conservationist. A couple of weeks later, when Chris broke his ankle on the job, he told me how you kept him company and patrolled with him, and I thought, 'He's a good friend.' And then months later Chris told me that things between them had changed and had such excitement on his face. My brother said to me, 'We're going to make a go at it.' And I thought, 'Wow, Chrissy is serious about this one. And Chrissy is never serious about anyone.' And I was there the morning after their first date when I walked in on…"

She did a jiggle with her body and grinned, making everyone laugh, and someone whistled.

"Real subtle, sis," Chris said sarcastically.

"My point is if there is one person who saw firsthand, sometimes third wheel, of their growing love affair, it was me. I know my brother. I knew when he started to fall in love before he did. And I know when Ciaran started to feel it, too. I was there for the breakfast dates and movie nights and all the in-between conversations. So if no one else gets it, just know that I do. And now that I understand so much more, I really get it. Ciaran, Chris, you two are truly made for each other. Your love was written in the stars. And I am so happy that I will continue in my first-row seat on this magical road of your lifetime of happiness. Congratulations to the happy couple."

They all stood up and clapped, including Ciaran and Chris again. She came over to them and hugged them both. "We love you, sis," said Ciaran.

"Thank you, little sister," Chris said right behind him.

"Hello? Is this thing on?"

They all turned to see Ted with the microphone in his hand.

"So for those that don't know me, I'm Ted Beals, eldest brother and leader of the ginger head clan. I had the honor of being the first of the Beals to meet Christopher Jennings. And within a few hours of meeting him, he told me that his cock is bigger than mine and challenged me to a duel." The crowd laughed loudly, and Chris smiled.

"No, really, I'm not kidding," said Ted with a smile. "He really did that. And that was before I found out he was the boyfriend. And I'm thinking, this guy could not be who my brother is hanging out with. Because there isn't an arrogant bone in his body, and no one in Ciaran's circle is cockier than me. Except maybe Sean."

Sean yelled an "Oy!" making everyone laugh.

Ted continued, "It is truly a case of opposites attract. But it works. And it works well. Since then, I've grown to love Christopher like a brother. I've caught a glimpse of him at his best and at his worst, and ya know, he's not so bad overall. It would be really nice if he stopped hitting on my wife, though, really."

"Never!" Chris yelled out, making them laugh again. Elodie stood up and blew her new brother-in-law kisses.

"So one big change that Chris has influenced my little brother is in his taste in music. Because Christopher loves music as I've discovered. Singing, dancing, playing the piano, and he's in tune with all the popular songs, not just Coldplay." Ted made a face, and they all laughed again. "So thank you, Christopher, for being the total opposite of Ciaran and being a brother to us all." Chris put his hand on his heart in gratitude.

"Now, in honor of Ciaran's newfound love of bands other than Coldplay, we're going to do a little karaoke—"

"Fuck off!" Ciaran yelled.

Ted pretended he did not hear. "And I chose the perfect song because I feel like the lyrics fit my brother's attitude perfectly when it comes to music, dancing, and parties. So Mr. DJ, if you will, hit it!"

Another Ed Sheeran song began to play, "I Don't Care", and Ciaran groaned loudly. Chris stood up and laughed. "Oh God, this is perfect. It really is perfect for you. Let's go."

"No," said Ciaran in bewilderment. "Absolutely fucking not."

Chris yanked on Ciaran's arm. "C'mon, you big baby. Like the lyrics say, let's sing and dance at a party you don't really want to be at."

Ciaran groaned again. But he allowed Ciaran to drag him onto the dancefloor. Ted joined him and began to sing. He put his hands on Ciaran's hips and moved them side to side.

"I hate you," Ciaran murmured to his older brother. Chris laughed and grabbed his hand, dancing really close to him. Ciaran relented and started moving his feet.

Sean ran up and joined them, pulling Rob with him. Quentin got up and pulled on Alastair's arm. They danced around Ciaran, who eventually let go and started jumping around throughout the song. Unaware of who started it, the seven men pretended to be in a chorus line and held arms, kicking their knees, then their feet. The crowd was also standing up, cheering, and singing along.

As the song ended, they hugged each other; then Ted grabbed the mic screaming, "Wait, wait, waaaait! That's enough for the speeches. Let's party like Commoners!"

CHAPTER 36

Revelations

As the night continued, the guests forgot about their place seating and mingled together. Chris introduced Ciaran to his Uncle Alieu, his mother's only sibling, who came from Senegal to watch his nephew get married. He brought with him his son Abdul and his daughter Yenoh. Chris, Clarissa, and Charity were excited to meet their cousins from Africa for the first time.

Ciaran also met Chris's aunt Lacey from the States, her husband Donald, and Chris's cousins Dougie and Maribella. They hadn't seen Chris since they were all teenagers, and he came to the US one summer before he began at Uni, and they happily greeted and congratulated him. Lacey shared stories about Ma Ami as a young girl and as a college student since Lacey and Amina had gone to school together. And Dougie talked about Chris being obsessed with an Irish boy two years younger than him that he was falling so hard for that he decided to leave his Uncle Ben's house and come to their house earlier than expected. That made Chris blush and Ciaran laugh.

Chris noticed that Collum did not sit with his sister Lacey and her family. He sat at a table all alone near the bar, and Chris was just fine with his father staying out of everyone's way. But Ciaran watched Hamish glide himself over, hold out his hand to introduce himself, and sit next to Collum. They talked for a while; then Dale and Graham joined them.

Ciaran tapped Chris, getting his attention to the men sitting together. He whispered in Chris's ear, "I wonder what they're gabbing about."

"If it's about me, I don't want to know," Chris said and looked away.

"Maybe you should," said Ciaran. Chris gave him a wry look. "It's the best time to approach him. If you want to." Chris sighed and didn't respond.

The couple moved around and sat at tables with their guests, making sure they spent time with everyone. When sitting with Ciaran's friends and Reservers, Bruno, who had not been with them the whole time, walked over with a small-framed curly-haired woman.

"So," he said loudly, getting everyone's attention, "This is my wife, Tereza. She's been dying to meet you all." All the Reservers looked up in shock.

Ciaran chortled, "Ho, ho." He stood up, grinned at Bruno first, and then shook her hand. "Very nice to meet you, Tereza. Thank you for coming to our wedding. It's an honor to have you here. You must know that we had no idea Bruno was married. He never talks about his home life."

"Yeah, we thought he was living in a hobbit hole somewhere," Tommy deadpanned, making the others laugh. Bruno glared at him. Tommy stuck his tongue out, knowing he was the safest he had ever been around Bruno, at Ciaran's wedding and in front of his wife.

She chuckled. "Bruno is like that. I'm not surprised. I hope it's not because he's ashamed of his Commoner wife. We've been married for twelve years and have four beautiful daughters."

"Commoner?!" Chris said in surprise.

"Twelve years?!" Felix exclaimed.

"Daughters, you say?!" Sahid said right behind him. "Sons maybe, but Bruno raising *daughters*?"

Bruno shot his Hunter a look. Tereza patted his hand. "Besa is ten, Denisa is eight, Rita is five, and Zamira just turned three." She took out her phone and handed it to her husband. "Show them the pictures of your daughters," she commanded. Bruno gave her a soft smile and began to show everyone at the table.

Tereza turned to Ciaran. "He talks often about his friends at the Reserve. And speaks very highly of you, Ciaran."

"Does he now?" Ciaran replied and looked at Bruno, who avoided his gaze. He turned back to Tereza. "That's very interesting, considering we spent the first few years snarling at each other when I came onto the Reserve at nineteen and he was twenty-five."

"Well, he thought you were arrogant and a know-it-all. And there is only one room for one arrogant, know-it-all on the Reserve." She winked. "But then Dale let you fight it out that last time," she said with a smile.

He chuckled. "Yes, Dale did." Ciaran looked up at Bruno again, who pretended he wasn't listening as everyone else commented on how beautiful the girls were, all curly brown-haired, with bright smiles and Bruno's green eyes. "I think we pummeled each other for a good twenty minutes before Sarah broke it up with a hex." He turned to Chris. "That's how I ended up on the night shift, so he and I wouldn't see each other."

"Oh, I remember him coming home that day cursing the day you were born," she said with a smile. "That mission to Chad changed things for the two of you. You asking him to be a part of that mission, in the role he was in, showed that you respected him." She patted his arm. "Thank you for that. He'll never admit it, but it meant a lot that you did that."

"It meant a lot to me that he accepted. I would face any mission with Bruno by my side," said Ciaran. "You heard that, Bruno?" he said louder.

"Fuck off, Ciaran," Bruno said without turning around. Both Ciaran and Tereza laughed.

Clarissa came over to them. "I'm going to drop Papa off at the house to relieve the babysitter and come right back."

Chris nodded, but Ciaran stopped Clarissa from walking with a touch on her wrist. He turned to Chris. "It's now or never."

Chris nodded again, then stood up. The three of them walked over to the table where the older men still sat together, talking and smoking cigars. "Gentlemen," Ciaran started talking first, "We just want to thank you all for coming. Dale, we forgive you tossing us around that one time."

"Bygones," Dale said with a shrug.

"Dad, thanks for being you. Level-headed, astute, welcoming, funny, and everything I aspire to be as a man and now as a husband."

Hamish smiled. "Cheers, son."

"Grandminister Graham," said Chris, "we appreciate your support throughout Christmas until now." Graham raised his glass and nodded.

Then Ciaran said, "And, Collum, we appreciate you coming and supporting our relationship. It means a lot to the both of us, but especially to your son."

Collum nodded, then looked at Chris, and swallowed. They stared at each other. Dale cleared his throat first and rose from his seat. "You know, I could use another drink. Ministers?"

Hamish and Graham both stood up. Hamish touched Collum's shoulder, and Graham touched Chris's. Dale grabbed Ciaran's arm and dragged him with them as they left Chris and Collum alone. Clarissa, getting the hint, followed them to the bar. Chris sat down next to his father.

"So," Collum began, "Ciaran went to jail for you, innit? Bar fight? That's what they told me."

"Yeah," Chris replied. "Bar fight." He began to play with the saltshaker on the table to find something to do with his hands.

"Seems like it was more than a bar fight if you needed a parliament minister to get him out of it."

"He didn't get out of it," said Chris, shaking his head. "He was in jail for five days, then went to a hearing. He pleaded guilty and got probation. Ciaran is still on probation. And he did it to keep me out of trouble, too."

"Hmmm... He's already a better match for you than that first one."

Chris stopped flipping the saltshaker in his hand. He gently put it down and turned to his father. "Remington?"

"Don't," Collum growled. "Never say his name before me."

"I'm sorry, Papa, for what I did," Chris said.

Collum looked at his son in surprise. But Chris continued.

"I'm sorry I threw you out of your home. The home you shared the love of your life with. That was cruel. But..." Chris looked away. "You were also cruel. You said the most god-awful things to me that I will never forget. It was homophobic and hurtful."

"You shouldn't have..." Collum started, then stopped. "Yes. It was homophobic and hurtful. I'm sorry, too." Chris looked at him, also surprised at the apology. "But..." Collum looked up. "You have to understand that it was hard for me to understand. It's not our way. Not the Jennings way. Your mum ... Ami ... she tried to tell me one day. All the time you were spending with the Bangladesh boy. I understood after she was gone what she was trying to tell me. And I could have accepted it if it wasn't for ... *him*."

"Remington."

"Don't!" Collum growled again.

"I'm sorry about that, too, Papa," Chris said softly. "I allowed myself to be swept up and away by him at a young age and—"

"Stop!" Collum said, banging his hand on the table, shocking Chris with his anger. He put his finger on Chris's face. "That was not your fault. It was his. That... That... fag—"

"Don't!" Chris said back, pushing his father's hand out of his face. "No more sissy, girly, flaming fruitcake, fag, wimpy, male whore bullshit coming out of your mouth. If you're pissed that Rem took advantage of me as a child, then say that. But don't make it about us being gay!"

Chris started to rise, but Collum grabbed his arm. "Sit down, Chrissy," he said gruffly. Then softened. "Please, son." Chris sat back down.

"He was a man," Collum said in a low voice, trying to keep his anger in check. "He was a man, and you were not a man. Not yet. No man should ever do what he did to a child. There was no excuse for what he did to you. None. I could have killed him. I should have killed him. It was wrong what he did. Wrong."

"I know that now, Papa," said Chris. "Ciaran helped me to see that."

Collum glanced over at Ciaran at the bar with his father, then back at Chris. "If you would have brought the ginger home first, as an adult, I could have..." Collum sighed. "It still would have been hard for me to understand because it's not our way. But it would have been different between you and me."

"I know. The introduction to my sexuality by finding out I was sexually groomed by an older man made it even more difficult for you to accept. But do you accept me now? Because this is who I am, Papa. I've had relationships across genders before Rem and after Rem. And now I'm deeply in love with my husband. Can you accept that, so I can have a father back in my life?"

Collum looked around. "Lots of gingers running around here. I would probably be more concerned with that than him being a man. But they're all alright with me. Especially the one you just got yourself hitched to."

Chris smirked at his father. "Glad to know I have your permission to start a family."

"A family? Really?" Collum said in surprise.

"Really," Chris said with a nod. "I've always wanted to be a dad."

"*Is dócha go mbeidh tú níos fearr air ná mar a bhí mé,*" Collum said.

Chris shrugged. "You were a good dad to my sisters. They adore you. I hope to have a brown-skinned, ginger-haired daughter love me just as much. Or a son."

"Aye. Ami would have loved to see that. Make it happen for her," Collum said with a smile.

Chris chuckled. "Deal."

Clarissa came over when she saw the smiles. "Are you ready, Papa?"

"Yes." Collum stood up and stretched. Chris stood up, too. "Chrissy," he began. But Chris cut him off by throwing his arms around his father. The old man hugged his son back. Both failed to hold back tears as they held on. Eventually, Chris let go first.

Collum touched his face. "I am proud of you, Christopher. Your mum is too."

Chris swallowed the lump in his throat to answer. *"Buíochas, Phápa."*

Collum kissed his son's face, then took his daughter's hand. She led him out the door.

Ciaran walked over to Chris as he watched his father leave the tent. "Okay there, love?"

Chris turned to him and kissed him. Ciaran pulled back first and wiped the tears from his face. But Chris felt something else. "Why are you trembling? I should be the one shaking from the intensity of that conversation, not you."

Ciaran gave him a weary smile. "I'll tell you later. Right now, I got a wedding present for you."

Chris smiled. "Really?"

Ciaran smiled and took Chris's hand. He brought him back over to their table. Ciaran pointed to two square boxes. "I had them custom made for us. Used that last sample of your blood for it."

"Oooh. Kinky," Chris mused. Ciaran picked one up, handed it to Chris, and held onto the other one. Chris opened it, and inside was a black link watch with an oval face and no numbers, just dots. "It's beautiful."

"Put it on," said Ciaran, as he opened up his box to reveal an identical watch.

Chris slid it on. "I can feel the ticking," he said as it pulsed on his wrist.

"That's not ticking," Ciaran said as he put his on. He took Chris's other hand and placed it on his chest. "It's my heartbeat."

Chris gasped and stared at Ciaran. Ciaran raised his arm and placed it on Chris's chest. They stood together and stared into each other's eyes for a full minute, feeling the other's heartbeat.

"Ciaran," Chris breathed out.

"No matter where in the world I am, you'll know my heart is still beating for you," he said.

Chris kissed him. "God, you're such a fucking romantic. I don't think I could ever top this."

"I'm good at what I do," Ciaran said smugly.

"I lied," said Chris. "I think I topped it for you."

"Really?" Ciaran said with a smile.

"A hundred percent," he said confidently, with a smile.

Chris took Ciaran's hand and led him past the DJ booth out the back of the tent. They walked a few feet away to the cliff's edge. "Turn around." Ciaran did. "What do you see?"

"Our wedding venue."

"What else?"

"Grass, trees."

"Land."

Ciaran was confused. "Land?"

"About three acres. And this clearing is right in the middle of it, overlooking the river below and the mountains of the Reserve. Wouldn't you want to wake up to that view every morning, every day of your life?"

Ciaran looked at his husband. "What do you mean?"

"I mean..." He took Ciaran's hand. "This grass, these trees, this clearing, all three acres are ours. And by the time we come back from our honeymoon, the framework for our dream home will be underway. Right here where this tent is."

"Christopher…" Ciaran said in shock. He looked around, speechless.

"You wanted a home in the woods overlooking trees and mountains, with enough privacy to be a Magus, and you shall have it. A three thousand-square-foot, two-story, four-bedroom colonial on your own land. Of course, we'll put up wards and such—"

"You're right, you topped it." Ciaran turned to him. "You're an amazing husband for this. If I could throw you on this grass and make love to you right now, I would."

"Can't. I'm wearing white. And so are you." Chris winked at him.

Ciaran kissed him. "One more hour, then we're gone from here."

"Oooh, now you want to consummate," Chris teased as they walked back hand in hand.

"I wanted to consummate in the trailer, but you were being an emotional ninny," he deadpanned.

Chris looked at him, wide-eyed. "Wanker!"

Ciaran smiled and kissed him again. "Reception is almost done. Then we start our forever."

"Then we start our forever," Chris agreed as they walked back in.

His cousin Dougie waved him over as Alastair tried to get Ciaran's attention. They kissed and went their separate ways to greet their guests.

CHAPTER 37

Happy

Ciaran was steadily watching the time for when the hour was up as he went around to spend time and thank everyone there. As he was walking over to Magna, Lucy, and Selma, he saw a glimpse of Chris at the table with his cousins and Ciaran's brothers, laughing loudly. He smiled to himself.

<You look happy over there,> Ciaran said to him.

Chris smiled. <I am,> he thought to himself. <Happiest day of my life.>

Ciaran smiled back as Chris's thoughts floated through his head, loud and clear. But then his mouth dropped in realization. He stopped in the middle of the floor and froze.

He had not tried to talk to Chris mentally all day, so he had no idea when it happened. But it finally happened.

He watched Chris continue his conversation with Sean and Dougie as they discussed the sights and sounds of New York City. <Happiest day of my life, too,> Ciaran said back.

Ciaran watched Chris freeze, and his own mouth slowly open. He raised up his eyes. <Ciaran?>

<Yes, love?>

<You heard my thoughts?>

<Yes, love.>

Chris stood up quickly and looked around frantically. *<YOU CAN HEAR ME?!>*

Ciaran found himself chuckling. *<No need to shout. You can whisper in your head, and I would still—>*

"Ciaran!" he said out loud.

"What's wrong?" Ted said with concern, also looking around.

"The *Ardenti*?" Alastair asked. "I've seen that look."

"What's that?" Dougie asked in confusion.

"I—" Chris looked around again, needing everyone else to shut up and stop asking questions. *<Where are you?>*

<Currently, I'm in your head,> Ciaran teased.

Chris moved away from his table. "Where are you going?" Sean asked.

Chris held up his hand to shush him and kept walking. *<Where are you, Ciaran?>* he asked again.

<Around.>

<C—>

<You know, I'm getting the appeal. I just Wisp'd home to see the range, and it's pretty damn brilliant.>

Chris stopped walking. *<You're at The Atrium?>*

<Cool it. I'm back already.>

Chris whirled around. *<Ciaran!>* He heard Ciaran chuckle in his head. *<Are you going to show yourself?>*

<Eventually.>

Chris briskly walked the length of the room again. He knew he looked mad; he was getting the attention of others. *<So unfair.>*

<Tell me you love me.>

<What?>

<Tell me that you love me.>

Chris stopped walking and looked up. *<I love you.>* He didn't hear anything back. *<Ciaran?>*

<It sounds like heaven to hear you say it this way. It's just vibrating around in my head, echoing.>

Chris smiled. *<Yeah. It does.>*

"Think I fancy hearing it out loud, though."

Chris turned around, and Ciaran was right there, grinning. "I love you, too."

Chris practically ran to him. They moved at the same time, crashing their lips into each other, grabbing faces, kissing in the middle of the tables. Their friends and family started hooting, clapping, and cheering.

Ciaran pulled back first and held Chris's wrists. *<It's time to go.>*

<Yeah, I think so, too.>

They made their rounds to say goodbye to their guests, hand in hand, and lastly turned to their eldest siblings. "We're leaving them in your capable hands," said Ciaran.

"We got it," Ted said confidently.

"See you in a month," Clarissa said back.

Chris looked at his new husband in confusion. "How are we—" But Ciaran held his hand and pulled him along.

They stepped out of the tent together, and the fairies followed them again, lighting their way to the edge of the cliff. Ciaran turned to him and held both his hands again.

"Ready?"

"For?" Chris asked curiously. "What are we doing, Ciaran?"

"Another surprise," said Ciaran slyly. "We're not going back to The International. We're traveling by boat and visiting Paralia Mirtos in Greece, then across the Ionian Sea to Sicily, farther up Italy to Santa María de Leuca, and back across to Albania. Our entire honeymoon is one full month of sailing at sea. Debony is already on the boat, ready for an adventure."

"Ciaran…" Chris gasped. "Okay, you're officially more romantic than me."

Ciaran smiled, squeezing his hands. "But the real surprise for us both is that we're going to Wisp there."

Chris chuckled. "You know you can't. That tent is crawling with Magi Council officials."

"I can," said Ciaran. "When you were talking to your father and we were at the bar, Graham turned to me and said, 'A wedding present.' And he tapped me on the head with his *dulé*, taking the trace off me."

"Really?!"

"He did," he said with a nod. "That's why I was shaking because it felt like I was being shocked with electricity, like when they put it on me. He said he used his discretion, and eight months' probation is long enough, especially after we saved Gullfelt. Magna signed the consent to lift the trace this evening, and Graham carried it out. And since we have the *Ardenti* and a tie-bind, I literally couldn't hurt you without hurting myself. So again I ask," he squeezed Chris's hands again, "are you ready to go on more adventures with me, husband?"

"Always ready with you, husband."

Ciaran kissed him. "Then here we go. Close your eyes and see the boat in my mind."

Chris molded his mind with Ciaran's. "I see it."

Ciaran wasted no time and Wisp'd with his husband.

Three Months Later

Chris was sitting on his swing on the back porch that Sunday morning with Debony sleeping on his lap, watching the sunrise, waiting for his husband to Wisp home. The leaves were turning golden and falling, and he made a note to tell Ciaran to magically clean up the expansive yard and the walkway leading to their path. Suddenly Debony woke with a start. She stood up on four legs, her back arched, her ears alert, her tail down.

Chris looked at her in alarm. "What is it, Debs?" She whined, jumped off him, and scurried back into the house.

He stood up and watched her with concern. He was about to follow her inside when he heard a roar in the distance. Chris slowly turned around. He could see it far off, but it was getting closer, closer. He put his hand over his eyebrows as a visor to make sure he was actually seeing what he was seeing. The figure that was as small as a bird along the horizon grew larger the closer it got to his home. He stood there watching, frozen in awe. The blue-black beast landed right on the field at the edge near the cliff. It lowered down to all fours and tucked its wings in. But its rider did not get off.

Chris walked slowly through the garden of Magi herbs to his white gated fence. Their land had wards on it so no other Magi could enter, so he knew the rider was no stranger. And neither was the dragon. He opened it and stepped onto the meadow. Keeping an eye on the young dragon, he made his way to the left side of her, about five feet away. Robetta watched him too, sniffing the air to catch his scent.

"Hello, beautiful," he said, greeting her first with a slight bow. She grunted at him in recognition. Chris came closer and touched her reptilian skin. He could see the areas coating her feet and her belly were beginning to harden like black glass. Like magnetite. Betta grunted again.

Chris finally stepped back and looked up. "And good morning to you, too. Forgot your key?" he deadpanned.

"Good morning," Ciaran said. "Fancy an early morning ride?"

Chris's mouth dropped. "Are you sure? Would I be safe?"

"Of course," Ciaran said confidently. "Especially with Betta. And you know you're always safe with me, love."

Chris nodded. Then he said to her softly, "Is that alright, girl? If I climb aboard?"

The dragon turned her face to give him more access to her neck. Ciaran put his hand out. Chris took it and hoisted himself onto the dragon in front of Ciaran.

"Now, hold on to her spikes like this." He showed Chris how to hold on like a motorcycle. Ciaran wrapped his arms around Chris's waist and held onto the set of spikes below Chris's. "Whatever happens," Ciaran said softly in his ear, "Don't let go."

<Never,> Chris responded in Ciaran's head.

Ciaran smiled and kissed the side of his face. "Let's go, girl. Hiyah!"

Betta rose up on all fours. "Whoa," Chris said as fear swept through him.

"We got you," Ciaran reminded him, as Betta turned around. She trotted to the edge and threw herself off.

Chris couldn't help the scream that came from his lips as she nosedived into the valley. He was sure the entire Drenova National Park heard him. But as she outstretched her enormous wings and plateaued, he could feel the wind rushing through him. Betta began to soar upward, high into the clouds, back toward the mountains. Chris closed his eyes and held on, feeling the beat of Robetta's wings vibrate throughout his body and the beat of Ciaran's heart against his back as they sailed into the rising sun.

Ciaran and Chris grow deeper in their *Ardenti* bond as they grow their family in Book 4: *The Ranger's Mages!*

BOOK CLUB QUESTIONS

1. This book picks up where book 2 left off. If you happened to read book 3 first, would you want to go back and read book 1 (*Beasts and Bromance*) and book 2 (*Ardenti*)?

2. The Oath is a pledge to protect and defend the magical world. If you had the opportunity, would you take The Oath? Why or why not?

3. What are your thoughts on the reason for Gérard Bruguière and Jaques Lemaître to build their charm school specifically for Generational Magi?

4. Eli and Fab mentioned that the *Ardenti* can sometimes be considered dark magic because of the intensity. List out the ways that *Ardenti* can be dark magic and light magic.

5. In book 1, Ciaran talks about the Magi Community's prejudice against non-magical humans, but Chris experiences it in Paris and in Gullfelt. Describe a time when you felt like a second-class citizen.

6. What do you think of Ciaran's decision for them to wait a few years before starting a family?

7. Compare the two dragon reservations, the DRA and the Canadian Dragon Preservation, and the pros and cons of both.

8. If you were Christopher, how would you have handled Jonathan Hinkley?

9. Who is your favorite Dragon Tamer? After three books, what is your favorite dragon?

10. A thread throughout the series is Chris's deep intuition that there is magic in his bloodline. What do you make of that?

AUTHOR BIO

Wife, mother, partner, daughter, sister, friend, social worker, life skills coach, and part-time erotic romance novelist, Eskay Kabba finds the complexity of human nature and creates romantic and erotic love stories. The characters reflect the notion that no one is all good or all bad, but we are all just trying to find love in hard places. Eskay pens erotic romance novels that celebrate the LGBTQ community, people of color, and interracial relationships. When not writing about the throes of passion, Eskay finds joy in spending time with her family and loved ones, reading dystopia and fantasy series, and binging popular shows from a streaming app.

Eskay.Kabba@gmail.com

Discover more at
4HorsemenPublications.com

10% off using HORSEMEN10